SEDUCED

SEDUCED

two celebrated erotic novels

Marcus Van Heller

CARROLL & GRAF PUBLISHERS, INC.
NEW YORK

Collection copyright © by Carroll & Graf Publishers, Inc.

All rights reserved

First Carroll & Graf edition 1995
Second edition 1998

Carroll & Graf Publishers, Inc.
19 West 21st Street
New York, NY 10010-6805

ISBN 0-7867-0550-7

Manufactured in the United States of America

Contents

The Devil's Advocate   vii

Roman Orgy   267

The Devil's Advocate

CHAPTER ONE

You stand at the office window, watching the purple-black pigeon who comes each morning to breakfast on the crumbs you spread for him on the ledge. You wonder: Where does he go on Sundays? Does he have a regular beat for handouts, like cops and whores and the old woman who comes in to sell shoelaces and condoms?

The pigeon teeters on one claw and stares with hateful eyes at your teasing forefinger. You think: It must be hell to take charity. Before he leaves, the dumb bbiiirdd will spitefully foul the window ledge. So much for your charity, Sport. Maybe the bird isn't so dumb after all.

You look up from the ledge and across the street. That imbecile in the penthouse suite is entertaining his chubby blonde secretary again. She sits on the corner of his desk, her round little rump near his elbow, and she swings her pretty legs while they both laugh at his killing wit. Later, when she's gone he'll take the hand mirror from his desk drawer, straighten his hair and tie, sit officiously in his big leather chair and read stories of cuckoldry and virility in Esquire *magazine. A real dude, he is. A real dude. . . .*

The door creaks open and you turn from the window. It"s Jackson, with the newspapers. Good old Jackson. The perfect secretary. He'd be as willing to whore as the little girl across the street if he had to keep his job. Well, maybe he wouldn't sit on your desk and make eyes at you – (or, come to think of it, would he?) – but he'd laugh his stupid head off at anything he thought you intended as a joke.

Only there aren't any jokes this morning. You joke when you're riding high. Right now, you're riding low. The case you lost was a big one. A very big one. And, when you lose a big one, it's no laughing matter.

You take the papers from Jackson and send him on his way. He gives you a small smile. A smile that lets you know he's pulling for you. All the pulling in the world can't help you on this one. You lost it and you lost it good. You'll appeal, of course, But with a case like the state has, the appeal is just a formality. You're nowhere, and you know it.

Sure enough, the Journal *has come through with flying colours. Banner headline and three photos. The big photo shows Cembretti and Morgan walking through the pen gates. Chair for Cembretti; life for Morgan. They must've had a hard time figuring that one out on the jury. Especially since Cembretti had been the one who squealed. Maybe the yo-yos figured that a clown like him was simply too dumb to live. All the bright ideas had been Morgan's, and if he'd run the show alone he'd never have been caught. So you're making a private bet with yourself on Morgan. Eight to five he finds some way of breaking out before the year is up.*

So much for the Journal. *Now you cheque out the* News. *They're playing it big, too. Banner headline and two photos on the front page, four more photos and six columns of type on the inside. Plus there's a special storey dedicated to you, the attorney for the defence. And with the storey is another picture – a picture of you, a head shot, one of your old ones.*

They would have to use that photo. You look like a fox with those ears. And that smile! More of a smirk, really; a nasty-looking twisting of the lips where a smile would be if one was there. And the eyes should be less disdainful. Successful criminal lawyers look honest and tough, like John L. Lewis; not like a damned Communist intellectual. . . .

But you don't spend much time contemplating the picture. There are other things that annoy you even more. Like the headlines DEVIL'S ADVOCATE BLOWS A BIG ONE. And the leads 'Criminal lawyer Conrad Samuel Garnett, who earned the nickname of "Devil's Advocate" by securing acquittals for dozens of alleged murderers, found himself advocating his first losing cause in three years yesterday as Rocco Cembretti and Dave Morgan were found guilty and sentenced, respectively, to death and to life imprisonment.'

How much do you want to bet the writer doesn't like you? Other-

wise, why would he have played up the middle name? Everybody knows you don't use it – that, in fact, you hate it. So why didn't the creep just write 'Conrad Garnett,' like all the other creeps did? Because this creep doesn't like you, Conrad Samuel. That's why. And, when creeps don't like you, they kick you. Especially when you happen to be down. Which you happen to be. For now.

Conrad Samuel Garnett. Samuel, as in the Book of Samuel. Funny that you should think of that. You never were the Bible-reading type.

But wait – didn't some broad once say something about the Book of Samuel? And didn't she always call you Sam from that day on?

Yeah. Sexy broad. The one with the long legs that fell open much too easily.

Elena?

Right. Elena.

Elena the creep.

What was it she used to say? 'Samuel the Devil. His Satanic Majesty, Conrad Book-of-Samuel Garnett.'

Now there's a notion for you. Have you got anything better to do than to be Lucifer this week? Limited engagement; matinees on Wednesday and Saturday. Auld Hornie in – In what? Or, more likely, in who?

Think of somebody you'd like to be in, Hornie Auld boy. No, not Elena. Elena belongs to last year, and besides Elena was much too easy. A self-respecting devil likes the more difficult cases.

* * *

They were on the beach together. He lay on his back, with his long fingers locked behind his neck.

She wondered if he was as dark in February as he was now. February. Six months ago. Six months ago, and three months before they had met. Only three months! Could he really have changed her so much in three months?

'Sam –' She moved closer. Close enough to touch his chest with the firm roundness of one of her breasts. Then she let her creamy soft thigh slip into place against his. Even through the dull white wool of her bathing suit, her hip thrilled to his touch. 'What are you thinking about, Sam?' she asked after a moment.

'I was thinking about the mating behaviour of the dung beetle,' he replied promptly.

Too promptly. She realised instantly that she shouldn't have broken the silence. Now he probably would go off on another of his ridiculous speeches, flinging still one more precious hour into the maelstrom of his rhetoric. Hurriedly she pressed closer to him. She brought her hand to his bare muscled thigh, then ran her finger along the white stripe on his blue swimtrunks. Her eyes captured the arched hair at his crotch, the insolent pride of that part of him that owned her most certainly and deeply.

'Our beach is nice today,' she said in a voice already husky. 'I've always wondered why no one ever came to this part of the beach.' She pushed her round pink toes into the silky sand, and her smooth knee touched his thigh. She hoped that her talk of the beach would divert him from the speech, from the exacerbating stream of solemnly voiced non sequiturs which already seemed to be taking form in his mind.

'An interesting animal, the dung beetle,' he went on, refusing to be diverted. 'Or, more precisely, an interesting insect. We must be precise, must we not? Imprecise talk leads to imprecise thought, and imprecise thoughts leads to chaos.'

'Sam,' she pleaded. 'Please don't start that again.'

'Yes, chaos,' he continued, ignoring her. 'But then, while the dung beetle is an insect, he also is an animal. No bias in the animal kingdom. Even the lowly insect is permitted to grace himself with the name of animal. Very democratic, really.'

'Sam,' she whined. 'Please.' Her hand worked its way over the seam of his trunks, and her fingers raked the bulge.

'Yes,' Garnett went on, unmoved, 'very democratic. Man is an animal and insects are animals. Even reptiles are animals. Very democratic. Democracy in action.' He shifted his hips, moving away from her probing fingers. 'But, of course, vegetables aren't animals. So maybe there's some bias in the animal kingdom after all. Bias and prejudice and oppression of minority groups. Damn it all, anyway, whatever happened to democracy? Is it completely nonexistent? Vegetables of the world, unite. You have nothing to lose but your – your what? What do vegetables have to lose, Elena?'

She sat upright. A tight, sour ball formed in the pit of her stomach. 'Why do you do this to me?' she asked. 'You know that I love you, and that I want to make love to you. Why do you torment me like this?'

He turned his face slightly towards her, his brows arching above his dark glasses in an expression of patient surprise. 'My dear,' he murmured, 'you're becoming a first-rate paranoiac. Seriously, I'm worried about you. You're only a step from the voices in the night and the spies with the death-ray machine.'

'Sam,' she sighed weakly.

'What makes you think I'm trying to torment you?' he continued, a small smile tugging at the corner of his mouth. 'This happens to be a very important philosophical question that I'm considering. Democracy – doesn't that mean anything to you? Think of the poor vegetables, denied the right to call themselves animals. Doesn't it offend your sense of justice? Don't you agree that they should unite? What can they lose? Their – their what. . .? Their vegetability, perhaps?'

A large tear formed in the corner of her eye and trickled down her cheek. 'Sam,' she said softly. 'I love you.'

'Of course,' he said soberly. 'But what about the vegetables? Don't you love them also? And if not, *why* not? Because they lack the apparatus with which to physically express their love? Elena, I'm ashamed of you. You're not only a paranoiac. You're a first-class bigot.'

Suddenly she could contain herself no longer. Eyes rimmed with red, she collapsed on top of him, her shoulders shaking, her throat choked with sobs. 'Why do you *do* this to me?' she demanded hopelessly. '*Why?* I think you'd almost like to see me go mad. But *why*? When I first knew you, you were cruel sometimes. But now you're always cruel. *Always!* You say things to hurt me, or to make me angry. And then you laugh. Just like you're laughing now. Just like you've always been laughing. You've been laughing at me since that very first night, when I was awkward – because I was a virgin.'

'Elena.' He seemed to soften. His mockery was sheathed, and she grew quiet under the touch of his long, tender fingers. Her hand went out to his, and she drew his palm to the soft flesh on the inside of her thigh.

'Touch me,' she whispered after a moment, urging her hand upward. 'Please touch me.'

Garnett grinned. He liked the sound of her voice. The eagerness was there, coiled tensely inside her throat. But with the eagerness was submission, total submission to his will. 'So you love me, do you?' he asked quietly.

She put her hand on his chest and trailed a route across his naked stomach to the bulge in his swimtrunks. 'Yes,' she answered weakly, 'I love you.'

Garnett said notthing, but his grin broadened. His fingers played on her bare leg. Then he slowly filled his palm with her flesh, and, gathering a fold of skin between thumb and forefinger, marked the white surface with a violent red patch. She clawed ineffectually at his belly, but the gesture said only that she had no heart for hurting him in return.

For several minutes, they lay silent and motionless. She did not look at him. She did not want to find him laughing at her. Then, suddenly, she bent over him and cupped her lips to his stomach. Her arms stretched out, one over his chest and shoulders, the other over his legs. She buried herself against him, and her shoulder found his crotch. Her arm slipped between his legs, and she drew his thigh to her face. Her lips brushed the hair which grew coarsely at the point where his swimtrunks met his leg. Her nostrils quivered as she breathed in the strong, pungent odour of his maleness. 'Oh, Sam, if only you could be nice to me again, I'd die with love. Why can't you be the way you were at first? Why don't you treat me that way any more?'

He looked down at her half-bare buttocks and the curve to her deeply tanned back. To please him, to tempt him with her sexuality, she had worn a one-piece bathing suit so small and high on her thighs that it all but cut into her flesh. Her creased hams were scarcely legally covered, and, when she first had worn the suit, he had found it amusing to make her walk with him on the crowded public beach, talking to her nonchalantly, reminding her of her flaunted undress until she was blushing and ashamed before the lash of hungry and envious eyes all around her. Now, though, it was no longer amusing. It was merely ludicrous.

Her lips inched upward on his thigh, finally coming to rest over the bulge in his swimtrunks. When he failed to react, she looked up at him. 'Tell me what's wrong, Sam. Tell me what you want me to do. And put your hand down there.' She guided it with her own. 'Yes, there.'

He waited until she had taken her hand away. Then he removed his from her hungry, upthrust mound and raked his fingers across her bare back. He said nothing.

'Tell me, Sam,' she pressed. 'Tell me what's wrong with me.'

He reached into her bathing suit and moved his fingers over her buttocks. She pressed harder against his crotch, then eased aside one of her shoulder straps and touched his thigh with her naked breast.

'You know what it is as well as I do,' he said, still manipulating her buttocks with his hand. 'You can't expect me to act towards you now as I did before I really knew you.'

'I don't understand,' she lied, knowing full well what he meant but perversely determined to hear him say it.

'I know just what you are,' he continued evenly. 'And what you are is not what you used to be.'

'What am I?' she whispered, lowering her head as if waiting for him to pronounce sentence upon her.

'You know,' he said. And then he did laugh. It was a

cruel, vicious laugh. A laugh which began deeply inside his lungs and shook his entire torso as it roared through his throat and out his mouth.

For a moment she lay silent. Her bare breasts quivered against his thigh.

'See?' he taunted. 'I told you that you knew.'

Suddenly she raised her head. 'What you think of me doesn't matter. Nothing matters, so long as you take me to bed with you and so long as you like the feel of me and the way I act under the bedcovers.'

'Or on them,' he amended sardonically.

'It doesn't matter.'

'Okay, it doesn't matter. I never said it did. It was you who started all this nonsense. I was very peacefully dissertating on the undemocratic ways of the animal kingdom when you – '

'No, Sam,' she cut him off. 'Don't start again.' She rose to her knees and tugged the bathing suit to her hips. Then she swayed towards him, reaching for his body with her bare breasts. 'Strip me,' she said.

He lay motionless, his eyes scrutinising her. 'Why?' he asked.

She sprang to her feet. The close wool of her swimsuit clung hotly to her loins, and she suddenly could not stand to be anything but naked, not even for a minute more. She tugged the hated garment over her hips and let it drop to the sand. Then she stood naked before him, her shadow falling across his body as she sacrificed all of herself to his gaze. 'I love you,' she said.

'What would you do if someone came along?'

'No one will.' Every cell of her body was alive with desire for him. She ran her hands down her sides, then inward across her flanks, caressing the soft flesh at the top of her thighs. Her hips weaved from side to side in open invitation.

'What if I told you,' he went on, 'that I had asked someone to come here today – two couples, friends of mine?'

'I'd say I didn't believe you. And, if I did believe you, I wouldn't care.' She tossed her hair out of her eyes and buried her knees in the sand between his legs, bending far forward.

His trunks having been tugged open by her feverish fingers, she reached inside and took hold of his manhood. Hardened, choking with willingness, the ruddy organ lifted its ripe, fruit-like head to the benediction of her kiss. She seasoned it with the flower of her lips, then tasted it with the moist tip of her tongue.

'You'd be terribly embarrassed if these friends of mine found you like this,' he reminded her.

She didn't answer. Stretching his foreskin to unsheathe the totality of his bright pink glans, she brought her face forward and closed her lips around the swollen tip of the organ. Her long blond hair would have fallen to cover their deed like a curtain, but, in an agony of lustful renunciation, she caught it with one hand and held it back from her forehead so that he could watch every movement of her mouth as she lovingly performed her ministrations. When he turned to one side, she reached around his legs and pulled his trunks down over his tightly muscled thighs. Her fingers clawed into the sand as she sucked his member deeply into her mouth. Her body twisted, belly-upward. Her thighs gaped. Her knees flattened outward.

Finally she stopped, but only to fling her arms about him and cover the saliva-slick organ with the creamy opulence of her large, soft, young breasts. She let her nipples be bruised by the ardour of her caresses, shaming their proud pink pout with the obscene wantonness of her raging desire. 'I love you,' she said. And she added: 'I make a mark in the back of my diary for everytime I do this to you.'

'Do what?' he asked, pretending bewilderment.

'You know. What I just did.'

'What did you just do?'

'I – I –'

'You can't say it, can you? You can't force yourself to say the words?'

'I – sucked – your – ' She let the sentence trail off.

He chuckled. 'You can do it, but you can't say it. You're quite a woman.'

Fiery waves of anger and desire coarsed through her. Desperately she crawled towards him on her knees and kissed his cheek. She gave him her breasts, her soft belly, her thighs. His hands briefly sought her buttocks, and she drew up to him, legs spread, for the touch of his fingers in her hot, damp crotch. 'I'll make an altar of sand,' she whispered in his ear. Lust – and lustful anticipation – choked her voice. 'I'll make an altar,' she repeated, 'and I'll be my own sacrifice to you.'

'To me?' he asked mockingly.

Her helplessness gnawed at her. 'To – to love, then,' she fumbled.

'Love?' he said quietly. 'You don't even know what the word means.'

The anger and desire inside her raged more furiously than ever. She flew at him, scratching blindly for his eyes, bruising her fists on his chest. 'I hate you!' she sobbed. 'I hate you, hate you, hate you! You son of a bitch! Why do you want to make me despise myself? Isn't it enough that you despise me?'

His strong fingers closed around her arms, and he held her away from him. Still, she could feel the hot, insistent thrust of his rigid organ against her belly. 'Build your altar,' he said after a moment. 'But don't try to deceive the gods.'

She crept from him, and on hands and knees, laboured at moulding a low table of sand. He watched the slight sway of her breasts as she moved her arms, and he smiled at the doggish attitude of her head as she bent to her self-appointed task. Low between her buttocks, the pink-brown slit of her womanhood winked at him, appearing and disappearing as her body moved from side to side. Seen that way, between the thighs of a kneeling or bending woman, he thought, the pretty aperture looked prettier and more interesting than from any other angle.

As she continued to work, he studied her entire body. He was struck by the changes which three months of sexual congress had wrought in her. She was, he thought, like a whip, growing better fitted to its task and to the hand of the wielder as the softening leather lost its stiffness and resistance. It was, he told himself, really a pity to discard such a well tempered tool. But there was nothing else to do. His interest in women was that of a fine craftsman who, with consummate skill and patience, shapes raw material to the pattern of his fancy, then goes on to work with new material. Elena now had reaped the full benefit of his talent. He had found her virginal and unaware, and he had made a woman of her. He had uncovered her capacity for suffering, and her tears had made her radiant. He had made her alert to her senses and to her shames. He had, in short, taught her to feel, to live. But, now that he had given her so much, she no longer had anything to give him. Thus, she would have to be discarded. Although she did not know it yet, today would be her last day with him.

'It's finished,' she said, turning on her hands and knees and looking across the mound at him. 'The altar is finished.'

He rose and started towards her.

She stood to receive him.

'No,' he instructed her. 'Don't stand. Kneel.'

She looked at him uncertainly for a moment, then complied.

Suddenly he found himself becoming excited. Her submissiveness, coupled with his knowledge that the sex act about to be performed would be their last together, stoked his passions. Tugging open his trunks, he advanced on her. 'Open your mouth,' he commanded – superfluously, for she had already anticipated his wishes. Then, seizing her by the hair, he thrust his throbbing engine between her lips.

Her fingers clutched at his buttocks, pulling them to her. Her tongue and teeth played hungrily against his swollen shaft. He forced her back on the rude altar, his veins aflame from her helpless acquiescence. The sand crumpled under the weight of their writhing bodies.

But he didn't want to complete their union in this posture. The last act, the final experience, should, he thought, be a total one — a total one for her as well as for him. It should be one she could remember him by, one which would burn forever in her brain.

Releasing his grip on her, he lowered himself into coital position. She opened her thighs and clutched his shoulders. He felt between her legs with his fingers, finding the hair slick and wet, the lips hot and trembling. His finger entered her, and he smiled as he felt her belly rise against his. He pressed, looking downward between their bodies as her hands found his manhood and guided it into place.

'Quickly!' she gasped.

He knew what she was asking for. She loved the sudden rape, the rending shock of his spear being driven violently inside her, gouging the tender folds of her womanhood. He had taught her to adore it, and she did.

Flinging her thighs wide apart, he tore into her with a savage fury. Her body buckled under the force of his assault. Her love-nest became dripping wet, and her eyes grew misty 'Make love to me,' she moaned thickly. 'Make love to me so hard that the whole damn altar comes tumbling down.'

Grinning, he seized her legs and wedged them between his body and hers. Then he began plummeting against her with hard, rhythmic strokes. With each thrust, her body trembled. Her fingers clawed at his shoulders. Her buttocks burned against his thighs. The white sand clung to her skin in sweaty, damp patches.

'Feel me!' she begged. 'Touch me! Do you like it? Am I soft and nice? Am I just the way you want me to be?'

He said nothing.

'Love me!' she continued. 'I want all of me to be exactly the way you like it, so you'll love me! You do love me when we're this way, don't you?'

His hands closed around her waist, feeling the life pulsing through her. He knew that she would spend in just a moment. Covering her mouth with his, he kneaded her breasts, then ran his hands down her sides and over her thighs, touching her as lightly and delicately as an assassin thumbs his knife.

'You love me,' she went on deliriously. 'You love me when we're like this. You love my breasts and my belly. And my mouth and my lips. Don't you? And my thighs and my legs. And my neck. And my tongue and my – my Don't you love me?'

She seemed hardly to know what she was saying, except that it was wanton and that it excited her and that it therefore would also excite him. She was scarcely aware of the baking-hot bed of sand on which they lay. She could have been lying on hot coals without noticing it. The sun burned fiercely through her closed eyelids, and everything – all existence – was to her just one brilliant globe of ecstasy.

'Love me,' she groaned. 'Lovveee me, Sam. Oh, please, please love me.' Then she fell silent as the long, slow, warm waves of orgasm inundated her.

He felt her body go slack beneath his. She was exhausted, her womb and belly fluttering weakly in the afterglow of the soul-shattering sexual explosion. Digging his elbows into the sand, he took his weight off her. His swollen organ, sucked of its juices, slipped slowly out of its moorings. The job had been done. And it had been done well.

For all of a minute, neither of them said anything. Then, smiling weakly, she told him: 'You've killed me. You've stabbed me, and now I'm dead.'

He smiled back. 'Dead?' His eyebrows arched. 'Then you should be buried.' And, not taking his eyes from hers, he grabbed a fistful of sand and let it sift through his fingers onto her sweat-streaked belly.

Her expression was one of puzzlement. She was sure that he was joking, but she had the uncomfortable feeling that the joke was on her. She tried a laugh that didn't quite come off. Then she smiled again and searched his eyes for a cue.

He did not return the smile. His face a study in sobriety, he took another fistful of sand and criss-crossed her damp skin with it. Then he seriously began to cover her body. He outlined her figure, built upon that foundation and soon had a heaping mound of sand which left only her head and her toes free.

'I can't move,' she said. And with the discovery came a sick feeling of fear, a feeling which twisted her insides and made her mouth go dry. 'Sam,' she repeated. 'I can't move.'

He didn't answer. He continued to pile sand on her. Then, at the top of the rotund mass, he sculptured a pair of breasts, a heavy belly and a gaping caricature of a vagina.

'I'm – I'm – scared, Sam,' she said weakly. 'I can't move, and I'm scared.'

He still said nothing. Stepping back from the pile of sand, he admired his handiwork. Then he pulled on his trunks, picked up her bathing suit and started towards the shore.

'Sam!' she cried. 'Where are you going?'

'To wash your suit,' he said over his shoulder. 'I want to get the sand all out of it.'

'Sam!' she called, louder. 'Sam, I don't like this game any more! Help me out of here, Sam!'

But he did not reply. All she could hear was the roar of the ocean as he walked away from her. Soon his broad, bronze shoulders disappeared behind the mound which covered her, and she was alone. She began to cry.

At the water's edge, he put his arm through one of the leg-holes in her bathing suit and looped the garment over his shoulder. Then he waded into the light surf and struck out in a long, slow crawl. Two hundred yards from the shore, he took the suit off his shoulder and let it float away. Then he swam back.

She was nearly hysterical when he returned. 'You had me scared witless!' she scolded him. 'I don't know what to do! You were gone so long that I was afraid something had happened!'

'Shut up,' he said quietly sitting on the sand next to her. 'You're boring me.'

'I was so frightened – ' she continued, as if by reflex.

Then, lowering her voice to a conciliatory tone, she added: 'Really, Sam. I began to imagine what would happen if you didn't come back, if the tide began coming in –'

'I wonder,' he interrupted, 'if you realise how easy it would be to kill you right now.'

Her face went white. She tried to cover her fright with a smile, but her eyes revealed the terror which raged inside her. 'Sam,' she said softly, 'don't talk like that, even if you're joking.'

'Seriously,' he went on, appearing to contemplate the sandpile which held her prisoner, 'do you realise how easy it would be? A handful of water in my cupped palm would finish you off. Not a mark. Not a sign of any struggle. When the tide came in, all the sand would be washed away. And, when it went out again, you'd be left naked on the beach. Naked and dead. The perfect crime. Accidental death by drowning. No coroner could interpret it any other way.'

'Sam' she gasped. 'Please! You're scaring me!'

He gazed at her curiously. 'So much the worse for you. I'm amusing myself, and that's what counts.' Smiling, he added: 'If you're smart, you'll pretend that you're not scared at all. Even an armchair assassin like me – a man who wouldn't dream of putting his thoughts into action – might be compelled to commit murder if he found that someone was actually terrified of him.'

'Well,' she replied quickly, 'let's not talk about it any more then. But help me out of here, will you? Really. I'm very uncomfortable. And I want to get dressed. Where's my bathing suit?'

He groaned mightily. 'Elena, Elena. Must you always nag? You know it bores me so.'

'But, Sam –'

'Shut *up*! I'm tired of listening to your voice. Besides, I need silence for a moment. I have to think up some excuse to break away from my friends when they get here.'

'Friends? Here? What friends, Sam?'

'Don't you remember? Didn't I tell you that I had asked some friends of mine – two couples – to meet us here today?'

'I thought you were joking.'

'I wasn't. And, if I'm not mistaken, they should be coming along right about – ' he glanced at his wristwatch ' – now.'

Her head jerked as she tried to bolt upright, forgetting for the moment that she still was imprisoned in the sandpile. 'Sam!' she exclaimed. 'They're coming here? Now? But I'm not dressed. I'm *naked*, Sam! Where's my bathing suit?'

He chuckled. 'Unfortunately, I lost your bathing suit in the water. And, also unfortunately, I have to leave as soon as my friends arrive. I've suddenly remembered an urgent appointment with a client.'

'*Sam!*' she sputtered, her uncovered toes curling in helpless fury. 'What are you trying to *do* to me?'

'Nothing, really. That is, what I'm trying to do is amuse myself. You happen to be the instrument of my amusement. But it's nothing personal. I'm not trying to do anything to you.'

'Sam!'

'Shut up. I think I hear them coming.'

From the distance, a quartet of voices wafted through the air. He stood and looked across the sand. 'Yes,' he announced, 'here they come.'

'*Sam!*'

'Now, now. Don't get yourself in an uproar. They're almost here.'

'But I'm *naked*!'

'I think you'll find them very sympathetic to your plight. They're quite nice people. One is a young clergyman, who's with his fiancée. The other is a sailor, with his girl friend. An odd combination, don't you think? I met them down at the public beach the other day.'

'Oh, for God's sake! Make them go away! Don't let them find me like this! Please, Sam I'll do anything you say.'

He laughed. 'But, my dear girl, what could you possibly do? You've already exhausted your entire repertory!' He patted the sandpile, as if to reassure her. 'Quiet, now. Here they are.'

The quartet appeared, all smiles and exuberance. The youthful, pink-faced preacher carried a picnic basket covered with a chequered tablecloth. The sailor carried a jug of wine and two blankets. 'Ah, right on time!' Garnett greeted them. 'Just like clockwork. And it's so good to see you! Permit me to present my girl friend, Elena. She's resting now, as you can see. But she's quite eager to meet you. Elena, say hello to Rose Briggs and, er – '

'Mabel Lamour,' coached the sailor's peroxide blond.

'Mabel Lamour,' repeated Garnett. 'And Doctor Green and Jack Doyle.'

The group exchanged how-do-you-do's, and the clergyman spread his tablecloth and began unloading the picnic basket. Garnett sat on the sand next to Elena, lit a cigarette and brought it to her lips. She puffed on it, then exhaled, her eyes glowering furiously.

'Well, it's a lovely afternoon, isn't it?' Garnett beamed heartily. 'Elena and I just took a very refreshing dip. The water's marvellous.'

'Yes,' agreed the Reverend Doctor Green. 'Rose and I were bathing earlier.'

'A lovely day for a picnic,' Garnett went on. 'What a shame, really, that I have to miss it.'

'Oh?'

'Yes, I have to meet with a client in just a few minutes, so I won't be able to stay. But I'll be back as soon as I can. And Elena will remain with you. I think you'll get along just fine together.'

'I'm sure,' smiled the clergyman.

Garnett brought the cigarette again to Elena's lips. 'Another drag, dearest? But aren't you smoking an awful lot today. Doctor Green, don't you think it's scandalous how modern girls smoke so much?'

'Well, ah,' the clergyman stuttered, 'I, uh, that is, ah, I try to be very liberal about these things. Uh one has to be liberal these days, you know. But, of course, I don't approve of extremes.'

'You tell 'em, doc,' the sailor agreed lazily from the blanket where, with his toe, he was tenderly tickling the belly of Miss Lamour.

Red-faced, the Reverend Doctor Green busied himself with the picnic basket. Garnett leaned overrr Elena's face and kissed her playfully on the nose. 'See dear?' he teased. 'Doctor Green disapproves of extremes. If you do smoke in the future, please be careful to do it moderately.'

'*Sam!*' she whispered urgently. 'Get rid of these people! Please!' When his only reply was a throaty chuckle, she added: 'If you do I'll show you a better time tonight than I ever have. Really, it'll be much better than it ever was. I'll think of new things to do. Things we've never done before. Honestly, I will.'

'Ah, Elena,' he answered aloud 'how can a girl let herself get so addicted to a vice? Really, it's unbecoming.' Then, turning to the clergyman, he said: 'But I must be off. Duty calls, and all that. Do forgive me. I'll try to get back as soon as I can. But if I'm delayed, don't let Elena bake too long in the hot sun. Be sure of that now, won't you, doctor?'

'Oh, yes,' the preacher volunteered. 'I'll take good care of her.'

'I'll bet,' interjected the sailor, just loud enough for everyone to hear but soft enough that all could pretend they hadn't.

'And Jack,' Garnett told the sailor, tucking his towel under his arm and starting towards the road, 'See that she gets in for a swim to get the sand off her. She'll surprise you.'

'*Sam!*' Elena called, trying to twist her head around to see him. 'Don't go! Please don't go!'

'Bye, dearest,' his voice came back to her.

'Sam – don't!'

But there was no reply. Garnett trotted across the beach to the hotdog stand at the side of the road. Then he bought a frank dripping with mustard and cold sauerkraut, ate it leisurely, ambled to his car and headed back towards the city.

Ah, Elena, he mused as the car raced along the highway. *If only you had grown hard and mean instead of soft and weak! If only you had become a woman instead of remaining a whimpering, simpering little girl!*

The more he thought of it, the more it annoyed him. What the hell did it matter if someone saw her naked? If only she'd learned to be as shameless in public as she was in private!

But he quickly pushed the thoughts out of his mind. Even now, a few short minutes after he had left her on the beach, Elena was already out of his life. Gone. Past tense. Maybe she'd phone his office once or twice. But his secretary would give her the brush-off, and eventually she'd stop trying. Then she'd fade into oblivion, just one more dim memory in a lifetime of dim memories, just one more piece of raw material which had been fashioned by the master craftsman and then was cast aside.

So much for Elena. If only she hadn't called him Sam.

* * *

Yeah, Garnett, so much for Elena. Yesterday's garbage. Who needs it? Whatever made you think of her, anyway?

Oh, yes. The storey in the News. And the way the writer used your middle name, 'Conrad Samuel Garnett.' And Elena was the only person who ever called you 'Sam'.

But is that the only reason you thought of her?

You're not sure.

And, the longer you ponder the matter, the more convinced you are that there was another reason.

Suddenly you remember that during the Cembretti-Morgan trial you saw a broad out in the spectator section who looked vaguely familiar to you. The first time you saw her was when you put Cembretti on the stand. The second time was when you were delivering your summation to the jury. Both times you were so involved in the trial proceedings that you didn't give her more than a passing glance. And she was all covered up with a big-brimmed hat and sunglasses, so you really didn't get a very good look at her. But the look you got was enough to let you know that you had seen her someplace before.

The whole thing didn't mean very much to you at the time. After all, you'd seen hundreds – thousands – of broads. So why pay special attention to this one? But now – now that you've made a connection between Elena and the business about your middle name – everything seems to fit into place. The broad out in the spectator section was Elena. It had to be.

Oh, well, so what? So she sat in on your trial for a couple of days. Big deal. Maybe she still has the hots for you. Maybe she's been having wet dreams about you lately – do broads have wet dreams? – and she wanted to see you in the flesh again. Who cares? Besides, you've got some important things to think about.

You glance at your watch.

Ten-fifteen.

You've got to get to work on that brief for the appellate court. They've given you four days to file, and you don't like to miss deadlines. Not that the appeal will do Cembretti and Morgan any good. They're both goners and you know it. Still, they paid a pretty penny for your services, so they're entitled to the full treatment.

And you've got to review the file on the Morrissey case. You've got a conference tomorrow afternoon with Morrissey's buddy's lawyer, and you're sure that the guy has a fast one up his sleeve. Might as well beat him to the punch.

And, now that we think about it, you've got to line up some fresh female action for the weekend. You've been so busy with the Cembretti-Morgan thing lately that you've let your social life slip. No time like the present to swing back into action.

You buzz Jackson and ask him to get the Morrissey file ready. Then you fold up the newspapers and stack them in a corner on your desk. Now to get to work on that brief. If you're lucky, you'll have it finished by tomorrow afternoon.

CHAPTER TWO

'There's a young lady here to see you, sir,' said Jackson. 'She claims to be a cousin of yours, but – ' The intercom hummed for a moment, and Garnett heard an exchange of voices in the background. Then Jackson said sceptically: 'She claims to be your cousin Clara.'

Garnett smiled. So there was a broad in the outer office. And she wanted to see him badly. Badly enough that she had resorted to a ruse so transparent that even Jackson could see through it. Any broad who was that desperate deserved a look-see. 'Blond?' the devil's advocate asked, playing the law of averages.

'Brunette!' declared Jackson triumphantly, certain that he had intercepted an impostor, possibly one with a vial of acid or a pearl-handled automatic in her purse.

'Oh, my *brunette* cousin Clara!' Garnett laughed into the intercom. 'Send her in!'

She was strictly from hicksville. Her clothes were last year's, and her hair-do was older than that. The blush that came to her cheeks when Garnett greeted her suggested that she still found it a novelty to have a man rise when she entered a room.

Still, she was quite a looker. Pretty face, good breasts, a nice flat tummy and great legs. Exactly the sort of diversion a busy criminal lawyer needs after slaving for two hours over a brief.

'I'm sorry to break in this way, Mr Garnett,' she apologised, 'but I just had to see you. It may be a matter of life and death.'

Garnett took her hand and favoured her with his professional, sure-to-con-a-jury smile. 'I invariably see anyone who uses even the slightest ingenuity to get past that secretary of mine,' he replied amiably. 'But the cousin business is pretty lame. Next time think of something better.' He motioned to a chair. 'Won't you sit down?'

'I *am* sorry,' she repeated. 'But this really is urgent, and I couldn't think of anyone else to turn to. I do hope you'll help me.'

Garnett made his way to this desk. 'Tell me all about it, cousin Clara, and maybe I will.'

She leaned back in her chair and tugged at the hem of her skirt. The 'cousin Clara' had made her blush, and the crimson in her cheeks heightened her attractiveness. She had, Garnett decided, an extraordinarily good face. The hair-do was atrocious, but the eyes were very pretty. And the nose was cute. And the cheekbones were nice and high. And the mouth was super-sexy, especially at the crest of the lips, where she had bitten off most of her lipstick. She stared at the floor for a moment, then said quietly; 'I don't know where to begin.'

Garnett flashed another smile – Warmer-Than-Cordial Smile Number Three – reserved for pretty young girls with problems. 'Suppose,' he suggested, 'you begin at the beginning. What's your name – I mean, your real name?'

'Clara. Clara Reeves. I'm not your cousin, of course. In fact, I'm not anybody's cousin. So far as I know, my older sister, Rita, is my only living relative. My parents are dead, and – well, I guess I'm just all alone.'

'And now you're in trouble.'

She leaned forward in the turkey-red leather chair. Her frown deepened. 'Not exactly. But I think Rita is. You see, she's – she's disappeared.' She paused, as if expecting Garnett to produce the sister from his vestpocket. When her revelation resulted in nothing more than a professionally interested 'Ummmmmm', she added: 'She's been gone for more than a week.'

'What's she running from?'

'I – I don't know. I mean, I'm – not sure – she – *is* – running.'

'Then why did she go?'

'I'm not sure she did go – voluntarily.'

'You think she's been kidnapped?'

Clara swallowed hard. 'Maybe. Or else – murdered.'

'What makes you think so?'

'I don't know. I mean, it's all so strange. I mean, she's gone away before without telling me where she was going. But never for this long. I mean, I think she's in trouble – or dead. Otherwise she would've phoned me.'

'How long has she been gone?'

'Twelve days.' Clara's eyes grew moist, and her lips quivered. 'Twelve days, Mr Garnett.'

The devil's advocate smiled reassuringly. 'Well, that *is* a long time. But you yourself said that she's gone away before without telling you. Maybe you're getting all worked up over nothing.

'Maybe, Mr Garnett. But I don't think so. I mean, I really think something has happened to her.'

Garnett took a pencil from the top of his desk and examined the eraser. 'Miss Reeves,' he said slowly, 'I can understand your concern. But, even if something has happened to Rita. I'm hardly the person to help you. Why don't you go to the police?'

Clara fidgeted with the hem of her skirt. 'Oh, you know. They'd only ask a couple of questions, then put her name on a "missing persons" list. But they wouldn't find her. I want to find her, Mr. Garnett. I've got to find her.'

'But Miss Reeves, I'm a criminal lawyer, not a tracer of lost persons. What do you expect me to do? The police have a department that was created specifically to track down people who suddenly drop out of sight. I'd suggest you contact them.' Looking into her eyes and smiling slightly, he added: 'Unless there's some reason you're afraid to go to the police – '

She blushed again. Her eyes were riveted to her knees. 'I *am* afraid,' she admitted softly. 'Rita's been acting strangely lately. I think she's involved in something, but I don't know just what.'

'What do you suspect?'

'I couldn't even guess.'

Garnett studied her hands, which were folded into tight little fists. 'Miss Reeves, if you expect me to help you, you've got to tell me everything you know. Suppose we go back to the beginning again. Where are you and your sister from? Where do you live now? What kind of work do you do?'

Clara took a deep breath and exhaled heavily. As she did, her breasts heaved, and Garnett couldn't help but notice their round, well-sculptured firmness. 'We're from upstate originally,' she said. 'When Rita was eighteen and I was sixteen, our parents were killed in an auto accident. We came to the city and moved in with our Aunt Madge. She died last year. Then we took an apartment of our own. Rita was working as a secretary at the time, and I had a job as a cashier in a restaurant. I still have my job, but Rita quit hers six months ago.'

'What has she been doing since?'

'Nothing.'

'Where does she get money to live on?'

'I don't know. But she always seems – or seemed – to have all she needed. She never was late with her half of the rent or food-money. In fact, she was always asking me if I wanted to borrow some.'

'Very interesting.'

'I know what you're thinking, Mr Garnett. But it isn't true. Or, if it is true, it isn't Rita's fault. Somebody must've tricked her into it – maybe with drugs or something. She just isn't that kind of girl.'

Garnett's eyes took another quick tour of Clara's body. He wondered just what kind of girl *she* was. Certainly not a swinger; all the evidence pointed away from that possibility. But it was hard to imagine her as a virgin, either. With a figure like hers, she was sure to have been propositioned a dozen times a day. Could she have said no to everybody? Unlikely. Or maybe not so unlikely after all. The subject merited further investigation.

'You say someone might have tricked her?' he asked. 'Who?'

'I don't know. But she's been running around with a pretty funny crowd lately. I wouldn't put anything past them.'

'Tell me more about them.'

'I'll tell you all I can, but it isn't very much.'

'Every little bit helps.'

She looked up at him and tried to smile. Then her eyes focused on the floor and she spoke in a soft, distant voice. 'I don't know when it began, but I realise now that for a long time Rita was keeping a lot of things secret from me. It wasn't at all like her. Why, all our lives, we've always told each other everything. But, last year sometime, while she was still working, she began spending weekends away from home. She'd leave Friday night, and she wouldn't come back until Sunday. I never saw any of the people she went with. She always drove off in her own roadster and came back alone. When I asked if I could go with her, she only laughed and kissed me on the nose, as if I were a silly little kid.'

'How old were you at the time?'

'Well, let's see, that was last year, so I was twenty. Anyway, after she quit work, she began staying away for longer than just a weekend. Sometimes she'd go on Thursday and not come back until Monday or Tuesday. I tried to find out where she went, but she never wanted to talk about it.'

Garnett took a cigar from the humidor on his desk and peeled off the cellophane. His eyes darted from Clara's breasts, which rose and fell rhythmically as she talked, to her thighs, which were outlined provocatively against her tight-fitting cotton skirt.

She continued: 'A week ago last Friday, Rita disappeared for good. She told me she was going away for a weekend in the country, and she drove off alone as usual. When she didn't come back by Tuesday or Wednesday, I began to worry. And, by Friday, I was petrified. Now here it is Wednesday again and I still haven't heard from her.' She took a tiny handkerchief from her purse and dabbed at her red-rimmed eyes. 'I'm scared, Mr Garnett, I really am. I'm sure something has happened to her. Otherwise she would've called me.' She covered her face with her hands, and her body shook with uncontrollable sobs. 'Oh, Mr. Garnett, where can she be, where can she be?'

Garnett crossed the room and sat on the arm of her chair. Her body yielded to his touch, and she buried her head against his chest. 'Now, now,' he said, stroking the back of her neck soothingly with his fingers, 'pull yourself together. Your fears probably are groundless. More likely than not, your sister went away with these friends of hers and stayed a little longer than usual, that's all.'

Clara lifted her head. As she did, her breasts came to rest against Garnett's thigh. He savoured the feel of them. 'Maybe you're right,' she said, dabbing again at her eyes. 'But I'm still worried. You see, I haven't told you everything yet.'

'Then tell me,' he urged, pressing firmly against her back. The action resulted in her breasts' being wedged tightly against him. He realised instantly that her brassiere wasn't padded.

'Well,' she went on, 'last Friday, when I really got panicky about Rita, I decided to try to find out something about those weekend parties of hers. I went through her drawers, and I found some pretty peculiar things.'

'What kind of things?'

'Well – uh – that is – '

'Come, now. Why can't you tell me?'

'I – I'm embarrassed.'

'But, my child, if you don't tell me, how can I help you?'

'Well – okay – I'll try.' She stuffed her handkerchief into her purse and stared across the room. 'You see, Rita had this one drawer that she always kept locked. I prised the lock open with a kitchen knife. I mean, I know it's wrong to go through other people's private property, but, I mean, I love my sister, and I was only trying to protect her. Anyway, I opened the drawer, and I found all sorts of unbelievable things.'

'For example?'

'This!' She took a large silver ring from her purse and thrust it into Garnett's hands. It held an enormous onyx, into the polished face of which, in fine gold, an exquisite figure had been wrought.

'A scorpion,' he said, balancing the ring carefully on his palm. 'Beautiful work.'

'A man's ring,' she pointed out. 'Rita never showed it to me. And I'm sure that it has something to do with her disappearance. Can't you just feel it? That's not just a ring; it's something evil!'

He laughed softly. 'My dear, a woman's intuition is a wonderful thing. But, if you expect me to believe that there's something sinister about Rita's disappearance, you'll have to produce more evidence than this.'

'Well, there is more evidence. In the drawer with the ring were some books. Terrible books. With horrible pictures in them. And the bookplates all had the same scorpion design as the ring.'

'What were the books about?'

'They were terrible. And the pictures were even worse. They showed men and women doing all sorts of horrible things. I couldn't believe my eyes.'

'What exactly were the men and women doing?'

'I couldn't tell you, Mr. Garnett. It's too awful. I mean, it's really hideous.'

'Were they being tortured and murdered and things like that?'

'Oh, no. Much worse. The pictures were – well, they were *dirty* pictures! *Filthy* pictures!'

'In other words, pictures of people having sexual intercourse?'

'Y—yes. And worse things too. All sorts of terrible things.'

During the conversation, Garnett's hand had slipped over Clara's shoulder and had come to rest casually alongside her breast. Apparently the girl had been so caught up in her narrative that she failed to notice it. But, Garnett realised, she soon would notice it, and, when she did, the result might be a lessening of the rapport which he presently enjoyed. Accordingly he withdrew it. 'Well,' he said, returning to his desk and lighting his cigar, 'what else did you find in the drawer?'

'A diary. Rita's diary. And it was just as bad as the pictures.' Again Clara's eyes grew moist. 'Oh, Mr Garnett, you wouldn't believe it. Someone had to be influencing her – someone horrible – or else she never would have written anything like that!'

'What did she write?'

'I can't repeat it. I'd die of shame. But it was awful. Really awful. It told about this vile gang of people she's been mixed up with, and all the terrible things they did at their weekend parties. I was mortified when I read it. I couldn't believe that my sister would get involved in something like that. Still, I can't deny the facts. It was her handwriting. And, judging from the way she described things, she actually enjoyed what they were doing. That's why I was afraid to go to the police. I knew that these parties must be against the law, and, if Rita really hasn't been kidnapped or murdered, I wouldn't want her to get arrested. So I came to you. I figured that if anybody could help me, you could.'

Garnett took a long drag on his cigar and blew a thin stream of smoke towards the ceiling. Through the corner of his eye he focused on Clara's breasts, the rhythmic rising and falling of which had accelerated proportionately to her mounting excitement. Suppressing a smile that begged for expression, he said gravely: 'A wise move, Miss Reeves. This is a serious matter and can't be handled too carefully. But, as you may realise, my fees are not small. Do you think you can afford me?'

She reached inside her purse and withdrew a little wad

of bills. 'I have about fifty dollars. If you want more, I'll sign a paper authorising my employer to deduct it from my salary.'

He chuckled. 'My dear girl, I normally get fifty dollars just for a conference like we've been having here this afternoon. To follow up on a case as complex as the one you've described would entail weeks of work, not only by me but also by private detectives and other people affiliated with my office. The absolute minimum I would charge is five thousand dollars.'

Clara's face went pale. Slowly she stuffed the bills back into her purse and snapped it shut. 'I'm sorry I took up so much of your time,' she said quietly. 'I guess I should've known that a famous lawyer like you would want more money than I ever could hope to pay.' She started towards the door.

Garnett waited until her hand was on the knob. Then he said: 'Don't go, Miss Reeves.'

She turned, and again his eyes drank in the exquisite lines of her body – the marvellously sculptured breasts, the trim and flat tummy, the gently rounded hips, the long and lovely legs.

'Ordinarily,' he went on, 'I don't waive a fee under any circumstances. But, frankly, this case intrigues me – and, if I may be so blunt, I also find you a very engaging young lady. Therefore, I'm gong to offer you a proposition.'

A glimmer of hope shone in her eyes. She smiled hesitantly and waited for him to continue.

'Let me see these books and this diary that you found in your sister's drawer. If I'm persuaded that she has, as you believe, fallen prey to a band of scoundrels, I'll do everything in my power to help rescue her and to bring the knaves to justice. There'll be no charge for my services.'

'Oh, Mr. Garnett! I *knew* I could count on you! I just *knew* it – '

'But,' he interrupted, 'I'll need your full cooperation. If

there is in fact a band of scoundrels, and if Rita has in fact become their prisoner, the only way she can be saved – and the only way we can get enough evidence to foil her captors – is if you personally infiltrate the group. The mission would be dangerous, and, I expect, quite disgusting. You'd be required to undergo a great many risks and to make a great many sacrifices. The question is: are you sufficiently concerned about Rita's well-being and about seeing justice done that you'll do whatever is necessary?'

'Gladly, Mr. Garnett! Gladly!'

'Then,' said the devil's advocate, motioning her back to the chair which she so recently had vacated, 'let's review the basic facts in the case. First off, you say that you and Rita have no other living relatives, is that correct?'

'Yes, it is.'

'And she hasn't had a job for approximately six months?'

'Right.'

'Then there's no one other than you who would have noticed that she's missing?'

'Yes, that's right.'

'No boyfriends, no girl friends, no other acquaintances?'

'None I can think of.'

'And you haven't mentioned this matter to the police or to anyone else?'

'No; no one but you.'

'No neighbours or friends?'

'No one, Mr Garnett.'

'All right. Now what about the diary and the erotic books? Are they presently at your apartment?'

'Yes.'

'Under lock and key?'

'Well, Rita's drawer is unlocked; as I told you, I opened it with a kitchen knife. But the apartment itself is locked, and Rita and I have the only two keys.'

'And you haven't shown the diary or the books to anyone?'

'Not a soul. I'd die of embarrassment if anyone saw them.'

'Very well. Now, about your visit to my office: did you tell anyone you were coming here?'

'No. I got off work by pretending I had a dental appointment.'

Garnett flicked the ash from his cigar and stared thoughtfully at the glowing coal. For a moment he was silent. Then, raising his eyes to meet Clara's, he said: 'Miss Reeves, you've handled this whole affair quite admirably. If you continue to exercise the sound judgment which you've displayed so far, I'm sure we can bring matters to a successful conclusion. As concerns your sister's safety, I'm rather certain you have nothing to worry about; if she had been murdered, her body would have been found by now and you would have been notified: therefore, it's reasonable to assume that she's still alive and unharmed. As concerns her whereabouts, we're still in the dark; but perhaps there'll be a clue among the contents of that secret drawer of hers. In any event, it would behoove us to examine the drawer carefully, and as soon as possible; we can plot our next move from there.'

Clara nodded. 'Would you like me to bring everything to your office?'

'No, that would be too risky. I don't think you're being followed, but, if you are, you'd be tipping our hand if you came here again. A better procedure would be for me to come to your apartment. Not too many people know me by sight, and whoever is following, if there is someone, might think I was just another of your boyfriends.'

Her smile suggested that she found the prospect of his being mistaken for her boyfriend a pleasant prospect indeed. 'I can see why you're such a successful lawyer,' she beamed. 'You certainly think of all the angles.'

He dismissed the compliment with a shrug. 'Write your address on this,' he said, handing her a pencil and a yellow legal pad. 'I'll stop this evening after dinner. Is nine-thirty convenient?'

'Very,' she replied, writing the address and returning his pad and pencil.

'Then nine-thirty it is.' He stoood, signifying that the interview was over. 'Now run along and try not to worry. I'm sure we'll get to the bottom of this in no time at all.'

She rose, smiling. For the first time all afternoon the smile seemed both genuine and confident. 'I don't know how to thank you, Mr. Garnett. I don't know what I would've done without you.'

'Think no more of it,' he smiled back. 'I'll get my reward when the case has been solved.'

She started towards the door. He followed, allowing himself enough room to ponder the niceties of her posterior construction before going forward to open the door for her. He scrutinised her hips and the tight press of her skirt over the outline of her rump. It wasn't hard to imagine her walking naked. He wondered what she wore under the cool summer suit, and he visualised a pair of sheer panties caught in the cleft between her luscious buttocks, their soft pink flesh showing through, a light edging of lace lending piquancy to the dish.

In the outer office, she turned to smile at him once more before she left. Standing in his doorway, he moved his lips in a final goodbye. She could not have realised it, but the words his lips actually formed were: 'Welcome to the club, sweetheart.'

'Jackson,' he said aloud after she had gone, 'did you know that I have a criminal mind? What is it they say – it takes a thief to deefend a thief?'

'Hahahahahahaha, you mean "to catch a thief," ' Jackson replied, 'but the point is well-taken, sir hahahahahahaha.'

Garnett closed the door and returned to his desk. *Well, Conrad Samuel,* he told himself, *Jackson has been given his little joke for the day; it remains now only to tip the waitress in the restaurant where you'll eat lunch, to run your hand under her dress and pinch her chubby little leg, and you'll have rounded out the morning and made a good start on the weakminded idiocies that constitute the afternoon's dull routine.*

CHAPTER THREE

She came towards him as though she were going to kiss him, and he involuntarily reached – or half-reached – for her before he realised that she wanted only to take his hat. Then he followed her into the living room, jealous of the light summer dress which clung so possessively to her young body.

'Would you care for a drink?' she asked. 'I read in the papers that you like gin-rickeys, so I bought some lemons and stuff.'

'How nice of you!' he beamed appreciatively. 'As a matter of fact, I'd love one. I'm really parched. But I don't like to drink alone. You'll have one with me, won't you?'

'Okay. But you'd better help me mix them. I usually make them too weak.'

She led the way into the kitchen, and he marvelled at the change which had come over her since her visit to his office that morning. There she had been nervous and awkward, a gangly kid from the sticks who didn't know her buttocks from home plate. Now, here in her apartment, she was the picture of poise and self-assurance – a lovely morsel, and a perfect hostess to boot.

He stood beside her as she squeezed the lemons and strained their juice over the sugar-coated cubes in the large cocktail shaker. Then he poured the gin, at the same time intoxicating himself with her smell – the heady aroma of young sweat and scented soap and good perfume. His glance dropped to her breasts; his mind was already between her thighs.

'Any news from your sister?' he asked.

'No. Not a word.'

'Well, don't worry. She's safe and sound. I'm sure of it.'

She smiled winningly. 'Believe it or not, I'm not worried at all any more. I guess it's because I know you're in my corner. You'd be surprised how much reassurance you've given me. But I guess it's that way with all your clients.'

'Yes,' he conceded immodestly, 'it generally is.'

She arranged their glasses on a small serving tray and carried it out to the terrace, which offered a commanding view of the river. Then they sat opposite each other on a pair of matching wicker chairs and touched the glasses together in a silent toast. A breeze rustled through the dusk as the moon rose suddenly over the water. Her skirt billowed, and he got a glimpse of her soft, marble-white thighs.

'Lovely view,' he observed pointedly.

'I like it very much,' she replied, evidently unaware of the panorama which interested him most. 'Rita and I had thought of renting a less expensive apartment, but, after we looked out at the city from the terrace of this one, we decided to forego a few other luxuries instead.'

'A wise choice, I think.'

'Yes, I think so, too – although I'll confess that I sometimes have second thoughts when the first of the month rolls around.'

They exchanged a few more banalities. Then the breeze lifted her skirt again, just as she uncrossed her legs. Apparently unnoticed by her, the hem came to rest high above the tops of her rolled stockings. Garnett sipped his drink and pitted his eyesight against the dusk.

If her legs had remained covered, he wouldn't have noticed anything unnatural about her posture. But, now that they were bare where the skirt had gently fallen back, she appeared to have taken a particularly suggestive position. Her knees were turned slightly outward, and the naked inner sides of her thighs gave the impression that more was being shown than actually was.

'I think it would be very thrilling to be a criminal lawyer,' she was saying. 'You probably get a great deal of satisfaction from defending an innocent man.'

'It's very satisfying,' Garnett replied. 'There's nothing quite like it.'

But his present source of satisfaction had nothing whatsoever to do with the practice of criminal law. While she was speaking, she had drawn up one knee. In so doing, she had bared to his sight the entire underside of her leg, from calf to buttock. It now hung there like a gigantic, ripe and somewhat ill-proportioned pear. It was funny, he mused, how much more there was to a woman's leg than a man ordinarily sees.

Her skin was pink under a light coating of tan, and he could even distinguish the line of lighter colour where her bathing suit had kept her upper thigh from tanning. Where the naked leg joined its twin on the seat there was – there was – no, it was growing darker, and there was nothing. Garnett sighed, but his disappointment did not sour him to the extent of forcing his eyes elsewhere.

Clara presently began to relate her life storey. The circumstances and the view being what they were, Garnett sat there silently and let her talk. She described her childhood with Rita, their schooling and the tired little tragedy of their parents' deaths. Then, just as she came to the part about their move from the country to the city, the breeze spitefully carried her skirt back down over her knees. Garnett suggested that they go inside and examine Rita's effects.

Clara led the way to the bedroom and flicked on a light. 'This is it,' she announced, tugging open the drawer.

Garnett carefully lifted it out of the bureau and placed it in the centre of the bed. Then he sat on one side of it and motioned for Clara to sit on the other. 'Exhibit A,' he observed, 'one pair of green silk panties.'

'Oh, those are mine!' she exclaimed, snatching them from his hand and running off to the closet with them.

'I thought this was Rita's drawer,' he said dryly.

'I – I was using that old silk thing as a dustcloth when I found what she hid in here.' Her face was ruddy with blushes, and he eyed her with considerable amusement. He wondered if her discovery had inspired her to masturbate, and, for a moment, he could almost see her worrying that hair would grow on her palm if she played with herself.

But he didn't pursue the matter. 'Yes, a dustcloth,' he said. 'I see.' Then he began picking through the drawer, lifting up objects at random and laying them on the bed as he finished inspecting them.

The first item which attracted his attention was a linen envelope. On its face was a Chinese letter, painted in delicate red brush-strokes. Inside: six condoms of extraordinarily good manufacture, printed in gay colours and curiously armed with an array of rubber spikes, knobs, dimples, nipples, fins, studs, tiny fingers, whiskers and bits of sponge.

Next came a book of etchings, hand-tinted with water colours, and a scorpion bookplate on the inside front cover. The workmanship was sumptuous. He lingered for a moment on one plate which depicted a pair of girls engaged in mutual cunnilingus while they swung through the air, supported by flying rings through which one girl had hooked her knees. Clara could not resist peeking at the drawing which intrigued him. He looked up suddenly and she swallowed hard.

Next was a small bocca-da-gazza case of shantung silk with a bone clasp. It contained two silver balls of a size slightly smaller than a walnut. Clara looked puzzled, and the devil's advocate offered an explanation. 'Japanese. It's called a rin-no-tamma set.' She nodded brightly, as if she really knew what he was talking about.

Next came three small books, each decorated with the now-familiar scorpion bookplate. The first was *Memoirs of Madame Condeux*, a well-known erotic classic. The second was *Sixty-Nine Delightful Ways To Sin*, less well-known but equally classic. The third was a two-in-one special, *The Art of the Tongue* and *Ten Inches Above the Garter*, both illustrated with photographs. Clara averted her eyes as he examined them.

Next came an object which was, yet was not, a male sexual organ. More precisely, it was a rubber replica, excellent in proportion and design, hollow rather than solid and therefore extremely lifelike to the touch. Obviously it had been made to fit standards which were quite exacting, especially with respect to size. Garnett got rid of it without overmuch delay, although it was indeed an admirable bit of workmanship. Indeed, its workmanship was its fault. It was too real. Even its colouring was perfectly human. Every vein was indicated, every nuance of tan and pink and red. Garnett could not touch it without thinking of himself as a sodomite. He gingerly placed it on the bed, observing as he did that Clara's cheeks were crimson.

Next he examined a small cat-o'-nine tails, but with only five tails. It was fashioned from the finest and softest of leathers – kidskin, to be sure – and braided by a master hand, tooled and worked with a wealth of fine design. He gave it an experimental flick, to which Clara did not react, then abandoned it alongside the other *objets d'art*.

Next came a small silver box, not unlike a snuff-box, containing a quantity of broken greenish-black shreds, not unlike tea. 'Cannabis,' he said, sniffing it.

'What?' she asked.

'Hmmmm? Oh, a sort of Indian tobacco. We'll have to try some of it sometime. It's hard to get because of the tax.'

Finally there was Rita's diary, a book of padded ivory leather with a ridiculous miniature lock which did not lock. The handwriting was soft, curling and barely legible. Garnett riffled through the pages, then set the volume on the bed alongside the box of marijuana.

The inspection having thus been completed, Garnett and his pretty young client sat in the midst of the artefacts of Rita's secret sex life like two castaways. For a moment neither of them said anything. Then Clara lit a cigarette and asked: 'What do you make of it all?'

'Very interesting,' replied Garnett. '*Very* interesting. But

I can't say that it proves much. The books are rare and some of the other objects are even rarer. Still none is rare enough that we'd be able to trace its purchaser.'

'How about the diary?'

He picked it up and riffled through the pages again, finally stopping at one of the more curious entries. 'I don't seem to be able to make out the handwriting,' he lied, knitting his brows. 'Would you read it to me?'

'Oh, but really!' Clara remonstrated. 'Why the words are just awful! I couldn't bring myself to repeat them!'

'Come now, don't be coy. How else can we investigate this thing?' He moved some of the objects on the bed to one side, sat next to her and thrust the little book onto her lap. 'Here. Start with this entry.'

She hesitated for a moment, then began reading in a low voice. 'It was wonderful last night, more wonderful than ever. But each time always seems more wonderful than the last.'

'Excellent!' he applauded. 'I couldn't make out a word of that myself. Read some more.'

' "I went to his apartment. He was waiting for me. We didn't say a word, but he kissed me as soon as I entered the room. When he did, our bodies touched, and I knew that he had been thinking of me, for I felt – felt – " '

'Go on. What's the matter?'

'I can't read that word.'

He took the book from her hands and studied it. 'Prick,' he informed her. ' "I felt his prick." You see, what she is saying is that when their bodies touched she felt his prick. Do you understand?'

'Yes, but I can't read words like that out loud to you.'

He chuckled softly. 'Dear, sweet girl. I'm sorry to have to ask you to do this. But your innocence will keep such words from actually touching you. I'm the only one who hears you say them, and I know that it isn't really you who's saying them; it's Rita. You must be Rita's voice for me, or else we'll never learn what happened to her. Every word in this diary may be important to us.' He put the book back in her hands. 'Come now, read some more.'

'I'll try,' she promised bravely.

'Good girl.' He patted her on the knee. 'I'm sure we'll get to the bottom of this yet.'

' "I knew that he had been thinking of me" ' she resumed bravely, ' "for I felt his – prick – pressing against my belly. We fairly ran into the living room, and there, before that great Chinese Bhudda, I pulled off my things. I shook the snow from my coat, then I stripped to the skin without once pausing. Meanwhile, my darling simply stood and stared while I undressed.

' "I was in a perfect fury to get completely naked, for I wanted the detestable clothes off me and my darling on me. Still, I remembered how he liked to see me in various stages of undress, so I took my time and let him see everything nice that there was to see about each stage. I looked back over my shoulder while I took off my snow boots. Then I took off my coat and dress. By the time my underwear was off, his eyes were shining. I was facing away from him, and I knew that, between my buttocks, he could see the bright pink lips of my sex. He always loved looking at me that way. Men are so silly, aren't they? Who can understand them? One glimpse of a girl's tendermost spot and their – their – pricks get stiff as a stick." '

'What's wrong, Clara?' asked Garnett. Why have you stopped?'

'I – I just can't go on. That – that word. That awful word!'

'But my child, it's only a word.' He folded his arms across his lap so that she could not see the physical effect which her hesitant pronouncing of the word had upon him. 'Wasn't it Shakespeare who said, "What's in a word?" '

'But, Mr Garnett, it's disgusting. It's the most disgusting word I know.'

'The *most* disgusting?'

'Well, maybe the second-most disgusting. Or the third.'

'But why should it disgust you?'

'I – I don't know. I really don't know.'

'Well, if we're going to get any place with this diary, you've got to purge yourself of this disgust. I'd suggest that you try saying the word aloud several times.'

'Several times? Without even reading it? Oh, Mr Garnett!'

'Try.'

'But – '

'You must.'

'Well – '

'I'm waiting.'

For a moment she was silent. Then her lips formed a letter 'p' and she whispered the word slowly. '*Prick.*'

'Again,' coached the devil's advocate.

'Prick,' she said a trifle louder.

'Again.'

'Prick!'

'Again.'

Her tone was firm and clear. 'Prick!'

'Excellent. Now resume reading.'

She lowered her eyes to the diary. ' "As soon as I was stark naked, I ran to the fire which was burning in the grate and stood by it, pretending to warm my behind. I wasn't merely pretending, though, for it had been terribly cold outside. Then my darling came to me and said that he would help me warm up. So I got a footstool and bent across it and had him switch me. That warmed both of us.

' "When he had given me a switching that smarted beautifully, he threw the birch rod into the fire and took off his clothes. I lay at his feet, adoring him while he undressed. My bottom was burning, and my insides were itching like crazy. Switching certainly is a wonderful invention! And, for me, it's certainly wonderful to belong so thoroughly to a man that he can even beat you!

' "As soon as he was naked, I asked his permission to kiss him. He said yes, and I brought my eager lips to his thighs and his belly and his – his prick." See, Mr Garnett? I said it. "But he wouldn't let me put it in my mouth, no

41

matter how much I begged him. Instead, he took me to the sofa and we stretched out, side by side, our bellies touching, and he teased me for a while.

' "I thought he never was going to let me have it, but at last he allowed me to hold it in my hand and play with it, and soon I was holding it warmly between my legs. I was anything but cold by this time, but still I was shivering because I was so passionate, and he teased me, asking if I wanted more of the switch. So I said yes, I wanted anything that would bring his — his prick with it. I was only joking, but he took me seriously, and went to fetch another rod.

' "There weren't any left, so he brought back a light watch chain and a wet silk cloth to spread over my buttocks so that the chain wouldn't cut me. He made me lie on the sofa, my face buried in a couple of big, soft pillows, while I took another whipping.

' "The second whipping hurt much more than the first, and I cried. Actually he was gentle with me. If he hadn't been, the chain could have been sheer torture instead of being nice and exciting like it was. Still, it hurt. But I wouldn't stop him for the world.

' "As he hit me, I could see his prick standing upright, erect as a hatrack, and the tears in my eyes seemed to make him go wild. When he pulled off the silk cloth and dropped the chain, my bottom was red as a lobster. It burned like fire. And I was on fire inside, too. I could hardly wait for him to leap on me. I flung my legs open and turned over onto my back. I was dripping with passion. He threw himself into the saddle just as hard as he could. By this time, his prick was bursting out of its skin, like an overdone hot dog, and he made love to me like a beast. I could see that he was no more thinking of me as who I was than I don't know what..." ' Clara looked up, puzzled. 'What does she mean by that?'

'It's just confused writing,' Garnett explained. 'Evidently she got so aroused while recalling her experience that she lost all track of what she was saying. Read some more. Maybe the matter will be clarified.'

' "I was just an instrument to him then," ' Clara went on. ' "I was just a – a – " '

'Well, what's wrong? Can't you make out the word?'

'I can make it out, but I can't say it.'

'Come, now. Try. What is it?'

'C-c-cunt. Oh, Mr. Garnett! That's worse than "prick"!'

'Read,' he commanded brusquely.

'I – I can't – '

'Read!'

'Well – all right. "I was just – a – a – a – *cunt*. If he had cut off my head and my hands and feet, it wouldn't matter. All he wanted was that one outlet for his fiery passions. I could do nothing but lay there on my back, with my legs around him and my hands helping him, until he reached his goals. When he came, it was if his whole body was filled with nothing but semen. I was inundated.

'At that moment, I loved him with all my heart and soul. I came again and again. There were green and yellow lights going off in my head, and the whole room swam round me. It was like a forest fire, spinning out all over me from inside my – my – cunt and from my burning buttocks. I clutched at him so hard that my nails pierced his skin, but I didn't care, and neither did he. It was glorious!

"Then it was over, and he told me to pick up my clothes and his, for we were going upstairs to bed and make love all night like a couple of minks." '

'Let's not bother with the upstairs part just now,' Garnett interrupted. 'I don't think it's very significant. Probably just a repetition of the scene on the couch. What's important here is the fact that she appears to be very much in love with this man – captivated by him, as it were – and unable to resist him. Obviously, he has her completely under his control.' He looked into her eyes. 'But, Clara, my child, you're trembling! What's the matter?'

'I just can't believe it,' she said weakly. 'My sister – my own sister – that she would – ' Garnett's shoulder was there for her to lean on, so she did. His arm went around her.

One hand came to rest against the tip of her breast, and he could tell that the nipple was distended. 'I don't know what you must think of me,' she said after a moment.

'Why, what's there to think? As I said before, you're only reading Rita's words. It isn't as if you yourself had done the things she described.' He paused. 'Or have you done some of them?'

'Oh, no. No! NEVER!!! Why, I've never even thought of them!' She looked up at him with dewy eyes. 'You do believe me, don't you? I never even heard of things like that until I found what was in this drawer.'

'But do you think about them now – now that you've found out?' His voice was persuasive. His gaze roamed to the closet where she had hidden her green silk panties, and her eyes followed his guiltily. 'Do you?' he prodded.

'I – I can't help thinking about it sometimes.' Her lips quivered. 'I guess that's terrible, isn't it?'

Garnett drew her gently towards him, then urged her body into a supine position on the bed. He soothed her and caressed her and finally kissed her, and he was pleased to find that she offered no resistance as he thrust his tongue between her lips. She seemed a little shocked at first, but soon she touched the tip of his tongue with the tip of hers, and he sucked on it passionately.

Abruptly, however, she backed away from him, her cheeks flaming with shame. Not wanting to let her think about what she had done, he spoke rapidly. 'You know,' he said, patting her hip, 'I have a plan that I think will lead to your sister. There's a slight chance, I suppose, that she'll return of her own accord, but, judging from what we read in her diary, it's safe to assume that she likes it wherever she is. So we'll have to find her – or, more to the point, you'll have to find her.'

'But how?'

'Well, I have a hunch. Do you remember the ring you gave me in my office – the ring with the scorpion design?'

'Yes.'

'Where do you think she got it?'

'From her lover.'

'Precisely. From the man she described in the diary – presumably the same man who gave her these books.'

'Yes!' she said enthusiastically. 'It has to be the same man!'

'Okay. Now, suppose that he's holding Rita captive – whether physically or by moral force. Either way, he's going to remember sooner or later that he gave her his ring and his books. He'll want them back, especially if he has reason to believe they might fall into the wrong hands.'

'Of course!'

'So let's give him an opportunity to get them back. Tomorrow we'll run an ad in the newspaper saying that the ring has been found. If he sees the ad, he'll make some attempt to contact us – or, more precisely, to contact you. When he does, if you play your cards right, you'll be able to infiltrate his group of weekend revellers.'

'Yes! And when I infiltrate them, I'll be able to find Rita and bring her back! Oh, Mr Garnett, that's a marvellous idea!'

Garnett's face grew sombre. 'But, Clara,' he said darkly, 'before you agree to the plan remember that it's dangerous. In order to infiltrate the group, you'll have to get into this scorpion fellow's good graces. In other words, you'll have to get him interested in you sexually.'

'You mean I'd have to – '

'Yes, Clara, you'd have to make him want to make love to you.'

'Oh, dear.'

'Of course, that part won't be difficult. In fact, considering the type of man he appears to be, he's almost certain to want you. You're so fresh and young and vital. And so beautiful. Why a man would have to be made of stone to resist you. And this scorpion fellow is anything but inhibited. When he meets you, he'll want to take you somewhere, perhaps in a car. And he'll want to kiss you. And hold you tightly, like this – '

'How awful!' she exclaimed, pressing her body against his in answer to his embrace.

'And he probably would squeeze your thighs, too. Like this. Then he would kiss you again.' He kissed her until her body went limp in his arms. His hands searched out her young breasts, and he pressed them hungrily. Then his fingers worked their way through the neck of her dress and squeezed the firm flesh of her soft, round breasts. 'He might even want to do this.' With his free hand he reached under her skirt and clutched the hot, damp altar of her womanhood.

'He wouldn't!' she spat, bolting upright. 'Oh, that's terrible!'

'Yes, it is. But if finding Rita depended on it?'

Clara bit her lip. 'Well,' she said hesitantly, 'I do love my sister very much. I suppose I'd do anything to save her. But – ' her whole body trembled ' – I'd never let him do that!'

'I thought so.' He sighed mightily. 'And I guess that's the end of Rita.'

'No! Wait! I would let him!' Her eyes took on a resolute expression. 'If Rita's safety is at stake, I'd let him do anything he wanted.'

'I don't think you could.'

'I would!'

'I doubt it. I don't think you could even undress in front of a man without dying of shame.'

'I could!'

'Then undress in front of me now.'

'Oh, my heavens, no!'

'See? I told you you couldn't.'

'I could. But why should I? Nothing depends on it now?'

'No, of course not. But, when something does depend on it, how will you be able to cope with the situation?' He shook his head sadly. 'I'm afraid it was a bad idea, Clara. Maybe we'd better turn the matter over to the police after all. You're willing to help, but I don't think you could go through with it. You're too timid.'

'I'm not timid. Or, at least I wouldn't be when the chips were down. I have plenty of nerve, you know. I really do.'

'Do you? Enough nerve to pretend that I'm this scorpion fellow and that I've just told you that I want you to undress, right this minute. That's just the way it might happen, you know. Without any warning.'

'I have plenty of nerve,' she repeated. She was blushing, but she stood up. Then, trembling quite visibly, she positioned herself directly in front of Garnett. 'Watch,' she said. 'I'll show you.'

Garnett was trembling also, although not as noticeably. It excited him immensely to see the beautiful young girl so overwrought. 'I don't believe you,' he taunted. 'I don't think you can do it.'

'Watch.'

She unbuttoned her dress at the front. It was belted, and, when she took the belt off, the garment fell open. Her skin showed pinkly through the space between the bottom of her brassiere and the top of her panties.

'There!' she said triumphantly. 'I did it, didn't I?'

'Not quite.'

'Do you really want me to undress?'

'I do.'

'But why?'

He shrugged, as if to say, 'I told you you didn't have enough nerve.' Then he laughed out loud.

She closed her lips tightly and gathered folds of her dress in her fists, raising the hem over her bare thighs to her hips. Garnett saw the lacy panties which he had only imagined before on the terrace. Then she hoisted the dress over her head, tugging with crossed arms to pull the tight-fitting cloth past the gorgeous bulge of her marvellous breasts.

Her underthings – what there was to them – fitted her like a dream. But the way she removed them was even more dream-like, and infinitely exciting.

At his nod she unfastened her brassiere. But she did it the hard way, slipping the straps off first and only then reaching behind her with one hand to undo the snap. When she reached, one luscious pink nipple peeped out. Then the snap fell open and the brassiere fell down her arms.

Garnett's mouth went dry with despair. Her breasts were beautiful beyond belief. The tips pointed upward, and the flesh was firm and high. They were the golden colour of melons, and just as round, with a splendid groove between them. He smiled wolfishly, mentally sinking his teeth into their creamy magnificence. 'You have more nerve than I thought,' he whistled under his breath.

She bent to take off one shoe, and her breasts swung forward like temple bells, slowly and resplendently. Then she took off the other shoe by lifting her foot behind her and reaching down towards it. This movement raised the exquisite globes and made them jiggle provocatively atop her chest.

Garnett's palms went sweaty. He wanted to reach out and grab the splendid spheres, to bury his face between them and bite them and lick them and suck them until his jaws ached. But he restrained himself. He couldn't risk frightening his quarry – especially not when she was so close to his grasp.

With her shoes off, Clara looked even more helpless than ever. Timidly, but resolutely, she began to unroll her stockings. The gesture was doubly exciting, for it not only revealed the marvellous lines of her long legs but also forced her to handle her own naked thighs – and therefore made her increasingly aware of her nakedness before a man's eyes. She leaned against a chair while she took them off, then dropped them onto the seat of the chair and stood before Garnett.

Now she was naked except for her panties. For an instant she looked into Garnett's eyes, as if hoping for a final reprieve. Then, when he said nothing, she pulled the lacy things off with the three quick gestures. First she slid her palms along her sides under the elastic band at the waist. She pushed the clinging material down her thighs and calves. Then she kicked them off her ankles.

She did not try to hide the diamond patch of black hair at her crotch, although her hands fluttered a little, as if she wanted to but was determined not to. Her face was flushed, but mingled with the expression of shame was a glimmer of triumph. She seemed to be saying: 'There! I told you I could do it!'

Garnett's lips parted in a small smile. 'You've never undressed in front of a man before, have you?' he asked quietly.

Her voice was even softer than his. 'Never.'

He motioned to her, and she sat beside him on the bed, covering her face with her hands. After a moment she asked: 'Do you still think I don't have enough nerve?'

He didn't answer. Instead, he guided her body into a horizontal position, then lay alongside her, resting on one elbow and looking down at her upturned face as he caressed her with his free hand. His fingers stroked her from head to knee, tickling her nipples, moulding her breasts, caressing her belly, gliding over her thighs.

'Why do you let me do this to you?' he asked.

'Because you told me to.'

'Is that the only reason?'

'Yes. You wanted to see if I had enough nerve to meet the Scorpion, and I wanted to show you that I do, that's all.' She bit her lip. 'I'm awfully ashamed of myself,' she added. 'I wish you wouldn't look at me when you touch me, or that you wouldn't touch me when you look at me. I feel terribly dirty inside, and I feel even dirtier when you look at me and touch me at the same time.'

'Aren't you letting me do this because you want me to?'

'No! Oh, heavens no! I don't want you to do it at all. I want to go away in a corner and cry. I hate it.'

'Do you hate me, too?'

'No I don't hate you. Men are like that, I guess. But I shouldn't let you do it – not for anything, not even for Rita. I didn't know you'd want to do this when you came here tonight, or I never would have asked you to come.'

'Even though Rita's safety may depend on it?'

'Even though — well, no, I can't say that. I guess her safety is more important to me than anything else.'

'But you don't like what I'm doing to you, even a little bit?'

'No, not at all. I despise it. I loathe it.'

He lit two cigarettes and placed one of them between her lips. 'Will you read some more of Rita's diary to me?'

'If you want me to.' She started to get up.

'No, I don't mean while you're clothed. I mean naked, like you are. Will you lie here naked and read to me?'

'If you say I have to, I will.'

He gave her a book. It was not Rita's diary. It was *Memoirs of Madame Condeux*. 'Read some of this to me,' he said, moving closer to her and feeling her with his body as well as with his hands.

'Why?'

'Because I want you to.'

'But why?'

'For no reason, except that I desire it.'

She trembled. 'Why are you doing this to me?'

'Does it matter?'

'Of course it matters.'

'Then let's just say that I'm doing it because I feel like doing it.'

'You're evil.'

'Yes.'

'And I thought you wanted to help me.'

'Did you?'

'Of course.' She stirred, as if she were about to get up from the bed.

Garnett heaved a sigh of exasperation. 'Don't you understand? I'm treating you the way the Scorpion will treat you. You can't be hesitant with him, you know. You can't refuse to do what he asks you, and you can't question him about why he wants you to do it. You must simply do it. Don't you understand that.'

She exhaled deeply, seemingly relieved. 'Yes, I suppose so. But for a minute I thought you were telling me things because you wanted me to do them, not because the Scorpion would want me to.'

'Well, now you know otherwise,' he lied. 'So stop stalling. If we do locate this scorpion person, you'll probably be obliged to do things more shameful than you ever imagined. If you're going to crack under the strain, I want to know right now, before we make any definite plans. If you break down and he finds out what you're up to, you may be in grave danger.'

Her eyes found his. They were fearful, but still resolute. 'I told you I could do anything,' she said. Her voice was very small, and her hands trembled so much that he wondered if she would be able to read from the page of the book.

'Now go ahead,' he instructed her. 'Tell me about the affairs of Madame Condeux.'

She steadied the volume on her lap and read in a quiet, quivering tone. ' "I was only fourteen when Robert, the young master of the house, and Henri, his friend, taught me a lesson I will never forget. I was going about some errand on this particular afternoon when Robert called me from his chamber in the upstairs wing. 'Marie, will you come here for a minute?' he said. I had no more entered the room when I felt myself seized from behind, and Robert's voice hissed: 'Shut the door, Henri, and help me carry her to the bed.' They deposited me on the bed, and, to my dismay and chagrin, began undressing me.

' "I had no defence. Even to call out would have been futile at that hour of the day, for there was no one to hear me, and the cook was in the kitchen away at the other wing of the mansion. In no time at all I was stripped quite stark. Then what a merry time they had with me! Fastening my wrists and ankles with their belts and ties, they bound me securely to the four posts of the bed. My arms and legs were spread wide. In this helpless position I was forced to endure their assaults.

' "After spending some time teasing and tickling me and pinching my budding breasts, they both undressed. Robert came at me first, but not, as I had thought, to make love to me. Instead, he knelt across my body, bumping his bottom on my belly, and, after rubbing his prick – " ' she said the word without hesitation ' " – across my breasts, on which it left a sticky wet trail, he summarily ordered me to open my mouth and let him invade me in that manner.

' "I, of course, had no intention of submitting to such a demand, and I withstood him as long as I could. But both he and Henri pinched and pummelled me and threatened me until I began to cry and was at last tearfully forced to submit. My cries seemed to have no effect whatsoever on the two savages. The young are so cruel.

' "Into my mouth his rigid member went. It felt enormous and my jaws ached. The corners of my lips threatened to split. His shadow fell over my eyes, and, through the gloom, I heard his voice demanding that I suck him. In truth, my choice was either to suck or to choke and suffocate, so I selected the former – a selection, I might add, which was strange and seemed horrible, but which, in truth, was not wholly unpleasant.

' "When I had sucked Robert's prick for what seemed like a long time, Henri wanted me to suck his, and this I was of course obliged to do. He mounted me in the same fashion as had Robert, and, with Robert remaining nearby, he put the swollen end of his terrible tool on my lips and rubbed it back and forth until I opened my mouth. Robert, meanwhile, rubbed his weapon against my tender slit.

' "I began to get very excited, and everything became vague. All I kept wondering was whether Robert was annoyed by facing Henri's back as they both mounted my body facing the same way. Having rubbed his shaft around and around my grotto until I was all wet, partly from his drool and partly from my own juices, he thrust it inside. My jaw ached and my legs hurt, and the straps and ties cut my wrists and ankles, but I was introduced willy-nilly to one of the many fashions in which a willing (or even unwilling, as I certainly was) young girl may conduct the entertainment of two or more men together.

' "The boys soon wanted to change places, so Robert took Henri's place and Henri began to stroke me in the natural place. My poor thighs hurt fiercely and my breasts stung so with the constant handling and abuse to which they had been subjected that I scarcely cared what they did to me as long as the business was quickly got through. The pleasure I had begun to feel was lost in my discomfiture and pain, and even when I felt Henri begin to shoot inside me and flood me with his spend, I did not any longer feel the least voluptuousness.

' "My only thought was to do everything I was told to do, striving only to keep my bonds from cutting too deeply into my flesh . . ." '

Clara closed the book and put it aside. While she had been reading, Garnett had been touching her more and more familiarly, pressing his fingers against whatever sexual part was mentioned in the reading and rubbing his penis against her thigh through his trousers whenever that organ was mentioned. Her legs had been induced to spread early in the narrative, and his fingers now rubbed between the lightly haired thighs, plucking at the pink lips of her womanhood and pinching lightly at her clitoris. She was in an agony of humiliation, the very picture of utter and devastated shame. She looked very young and crushed, and somewhat bewildered to find herself in such circumstances.

'Let me feel your bottom now, Clara,' Garnett said softly. 'It looks so pretty and white, and so soft.'

'You are feeling it,' she murmured, but she obediently lay on her side as he pushed her in that direction and offered him her pert rump from the back. He fondled the plump buttocks, luxuriating in their young, firm, softness. He tickled her along the cleft and put the tip of his finger into her. She covered her face with both her hands, and her shoulders shook when he took his finger from that orifice and brought it to the one in front.

'You're not really going to do anything to me, are you?'

Her voice was shot with fright. She turned her eyes up to him and added, almost as an afterthought: 'Please?'

But Garnett had had enough of the game. He had torn down her defences, and he knew that he could take her whenever he wanted her. So now there was really no point in taking her. Once he had taken her, she would never be ashamed again. And, nothing pleased him as much as her shame.

What a pity, he mused, that she wasn't a Catholic. If she had been, she could screw like a snake in a barrel of snot and still be ashamed every time. But it was pointless to contemplate hypothetical situations. She wasn't a Catholic, and, whatever she was, she would have to do. Besides, there were damned few religious Catholic girls who were as beautiful and as fresh-looking as she was.

'No, my dear,' he promised, 'I'm not going to do anything more to you. I only wanted to see if you really could make the sort of sacrifice which this scorpion fellow – if there is in fact such a person – may demand before you can learn anything about Rita. I see that you can. But it pains me to think of you as a –' He let the sentence trail off.

'I am one now, aren't I?' she said quietly. 'I let you do these terrible things to me, and now I am one.'

He didn't answer.

'But it doesn't matter,' she added quickly. 'I'm doing this to help Rita, and that's all that counts.'

'Right,' said Garnett, getting up from the bed. 'And on that note of steel-willed determination let's bring tonight's little session to a close.' He reached into his jacket pocket. 'Here's the ring you gave me this afternoon. When I leave here I'll place a want ad in the newspapers describing the ring and saying that it was found in the street. We may get an answer immediately, or we may never get an answer. But, either way, we'll have taken a step towards our goal.'

Clara sat on the edge of the bed. 'May I put on my clothes now?'

'Of course, I'm ready to leave, and you won't want to walk me to the door naked, will you?'

She laughed in spite of herself. 'No, I wouldn't want that.'

'So, chin up. As I said before, try not to worry about your sister. I'm sure that she's alright.' He watched her dress. 'If you have any reason to talk, phone my office. I'll tell Jackson to expect your call, and he'll put you through to me without any delay. But don't come to the office. Someone may be following you – especially after the ad appears in the papers – and it would be dangerous to tip our hand.'

She snapped her bra shut and pulled her dress over her head. Then she led him through the living room to the door. He kissed her on both eyes, then on the lips.

'Now you can go off to that corner of yours and cry,' he said, smiling. 'I'll see you soon.'

CHAPTER FOUR

She draws her chair around the corner of your desk. It is very important to her that you get a good view of her excellent legs, and she says 'Mister Garnett . . .' Her red hair spreads around her head like a halo, and her voice is that of an angel. 'I'm in terrible trouble, and you're the only person who can get me out of it.' She allows two big tears to well up in those innocent green eyes. 'You see, I know this man – Abie the Goat they call him – and right now he and some of his friends are in jail on a counterfeiting rap – charge, and they're afraid the district attorney is going to throw the book at them. They told me to get the best criminal lawyer in town to get them off. Of course I came straight to you.

'Of course,' you echo softly.

'For an ordinary lawyer, it would be a real rough case. But for you, it'll be a breeze. I just know you can get them off without half trying.'

She draws her skirt a bit higher and crosses her legs, showing a generous portion of white meat. The fan which you have set in action against the mid-afternoon heat ruffles the frills on her blouse, drawing your attention to them. She leans forward encouragingly, and her breasts strain maturely against the black gossamer fabric of her shirtwaist, so cool and soft against the crisp white tailored suit. You have to give her credit, she has a quick eye for the direction of your gaze, and she's anxious to be as obliging as she can. You look far into her blouse through the transparent material. The two melons on display are really ripe. These well-kept molls have what it takes and know how to dress it up.

Slowly, deliberately, you light a cigarette. You don't offer angelface one. If she wants a cigarette, she can smoke her own. Garnett's

Law: 'Never do anything for anybody unless you're sure that the profit derived from your generosity will far exceed the expenditure.'

You lean back in your chair and assume a business-like expression. 'Of course,' you say, 'I'll have to speak to your pals before I can agree to defend them. Then, if I decide to take the case, I'll want a ten thousand dollar retainer plus two hundred a day and expenses for every day I spend in court. And, no matter what I decide to do, I'll want another hundred for today's conference, and for my visit with your boyfriend.'

The tears are back, for real this time. Her lower lip quivers and her voice trembles as she says: 'He's not my boyfriend, and I haven't got that kind of dough. Not now. Once you get Abie off, I can pay you whatever you want. But now . . . a hundred bills is all I've got in the world.'

You study her face for a minute, watching the silence grating on her nerves. Then you say, 'If he's not your boyfriend, just what is your relationship to Abie the Goat?'

'Relationship?' she echoes, like she's never heard the word before. 'Why there is no relationship between me and Abie. He's just somebody I know, like an acquaintance. You don't think that I'd get involved with anybody like a counterfeiter, do you?'

What you are thinking about her right now would melt even this little ice cube's composure. But you're in a kindly mood, so you don't say anything; you just smile.

'Please, Mr Garnett, you must believe me. My friends are all very high class types. I don't ordinarily have anything to do with people such as Abie the Goat. I certainly wouldn't have even spoken to him if I had known what kind of person he was. But I must get him off. I just must. It's a matter of life and death!' Her eyes widen as she realises she's said too much.

You give her another minute of silence and then you ask, keeping your voice very low, 'Whose life . . . or death?'

'Mine.' Her own voice is scarcely audible above the whirring of the fan. It's her turn at the silence bit. She waits for more than a minute before she says: 'All right, I'll tell you the whole thing. You see, I met Abie through my room-mate. Of course, like I said before, I didn't know he was mixed up in the counterfeiting business, honest I didn't. Anyway, I went out with him a couple of times, just for *drinks and laughs, that's all. This was about a month ago. The first time I saw him, I mean. Then, after the couple of times we went out together, he stopped calling. Well, I didn't think anything of it, except maybe he didn't think too much more of me than I did of him. He wasn't my type, you see.'*

Her glance makes it very clear that you are her type. How flattering.

'Anyway,' she goes on, *'I'd actually forgotten all about him until yesterday, when this man came to see me. A man I'd never seen before. He said he was a friend of Abie the Goat's, and that Abie and some other guys were in jail on this counterfeiting rap.'*

By now her high-class pretensions have fallen by the wayside, and you notice with inner amusement how easily she has slipped into a vernacular she claims to know nothing about. She is saying: *'He told me that Abie said to get him a lawyer, the best there is. If I didn't, the man said, I'd be killed. So you see, Mr Garnett, my life is at stake. And you're the only person who can save it.'* She gazes at you appealingly, and the skirt slips a little higher. *'I know what a mess I've got into. I should've been more careful about going out with a man I didn't know anything about. I've been a very foolish girl. You know, if my daddy were alive today, he'd probably spank me for my foolishness, big as I am?'*

'So you think you ought to be spanked?' You take a final drag from your cigarette and glance along the line from her knee to her hip, the full line of her nicely rounded thigh. Her skirt is drawn tight along the upper part of it; it looks as though a hand applied there would cause a fine, resounding smack.

'Don't you?' she asks you coyly. She watches you grinding out your cigarette in the heavy glass ashtray, and a little smile comes to her lips. That smile would play hell with a jury . . . an all-male jury, of course.

'So you want me to be the big, understanding, gently reproving daddy, do you? You wouldn't by any chance be trying to arrange for my services on the promise of how warm that little fanny of yours can get, would you?'

You reach out suddenly and pinch her thigh. She doesn't move her leg, but she makes her eyes bigger. You can see her calculating whether to register coy surprise or lascivious promise. Her purse *drops to the floor and she reaches to pick it up, stretching her leg out towards you. You feel the silk clad muscles under your hand, and, you run the hand under her skirt. 'Come here and sit on my lap.'*

She's certainly prompt. Her buttocks spread comfortably on your thighs, and she puts one arm around your neck, pressing her breasts against your chest. Your hand fits around one of her buttocks and squeezes. She's pleasantly soft.

Next, you feel along her hip and down her thigh to the knee. You raise her skirt and look at the milky prettiness of her legs, the laciness of her high-cut panties and the swelling temptation which they mask. You open her blouse and remove one of her breasts from the brassiere. You fondle it for a moment, then tuck it back into its cradle.

'I'm going to spank you just the way your daddy would,' you tell her. You remove her gently from your lap, and brush the papers from the desk into the top drawer. 'Come on, lift your skirt.'

You look at her standing there, placidly holding her skirt up, awaiting your pleasure. She isn't a bit frightened. When they put her together, they left out fright and put in a double portion of shrewd whorishness.

You make her turn around so that you can see your target. And quite a target it is. Just the way you like them. Two full, white globes. A beautifully matched set. This is going to be even more fun than you'd thought.

You lock the door. Then you flip on the intercom and tell Jackson that you don't want to be disturbed. You lean casually against the desk and watch her standing there, her skirt still up around her hips. You tell her to take her panties part-way down. You figure she'd take them off and hang them out the window if you asked her to. But there's no necessity for that. And you're a reasonable man.

She complies with your request, and you tell her to bend over the desk. She places her head on her purse and grasps the edges of the desk with her hands, so that her buttocks rise until they're well within your reach. You fondle them in turn, then slap them briskly with your whole palm.

'Ooooooh!'

'Not coyness, but shock. You didn't hurt her, but you did surprise the hell out of her. You point out to her the impracticality of yelling

in an attorney's office, and right away she's apologetic. She promises to be quiet. She won't make the slightest sound, she says. She knows that she deserves a spanking, she says. You resume.

The lace panties flutter. Her heels fly up. She reacts very nicely to the spanking. You give it to her mildly, not really hurting her. But the slaps do sting a bit – you can tell from the bright red splotches that are appearing on her white, satiny skin.

You spank her for a long time because, you tell her, she has been a very bad girl this time. Fun for the feebleminded, you think. And then you notice that your penis is rapidly hardening. Funny that it should be sexually exciting to paddle a girl's bottom. But you like the idea of having a girl whom you've known less than twenty minutes so much under your power that you can slap her bare bottom.

She has stopped yelling, just as she said she would. But she sucks her breath in hard each time your hand makes contact with her flesh. She doesn't particularly care for spanking, but she's far too old a hand at high-class whoring to complain, especially since she's extremely anxious to please you.

You don't disappoint the lady. You unbutton your trousers and take out what's inside. The large, upthrust instrument looks a little ridiculous against your well-creased trousers and fitted jacket.

She looks at it and at you. You tell her to lie down again. She does, and you come up behind her, slapping your rigid tool gently against her buttocks. She seems to like the feel of it, for she twists her head back and gives you a nice, lewd wink. What a sweet little tart she is.

You look at the delightful little cavern between her legs and insert a finger in it. She appears to like that, too. She wriggles and clutches the edges of the desk wildly. Well, this is a day of new experiences. You've heated up a pro.

You rub the tip of your organ between her buttocks, then slide it gently between her legs. Now she really wants it. She shoves her buttocks back towards you, reaching for it with gaping lips. You slide the tip of the organ between them and it disappears practically before you know what's happening. Well, what do you know? An educated vagina. Verily, there's nothing like professional work . . . all too rare these days.

*She lets out her breath in a lascivious gasp. Suddenly she giggles.
'Daddy would never have done anything like this to me.'*

You're not so sure about that, but you don't see any reason to insult the memory of the dead, so you keep your lip buttoned and concentrate on what you're doing. You don't really have to concentrate, though; just relax and enjoy it. She's doing enough work for both of you. She's rotating those buttocks as though they were made of rubber, giving it to you wide open. She isn't holding back a thing. You're in her as far as anybody has ever been, and if you go much further you'll probably come out her throat.

'If you want me to do anything else,' she gasps, 'Just tell me, and I'll do it. Do you want to see me again tonight? Or any other time? You can have me like this, or give it to me any way you like.'

She means it litreally – Any way. Snap it up, chum, it's a bona fide offer. Spank her, make love to her, wipe your feet on her if you want to. Her life is on the line and she'll pay to the best of her ability in the only coin she's got. And the best of her ability is damn good.

You draw her buttocks against you, and you feel yourself going even farther inside her than you'd thought you could. You hold her hips with one hand and reach around with the other to tickle her. She's really giving you her all now. She rolls and groans. It might be an act, but if so, it's an excellent one. Rotate your weapon inside its lovely, warm, wet sheath, and watch the fan blow the hair across the back of her neck.

Suddenly everything gets hazy and dark. You stop noticing things. In . . . in . . . IN!! That did it! The warmth wells up inside you. This time you're going to explode for sure. Your fluid floods her . . . it's all over.

You drop into a chair. Somehow you don't feel much like standing – or doing anything else, for that matter. She looks at you as though asking permission to let her skirt drop. You nod.

The telephone rings.

Perfect timing.

You motion her to get on her knees and kiss your almost-limp organ. Then you pick up the receiver.

'This is Clara Reeves,' a clear voice says.

You can see her in your mind's eye, and you amuse yourself imagining the expression on her face if she could see you now, with a petite redhead delicately washing your parts with her little pink tongue.

'I just got a call from a woman,' the voice continues. 'She says the ring belongs to a friend of hers. She wants me to meet her for tea at the Clive Hotel. I said I'd be there at four.'

'Fine. A Woman, eh? Well, try to make friends with her. And under no circumstances give her the ring until you've found out something about her – and her friend. Get her to tell you where she lives, then cheque it in a phone book.'

The girl on the floor is running her tongue along your shaft, holding it like an asparagus stalk in her fingers and nibbling at the tip. She puts her mouth full on it and kisses it, smiling up at you. We aim to please, the smile says.

'Don't worry,' the voice on the phone assures you. 'I'm not simply going to hand the ring over. And I'll see you tonight to tell you what happens, if – if I come back alive.'

You smile.

She says: 'Will you come to the house again – tonight – about ten?'

The redhead is taking it in her mouth, pressing her rouged lips on the bare flesh. Her lipstick is marking your organ. That's fun.

She squeezes you between the legs and tickles you with one well-manicured finger. You slide forward in the seat and motion for her to pull your trousers down.

Now she runs her finger down the groove between your buttocks. You slide forward even more, letting her slip her forefinger into the hole. Wondering how much longer you'll be able to control your voice, you say into the phone; 'Yes, I'll come up to the house. And don't worry. You'll come back alive. Just be careful.'

She tells you she will be, and you tell her that you've got to run. She hangs up and you do likewise.

The redhead is still kneeling at your feet, dragging her mouth up on your organ and pressing it down with an expert side-to-side movement of her head. You let your mind go, and your body becomes one mass of sensation.

She goes faster and faster, and your hips begin to jerk spasmodi-

cally. She squeezes and presses your buttocks, and her tongue flicks around the lip of your shaft in rapid circles. 'GOD . . .'

You open your eyes. She is leisurely cleaning you off with her tongue.

You say: 'You might as well get up now.'

'You don't want to do anything more?'

'No. We've done everything we're going to do, toots. Now fix yourself up so you can make a handsome exit.'

She stands and puts on her panties. She straightens out her skirt and adjusts the ruffles on her blouse. She takes a gold make-up kit and a mirror from her purse, and works small miracles with them. She pins back her hair into an identical facsimile of the coiffeur she had had when she came in. 'I feel so much better about everything now,' she says casually. 'I feel just the way I used to when I'd been naughty and had something on my conscience for a long time, and then daddy gave me a good spanking and I felt all . . . well, forgiven and everything.' Just the right note. You have to give her credit.

'How soon do you expect to need another spanking?' you ask.

'As soon as you think I need one,' she says.

'So it's a permanent arrangement? I just go on spanking you and punishing you in whatever other ways I see fit for as long as I see fit. Is that it?'

'It can be that kind of an arrangement if that's what you want.'

'No. I think you've been punished enough.'

You see the surprise in her eyes. She hadn't thought it would be that easy. She's almost afraid to ask, but she knows she must: 'And Abie the Goat? You'll see him? You'll take the case?'

'Don't worry your pretty red head about it. I'll take care of it.'

She pecks you on the cheek and turns to go.

'Haven't you forgotten something?' you ask.

'What?'

'The hundred bucks I told you it would cost you for the conferences with you and Abie the Goat.'

She blanches. She had thought she had you hooked. 'But I told you, a hundred dollars is all the money I have. I can't just give you all of it.'

'All right, make it fifty, then. After all, you have shown me how

really sorry you are that you got involved in all this. But I want it now. Cash.'

By this time she's recovered her poise. She doesn't bat an eyelash. Opening her purse, she takes out a roll of tens and counts off five of them. As she hands them to you, she even manages a smile. She's a realist, this girl. She knows that a fifty buck fee for a conference with the best criminal lawyer around is quite a bargain. As she starts to leave the office you goose her and she emits a coy, girlish giggle that any virgin would be proud to call her own.

'Goodbye . . . daddy,' she says and walks undulatingly out of your life.

You flip the intercom switch and tell Jackson you want to see him in your office. When he comes in you tell him to call the Tombs and get a line on a forgery pick-up. Alias Abie the Goat. 'Then,' you tell him, 'call Judge Harwin's residence and get his son on the phone. Tell the kid I want him here nine o'clock tomorrow morning. I've got a case for him.'

You're very pleased with yourself. In one fell swoop, you get a broad out of your hair and you repay the judge's favour. Very clever. You always like to throw the cases you won't touch to struggling young lawyers, especially ones like the judge's son, who don't need the money but can use the court experience. And young Harwin won't have to worry about damaging his rep when he loses the case, 'cause he hasn't been around long enough to build up a rep to lose.

All in all, a very satisfactory solution. You smile as you imagine the expression on the hooker's face when she looks for you in court and sees Harwin Jr instead. Too bad. But it's her own fault. She's certainly been around long enough to know that you shouldn't play the game if you haven't got the chips. Abie the Goat! How could the great Garnett ever defend a goon with a monicker like Abie the Goat?

CHAPTER FIVE

Clara was terribly excited when Garnett visited her that evening at ten. No sooner had she ushered him into her parlour than she announced: 'I've met part of the Scorpion's gang! I'm sure I have!'

They sat in the big couch, side-by-side, and she told him all that had happened.

'This woman called me,' she began, 'and said that the ring belonged to a friend of hers – I told you that over the phone, didn't I? Well, I met her at the Clive. She calls herself Mrs Mason, and I guess that's her name, all right. She's in her early thirties, I think, and she's very pretty. You know, like a countess in *The Three Musketeers* or something. Anyway, she's very fascinating and very European. The name Mason doesn't fit her at all. She has dark eyes and hair and a husky voice. She's very cultured. I kept thinking about international spies and things like that all the while I was with her. And she has the tiniest feet I ever saw!'

Garnett smiled. The girl certainly had enjoyed herself; in fact, she had sponged up all the thrill there was to be had.

'She didn't say anything about the ring right away,' Clara went on. 'We took a table in the Clive and ordered tea and cake, and she was very pleasant to me. She had brandy in her tea, but I was afraid of sleeping drugs and stuff so I said no to the brandy. My, she was nice, though. Before I knew it she had invited me to come and visit her at her home in the country. We talked about all sorts of things for quite a while before she asked about the ring. But I didn't have it with me. I told her that I was afraid I'd lost it, and she seemed quite disappointed. But she went on and described it perfectly. Even the little nick in the silver – did you notice it? I couldn't refuse to give it to her after that, and I asked her if she could come home with me and get it. But she said she was expecting a friend and couldn't. Instead she asked if it would be all right to send her brother-in-law with me to get it, and I said of course that would be all right, so she made a phone call, and we had some more tea, and then a man came and joined us at the table. She introduced him as John Webster, and said he'd drive out with me and get the ring.

'Mrs Mason and the Webster man were very friendly, and I somehow got the impression that he had been an old flame of hers. Either that or she's known him better than a married woman should know a strange man, even her brother-in-law. Anyhow I didn't believe he was any relative of hers. From what I found out later about him, boyfriend or not, he probably knows her too well.

'We finished tea finally and Mrs. Mason wanted to know if I could come out to her place in the country tomorrow. I promised to phone tonight and let her know. She said I could call any time after eleven. Then I got into the Webster man's car.

'He was nice, I guess, but he insisted on complimenting me all the time. And they were very personal compliments, too. All about my bosom and things like that. But he didn't do anything until we arrived here at the apartment. Then, after I had given him the ring and we were both sitting here with a drink, he suddenly put his arms around me.

'I hardly knew what to do. I just sat still while he ran his hands over my arms and back. I let him kiss me a couple of times, and I opened my mouth when he seemed to want me to. Then he told me to lean back in the chair while he felt one of my breasts. I was awfully scared. I didn't know whether he was the Scorpion or not – but I'm sure he wasn't; he wasn't the sinister type at all – and I was determined not to seem scared or surprised, so I just smiled at him and encouraged him. I wanted these people to think I was their type, so it would be easier for me to get mixed up with them and find out about Rita. Was that right?'

Garnett nodded sagely. 'Webster probably was just testing you. Anyway, he felt your breasts and you smiled at him, then what did he do?'

'He slipped his hand up under my dress. I hated to have him touch me. I didn't really like him at all. But I kept on smiling and acting as though that were just what I wanted him to do. Then he suggested that we come over here to the couch.

'Once we were on the couch together he became very insistent. He began to handle my legs and to put his hand all the way under my dress, and right away he asked me if a man had ever – had me. I told him no, and I winked at him, so he wouldn't know whether I really meant it or not, and he said that if I wasn't kidding I was making a big mistake and missing a good deal. Then he told me that if I wanted to be made love to – and he said he couldn't understand any girl not wanting to – I should positively go to one of Mrs Mason's weekend parties. But he went on to say that I ought to look him up first. Then he began feeling my thighs again.

'I knew it wouldn't be long before he'd want me to take my dress off, just the way you said, and it wasn't. He had been pushing my skirt up along my legs until he could feel between them, and, while he was pushing the skirt up, he had been trying to push me down on the couch with his shoulder. Finally I was lying down.'

She paused and appeared reluctant to go on. 'What's the matter?' Garnett asked. 'Have you forgotten what happened?'

She shook her head and turned crimson. 'I haven't forgotten a thing.'

'Then tell me. What did he do next?'

'He made me take my dress of, and everything else besides – my underwear and my stockings and everything.'

'While you were lying on the couch?'

'Partly while I was on the couch, partly while I was standing in front of him.'

'And then he had you lie down with him again – naked?'

'Yes, that's right. I had to lie down with him – naked. It was almost like with you. I don't mean to sound like I'm putting you both in the same class; I didn't like him at all – he wasn't nice or anything – but it was almost like it was last night. What he did, I mean. I had to lie in his arms while he felt me and prodded me and fingered every single part of my body. Every single part!'

'You mean he examined your vagina too?'

Clara swallowed hard. 'Uh-huh, that too. He made me spread my legs open and let him feel me there, and then he put his fingers inside.'

'And he still had his clothes on?'

'He did then, but he took them off right after that. He made me sit up, and he wouldn't let me cover my breasts with my hands, and he made me look at him while he undressed. He made me tell him that I had never seen a man naked, and its seemed to delight him to be the first man I ever saw. He especially wanted me to say that the hair over his – thing, surprised me. But I said no it didn't because I had hair there, too. He looked a little sore about that. Then he came back to the couch with me' – she smiled as she noticed that Garnett was laughing silently over her last sally – 'and he stood up in front of me and made me touch him. He took my hand and put it on his – on – oh, do I have to tell you all this?'

Garnett rose from the couch and turned out all the lights except one lamp over in the corner. Then he sat with her again. 'If you can't tell me, show me,' he said. 'Where did you have to put your hand?'

Clara timidly brought her hand to his trousers. 'There,' she said.

'He made you touch his prick, you say?'

'And that wasn't all! After I touched it, he made me hold it in my hand and look at it while it grew big and fat and stiff, and the skin on the tip stretched and got shiny and looked like a plum.' She stopped, as though she just realised that she had been more appreciative of the enterprise than an unwilling little innocent should have been. Then, blushing slightly, she added: 'He made me hold it in both palms and – and –' She made a vague up and down gesture.

'Perhaps you'd better show me exactly what you mean. I see you don't like to say it right out. Go ahead, show me. I won't look at your face while you do. Open my trousers.'

She seemed unable to believe at first that he was serious, but he nodded at her questioning look and she bent in a confusion of blushing and tried to unpuzzle his zipper fly. 'Oh, Mr Garnett,' she exclaimed as she bent to the task. 'I'm so ashamed of myself. I did something so dirty today that I can't believe I did it.'

'Yes,' he said, 'I can see that. But this is the price you must pay to find your sister. If you love her, it won't matter.'

She fingered his tool gingerly, dropping it confusedly now and again from one hand to the other like a hot potato. It was hot to the touch, and it became incredibly stiff in her grasp. She moved her hand to and fro, illustrating the manner in which she had been obliged to manipulate the member of Mr Webster. Garnett's engine grew bigger, and she moved her hand faster.

'He made me do it faster, too,' she confessed, 'and he grew very excited. He seemed to be trying to pull my head towards it. At last I wouldn't do it any longer. My wrist was tired, but I didn't tell him that was why I stopped. That was when he lay down with me for the second time.' Garnett took Clara's hand and closed it more firmly around his shaft, which she had almost released while speaking. She added: 'He was feeling me –' she guided his hand – 'there.'

Garnett reached far under her dress and into her crotch. He was a trifle surprised to notice that she didn't have any panties on this time.

'He was doing everything you did there with your fingers,' she went on, 'and he made me play with his – thing – again.'

'And you were ashamed,' Garnett suggested softly.

'Oh, yes, I was horribly ashamed. But I had to keep doing it. He didn't feel like you do.'

The devil's advocate looked at her questioningly.

'His – thing – had more skin on it up at the end,' she explained.

'His foreskin,' Garnett advised her, amazed at her ignorance of so common a phenomenon as circumcision. Didn't little girls take care of babies any more?

She went on: 'He said he didn't know whether he should make love to me or not, but that if I did what I was doing well enough he wouldn't have to. So I did it as well as I could, but my wrist was killing me. Anyhow I did everything he told me to, and just like he told me to do it. I pulled his – thing – and rubbed it and tickled it, and I took the heavy things underneath in my other hand and squeezed them a little. I let him tickle me and rub me as much as he wanted to. I was afraid that if I stopped him he would make love to me, and I pretended to be enjoying myself very much. When he asked me how I liked it, I told him that I'd never felt anything so great in all my life.'

'That was true, wasn't it,' Garnett chuckled.

'Yes, but I hated it! I *hated* it! And I was so afraid that someone would come in and find us there like that even though I knew that no one was around. The slightest noise made me jump like a bank robber.'

'Bank robbers don't jump. They have nerves like iron.' Garnett worked his finger more insistently in her dripping-hot, grotto. 'I suppose he was doing just about what I'm doing?' He put a good deal of feeling – and rotary firmness – into the movement.

'He was using two fingers,' she confessed shyly.

Garnett corrected this error promptly and found that two not only fitted more snugly than one but also worked twice as well. The twisting motion was even more interesting, and it did not hurt her a bit. This year's virgins had more leg room than the earlier models, he decided. Come to think of it, though, this kid was only technically a virgin – and she wasn't going to stay that way any longer than it amused him for her to do so. 'How long did this go on?' he asked her after a few minutes.

'Just about as long as we've been doing it. Then –'

'Then *this* happened!' Garnett finished for her in a tight voice.

'Oh, Mr Garnett! How could you?!' she cried, wiping her hand on the handkerchief which she snatched from his breastpocket. She sat up, wringing the handkerchief between her fingers and accusing him bitterly. 'You're just as beastly as he was! Oh, I didn't expect this of you!'

Garnett grinned. 'But it's only natural, my dear girl. If your handling had this same effect on Webster, you should have expected that it would have it on me. Isn't that true?'

'No! You should have used self-control!'

'I suppose so. But it wouldn't have been much fun. Life is too short for self-control. Anyway, what happened after Webster ejaculated? Did he do anything else to you?'

'No, he left right after that. But, before he went, he told me to be sure and remember Mrs Mason's party tomorrow. I suppose I have to go, don't I? Now that the ring is gone I can't simply let her forget me.'

'Yes, you'll have to go – poor girl. Have you looked in Rita's diary to see if she mentions Mrs Mason or Webster?'

'She doesn't use any names at all. She calls people A and B.'

'How inconsiderate of her,' Garnett sighed. 'How goddam inconsiderate.'

CHAPTER SIX

'I would have sent someone to meet you,' Mrs Mason apologised as she held the car door open for Clara, 'but when we have a party we always send the servants away. Just so they won't have anything to gossip about, you know. I hope you weren't worried when you found yourself alone at the station.'

'Not worried, exactly, but I was beginning to wonder if you had forgotten about me,' Clara replied as she climbed into the front seat of the touring car.

Mrs Mason put the machine in gear and they shot away.

'We're having a lot of people there,' the older woman went on. 'With you I believe it makes thirty. It looks as though the party will last all week. I hope so. We like long parties. They have a dream-like quality about them after a while, don't you think? As though none of it were real?'

'I don't know, Mrs Mason,' Clara smiled. 'I've never been to a long party before, not even to one that lasted a weekend.'

The exotic-looking woman at the wheel broke into a throaty laugh. 'But you mustn't call me Mrs Mason,' she chuckled. 'It's such a stuffy name – it makes me sound like a spinach packer's wife. My name is Blanca. And you say that this will be your first marathon party? Then you will stay the week won't you? I think it's going to be lots of fun. Of course you'll meet many strange people, but you mustn't let that bother you. Just pick out the ones you like and leave the rest alone. That's what I always do. You can't expect to like everybody or to have everybody like you, can you? And when I find I'm not having fun any more I just pack up and go back to town. But I'm sure that you'll have a marvellous time, Clara . . . your name is Clara, isn't it? I'm very stupid about names and things like that.'

'Yes, Clara – Clara Morrow,' said Clara, having assumed an alias for the adventure.

'Yes, of course. Anyway, as I was saying, I'm sure you'll have a good time just as long as you care to stay. You're very pretty, so a good time is practically a certainty.'

'Being pretty is essential to having a good time?'

'It helps a great deal. Men are very superficial that way. That's why there's so much divorce these days.'

The car turned off the highway and onto a winding private road. At the end of the road was a huge wrought-iron gate. Blanca Mason stopped the car in front of the gate, got out, unlocked the phone box on the gate post and spoke into the receiver. Almost as soon as she returned to the car, the gate rose automatically. The car spun through a lovely, wooded park. Butterflies fluttered, rabbits scampered and several deer bounded through the trees to safety as the automobile roared past. Then the house came into view. It was very large, in the Victorian manner; very imposing and dignified. It made the people in slacks and shorts, lolling on the great, shadowy, arched porch that ran around both sides of the huge manse, look strangely out of place.

'At the moment there are no noisy drunks,' said Blanca as she jockeyed the car to a smooth stop. She crooked a finger at a man who was passing and pointed at Clara's overnight bag in the back of the car. Without a word, the man lifted the bag and followed the two women into the house.

'I'll show you to your room,' said Blanca, 'and there my pretence of being a good hostess stops. If you want to meet people you'll have to stop them and ask them who they are. That's what I do.'

The man who had carried the bag now put it down at the door of Clara's room and disappeared before she could thank him. A very thorough disappearance it was, too, for she never met him again about the place.

'Is there anything you want before I leave you?' Blanca asked, throwing open the door of Clara's bathroom and indicating it with a motion of the hand.

'No, not a thing. Thank you very much. I'll be just fine.'

A young man was passing through the hall, and he calmly stopped in the doorway and looked in, eyeing Clara coolly.

'Ah, Derek!' Mrs Mason exclaimed. 'I was hoping you'd turn up this week.' She patted Clara's arm in farewell and left with the young man, ruffling his hair with one hand and caressing his shoulder with the other. His hand slipped familiarly over her hips as they passed out of sight.

As soon as Clara had put her things away in the scented drawers of the bureau and on the sacheted hangers in the closet, she went down the curved staircase that led to the hall and parlour. At the foot of the stairs stood a brown-skinned man in a shocking pink turban, talking to a vivacious blonde who appeared to be no older than fifteen. The blonde's breasts were very prominent under her sweater, which was several sizes too small – or just right, depending on how you felt about that sort of thing. A pimply-faced youth, with a rather scraggy beard, was clutching a brandy goblet full of a dark green liqueur, and talking to a beautiful Eurasian in a slit skirt. Meanwhile, a tweedy-looking woman glowered at him over two fingers of straight Scotch. In the corner a drunk sat alone, entertaining himself by blowing a tuneless sort of a chant through a muted clarinet. The mute was obviously an impromptu one, being nothing more than a wadded-up brassiere of black lace, with one strap hanging out of the bell of the instrument.

'May I read my poems to you?' inquired a heavily accented masculine voice in Clara's left ear. 'I write them in white ink on black paper, and I read each one only once to the woman of my choice.'

The owner of the voice materialised. He was handsome

in an aquiline way, with a leonine mane of jet black hair. In his hand was a sheaf of black paper that was as dog-eared as an old telephone book.

'Only once?' Clara asked with a smile.

The poet bristled. 'Positively. Only once to each woman of my choice.' He took her by the arm and led her into a conservatory which was full of harps, potted plants and pianos. 'We have to take our clothes off, of course,' he went on, whereupon Clara released her arm from his grip and hurriedly quit the room. She walked out on the terrace, where a blowsy woman promptly pounced upon her and kissed her on the mouth.

The odour of liquor was strong on the woman's breath. She offered Clara a glass of whiskey with a sprig of mint on the rim, and when the girl politely refused, she downed it herself.

'My name is Legion,' she said mixing herself another drink. 'Honest it is. Helen Legion. But for reasons I myself am not sure of, I call myself Jan. Have you ever been told that you are very beautiful?'

'Mrs Mason said that I was pretty,' said Clara, blushing.

'But your Mrs Mason doesn't want to go to bed with you, dear, and I do. My, you're beautiful. Very very beautiful. And so young! Do you like to sleep with women?'

'I – I – kick in my sleep,' Clara stammered. She hastily poured 'Jan' another drink. The woman accepted it, draining the glass with a single swallow.

On the lawn, not too far from the terrace, stood the poet, clasping his black poems in one hand, and the breast of a tall, heavily made-up woman in the other. The woman was laughing and the poet was saying loudly: 'Let me run barefoot through your hair!' A boy and a girl of college age shared an armchair in a corner. They were kissing and embracing rather athletically. The girl's skirt was high on her legs and it appeared that the couple was – oh, but people wouldn't do that in broad daylight, under the noses of any number of other people – or would they?

Farther down on the porch a giant of a man with an enormous bald head was roaring at another giant with a beard. Everyone seemed to shout or to murmur. Nobody just talked. The baldheaded giant was saying, 'But only tvelf yirs oldt! At dot aich she still haf no hair betveen her leks!' The bearded giant stroked his beard thoughtfully and murmured so that anyone on the porch who cared to could hear — for a giant's murmur is an ordinary man's bellow — 'Potzibly, potzibly . . . baht tonight!'

Suddenly Clara saw John Webster. 'There you are,' he called. She appeared actually glad to see him, although on the previous afternoon she had certainly acted as though she never wanted to see him again. Her change of attitude didn't seem to surprise him in the least, and he was all smiles and charm as he took her by the arm and rescued her from the woman whose name was Legion.

'I hoped you'd turn up,' he said. 'How was your trip up here? Did Blanca come to meet you? Who else have you met besides "Jan"?' As Clara answered his questions, they walked about the grounds, past towering cacti and through a rock garden with artificial streams at the edge and ridiculous little Chinese bridges spanning the streams.

There were a great many more than thirty people here. And all of them were engaged in the same sport — with variations of course. They lay under trees and bushes, on knolls and hillocks, in dales and vales. One adventurous pair even lay in the little brook beneath a Chinese bridge. And what they were doing was rather obvious.

On a padded double beach chair not far away lay a man with a woman curled between his legs. The woman, clad only in a bathing suit halter, was calmly kissing and licking the man's love instrument. Watching from a nearby bench, a young man with platinum blonde hair and false eyelashes gaily shouted *bon mots*. As Clara and Webster walked by, he fished an ice cube out of his drink and threw it at the woman on the beachchair. It hit her squarely between the legs and stuck there. She came up with a little scream and leaped to her feet, stamping to get the ice cube out.

'It's all very – free, isn't it?' Clara stammered.

'Hmmm? Oh, that?' Webster's eyes picked up the direction of her gaze. 'They're only doing what they want to do. And that's the one rule at Blanca's parties. "Do what you want." You know, from Rabelais.'

Clara nodded in a cultured way.

'No, there are two rules, I guess,' Webster went on. 'Do what you want is number one. Don't pretend that you came here to do it to your own wife or husband, is rule number two. Sensible, isn't it? If a guy is jealous, he stays home and keeps his wife there, too. If he comes here, he wants some fresh tail for a change, so why shouldn't his wife have a change, too?'

'But aren't they in love with each other?' Clara asked.

When Webster just laughed, she tried a new tack. 'Do you mean that all these people come here to make love to each other's wives and husbands?'

'Not all. A lot of these people aren't married.'

'But does everybody come here to make love?'

'Mainly, I suppose. Or to take drugs or eat horse-meat, or to satisfy whatever other private vices they have. This is a sort of private world where outside rules don't go. That's why the gate down the road is locked. It keeps the public out. And since "love" is the one thing most firmly restricted out there, there's bound to be a lot of it here. Yes, the place is just lousy with "love," if you insist on calling it by a pretty name.'

'A love-cult, in other words,' said Clara, with a fine but rather awkward contempt. 'Love as a fine art, and other Greenwich Village phrases.'

'No, sugar-pie. Not love. Sex as a fine art. And if you stay here very long you'll find out what a fine art sex really is. One of the finest. Ask that baldheaded Russian back on the porch if you want details. He writes books about it – in Russian. The pictures are in Esperanto, though.'

Clara snorted daintily. 'Some way to make a living.'

Webster laughed.

'How long has this been going on?' the girl asked him.

'Oh, for years, I guess. It's a kind of social experiment with Blanca and her husband ... Have you met him, by the way? He's always around somewhere. Very quiet and very distinguished looking. Greying at the temples and all that. He and Blanca are a couple of cool customers. This experiment of theirs – they want to see if people can live the way they want to and still stay recognisably human. Even if it doesn't work out, it will have been lots of fun, and nothing worse ever happens here than happens at a Jersey City political stag party.'

'Whose ring was that that I gave you?' Clara asked suddenly. 'Mr Mason's?'

'Blanca's husband isn't named Mason,' Webster replied evasively. 'That was her first husband's name. Some rich American creep she married in Europe to get her into the country. She comes from Trieste, you know. About that ring, if you don't know whose it is, I think the best way for you to find out is to see who's wearing it.'

'It's a man's ring, isn't it? Is he around now?'

'I haven't seen him, but he will be around, I can promise you that.'

'When?'

'Sooner or later. You can't miss him.'

'Why are you so mysterious about him?'

'Because I love mysteries, honey-babe. But why talk about these mundanities? Let's talk about life and how to prevent it. Has anyone ever told you what a luscious bottom you're waltzing around with?'

'Has anyone ever told you that the line you're waltzing around with is not only vulgar but also trite and highly unimaginative?'

Webster appeared to be both surprised and miffed by this spirited outburst, and disdained to answer it. They walked along in uncompanionable silence until they passed the green tile swimming pool and Clara observed: 'Well, at least they don't swim in the nude.'

'Swim naked? No, not in the daytime. This isn't a nudist camp. But you could swim naked in the daytime if you wanted to. I don't know, though. Somehow clothes are more interesting for the afternoon, especially when you think how few really handsome bodies there are, except on very young girls.'

'Do you mean on or on top of?' Clara asked with an air of bawdy daring.

Webster looked amazed, and then gave a little laugh. 'Well, you're coming along fine now, aren't you?' he asked, handing her a drink from an improvised bar set up on the lawn.

'I'd prefer to have something to eat,' she said. 'I haven't had anything since breakfast.'

'Haven't you learned yet that in this household one drinks when one is thirsty – or even when one is't – and, in the same spirit, one finds one's own meals when one is hungry? There are no huge gourmet dinners at this party.'

'Oh,' said Clara, 'I see.' She took the drink Webster offered, and promised to call him Johnny at his insistence. 'Not Jack, mind you,' he cautioned, leading her back towards the house.

Once inside, he brought her into a small deserted drawing room that was out of the main stream of guest traffic. It was tastefully furnished with a radio, a couch, armchairs, a rug, a few wall hangings and an enormous bunch of cut flowers arranged artfully in Japanese style in a globular vase on the sill of the open window.

Webster seated himself next to her on the couch and asked: 'How did you feel after your little lesson yesterday?'

'Must I have felt some particular way?'

'No, I suppose not. But it would be polite to pretend that you did.'

His debonair ease appeared to incense her. 'Well, I did feel something,' she said, jumping up and stamping her little foot prettily. 'I felt ashamed and miserable. I wished that I were dead – or that you were!!'

He pulled her around to face him and grabbed her thigh. Then he pulled her between his legs and pushed her down so that she was sitting on the sofa again, but this time with her legs over one of his and under the other.

'That's no way to feel,' he told her. 'Or maybe it is, for a girl like you. Would you like me to make you feel ashamed and miserable again today? Do you like that?' He gave her a shrewd look.

'Of course not,' she said. 'Don't be ridiculous!' She extricated her legs from his and took the drink he offered.

'I think I'll give you another lesson anyway,' he told her. 'I like that way of making you feel ashamed. Wouldn't you like to do what we did yesterday?' His hand was slowly creeping under her skirt.

Clara moved a few inches away from him, but he moved right after her. He tried to kiss her, and she hurriedly occupied her lips with the glass.

'You were very pretty with all your clothes off,' he told her. 'Very pretty indeed. Especially those little pink buds of yours. And the way you acted was very pretty, too, mainly because you thought you were being so very wicked and couldn't help yourself – didn't you?'

'Yes,' she said in a small voice. 'What we did was terribly wicked.'

'Well, that's a matter of opinion. But I'm rather glad you think so. And it would be just as wicked if we did it again, yes?'

'It would always be wicked,' she replied solemnly. She sipped at her drink before saying: 'You did a bad thing to me.' She sounded exactly like an eight-year old who feels she has been unjustly punished.

'I'm going to do it to you again,' he chuckled.

He was feeling her thigh, reaching up between her legs with agile fingers. Suddenly his hand was between her legs, spreading open the hair and the lips of her sex. She began to pull away when his hand came out from under her dress, but only for a moment – long enough to be raised to his lips. Then it dipped back under her dress and seized again, and she gasped as his wetted finger slipped down through the lips of her tender spot. His other arm slipped around her waist, his fingers pressing into her belly.

He rolled towards her and rubbed against her. His sex pressed her thigh. She covered her face with her hands. The liquor glass rolled across the carpet and broke.

'Oh, don't,' she said, 'please don't. Please.'

He took her limp hand and guided it into place around his member. By this time his finger was burrowing deep inside of her. 'Open your legs,' he murmured.

But she closed them tightly – on his hand, of course.

'Now listen,' he said, 'take me to your room, or otherwise, so help me, I'll make you undress right here. I swear I will.' His voice was very thick – whether from lust or liquor it was impossible to determine – as he said, 'I'll make you do it right here, where anyone can see us if they walk in. Come on, I'm going to take you to your room and undress you and make you play with me again.'

She rose with seeming reluctance, one hand covering her face, her body drawn back. He led her by the arm towards the staircase. She followed unsteadily, protesting softly but ineffectively.

They went up the stairs and she showed him the room Mrs Mason had given her. He pushed her in and closed the door after him.

'I don't want to!' she cried, running across the room away from him – but, unfortunately, in the direction of the bed. 'I don't want to!'

He picked her up bodily and dropped her on the bed. He took her shoes off and then her stockings, pinching her thighs as he did so. He made her lift her buttocks while he pulled her skirt up past her hips, then made her sit up while he hoisted the garment over her head. He leaned towards her and reached behind her to unsnap her brassiere.

Then he pushed her back on the bed and kissed her.

She lay still while he pulled down her panties. Then, as if resigned to her fate, she kicked them off, and they hung on one ankle. She left them there and covered her face and breasts with her arms.

Curtly, Webster ordered her to uncover her eyes and to watch him while he undressed. Slowly, she lowered her hands and turned her face towards him. 'All right?' she asked.

'Fine,' he said, as he slipped out of his shorts and came towards her, his member standing out stiffly in front of him.

'Now play with me the way you did yesterday,' he said. He closed her hand around his shaft and made her rub its skin gently up and down.

'Don't look away from it,' he told her, lying back on the bed and drawing her nearer to him, closing her other hand on the rest of his sex. 'I want you to see how big and wet you make it get when you do that to it. Bend closer. Don't be afraid of getting your fingers in the hair.'

He made her stroke the hair of his pubis, made her take up a fold of his pouch with the little finger of the same hand that was fondling him. That caused the two storage bags to bounce up and down, which seemed to please him mightily. 'Now we're going to do something new,' he exclaimed, springing off the bed suddenly. He made her get up, too, and had her stand facing him. Then he pressed his body against hers, rubbing her belly with his monstrous machine. She took the great stalk between her palms, rubbing its tip over her fair skin, up and down the line of almost invisible hair that ran from her navel to her Mount of Venus. Webster put his hands on her hips and caressed her buttocks while his member poked into her navel. Then he bent her backwards towards the bed.

'Put it between your legs now,' he ordered, 'rub it in your love nest.'

'I won't! Oh, no, I can't.' Clara appeared close to hysteria. But Webster was not impressed. Although he did not employ sheer brute force to make her do the things he wanted, his technique was hardly one of seduction.

'I like a certain amount of resistance occasionally,' he

said, 'but this is getting tiresome. Perhaps you shouldn't have come to Blanca's party.' His voice had a cold edge. 'this seems to be the wrong place for you, my little eskimo-pie.'

Clara relaxed in his embrace. 'Oh, no,' she cried. 'I want to stay. It's just that . . . all this is so new to me. Please be patient.'

He grimaced. 'Sure,' he said, 'I'll be patient. Just cooperate, and I'll be real patient.' He placed his shaft between her legs, rubbing it in the depth of the curly black hair which surrounded her Mount of Venus. The tip of his organ slipped between the lips of her spot, and he rubbed it up and down. After a while he guided her hands to the crucial spot, and embraced her, putting his own hands on her buttocks. 'That's better,' he said.

He began to rotate his hips, and pretty soon there was quite a bit of heat being generated, what with the friction caused by her hands and the rotation of his hips. He made her look down to watch what her hands were doing. 'I'll teach you to really like all of this,' he promised her. 'Yes, you'll like it all before we're through. You'll be begging for it, see if you're not.'

'But I'll never like *you*,' she hissed – in a delicate, ladylike way, of course.

This seemed to infuriate him. 'Kneel down,' he ordered her roughly.

'Kneel down? In front of you?' Clara's tone was incredulous.

'Yes, right down on your knees. Don't be bashful. This isn't going to hurt you any more than anything else has.'

Almost as if in a trance, she obeyed. Her knees sank into the soft rug; her eyes were on a level with Webster's hirsute masculinity. Slowly she sank back on her haunches.

'Do you know why I made you kneel?' he asked. He brushed her hair back from her face and gazed down into her tear-filled eyes.

'No.' It was almost a sob.

'Because I want you to lick me. . . . Yes, there!' He

caught her by the ears before she could leap to her feet. 'Lick it, Clara!'

'Oh, no! Please – Johnny! Don't make me do that!'

'All right,' he said mildly. 'You don't have to do anything you don't want to do. That's the rule here. I just feel bad about having to tell Blanca Mason that you're here to spy on her.'

Her voice was little more than a whisper. 'What makes you think I'm spying?'

'What else? I really don't know why you're here, and I won't try to find out either, if you do what I ask you to. But I do know that you're not one of us. I think you're interested in that ring. Now are you going to do as I say?'

The girl nodded slowly.

'Will you do everything I say?' he pressed. 'For as long as you're here, will you come to me whenever I tell you to, and undress and do whatever I want you to?'

'I – I guess so,' she mumbled. 'Is this the way the rule about doing only what you want to do works out?'

He grinned. 'I'm doing what I want,' he said. 'If that means that you have to do things that you don't want to do . . . well, this place is just an experiment, all the details haven't been worked out yet.' The smile left his voice, and he bent towards her, his organ brushing her cheek. 'Lick it now,' he ordered.

She turned her mouth to it dutifully and . . . 'I can't,' she whispered. 'I just can't.'

'You'd be surprised at what you can – and will – do. Lick!'

She brushed her lips against the member and started to pull back again, but his fingers wound in her hair. He pushed her face against his weapon. 'With your tongue,' he said. 'Don't just kiss it.'

She opened her lips and her tongue barely flicked across the tip of his shaft. She made a wry face.

'That's not enough,' he said. 'You've got to lick it a good deal more than that.'

She licked it several more times. Soon, under his orders,

she was licking it with all of her tongue and sliding her lips up and down along the sides.

'You're licking my cock, aren't you Clara?' he said suddenly.

She nodded.

'No. Speak up,' he insisted.

'Yes, I'm licking it,' she said softly.

'What are you licking?'

'Your – your – '

'Go on, say it. You're licking my prick, aren't you?'

'Yes,' she replied slowly. 'I'm licking your prick.'

At last he told her that she could stop. She pulled her lips away, as from a hot iron. He seemed to resent that, and made her kiss the top of his instrument again.

By now, her spirit seemed truly broken. This time when he said she could get up she did so only very slowly, as though she were half asleep. He laid her on the bed and straddled her chest, kneeling. He then told her to press her breasts together. When she had done so, he lay his shaft in the groove. Then he bent forward and made her lick it again – the moisture having dried while he had been getting onto the bed.

As soon as the stick-stiff penis was thoroughly wet again he began to rub it between her breasts, faster and faster, tilll he began to growl under his breath and clutch at her shoulders. Suddenly his hips began to jerk wildly, and he ejaculated all over her throat and shoulder. Then he rolled off her heavily.

He lay motionless for a moment. Then wordlessly, he rose and began to dress. When he had finished, he turned to her and asked: 'Are you coming downstairs again?'

'No, I think I'll just stay here for awhile,' she answered.

He shrugged and walked out without another word, closing the door behind him firmly as he left.

CHAPTER SEVEN

When Clara woke up it was almost evening. The sun was setting and she stood at the window while the sky turned from flame red to bright pink to milky lavender to palest silvery grey. Then, as the colours darkened, she began to dress. She put on a princess gown – with pink lace setting off its white chiffon loveliness at her throat and at the hem – stepped into pink pumps and wandered out into the hall and past several bedrooms to which the doors stood invitingly ajar. But it was a room at the very end of the corridor, whose door was firmly shut, that Clara finally entered. She had knocked timidly, waited for a moment, then tried the door. It opened, and she found herself inside a room more than twice the size of all the others on the floor.

The room was sumptuously furnished in green and black: pale green wallpaper, black fur rug, green velvet drapes covering a window which was set into the small, L-shaped alcove at the far end of the room. The main feature was obviously the bed, which stood on a dais in the exact centre of the chamber. It was huge – at least one and a half times the size of an ordinary double bed – and its black satin cover accentuated its enormity, as did the green velvet canopy which hung over it, supported by four black-veined green marble posts.

Clara crossed the room slowly and ascended the marble steps which led to the colossal love-couch. She peered up at the canopy: her own face peered back at her, reflected in the mirror which was very cleverly inlaid into the pale green sateen lining of the canopy. Whoever had designed this room hadn't missed a trick.

She hastily quitted the dais and went into the L-shaped alcove. Suddenly, Clara was not alone in the room. While she had been standing by the window, hidden by the thick velvet drapes, a man and a girl had entered. Clara stood stock still, as though she were rooted to the spot, and remained there, protected from sight by the curtain, which was hung in such a way as to afford anyone standing in the alcove a perfect view of the bed. Unaware of their captive audience behind the curtain, the two players in the comedy that was about to unfold prepared to speak their opening lines.

The girl was about six years older than Clara and very pretty, with honey blonde hair which fell gracefully about her shoulders. The man appeared to be about thirty, and in a lean, dark way was as handsome as the girl was pretty. Both of them were slightly out of breath, as if they had been running before their entrance into the room.

'Close the door,' the girl said. 'And you'd better lock it.' She was wearing a white skirt and a white sweater with a red fleece college letter sewed on to it. She removed a black leather belt from her waist, then pulled the sweater over her head.

The weave of the wool had left its mark on her bare breasts. She rubbed them briskly with her palms. The man came up behind her and began to fondle her breasts, saying: 'You know you don't have to do that when I'm around.'

She laughed, and he suddenly lifted her, still wearing her skirt and stockings and shoes, and carried her to the bed. She laughed again, and he began to strip, while she slipped out of her skirt in one quick, graceful motion. 'I knew you weren't wearing anything under your trousers,' she said. 'I could see the shape of your penis right through the fabric.'

'You were looking at it, were you?'

'Of course I was – and at every other man's, too. I was wondering how much longer I could last without a man inside of me.'

'It hasn't hurt you to wait,' her companion grinned. He took off her shoes, studied her for a moment, then put them back on. 'You look more like the filthy bitch you are when you keep them on,' he smiled tightly.

'I am a filthy bitch, aren't I?' she asked, smiling back. 'What's more, next time I won't wait. I'll go and have a ball with whoever wants me.'

'You're getting next time mixed up with last time. Last time you didn't wait.'

'Aw, Roy, there were only three of them. And the whole three of them together didn't please me as much as you could have.'

'But you liked it enough to ask them for a second round — and a third.'

'That was just because I was so excited.' She took his shaft in her hands as he lay down beside her. 'You know how excited I get when strange men make love to me — especially when there are more than two.'

The man felt between the girl's legs as she spread them wide. Then the couple's bodies curled towards each other, heels to head. They kissed each other's bellies.

The girl rubbed the man's organ gently, holding it between the palms of her hands. Then she began to rub it harder, licking the tip.

'Are you going to let Hanley make love to you any more?' the man asked her.

'Yep.'

'I thought I told you not to let him any more.'

'I know you did, but I'm going to let him anyway.' The man made an exclamation, and the girl quickly jumped from the bed. 'Wait, wait,' she cried. She ran across the room to the spot where she had discarded her belt. Swiftly she snatched up the black leather strap and ran back to the bed, flinging herself down and handing the belt to the man simultaneously. 'Go ahead,' she cried, 'beat me, beat the daylights out of me.'

She rolled over onto her stomach, throwing her legs open so that her sex gaped widely between them, waiting for him to strike. The leather hissed and bit into the skin of her back and loins. She quivered and laughed. The belt fell again – across her loins and buttocks this time – and, where it had fallen, half a dozen red lines appeared. Her buttocks trembled.

Now the man began to apply all of his strength to the beating. The girl laughed loudly, and the laugh was the clear laugh of actual pleasure, not the uncontrolled shrilling of hysteria. 'Harder,' she begged. 'Beat me harder!'

The request was obeyed. Time after time the lash whistled through the air and landed on her tender white skin. Welts rose on her back and buttocks, and, on the first welts, other welts, at crazy angles to the first ones. 'Now ask me if I'm going to let Hanley have me,' the girl exclaimed.

'Are you?' he roared.

'YES. I AM!' She laughed again, and he whipped her wildly, lashing her thighs and her calves, and even letting the blows fall between her legs.

Blood suddenly appeared and at the sight of it, the man's member, which had been standing rigidly out and erect all the time, suddenly began to spurt and he stopped lashing for a moment. The girl whirled and flung her arms around his waist, lapping up the fluid as it spurted and getting it all over her face. Then she rolled over again – on her back now – and spread her legs. She opened and closed her grotto with both hands as she waited for him to recover from the efforts of his orgasm and beat her some more.

After a minute, he resumed his whipping, but concentrating his blows on her belly and thighs. 'I'm going to let Hanley take me,' the girl cried, 'and you can't whip it out of me! I want my bottom whipped some more.' She rolled over and propped herself up on her knees and elbows, dropping her head and jutting her buttocks out. He slashed at the twin targets until they bled.

The girl kept her face buried in a pillow, while her hands involuntarily clutched at her own hair. Finally, she fell prone and writhed wildly as the beating rose to a climax.

'Oh, oh,' she cried. 'I'll spend right now if you don't stop!'

'Are you going to let Hanley make love to you?' His voice was like thunder, his face a cloud.

The girl's answer shrilled like lightning: 'Yes! Yes, I'm going to let Hanley make love to me. And anybody else that wants me. Go on and beat me. When I reach my climax I'll pretend Hanley is inside me and some stranger has his prick in my mouth!'

She thrust both her thumbs into her mouth and began to suck them noisily, while her hips wriggled and writhed wildly. The man flung the belt aside and threw himself on top of her, levering over and vaulting between her legs. She threw her legs high and drooped them on his shoulder, her body bent in half like a jack-knife. Their arms and legs tangled and they both began to laugh. The man's weapon drove into its target and her buttocks became wet and shiny with love-juice as the big sword jabbed in and out of its sheath.

They remained locked together for less than a minute before the man's body began to jerk spasmodically and the girl dropped one leg to encircle his waist, bucking him high in the air with almost demonic strength as she screamed that she was coming to a climax. Then the man disengaged his limbs from the woman's and they both sprang off the bed, seemingly more energetic than they had been when they entered the room.

The man took a corner of the green velvet drapery which hung down from the canopy and wiped the sweat from the girl's back and buttocks. Then they raced to get into their clothes, while the girl laughingly commented on how funny the man's buttocks had looked in the canopy mirror as they jolloped up and down while he was making love to her. The pair finished dressing and left the room in the same manner in which they had entered it – on the run.

As soon as the couple's footsteps faded, Clara also quit the room. As she started to descend the stairs, she met Mrs Mason.

'Why, hello, Clara,' chirruped the hostess. 'How are you getting along? Are you all right? You look a little pale.'

'Hello, Blanca. Yes, I'm fine, thank you. I was just wondering about dinner.'

'Dinner? Why I believe there are some people eating now. Join them if you like their looks. We eat anytime here. The kitchen is well-stocked, I believe. Somebody flew in some trout from the mountains just today. They're delicious. Or have some man cook a plate for you. Get one of the girlish-looking men. They're all marvellous chefs. And you'll find plenty of them to choose from.'

She paused with her fine, white hand on Clara's shoulder and stroked the girl's silky black curls. 'My, you really are pretty, aren't you?' she asked. She squeezed Clara's arm and went on, 'Well, if you're only hungry you won't need me.' And she continued up the stairs.

CHAPTER EIGHT

Clara had been in the library for twenty minutes and had not yet found a single book with a scorpion bookplate like the one she had shown Garnett. She was crouching in front of a low shelf, and, as she rose, her shoulder struck a small table on which a huge porcelain flower vase had been standing. The vase fell to the floor, splattering its contents over the hem and lower skirt of the dress of a woman who had been unobtrusively reading in an armchair near the table.

'I'm so terribly sorry,' Clara fluttered. 'I didn't know I was so close to your chair.'

The woman smiled. 'Don't worry about it, my dear,' she said as Clara kept repeating her apologies. 'It makes a woman twice as interesting if she changes her dress in the middle of the evening. But,' she added, 'if it will soothe your conscience any, you may come along and keep me company while I change.'

'Oh, yes,' said Clara, 'that *would* make me feel better. I'd be glad to come.' She followed the older woman out of the library.

Clara's new companion was one of those not-young, not-old women whom one so often finds at smart country houses. She was probably close to forty, but she could have passed for thirty with ease. She had grey eyes and a nose that tilted slightly at the end. Her step was that of a girl of twenty and her eyes were as bright and lively as those of a baby. But, over all these varied youthfulnesses, there was a rich cloak of maturity and poise.

'I haven't seen you here before,' she said.

'This is the first time I've been here,' Clara replied. 'I've just met Mrs Mason.'

'Blanca is wonderful, isn't she? And it's an exhilarating place, too, don't you think?'

'I'm not used to it yet, and some of the people frighten me a little.'

The woman laughed – a tinkle of tiny silver bells. 'The people frighten you only because you see them acting perfectly naturally, and you're used to people who act perfectly unnaturally – that is to say, people who are always keeping up pretences. At your age, you don't realise what a wonderful place this really is. This is the way the world ought to be, but isn't. A perfect anarchy. When you catch on to what it really means you'll appreciate it more and more.'

'But it seems as if everyone wants to make love to me,' Clara sighed. 'and they just grab.'

'Of course,' the woman laughed. 'Doesn't it make you feel good to have men really come out and try to grab you for a change, instead of hinting around the edges for hours and trying to liquor you up and put their hands all over you on the sly? I much prefer the out-and-out grabbers myself.'

'I should think it would infuriate your husband to have his wife grabbed at,' said Clara.

'Why should it? There's always someone else's wife for him to grab at. Only a lazy man can complain about such a system. If it hurts a man's vanity to know his wife is bored with his sex technique, well, he can polish up his vanity by working on some other wife who's bored with her husband. A lazy man wants to keep his own wife to himself even after being bored with her brand of loving for years simply because it's too much effort – physical or mental – to get somebody else's wife.'

'But what about jealousy?' Clara asked.

'What about it? I suppose it exists. And, when it does, it's good for people. Gives their adrenalin glands a workout.

At least they feel some sort of emotion for a change. Too little real emotion and too much fake emotion is what's wrong with the outside world. Self-hypnosis or hysteria or plain fraud masquerading as emotion. Most of it is just sentimentality, anyhow. You see me. My husband is here somewhere. He's with a woman. I don't know who. I hope she's pretty and I hope she's giving him a good time – but not a better time than I can give him when we get home. See? When we go travelling, we pick up a young couple if we can, and trade partners. I like a young man to compliment me and sleep with me, and my husband likes to have a pretty young girl fuss over him and make love to him. It makes him feel important. But we love each other, and we always come back to each other.'

'It sounds too simple,' Clara said. 'There must be something wrong with it.'

'You aren't very experienced, are you? Please don't be offended. I don't mean to be condescending. But an experienced woman either knows better than you seem to, or she's made a mess of her life. At least that's the way I see it. You see, I'm not trying to hold a husband. I don't need a meal ticket. I can earn my own living. I love my husband, but my big project in life is not to try to hang on to him. What I'm really trying to do is get on with the business of living a life as successfully and as happily as I can. Insofar as I succeed or fail, I keep or lose my husband, too – or at least his love, because he's no dummy. He wouldn't be able to love me if he couldn't respect me as a human being.'

Clara appeared impressed, but she asked: 'Do you believe that all the people here think like that? The people I saw making naked love on the lawn?'

'I don't know what they think. These parties are a kind of emotional explosion. You can see violent things around here if you want to: things that would bring a police raid if they got out. No one is forced to stay and watch, though, and no one is forced into participating. I stay because I like to be thrilled, and some of the things that happen here thrill me. It isn't always the things that I think are nice that thrill me. Sometimes it's things that I realise are pretty beastly and vicious. But you can't pick the things that are going to thrill you, and it isn't very sensible to fight against being thrilled. You just get neurotic that way, and you don't have any fun. I'll watch or do anything that makes my heart beat with excitement, as long as I don't ruin my health or go to jail for it. That's part of my way of getting everything I can out of life.'

They had reached the woman's room, which was in an annexe to the main house, and Clara entered after her. The woman took off her damp dress and put it away. She stood before the mirror and both women gazed at the reflection of the older woman's body. Her soft breasts did not thrust out like a young girl's, but they had a full heavy sensuousness that was very attractive. The woman put a dab of lipstick on her mouth and two more dabs on each of her full, dark-brown nipples. 'Kissproof,' she said. 'It doesn't stain the dress, and the men like the look – and the taste – of it.' She put perfume behind each ear and at the base of her throat, and touched it to her nipples, too. She cast a sidewise glance at Clara before sliding the dropper of the perfume bottle down under the band of her panties into her navel and across her Mount of Venus.

'If you want to help me,' the woman said, 'you can find a black dress in the closet. It's the one with the fringe at the neck.' She took off her grey slippers and put them in the closet. Clara searched for the black gown in a second closet.

'Shoes, too,' the woman called. Clara laid the dress out on the bed and put the black shoes with the high-tying straps on the floor near the bed. 'And with a black dress I'll have to wear black step-ins. I hate to disappoint the men,' the woman went on. 'Or anyone,' she added with a tinkling laugh. 'The step-ins will be somewhere in that lower drawer.'

Clara fumbled through the drawer. 'Tell me,' the

woman continued, 'what did you expect when you came out here? Not people playing bridge and listening to the radio and talking about their jobs and businesses back in town?'

'I didn't think it would be like that,' Clara replied, 'but I don't know what I did think it would be like. I don't think I expected to find Chinese girls, and men with turbans and beards, and poets who want to run barefoot through my hair.'

The woman laughed again. 'I think I know what you were looking for. A grown-up college crowd. Telling dirty jokes and kidding around and doing a lot of drinking and nothing much else. Well, we've got some of the old boys from Princeton, too. There are all kinds here. . . . These stockings aren't the right shade. See if there's a darker pair, will you please? More purplish and less grey.'

'I haven't met Mrs Mason's husband yet,' Clara said, continuing to rummage through the drawer. 'What's he like?'

'Him? Marvellous. Beautiful when he's naked. Slender hips and balls like church bells. He has the same effect on women that a bull has — they gasp when they see him. I know I did the first time I went to bed with him. I was still gasping the next morning, too, but for quite another reason entirely. We're quite good friends.'

As the woman spoke, she began rolling on the stockings that Clara had given her. She stood on one firm leg, pointed the other like a dancer and pulled the sheer silk along the lovely limb as though she were in love with its perfection. Her buttocks were high, with no hint of a sag, and they were just full enough to bulge slightly. In back, just above her buttocks, were two delightful dimples.

'How many men have made love to you?' the woman asked casually. There was a long silence, and then Clara said: 'Two.'

The woman did not question her. She remained silent for a moment. 'I was trying to remember how long ago it was that I had only been had by two men,' she said at last.

'I don't believe I had much fun with them at the time. I didn't know a thing about having fun in bed – or under a bush for that matter. I was just plain uninformed when it came to sex. Today, one of these first two lovers sends me flowers and the other has a wife and a shoe business in Seattle. Don't you think it's depressing to have one's first lover grow into a wife and a shoe business in Seattle?'

'I never think about things like that,' said Clara. 'But tell me – would you let these same men make love to you today?'

'The one who sends me flowers, yes. I'll go to bed with almost any man who sends me flowers. I'm a sucker for flowers. Especially camellias. I love them. But not the shoe business, and a fat wife with woman's troubles. No, that dope will have to sleep with his own wife. That's what he got her for in the first place. Damn him, even if he sent me flowers I wouldn't go to bed with him again.'

As she spoke, the woman turned around, and Clara could see her whole nakedness for the first time. She caught her breath and gripped the arms of her chair with all her strength.

The woman just stood there, chattering away and fixing her stockings, not noticing the horror-stricken expression on the young girl's face. She stood with her legs planted firmly apart while she half turned her head towards the mirror and readjusted a lock of hair that had escaped from her carefully curled coiffure. The lines of her body rose in sleek slopes from her full thighs to her shoulders. Her breasts, the nipples turned slightly away from each other and still glistening with the perfume and lipstick on them, gave her shoulders an added solidity, balancing the gorgeous roundness of her hips. Very low on her belly, several inches below her navel and just above the curling mass of pubic hair – was a crimson mark the size of a half dollar – a mark which looked as though it had been burned into her flesh. It was a deliberate, manmade thing, obviously not a birthmark or a scar. It was shaped like a scorpion.

CHAPTER NINE

The woman began to search for her step-ins. She found them laid out neatly on the chair near her dressing table. 'Thank you, my dear girl,' she said with a smile. 'You make a marvellous lady's maid. In fact, you're so good that I'm reluctant to let . . .' Her voice trailed off and her smile was replaced by a perplexed frown as she looked at Clara's obviously horror-stricken face. 'Whatever is the matter?' she asked. 'You look as though you've just seen a ghost. And you're pale enough to pass for a ghost yourself. Are you ill, child?'

'No, no, not at all,' said Clara with a thin tight-lipped smile. 'I'm just feeling a tiny bit faint. It's nothing to be alarmed about. You see, I haven't eaten any dinner. As a matter of fact, I haven't eaten since breakfast. But I've been drinking – and quite a bit more than usual, I'm afraid I guess a large quantity of alcohol on an empty stomach will make almost anybody queasy. And it is a bit warm in here, don't you think?'

With this last sentence, Clara's voice assumed a voluptuousness that it had not contained before, and the woman looked at her thoughtfully. 'Yes,' she said, 'now that you mention it, it is rather warm in here. Strange that I didn't notice before. Well, I'll just dress quickly, and we can go for a stroll in the garden to cool off. After you have some dinner, that is. You know, my dear, you really need someone to look after you. Do you live with your family?'

'My parents died in an accident. I've no family at all. Except my sister, that is.'

'Oh, does your sister look after you?'

'No. Not any more. In fact, she seems to have been having some trouble looking after herself.'

'Oh, poor little . . .' The woman broke off abruptly and laughed in an embarrassed fashion. 'My goodness,' she tittered, 'I don't even know your name.'

'Oh, do forgive me. It's Clara . . . Clara Morrow.'

'Clara. Spanish for "clear." Clear . . . pure. How very appropriate.'

The smile took the sting out of her sardonic tone. 'My name is Alice Burton. And I apologise for keeping you from your dinner. Do come and hook my brassiere for me, will you?'

She slipped her arms through the slender satin straps and turned her naked back towards Clara, who fumblingly hooked the garment's three hooks into its three eyes. Her fingers lightly brushed the woman's warm shoulders and, for an instant, rested there. Alice promptly turned, caught them in her hand and gave them a quick, affectionate squeeze.

The older woman now crossed the room and sat on the edge of the bed. Picking up the stockings Clara had chosen for her, she extended one. 'Here,' she said, 'put it on for me.'

Wordlessly, the girl took the stocking, drew it over Alice's tiny foot and carefully pulled it up over her thigh. Smoothing the silk, she then slipped a black satin garter into place over it. Alice prettily extended her other leg, and Clara repeated the performance. As she drew the garter on, she stammered: 'I . . . I . . . don't think I got the seams straight. If you'll stand up, I'll . . .'

Alice didn't wait for her to finish the sentence. She rose gracefully and turned, spreading her legs slightly apart so that Clara could hold on to one of them for support as she adjusted the stocking on the other.

Somehow, as Clara fumbled with the seams, her face became pressed against Alice's thigh. She attempted to rise, but Alice's hand was planted firmly atop her head. She dropped back on her haunches. The older woman then lowered her hips back onto the bed and hugged Clara's head to her thigh. Clara remained in that position the better part of a minute, then suddenly pulled away.

'Was I mistaken?' mused Alice aloud.

'What do you mean "mistaken?"' Clara asked in apparent confusion. 'About what? What do you want from me?'

'Don't you know?'

The girl shook her head.

Alice smiled and began stroking the girl's silky hair. 'Just a few moments ago,' she said very softly, 'you acted as though you knew. As if you wanted it, too.' She raised one thigh and gently brushed Clara's cheek with it. 'But I don't want to force you to do anything you don't want to do. Anything you do with me you must do because you want to; because you like me; and because I like you.'

At this, Clara lifted her head and smiled back. 'Be patient with me,' she said softly. 'Please . . . be patient.' She rubbed her chin against the softness of the woman's inner thigh and again offered a bitter-sweet smile.

Alice slowly drew the girl's head back into place between her legs. Clara's mouth pressed the lace fringe of the woman's panties, and she kissed first the broad expanse of thigh, then the warm, perfumed groin. 'Put out your tongue,' Alice whispered.

Clara touched her tongue to the softest part of the woman's thigh and ran it along the milk-white inner side. She fastened her fingers over the top of the panties to draw them down. Her lips, under the crotch of the wispy garment, touched a few curling hairs that escaped through the legholes. Her tongue dragged sideways over the perfumed petals of the woman's lotus-bud. She pushed the panty crotch to one side with her hand.

Suddenly Alice backed away. 'Get up now, dear,' she said sweetly. 'It's early yet. We have all evening.' She rose from the bed and swung one thigh across Clara's head to step free of her, then recommenced dressing as Clara, dishevelled and apparently distraught, got to her feet and started towards the door.

'Where are you going?' Alice asked, catching Clara's fleeing reflection in the mirror.

'To my room,' Clara answered. She lowered her eyes and added in a voice so low it was barely a whisper: 'To wash my face.'

Alice came to her side and took her wrist. 'No, you mustn't do that. I don't want you to wash your face.'

'But it makes me feel ashamed to stay this way.'

'Then that's all the more reason for staying that way. My goodness, child, if you've never been ashamed of yourself before, you must have been leading a terribly sheltered life. Shame is like wine to a woman; she grows drunk and wanton and glowing on it. How old are you? Twenty?'

Clara nodded.

'Twenty-years-old, and never drunk on shame; never crept to your room and bed feeling wonderfully dirty and used and degraded? My poor little Clara, you have a great deal to learn. So we'll call this your first lesson. You will not wash your face, Clara, any more than I will wash the stains of your lip rouge from my thighs. Those stains will stay there, do you understand? I want you to remember them and think of them every time you look at me tonight?'

She raised her dress to reveal the splotchy marks left by Clara's lips on her thighs. 'Shame wells up inside of you until you think you'll die of it,' she went on, 'but it never fails – all of a sudden the shame is gone and in its place is a wild exhilaration. You'll see, Clara, you'll see.' She paused and gazed at the girl tenderly, almost maternally. 'Don't wash up, but do straighten your dress and comb your hair. As soon as you're presentable, we'll go downstairs and get you that dinner I've been promising you.'

In less than ten minutes, Clara was comfortably reclining on a lounge chair, a heaping plateful of steaming hot spaghetti and meat balls on a tray across her lap. On a small table at her side sat a basketful of warm garlic bread and a glass of red wine. Alice Burton, seated on the other side of the table, raised her own wine glass. 'To our love affair,' she smiled. 'And to shame.' She waited until Clara lifted her glass in apparent acknowledgement of the toast. Then both women drank.

The next hour passed quietly. The wine and food seemed to relax Clara, and she was soon chattering away with Alice Burton and a few other people who had joined them. She did not seem the least bit embarrassed – and, in fact, she had quite captivated the blasé little group with her native air. It was thus that John Webster found her, in the midst of four or five people, laughing animatedly, her cheeks flushed and her eyes sparkling. 'Here you are!' he beamed enthusiastically. 'I've been searching everywhere for you.' He took Clara's arm and helped her to her feet.

'But she belongs to me now,' Alice Burton objected.

'Then I'll see to it that she comes back to you,' he replied amiably.

'You'd better,' she warned coolly. 'I have plans for her.'

Webster led Clara down the terrace steps and off towards the garden. 'Where are you taking me?' the girl asked.

'To meet two friends of mine,' he said, hustling her past the sundial and into the darkness of an arbour with a cushioned double swing chair hanging between two great oaks. 'You seem to be such a great believer in marital "togetherness" I thought I'd show you a little sample of it.'

'What took you so long?' a woman's voice asked out of the shadows.

'I had a hard time finding her,' replied Webster.

'We almost didn't wait,' said a masculine voice. 'Look what happened.'

The couple was lying in the swing chair, their limbs intertwined. In the darkness it was impossible to fathom where the male left off and the female began.

Clara turned away. Webster tightened his grip on her forearm. 'Just where do you think you're going?'

'Back to the house. Can't you see that we're disturbing your friends.'

Peals of laughter greeted the comment. 'I told you she was naive!' said Webster triumphantly.

Turning to Clara he added: 'We're not disturbing them, honey. We're going to help them out. You know – entertain them a bit, inspire them.'

The three friends laughed again.

'Oh! Take me back to the house,' Clara begged. 'Please, Johnny.'

'Listen,' said Webster roughly. 'Don't start the innocent virgin bit again. It won't work. He lowered his voice and said softly into Clara's ear. 'Unless you do exactly what I tell you to, I'll strip you right down to the skin and take you back to the house like that . . . to Blanca!'

'I'm not afraid of her,' said Clara defiantly.

'You should be. Remember that I know things about you that she doesn't.' He felt her resistance lessening, and, interpreting this as a sign of acquiescence, said aloud: 'Sorry, folks. The little lady's still kind of shy. But she's got over it now, haven't you, baby?'

Clara nodded.

'Haven't you?' he repeated harshly.

'Yes,' said Clara. 'I've got over my shyness now.'

'And you don't mind undressing now, do you?'

'Undressing?' There was a note of incredulity in her voice as she echoed the word.

'Yeah. Undressing. You know – taking your clothes off.'

More laughter from the swing.

'Don't answer. Just strip,' said Webster.

The girl began to obey, taking her dress off slowly, as though she were in a trance. Next came her shoes and stockings, then her slip. Finally, with great hesitation, she removed her brassiere. Then she stood facing the swing, her arms crossed over her pretty, pink breasts.

Webster tugged at the waistband of her panties. 'I said to take off everything,' he commanded in a voice that brooked no argument. And then, in a gentler tone, he added: 'You've got a beautiful body, darling. Did I tell you that? You should be proud of it. You should want these people to see it. The way I want them to see it because I'm proud of it. Proud that it belongs to me. That I can do whatever I want with so much loveliness.' As if to prove his domination over her, he violently tugged the seat of the panties over her smooth, round buttocks. 'Take them off,' he snapped. 'Now.'

Clara began to cry softly, whispering. 'Oh, no,' over and over again, like a litany. But she obeyed.

Grinning lasciviously, Webster clutched her breasts and squeezed tightly. Then he manoeuvreed her hands onto his penis, which he had removed from his trousers and which now stood bravely and sturdily erect. 'Rub it between your legs,' he said.

Clara did so as a tiny gasp, which welled into a shriek, emanated from the swing, indicating that the couple ensconced there had not been paying full attention to the activities being staged ostensibly for their benefit. The shriek was followed by a duet of giggles, and suddenly the couple bounded off the swing. The man knelt at the base of one of the oaks and fumbled around for several seconds. Then he struck a match and with it lit a small kerosene torch. Carrying the torch, he sat beneath his partner on the grass, not two feet away from where Clara and Webster were standing. Promptly a second act of copulation was begun.

The tiny flame of the torch flicked and quivered, shedding a soft glow around the entangled couple. 'No, No, No, NO!' cried Clara, her voice rising hysterically. 'I can't bear her to look at it!'

Webster gripped her by the shoulders, his fingers digging into her flesh. 'Stop it,' he hissed. 'Just stop it.' The force of his grip and the authority in his voice seemed to have a tranquillising effect on the girl, for after a moment she relaxed visibly.

'All right, now?' asked Webster.

Clara nodded dumbly.

'Then forget the lamp. Just forget it. Pretend you're still in the dark. Just you and me. In the dark.' He had softened his voice, and he spoke the last words in an hypnotic sing-song. He held Clara almost tenderly, gently stroking her hair. When he felt the tension go out of her he again placed his organ in her hands. 'Rub,' he whispered.

She held the rigid device against her own hairiness, rubbing it between her palms and against the flesh of her groin.

'Spread your legs and rub it against your pussy,' Webster commanded.

She pressed the large bud of the swelling stalk between the soft petals of her dear little flower. She stood on the tips of her toes, rocking back and forth. Presently, dew covered the sweet petals – liquid from Webster's rigid watering can, and liquid which flowed out of Clara's little well.

Webster toyed with her buttocks and her breasts, bruising her nipples against the roughness of his jacket as he pressed her close to him. He curled his fingers and ran his nails lightly along her sides to her thighs.

'You tickle,' she said with a giggle.

Unsmiling, he told her to kneel in front of him.

When she complied, he said: 'Lick it. Lick the part you had between your legs.' He pushed her head close to his crotch, close to his swelling love instrument, and repeated his demand.

Clara dutifully obeyed him. She ran her tongue slowly up and down his organ, making it lurch stiffly. Then she curved her finger around it and held it firmly as she licked the sides and the bare tip.

'Good,' said Webster. 'But not good enough.'

She held it up and licked beneath it, up and down the underside where the rim of the head came together in the little slot at the tip. Webster's hands gripped her head tightly, holding her mouth fiercely to its task.

Suddenly the other woman sprang up and came to kneel beside Clara. Her naked thigh touched Clara's, her fingers slipped over the fingers which clasped Webster's shaft. Her voice whispered voluptuously into Clara's ear, 'Lick it with me, honey.' She then faced Clara, pressing her own cheek against Webster's thigh. Her full, sensual lips buried themselves in his groin. Then they touched Clara's lips, kissing them over the arc of Webster's maleness. Her tongue flickered out, wetting Clara's lips with its hot moisture, brushing across Webster's member, then returning to Clara's lips.

'Lick it with me,' the woman repeated urgently. Her tongue pressed more firmly against the side of the shaft, forcing it harder against Clara's mouth. She placed one arm around Clara, and feverishly stroked the girl's breast. Her own breast brushed Clara's other breast and their nipples kissed. Then she slipped her hand down to Clara's buttocks, avidly caressing their round fullness. She tried to push the head of Webster's swollen organ into Clara's mouth, but Clara slid her lips away and tucked her tongue under the head.

The woman's tongue covered Clara's, tickling it teasingly. Clara curled her tongue in the other direction; the woman's tongue followed, licking more insistently and firmly. At last the woman drew Clara's tongue into her mouth and sucked it, lipping Webster's manhood at the same time. Then she drew his weapon into her mouth, sucking it and Clara's tongue simultaneously. Her lips pressed the organ firmly against Clara's tongue, so that it was being licked by Clara and sucked by the other woman at the same time. Webster's hips began to plunge back and forth, back and forth, and Clara violently pulled her tongue free.

The other girl's mouth stopped working and she pulled her lips away with an audible pop. 'Don't you want to suck it too?' she asked.

'No!' gasped Clara. 'Oh, no.'

'Then lick it.'

She pushed Clara's face against Webster's groin. 'Lick!' She waited for Clara to obey before she replaced the end of the organ in her mouth, compressing her lips tightly around it.

Then she slipped her hand through Webster's open legs and tickled the groove between his buttocks with one delicate finger. Meanwhile, Clara dutifully continued to rub the base of the shaft with the tip and blade of her tongue.

Suddenly, the older girl's face convulsed. Her lips grew wetter and she sucked more noisily than ever. Webster's hips were gyrating wildly, and his legs trembled and pressed more firmly against the girl's cheeks.

Webster suddenly pushed both women away, and stepped back. Clara's whole body drooped, and she closed her eyes, a relieved expression on her face. She remained there until she felt the man's member once again rubbing her lips. Even then she didn't open her eyes. She merely stuck out her tongue and resumed her former task. After awhile, she opened her eyes, raised her head ... and gasped. It was not Webster who towered above her, but a stranger – the man who had just witnessed the little scene in which Clara had participated.

Clara's eyes widened, and she pulled away. The man quickly grabbed her body between his knees and placed his hands on her shoulders. The other girl, who had already begun to suck this new lollipop, also placed her arms around Clara.

'You're not going to stop now – after you've begun so well, are you?' the man queried mockingly.

'I didn't realise,' cried Clara. 'I didn't know ... I don't know you ... oh ... please ...'

'It isn't any different, honeychile,' the other woman said. When she spoke out loud, her voice carried the heavy langourousness of the deep South. 'You didn't even know the difference till you looked.

'But if it will make you feel any better, why, just pretend it's Johnny you're loving up.'

Clara appealed to Webster, now seated in a corner of

the swing, watching dispassionately. 'Johnny,' she said, 'do I have to?'

'Yes, Clara, you have to.'

'Oh, please don't make me. Please take me back to the house.'

'When you've finished what you've started. This is a funny time to turn squeamish, don't you think? You've already licked one man. I can't see why you should object to licking another. Don't they all taste pretty much alike, Mary Lou?' he asked, addressing the other girl.

'Practically,' she laughed. 'Make her suck it if she doesn't want to lick it. Maybe it would be fun to see your virgin girl friend suck my husband. Arnold, darling, have you ever been sucked by a virgin?'

The man glared at her. 'Can it,' he said, 'and get back to work.'

The girl reached for her husband's love instrument and rubbed it against Clara's mouth, whispering in her ear as she did so.

Clara flushed. 'No!' she spat. 'That's disgusting! I'd never say such a thing.'

'Say it, or I'll have Johnny make you swallow Arnold's come.'

Clara lowered her eyes and said softly: 'I like licking men. I want to do it again.'

Arnold smiled and arched his hips forward. 'That's the spirit, kid,' he said. Clara resumed lipping his organ, rubbing her mouth up and down the sides of the penis as though she were playing a flute. She mouthed it up and down to the tip, finally nibbling on the tip itself. Mary Lou came in on the downstroke, and the two wet tongues played an andante up and down the length of the instrument. Then, when the jerking motions of his hips told the woman that her husband was about to reach his climax, she put the tip into her mouth and pressed forward until her lips almost reached his pubic hair.

Clara drew back as Mary Lou began sucking violently,

driving her mouth up and down and shaking her head from side to side.

When she had finished, she rose and began to dress. Clara remained seated, as though she was too dazed to move. She remained there, squatting on the flagstones, until Webster touched her shoulders and silently held out her underwear. She then rose and stepped into her panties. She extended her arms and he slipped the straps of the brassiere over them. Then he hooked the hooks in the back and slipped her dress over her head.

Finally he handed her her evening purse, saying: 'I suggest you powder your face and put on lipstick. That is unless you want everybody to know what you've been doing for the past hour.'

Clara blanched and immediately withdrew her compact from the purse. When she had finished making herself as presentable as possible, Webster said: 'Come on, now, we're going back. After all, I did promise Alice I'd return you to her.'

CHAPTER TEN

Alice Burton dragged on her cigarette and sensually blew the smoke out through her nostrils. 'Aren't you drinking rather heavily?' she asked Clara, watching the girl down two straight shots of Hennessy Seven Star in as many gulps.

'I haven't had anything else to drink but the wine for dinner,' said Clara, reaching for a glass of ice water. For a moment she held it in her hand – a hand which trembled so much that Alice could hear the ice cubes tinkling against the glass. Then she lifted it to her lips, gulped down the contents thirstily, and poured herself another jigger of cognac.

Alice waited until the girl had put down the shot glass. Then she said softly: 'You've really been through the mill, haven't you? Would you like to tell me about it?'

Clara gulped. 'No! Oh NO! I *couldn't*. I don't even want to think about it again.'

'All right, dear. I won't force the issue. Shall we just go out on the terrace to clear our heads? The cigarette smoke is really dreadful in here, isn't it?'

'Yes. All right,' agreed Clara. She followed Alice out onto the terrace and sat opposite her in the same deck chair in which she had been sitting less than two hours before, amusing Alice's friends with her naive banter.

'It seems like two years,' she said suddenly.

'What seems like two years, Clara?'

'The time that's passed since the last time we sat here. I was so happy then. Silly little baby. Being cute for all the grownups. Making them laugh. Oh, I'm funny all right. A real laugh riot.' Her voice broke with a sob, and she buried her face in her hands.

Alice, who had been standing at the railing of the terrace, moved next to the girl, placing her arms around the shaking shoulders and lightly stroking the tousled hair. At last the sobs ceased and the shaking body grew still. Clara drew away from the warm shelter of Alice's arms and sat erect, drawing her knees up and hugging them to her chest. 'Thank you,' she said, in a barely audible voice, 'for being so good to me. I don't deserve it.'

'Don't be silly,' replied Alice sharply. 'I'm only being nice to you because I want you to like me. If I weren't interested in you, Clara, I wouldn't have ever suggested that you help me change clothes. I probably wouldn't even have been so nice about your spilling water on my dress.'

'Oh!' Clara opened her eyes very wide. 'I didn't realise . . . that is . . . I mean. I didn't think . . . I mean . . . Oh, dear, I'm so confused.'

Alice laughed softly and patted Clara's hand. 'I know, lovey, and that's what interests me about you: your innocent confusion. You know, Clara, you're not the type of girl one expects to find here. I've been wondering just what it is that makes you stay . . .' She waited for Clara to say something, but the girl remained silent. 'If you don't enjoy yourself here,' Alice continued, 'you should go home. Where life is safe and sane. Where you won't see too much; where you won't scorch your pretty tinsel wings.'

'I don't understand what you mean.'

'And you won't understand until it's too late, I suppose. You know, you really have seen nothing terribly shocking yet. Don't you realise that? You think it's been like a nightmare, don't you? You think the things you've seen and done are utterly depraved. Well, my dear, you're wrong. Although I don't know exactly what you did tonight, I can take a pretty fair guess. I know John Webster and I know what his tastes are. That's why I let you go with him. Because I knew you'd be safe in his hands.'

'Safe?' Clara gasped. 'Safe?'

'Yes,' Alice smiled. 'Safe. You see. I told you you hadn't seen anything yet. Just listen, Clara, listen to the conversations around us. Listen carefully . . .

The two women sat silently for a moment, and strange voices wafted through the night air.

' . . . sent his wife into their son's bedroom, naked, with two bottles of champagne. A kid of fifteen; never drank a drop before . . .'

' . . . a wonderful place. . . . Completely integrated . . . In a coffin, on top of a white woman – with black candles lit at both ends. Terribly dramatic. And perfectly discreet.'

' . . . an incestuous family, all five of them, including the grandfather. Charming people.'

' . . . but after she'd been to bed with him and then went to New Orleans and Switzerland, she couldn't think of anything better to do with her sixty thousand a year and her million dollar education and six languages but get the Doberman to make love to her while the Pekinese curled up underneath and lapped her – that's why they call them lap dogs, you know – at the same time . . .'

'I feel rather tyred,' said Clara. 'I think I'll go to bed now.'

'Do you want me to take you back to your room?'

'Yes, please.'

The older woman helped the girl to her feet, put her arm around the slender waist and walked her into the house and up the staircase.

'Here it is,' said Clara, stopping in front of the door and fumbling in her purse for the key. At last she found it and placed it in the key hole.

The two women entered the room. Clara took the key from the lock, closed the door and replaced the key in the keyhole on the inside of the door. She paused for a moment, then locked herself and Alice in.

The woman stood quietly, watching, waiting for Clara to make the next move. But the girl seemed rooted to the spot, as though locking the door had sapped her of her last ounce of strength.

Alice went to her side and prodded her gently. 'Come to bed, dear. It's way past two a.m. and you're exhausted.'

Clara obeyed, moving towards the bed as though in a trance.

Alice switched on the small bedside lamp. 'Take off your dress,' she said, crossing the room to turn out the overhead light. 'And I'll take off mine in just a minute. Then I'll come back to you and we can make love. That is, if you really want to. If you don't, tell me now and I'll understand. But tell me now.'

She took the girl's continued silence for assent, and slipped her dress off and hung it neatly over the back of a chair.

Glancing at Clara, she saw that the girl was still fully clothed.

'Your dress, dear,' she said in the tone one uses with a recalcitrant six-year-old. 'Take it off.'

Clara obeyed, sitting up to do so. Then she fell back heavily on the bed as the dress slipped to the floor.

Now Alice returned to the bed and gently began stripping off Clara's underclothes, pausing occasionally to stroke and audibly admire the slender young body under her hands. As she stripped off Clara's stockings, she exclaimed: 'Why, your knee is badly scraped. But your stocking isn't even snagged. Now I'm beginning to understand. So John had you act out one of his little dramas, did he? He wasn't content with you as an audience, eh?' She paused. 'But why did you go along with it, Clara? *Why*? If you don't like these libertine excesses, why don't you leave here? You're free to go at any time, you know. Are you a masochist? Is that it? Is that why you stay here? Because you like to be hurt and humiliated? Tell me.' She bent over the girl, cupped the wan, heart-shaped face in her hand and gazed at the soft blue eyes. But she could read nothing in them.

'Please,' begged Clara, twisting her head away, 'I don't want to talk about it. Really I don't. Not now, anyway.' She sat up and put her arms around Alice, awkwardly unfastening the hooks of the black brassiere which, earlier in the evening, she herself had fastened. Then she slid her hands down to the slender waist and tugged gently at the waistband of the flimsy black step-ins. Alice arched her buttocks while Clara pushed the thin garment over her ample hips. She began to draw it down over the shapely legs when suddenly she stopped, and, with an exclamation, bent over the woman's mid-section. She put out one finger and tentatively touched the scorpion brand, as though she expected it to sting her. 'What's that?' she asked.

'So that's what startled you when you saw me nude earlier tonight,' she chuckled. 'It's a kind of tattooing.'

'But it's burned in. Didn't it hurt terribly? And why a scorpion? And in such a place?'

'One of my lovers put it there. He wanted a scorpion and he wanted it there, so that's why. And it didn't hurt when it was put on. He used an anaesthetic salve.'

'I didn't know there was such a thing. But then it seems like everything here is new to me, doesn't it?' Clara gave Alice a shamefaced smile. Then her face went serious again. 'But didn't your husband object?'

'Never mind about my husband and the scorpion,' said Alice. 'I don't like to talk about other lovers when I'm with you. Look! Your lipstick is still on my thighs. I told you I wouldn't remove it.' She took Clara's hand and guided it to the grotto where the now faded and smeared lip rouge obscured the smooth whiteness of her thighs.

'Have your thighs ever had lipstick on them?' she asked.

'No. I've never ... been with a woman before,' said Clara.

'So. I'm the first, am I?'

Clara nodded.

'Well, then, it's up to me to teach you the joys of lesbian love. If you don't enjoy this evening, it'll be all my fault.'

During the conversation, Alice had been rubbing Clara's nipples with the flat of her hand. Now the two bullet-like protuberances stood out sharply, and the older woman leaned over and delicately took one between her teeth and gnawed it lightly. Then she began tonguing it, moving in ever-increasing concentric circles which soon covered a good sized area of Clara's breast.

'Oh!' said Clara. 'That feels nice!' She sounded surprised.

Alice lifted her head and smiled at the girl. 'I'll show you something else that's nice,' she said, and taking her own breasts in her hands, she rubbed the nipples against Clara's until they, too, grew hard, and began to tingle. Then she drew Clara to her and held her tightly. Their two bellies rubbed together, the strands of hair between their legs intertwined.

Alice gently forced Clara's thighs apart with one of her own, and began moving that thigh up and down against the mouth of Clara's treasure trove. 'Relax,' she whispered. 'Just let yourself go. Stop thinking. Let your mind merge with your senses. Feel, Clara, feel! Feel how nice it is, how warm. Very, very warm. She spoke in a low monotone, almost as though she were trying to hypnotise the girl. And indeed, the words did seem to produce a hypnotic effect, for Clara's body relaxed, and the lines of tension on her normally smooth young face had vanished.

Alice continued to move her thigh up and down, up and down, feeling with satisfaction the warm moisture spreading out of the little girl's oven and onto her own flesh. 'Take my breasts in your hands,' she whispered. 'Excite me as I excite you.'

Clara complied, awkwardly crushing the woman's swelling globes in her moist palms. As she did so, Alice began to rub her own slit against one of Clara's legs. She was already quite excited, and she could feel Clara stiffen as the hot moisture spread over her thigh. But then the girl relaxed again and continued to toy with Alice's breasts.

'Put your hands on my buttocks now,' said Alice. 'But slowly. Work your way down. Explore me. Learn my body. Learn the things which excite me.'

Clara looked puzzled, and Alice smiled. 'Never mind, I'll explain all that later. Right now, I just want you to feel pleasure.'

Clara obediently but awkwardly ran her hands down Alice's body. Her awkwardness kindled a flame in the older woman, who began squirming and more insistently rubbing herself against the girl's leg. Clara then reached for the woman's buttocks and began patting them with one hand as, with one finger of the other, at Alice's instruction, she explored the valley between the two ripely swelling mounds. Suddenly Alice gasped as Clara's finger slipped between the lips of her love nest.

'Oh, that's good!' she moaned. 'Keep it there! Don't take it away!' She pushed the girl onto her back and pressed her own delta firmly between Clara's legs. She began to push her hips back and forth so that the two plants which flowered between their legs rubbed petals. Alice began to bite and suck at Clara's nipples as she rocked back and forth, and was rewarded with another gasp from the young girl. 'Oh Don't stop, Alice! Please don't stop!

'I won't darling, I won't.'

And she didn't stop until she felt the spasm welling and breaking through the girl's body, until the girl herself went limp whispered: 'I don't feel a thing any more.'

Alice would have smiled had she not been so excited. Instead, she rolled off Clara and onto her back, spreading her legs wide. 'Do it to me, now, Clara. Do to me what I just did to you. I'll show you how.' She pulled Clara between her legs. 'Make love to me, child. Love me with your sex, the way I loved you with mine. The way Johnny loved you tonight.'

'Oh!' Clara gasped. 'But he didn't . . . that is . . . I . . . oh please, he didn't make love to me and I don't want to think about it any more.'

'Tell me about it,' Alice commanded. 'Tell me about it while you make love to me, while you excite me and set me on fire. Tell me, Clara, what happened tonight?'

'I told you, I won't talk about it. You didn't want to talk about your lovers while you're with me. And I don't want to talk about mine.' Then, all traces of reluctance suddenly leaving her voice, she said quickly: 'But if you really want to know, tell me about the man who put the scorpion on your stomach and I'll tell you all about what I did with Johnny.'

'Touché,' laughed Alice, pressing herself ever closer against Clara and gently guiding the motions of the girl's body with motions of her own. 'But I pass for now. Let's make love, and we'll talk later.'

After a great deal of awkward experimentation on Clara's part, Alice reached a climax. Then she lay quietly at Clara's side, smoking a cigarette and idly stroking the girl's thighs and lower stomach. Suddenly she said: 'Clara. You told me Johnny didn't make love to you. That means he made you suck him, didn't he?'

'Oh, no. I'd never do that! Mary Lou sucked him while I licked.'

Alice suppressed a laugh. 'I see,' she said, as she stubbed out her cigarette. 'Would you like to lick me, Clara? While I lick you? Shall we lie here and lick each other?' She kissed Clara's hip and then the fleshy part of her inner thigh, brushing against the swelling Mount of Venus with her cheek.

'No!' cried Clara. 'Oh no! I just couldn't. You won't make me do it, will you?'

'Why, of course not, darling. I won't make you do anything you don't want to.' Inaudibly she added: 'Not tonight, anyway.' She continued in a normal voice. 'But you won't mind if I do it to you, will you?' Without waiting for an answer, she kissed Clara squarely between the legs. Then she extended her tongue and began exploring Clara's delightful rose bush.

'You've done this to a lot of girls, haven't you?'

'We're not going to talk about our sexual experiences any more this evening,' came the reply, the sound of Alice's voice muffled between Clara's thighs. She went back to her task with renewed ardour.

'It's you who should be ashamed now,' said Clara suddenly.

The woman again, stopped tonguing. 'Perhaps I am,'

she said. 'But if I am, it's part of the thrill I get. I told you before, shame is like wine; it goes with a good meal, heightens the taste of it and makes you high.'

'And that's why the mark on your belly is there. It's a mark of shame, isn't it? Did you want it there so that every man who made love to you would know about all the terrible things you'd done?'

Alice laughed. 'Really, Clara. You have the most vivid imagination I've ever encountered. And I hate to disappoint you, but I haven't done all that many "terrible" things.' While she was speaking, Alice's fingers had replaced her tongue, busily exciting and inflaming the swelling petals of Clara's sweet bush. Now Alice bent once more again to tongue the flowerlets, as Clara's body tensed and began to move in response to the probing fingers.

'Rub inside,' Clara said, and the woman slipped her tongue deep into the warm, moist cavern. To Alice's surprise, Clara now slipped her finger inside Alice's well and began to move it vigorously up and down. Alice began to suck again, harder than ever.

'Oh, stop!' Clara cried. 'Stop!'

But Alice did not stop. She continued rubbing back and forth against Clara's finger, and sucking and licking the girl's love parts.

'Oh, I'm going to explode!' cried Clara as, suddenly, the woman's finger intruded between her buttocks and plunged violently in and out. She twisted and writhed around.

Now Alice moved so that her Mount of Venus was about an inch from Clara's face. The girl, thrashing wildly, turned towards the dripping wet grotto. She reached out her tongue, licked the tiny petals and began to suck them violently, as her hips gyrated ever faster.

Alice threw her head back and smacked her lips, then bent forward again and nipped the soft flesh of Clara's little pink lips.

Clara screamed. A violent spasm shook her. She opened her mouth, and Alice pressed against it harder than before.

Clara stuck her tongue into the gaping cavern of Alice's sex and reached a second climax.

CHAPTER ELEVEN

The following day, Clara stood at the train station waiting for the 10:06 express. Suddenly a car horn honked, and a female voice called. 'Clara, Clara Morrow.'

The girl turned and walked in the direction of the horn and the voice. The car was Mrs Mason's, and Blanca herself was at the wheel. 'You're not leaving us so soon, are you?' she asked, a note of regret in her voice. 'And without saying goodbye?'

'Oh, no,' replied Clara. 'I'd never do that. It would be bad manners. No, I'm merely going into town for the day. I would have told you, but I didn't want to bother you. With so many guests coming and going, you can hardly be interested in the whereabouts of one rather colourless young girl.'

'Colourless? Oh, my dear, you underestimate yourself. Why I've heard your name mentioned at least a dozen times this weekend. You've made yourself very popular, you know ... Oh, do forgive me. There you are standing outside while I'm sitting here comfortably. If you're going into the city, why don't you come with me? I'd be glad to have some company for the ride. I do so hate to drive alone.'

'Thank you ever so much,' said Clara, settling down on the seat next to Mrs Mason. 'I have an appointment with a friend that I simply must keep. And I dislike riding on trains — they're so noisy and dirty!'

'A man friend?' asked Blanca. 'A very particular one?'

'Yes, a man. And I hope very particular.'

Blanca laughed loudly. 'Now I see where your popularity comes from. You're quite clever, aren't you? Well, my pet, whatever kind of friend he is, if you would like to, please feel free to invite him to come back with you – or to join you in a day or so, if he can't get away from work just now.'

'You're very kind,' said Clara, 'but I've already imposed so much . . .'

'Nonsense. We love having new people, that's what makes our parties so successful; new combinations of people. And the more the merrier, so do invite him – for me.'

Clara got out of the car a few blocks from Garnett's office, thanked Blanca for the umpteenth time and hurried off. When she arrived in the office, red-cheeked and breathless, the ubiquitous Jackson materialised and immediately escorted her into the inner sanctum.

'Where have *you* been?' snapped Garnett as soon as the secretary had closed the door behind himself. 'I've been worried as hell about you.'

'Have you really?'

'Yeah, I have. Why didn't you phone?'

'Because I was afraid of being overheard. There are extensions all over the house. Anyone could have listened in while we were talking – accidentally or on purpose.'

'Oh?' Garnett's saturnine brows lifted questioningly.

'Yes!' said Clara. 'I know definitely of one person who is very interested in finding out why I'm at the house – which, incidentally, is a very peculiar place. Why, do you know that – '

'Wait a minute,' said the attorney. 'One thing at a time. Just who is it that's so interested in discovering your reason for being at the party? And why is that person interested?'

'It's John Webster – Blanca's "brother-in-law" – and he wants to know why I'm there so that he can blackmail me. To tell the truth, he is blackmailing me. He says he doesn't know why I'm there, but if I don't cooperate with him, he'll make up a reason.

Once again the eyebrows went up. 'And just how much does his silence cost you?'

Clara blushed violently and lowered her eyes.

'That much, eh?' Garnett grinned. 'Well, we'll leave that to later. Now tell me what you found out.'

'Well, as I said before, it's a very peculiar place. It's full of weird people, all of whom are there for two purposes: to drink as much free liquor as they can and to have as much free sex as they can. And it sure is free!'

Garnett studied Clara's face thoughtfully. 'My my,' he said sarcastically, 'listen to the little cynic.'

'Well, it's true,' insisted Clara. 'Those are the only reasons people go there. You'll see.'

'What do you mean, I'll see?'

'Oh. I almost forgot. Blanca – Mrs Mason, that is – invited you to come back with us this afternoon. She drove me in just now.'

'She invited me? You told her my name?'

'No, of course not, silly.' Garnett winced inwardly at this endearing appellation. 'I said I had an appointment with a friend, and she said to bring him back with me – if my friend was a him and if I wanted to.'

'Do you want to?'

'Oh yes! I'm not a very good detective. I haven't found a trace of my poor sister. But I did find a cat o'nine tails just like the one I found in her drawer. And I discovered a scorpion in an extraordinary place! On a woman's stomach! Branded in!'

The attorney looked sharply at Clara. 'Are you sure of that? It couldn't have been a birthmark or a scar?'

'No, it couldn't have been a birthmark or a scar. I examined it very closely.'

Garnett snorted. 'You did, did you? And the lady just lay still while you examined her belly – with a magnifying glass in your hand, perhaps?'

'Sometimes,' said Clara, 'you can be positively beastly. If you don't want to help me – if you think I'm wasting your time with my silly problems – then just tell me. You're certainly not obliged to do this, you know.'

'Yes,' said Garnett quietly, 'I know. And when I want out, I'll let you know. Right now, though, I want you to go home and look through your sister's drawer again. Perhaps now that you've been to the house you'll recognise or understand something that held no significance for you before you went there.' He smiled. 'But, before you go, have you told me everything that happened yesterday?'

'I don't know what you'll think of me,' Clara blurted, 'but I just couldn't help what happened. Honestly I couldn't. That John Webster made me do the most awful things! I'm so ashamed today, I wish I could just shrivel up somewhere and die.'

'Nonsense,' said Garnett heartily. 'A young, beautiful girl like you shouldn't talk about wanting to die. Now tell me exactly what happened. Confession is good for the soul, you know.'

There followed Clara's highly dramatised version of the incidents of the previous day. When she finished speaking, Garnett said: 'We'll go into it more deeply at your place when I come to pick you up to meet Mrs Mason. And before I get there, look over that diary again. The whole key to your sister's disappearance may be in it.'

CHAPTER TWELVE

'Do you want to inspect the drawer out here?' asked Clara as Garnett stood in her living room, looking strangely awkward among the china figurines, lace doilies and tatted rugs.

'No, don't bother to bring anything out here. I can conduct my examination just as well in the bedroom.'

Clara led him into the room. She unlocked the drawer and pulled it open. Garnett took the cat-o'-nine-tails from it. He weighed it in his hand and dangled the light leather straps. 'You say you found one just like this at the house?'

'Well, not exactly, but almost. The one at the house looked heavier, but I could be mistaken.'

He examined the torture-implement carefully. 'It's very cleverly made,' he observed after a moment. 'A soft enough leather so that it won't cut the skin, but heavy enough to sting. If the other one cut, it must have been quite a bit heavier. I wonder just how intimate Rita was with this one.' He took the diary from the drawer, and, sitting down on the bed, proceeded to leaf through its pages. At last he said: 'This seems to be what I'm looking for – can you make it out?'

Clara took the diary. He pointed to the passage he wanted her to read. She sat on the bed beside him, drawing one leg under her, and began:

' "... F. was very angry when I told him. Or at least he pretended to be. He said I deserved to be severely punished for getting drunk and spending all night at C's. Next time, he said, I would be more apt to remember when I had an appointment with him.

' "He told me to take off all my clothes, and, when I had stripped, he sent me to the closet where he keeps the whip and made me kiss it and then bring it to him. He took it from me and swished it through the air until all the tails whistled. I started to imagine it whistling like that over my naked bottom, and I began to feel excited. He told me to go into the other room. There, he switched my ankles lightly, just enough to make me dance and to yearn for the switching to begin in earnest.

' "In the room was a very large leather armchair, and F. pointed to it with the lash. 'Stand on that,' he said. I obeyed, and he made me bend over the back of it with my head dangling towards the floor and my legs spread wide to steady me. I couldn't see him, but I could hear him moving behind me, swishing the lash through the air. Not knowing when the first blow would fall added to my excitement, which was rapidly reaching fever pitch. He must have realised this, for he began teasing me by laying the whip on my buttocks and then drawing it away so that the thin leather slithered snakily over my thighs. I waited anxiously for him to strike, but the moments passed and nothing happened.

' "At last I heard the swish of the leather. I closed my eyes, biting my bottom lip so that I would not cry out and discourage him from striking fiercely, the way I needed to be struck. The lash hissed and struck – empty air.

' "I could bear it no longer. I raised my head and begged him to begin. I was ready to go down on my knees and plead for it when the lash fell. The leather stung my bare flesh sweetly. Again he struck, this time harder. My bottom smarted excitingly. It was marvellous. I wriggled as I waited for the next blow. He whipped slower than most of the others had. I loved it that way.

' "After a few lashes, my buttocks began to burn all over. There was not a spot which the whip hadn't touched, and it fell time after time on places already heated with two or more previous kisses of the lash. He beat me for several minutes, focusing his blows on my bottom alone; he did not so much as tickle any other part of my body.

' "Before he had finished, my buttocks were aflame. He seemed to sense that I had got as hot as whipping alone could make me, for he stopped and made me promise never to be late again. Then he helped me down from the chair and made me bend over one of the big arms of it. I felt him lay his hands on my backside, and felt his thing pressing between my legs.

' "In a moment he was in me. Later, he took me brutally from behind. It was glorious." '

'That's enough,' said Garnett. He glanced at Clara's pretty knees as he took the diary from her. With a flippant gesture he lifted her skirt with the stock of the lash and coolly appraised her thighs. 'I wonder if this one was the one he used,' he mused, flicking Clara's calves lightly with the leather strips.

'How can you?' wailed Clara. 'How can you be so callous? Didn't you listen to what I just read? Oh, my poor sister. She's been debauched and ruined by those horrible people. Imagine, wanting to be beaten. Poor, poor Ruthie.' Clara buried her face in her hands and sobbed loudly. 'And now,' she continued, 'they're trying to do the same thing to me. They want to debauch me, too.' The face went back into the hands, and the sobs recommenced.

Garnett leaned over and patted her leg, having put his hand quite far up under her dress to do so. 'Do you know,' he said, 'that when I look at you I just can't believe that you did all the things you told me about? It just doesn't seem possible.'

The sobs grew louder.

'Perhaps what you need is for me to use this thing on *your* bottom,' he muttered. 'Then you'd really have something to sob about.'

Suddenly he pulled her down on the bed with him. Holding her with one hand, he unzipped his fly and took out his love instrument with the other. Then he leaned over the girl pulling her dress up to her hips, and pressed his organ against her bare flesh.

'You need either to be whipped or to be made love to,' he said. 'Perhaps both.' He pulled down her panties and put his hand over her delta, his fingertips just touching the thin slit between her legs. Then he rubbed his maleness along her thighs.

'Why must you do this to me?' whispered Clara. 'You know that I couldn't help what I did with the others. You know that.'

He ignored her words, gently removing her clothes and sliding her off the bed and onto the scatter rug beside the bed. He told her to kneel between his legs, and, robot-like, she did so. She appeared to have lost the last vestige of her resistance.

'Do you swear to me that you haven't had a man inside you?' Garnett asked.

'I swear,' cried Clara.

'Then show me what Webster and the other man made you do.'

'Why?'

'Because I asked you to.' He dropped the pretence of coherent reasons somehow connected with finding Rita. 'Unless you show me just what you did I'll give you both the whipping and a loving.' He took her hands and pressed them around his organ. 'He made you hold him this way, you said. Then what did you do?'

Clara just sat for a moment, but finally began to lick him as she had licked Webster and Arnold.

'And while you were doing that, what was Mary Lou doing?'

'She was sucking Webster and my tongue at the same time. Filthy creature. She threatened to make me do it to her husband if I wouldn't go on licking him after Webster was finished with us.'

'How could she make you do it?' asked Garnett sceptically.

'She and her husband were both holding my head. Then

she took his — you know what — and put it against my mouth in front. Like this.'

'Are you sure,' Garnett asked, 'that it wasn't like this?' He moved quickly and suddenly slipped the head of his member into her mouth, at the same time placing his hand at the back of her neck to prevent her from pulling away.

His lip curled in slight sardonic triumph. Give him three more days, he mused, and she'd be begging for it. They always did.

He slid the organ a little further into Clara's mouth, then took it out. She crumpled into a small naked heap at his feet, the back of her hand flung across her mouth. He looked down at her scornfully.

'See how easy it would be for me to make you do that?' he asked, thrusting his words into her silence. 'But I don't want to just yet. You will when I want you to, though, and you'll swallow, too.'

She shook her head mutely.

'Oh, yes, you will,' he chuckled. 'You'd be amazed at what women can do.'

But he was tyred of talking and playing games. All this kid stuff had inflamed his shaft, which now stood out rigidly from his body. He prodded the girl with his hands, and she quietly obeyed his unspoken injunction to sit up.

'Lick me, Clara,' he said, and was given the double satisfaction of feeling her tongue on his sex and of knowing that he had practically broken her spirit.

She licked him thoroughly and wetly, slobbering over the organ juicily and coming very close to — but not quite — taking it into her mouth. He could not understand why she made such a point of not sucking it, when she seemed to have no qualms at all about licking it. After a few minutes he made her stop.

'Now hold it at the base of your neck,' he told her. 'No, keep moving the skin up and down with your hand!'

She pressed the tip into the hollow of her neck and held it there while he discharged. The liquid splattered over her throat and trickled down her shoulders. He sat up and wiped her with his handkerchief, saying: 'You do it quite well and enthusiastically for a girl who has done it only three or four times.'

He rubbed his softened member over her parted lips and laughed when she drew back as though she had been stung. 'It won't kill you,' he said as she wiped her tongue on the back of her hand. 'Now, put on your clothes. We have an appointment with your Mrs Mason.'

He was toying with the whip, and, as she bent over to pick up her panties, he touched her quickly on her vulnerable buttocks with the leather thongs. 'The Scorpion's sting,' he suggested quietly, watching the pink streaks turn white and disappear on the young girl's tender flesh. *All right, old man,* he chided himself, *that's quite enough. No cheap theatrics, please.*

CHAPTER THIRTEEN

Blanca Mason extended her hand and smiled warmly at Garnett as he and Clara stopped in front of her car. Her smile seemed to flicker into something more than mere cordiality, and Garnett's eyes appeared to take on a new glow of understanding.

'Mrs Mason, this is my friend, Mr Douglas,' said Clara.

'How do you do?' said Blanca, flashing the attorney another smile. 'I'm so glad you're coming with us, Mr – uh, Douglas, isn't it?'

Garnett nodded affirmatively.

'We're all just crazy about Clara,' Blanca continued. 'I'm delighted to have any friend of hers come and stay with us.'

Garnett acknowledged this pleasantry with a smile and an inclination of his head. 'Do you think we have time for a cocktail before we start?' he inquired.

'An excellent idea,' tinkled Blanca. They swept Clara between them towards a cocktail lounge that Garnett said was just around the corner. By the time they had seated themselves and ordered – a pink lady for 'Mademoiselle,' a gin fizz for 'Madame' and a Jack Daniels on-the-rocks for 'The Gentleman' – Mrs Mason had become Blanca and Mr Douglas had become Conrad and they were laughing and exchanging witticisms as though they had known each other for years.

'Haven't we met before, Conrad?' asked Blanca quietly during a lull in the conversation.

'You insult me when you ask if I could forget a lady as

lovely as you are,' Garnett smiled. Peering deeply into her eyes, he added, 'There used to be an actor who resembled me, a Britisher – Leslie Banks – and people always seem to imagine they'd met me if they've seen his pictures. Myself, I've been a recluse of late.'

'Fleeing women?'

'Pursuing the dollar.'

'How very dull.'

'Sickening.'

Blanca reached across the table and took his hand in hers, bending over it intently. 'I foresee a change,' she said, running her enamelled nail along one of the lines in his palllm.

'Wonderful gypsy!' he cried heartily. 'Shall I flee women?'

'I see many opportunities to flee.'

'Tell me more. More, and I shall shower you with gold.'

'I do not tell fortunes for gold.' The corners of Blanca's patrician mouth flickered into a smile. Then she gently relinquished Garnett's hand and lifted her cocktail glass to him and to Clara. 'To love,' she said gayly. She looked into his eyes for no more than an instant, but, in that time, they seemed to hold a lengthy conversation. Then he turned away, signalling to the waiter to bring the cheque.

They rose to leave, and Garnett lingered behind for a moment to count his change. As he slowly followed the two women, he amused himself by comparing their two sets of buttocks – now, of course, decently skirt-encased. It was, he observed, an interesting comparison.

CHAPTER FOURTEEN

'You know,' said Garnett, 'you were right. I think I've seen more liquor consumption and more sexing in the last half hour than I see in a year outside.'

He and Clara were seated in a relatively secluded corner of the terrace, from which could be seen a good portion of the front lawn and most of the terrace itself. As he spoke, he let his eyes wander over the ever-changing, constantly varying scene.

Little had changed since the time of Clara's arrival two days previously. The woman whose name was Legion was still consuming much whisky and little water from glasses with sprigs of mint on the rim. The poet, with his black sheaf of poems, was still on the lawn – although the tall, overly made up woman had vanished and in her place stood a small, mousy girl with rimless glasses and buck teeth; she was much too flat-chested to grasp by the breast, so the poet was contenting himself by clutching one of her hands to his own breast while declaiming: 'I would love to run barefoot through your hair.'

And, while some of those who had been part of the scene two days before had vanished, they had been replaced by others whose activities were strikingly similar to those of their predecessors. In a chair not too far from Clara and Garnett, where two co-ed athletes had once worked out, now sat another co-ed couple, a strikingly handsome one. He was blonde, with aquiline features and a lithe body clad in stylishly expensive sportswear. She was as lovely as he was handsome. She had close-cropped black hair, long silky eyelashes and a tip-tilted nose. She was also dressed expensively and well, and wore enough make-up to enhance her charming features but not so much as to be brassy. They shared the armchair comfortably, holding hands and talking avidly. Garnett watched them with a wry smile, until Clara said: 'They do seem out of place, don't they?'

'Out of place?'

'Yes. That couple you're looking at. Just sitting and holding hands. They're obviously in love with each other. I mean – they're so normal.'

Garnett started to laugh. He laughed until his face turned red and his eyes filled with tears.

Clara looked puzzled. 'What's so funny? Are you laughing because to be normal here is abnormal? Is that why?'

Garnett sputtered into laughter again, but this time managed to control himself. 'Poor little Clara,' he said. 'Look closely at your "normal" couple. See the one with the black hair?'

'Yes. Isn't she beautiful?'

Garnett guffawed. 'Beautiful, yes; a she, no.'

'What?'

'My pet, she is a he. Under those chic trousers, there beats a fourteen karat male.'

'I don't believe you! How do you know?'

'You develop an eye for these things after a while. But never mind. I'm more interested in meeting some of your new friends. Like this brother-in-law of Blanca's, for instance.'

'Webster,' said Clara. 'I don't know where he is. But he'll probably turn up sooner or later. As soon as he finds out that I'm back he'll no doubt come looking for me. Unless he's found some other poor innocent to torment.'

'And your Mrs Burton. Do we have to wait for her to find you, too?'

Clara laughed. 'No. She's around. I saw her for a few minutes while you were with Mrs Mason. Which reminds me, where did you go with her for a whole hour?'

'That sounds as though I'm the person who's being investigated.' He smiled. 'She took me for a walk around the grounds.'

'She didn't bother to take *me* for a guided tour. She didn't even tell my fortune.'

'Perhaps your sex appeal isn't as potent as mine where she's concerned. Or perhaps,' he added maliciously, 'she felt you were more Alice Burton's type.'

'That's not funny.'

'It wasn't meant to be.'

'Oh, Conrad, stop stalling and tell me what you found out.'

'I didn't learn anything new. Blanca Mason talks very well, but she's a careful woman. She said absolutely nothing of any significance that I could communicate to you – but then the significance might be more apparent if the association were more easily comprehended.'

'Oh, stop teasing me with all that legalistic double talk. She didn't tell you a thing of interest and you know it. You're just trying to pretend she said some things that only you, with your great mind, can comprehend, because you want to avoid telling me that you spent a whole hour doing nothing but flirting with her.'

Garnett laughed condescendingly. 'Please, Clara, give me time. After all, I've only been Hawkshaw Douglas, Secret Operative Six-and-Seven-Eighths, for five hours and – ' he consulted his watch ' – thirty-five seconds.'

'But we must do something!' said Clara impatiently. Every hour Rita is gone . . .'

'Is one more hour that she's enjoying herself, I imagine.'

'You're heartless. My poor sister has been debauched, corrupted, perverted and . . .'

'You're being redundant, my dear.'

' . . . lord only knows what else, and you sit here saying she's probably enjoying herself. No one enjoys those things. She was probably forced to write that diary, that's what I think.'

Garnett's amused, slightly ironic expression showed what

he thought of her idea, but he remained silent as she babbled on.

'... So we've got to find her, and soon. Before something even more terrible happens to her.'

'In that case,' Garnett smiled, 'shall we take up our sleuthing again? Wander around and listen to a few more conversations?'

'All right, but I'll need my cardigan. It's starting to get chilly. I'll just run upstairs and get it. I won't be a minute.'

'I'll go with you. Perhaps the vanished Mr Webster is hiding under your bed, sniffing your chamber pots.'

Clara glared at him. 'There are no chamber pots here,' she said as she rose and led the way back into the house.

'I like your view better than mine,' Garnett said, gazing out the window overlooking the lawn. 'The sun shines through the girls' dresses better on this side of the house than it does on my side.'

'But the sun went down over an hour ago,' objected Clara.

Garnett laughed. 'You're not missing any tricks today. But I think Blanca gives the girls the rooms with the best views because the men spend most of their time in the girls' rooms anyway.'

Clara slipped the cardigan over her shoulders. 'Hmmph! The girls here aren't the kind that wait for men to come to them! Well, come on, I'm ready to go back downstairs now.' She turned to leave, as Garnett stood watching her with an expression of surprised admiration on his face.

'No,' he said, more to himself than to the girl, 'you're not missing any tricks today.'

He followed Clara out of the room and down the hall, past a man in travelling clothes and carrying a small Gladstone, who had just come out of a room on their left. 'Checking out,' Garnett murmured. 'Grand Hotel – but don't bother to leave your keys at the desk. Here, let's see if I'm right about the rooming system. We'll look in his room, and five will get you ten that it looks out on the kitchen yard.'

He touched Clara's arms and they walked down the hall towards the room. He had just put his hand on the door knob when suddenly he paused and stiffened. 'That – was peculiar,' he said. 'Did you see it?'

'No. What?'

'A girl came out of the corner room looking as though she'd just kept an appointment with God. Then the door was shut behind her very quickly.'

'Don't be blasphemous,' chided Clara. 'It was probably just a . . .'

'Hell's bells, girl! I see something I think might be important, and all you can say is "Don't be blasphemous"? For all you know, your sister could be locked in that room! And – look!'

A woman in her thirties now approached the door from the opposite direction. She was partially obscured by a turn in the hallway. She knocked, and, after a slight delay, she was admitted.

'That was rather odd,' said Clara. 'But . . . do do you really think Rita's in there?'

'I didn't say I thought Rita was in there. I don't think she is. I said that she could be there. We can't ignore even the most improbable or seemingly unimportant leads.'

Clara smiled apologetically. 'You're right, Conrad. I'm sorry I mistrusted you. It's just that sometimes you don't seem to take this investigation very seriously, so I didn't realise how concerned you are.'

He patted her shoulder. 'That's all right, kid. I know you're under a lot of tension.' He paused. 'But, I really am curious about that room. Why don't we sit on this chest here for a while and wait and see what happens?'

Time passed slowly. Garnett was growing bored looking at the tapestries and banners on the slightly yellowing walls and listening to Clara's ceaseless chatter. Then, suddenly, she said: 'Listen! Do you hear something? A sort of scuffling?'

He cocked his head towards the door. 'I think so – and a woman's voice. Can you hear anything she's saying?'

At this point, footsteps began tap-tapping down the hallway, growing louder as they progressed. Garnett grabbed Clara, and they embraced passionately. Burying his lips in her neck, he whispered: 'Don't look up. Let her think we're just lovers.'

The footsteps passed without slowing down and continued down the hall. They then stopped, and someone rapped on a door. Garnett released Clara and looked up just as a titian-haired girl disappeared into the room which he and Clara were keeping under observation.

'You still think there's nothing weird about it?' asked Garnett.

'No. I agree with you. Something extraordinary is going on. There's that noise again. Hear it?'

'Yeah, I hear it. You know, whoever's in there is running the place like a speakeasy – but rather indiscriminately, wouldn't you say?'

'Maybe – maybe they're drug addicts!' exclaimed Clara. 'And that's where they go to take their drugs!'

'Perhaps,' grimaced Garnett. 'But, just offhand, I'd say that in this place it's probably considered quite *au fait* to smoke your opium in the drawing room. Besides, that would hardly explain the scuffling.'

'I bet I could find out what it is!' Clara exclaimed suddenly.

'Yes? How?'

'Come on. You'll see.' She tugged at his hand until he rose with a shrug of his shoulders and followed her back down the hall to her own room. She opened the door, pushed him down in the most comfortable chair, handed him a copy of the *New Yorker* and said: 'Don't go away. Lady Sherlock shall return.' Then she bounded towards the door.

'It might be dangerous,' warned Garnett as she reached the threshold.

'Don't worry,' she flashed him a smile. 'Us detectives can take care of ourselves.'

Then she was gone. Garnett glanced at his watch, then settled down comfortably to read the *New Yorker* and wait.

CHAPTER FIFTEEN

It was half an hour later by Garnett's watch when the doorknob turned and the door opened very, very slowly.

He looked up. 'Good lord!' he exclaimed. 'What happened to you?'

Clara leaned against the door. Her make-up was smeared, her clothing rumpled and her hair dishevelled. Her eyes were red from crying, and the tears were still wet on her cheeks. 'They whipped me,' she said hoarsely. 'They whipped me.'

She staggered across the room. Garnett met her halfway and carried her to the bed. As he laid her down, she rolled over on her stomach, burying her face in the pillows and sobbing unrestrainedly.

Garnett very cautiously lifted her dress over the back of her thighs. The flesh was pinkly striped, but not raw. He raised her dress higher and then gently pulled down her panties, sliding one hand under her waist to raise her from the bed as he did so. Her buttocks, like her thighs, were not raw, but they were bright red. 'Who did this to you?' he demanded.

'The people in that room. Three men and a girl.'

He moved her head off the pillow and onto his lap. He stroked her hair and said: 'You know, your buttocks look very pretty like that. All pink and red. But they probably don't feel very nice. Have you got any cream or salve? That might take the sting down a little.'

'There's sun tan lotion on the little table right next to your hand.'

He found the bottle and scrutinised the label for several seconds. 'This should do it. Now just lie still and I'll put some on. It'll have to be rubbed in well, but I'll try not to hurt you.' He moved his fingers lightly over the smooth flesh, working the oil into it with just the tips, not pressing at all. He rubbed the lotion into the horizontal lines where her buttocks joined her legs, and also, extraneously between her thighs. 'Tell me how it happened,' he said.

She was silent for a moment. Then she said in a small, colourless voice: 'I just knocked on the door. It seemed like such a wonderfully simple solution. It was simple, all right, and so am I! When I knocked at the door, it was opened at once and a man took my arm. There was only a dim light, and I couldn't see anything for a moment. Then, when my eyes adjusted to the light, I saw three men and a naked woman lying on the bed.'

'Tell me more,' prodded Garnett eagerly.

'At first I thought I had been right about the drugs, because she was lying limp, with one arm and her head dangling over the edge of the bed. But then she raised her head and one of the men went to the bed. For the first time I noticed that her ankles were strapped to the bed posts. Then there was a knock on the door, and the man who had taken me by the arm let go and went to let in the girl who had knocked.'

'Did you recognise her?'

'I think I've seen her around. It was pretty dark in there, but she looked like someone Alice Burton was talking to the other night. The girl came over to me and said: 'May I watch you before my turn comes?' I was terribly confused. I didn't know what to say. But I was afraid to let them know I had no idea of what was going on, so I said yes. Then the girl said: "I'd like to help, if it won't spoil it for you. It always makes it better for me if another girl helps." '

'What did she mean by "help"?'

'I didn't have the vaguest idea. But it seemed rude to say no to someone who offers to help you – or so I thought then – so I thanked her and said of course she could help.

In the meantime, the other woman was being unstrapped and helped off the bed by two of the men. "That was beautiful," she said. "I'm sure to have a fabulous evening, feeling the way I do now." '

'What happened then?'

'I began to wonder if perhaps these people gave seances, which would account for the darkness. Or perhaps they were physical therapists, which would account for the woman's nudity and her comment. Then the girl said: "I always try to imagine how other people will act. You like to pretend that you hate it, don't you? Girls as young and feminine as you usually do." She didn't seem to notice that I didn't answer, or maybe she took my silence for assent. Anyway, she rattled right on. The woman who had just got off the bed now spoke up. "I think I'll stay and watch too," she said.

'Suddenly one of the men said: "Well, let's get on with it. Take off your clothes."

' "Oh, no," I said. "I couldn't."

'The man standing beside me laughed and said: "If that's the way you like it, we'll take them off for you!"

'He picked me up and carried me to the bed. I was kicking and screaming. I tried to tell him that it was all a mistake, that I had knocked on the wrong door, but he just laughed harder. Then the other two men came over, and I realised that I didn't have a chance, so I let them strip me.'

Garnett glanced at her buttocks and saw that all the oil had been soaked up and that the skin was again dry – even slightly parched He poured more oil onto her succulent spheres and began to rub it in.

She resumed: 'Two of the men held my arms while the third went to get something – a whip, it turned out. When I saw it, I began to cry and plead with them to let me go. I promised that I wouldn't say anything to anyone. But that only made them laugh, and the woman who had just been on the bed said: "You know, that's the most convincing performance I've ever seen." '

'How gauche.'

'Yes. Anyway, one of the men began to beat me. It was just horrible! All those people were watching me, and I didn't have any clothes on. The men had made me turn over with my face down and had strapped my ankles to the bed posts just like they'd done with the other woman. It was awful.'

'I can imagine.'

'At first I felt more shame than pain, but then the lashes got harder and harder. I began to squirm around, and, the more I moved, the more my tormentor beat me. Oh, God, it was awful!'

Clara appeared lost in her narrative and didn't seem to notice that Garnett had spread her legs quite far apart in his efforts to thoroughly grease every inch of the injured area. Now completely open to his vision – and to his fingers, which crept ever nearer – were all of Clara's feminine goodies, enticingly displayed between her lovely, marble-white thighs. Carefully, Garnett rubbed and rubbed, working his way into the crease of her thighs. If he noticed that the oil had dried on his fingertips long ago, he did not let on.

Clara continued: 'The girl stood beside the bed the whole time watching. Then, after what seemed like hours, the man stopped and she raised her hand. I saw that she too had a switch. It was smaller than the one the man used, more like the one in Ruth's drawer. She began to switch me on the backs of my thighs and between them. She beat me much more quickly than the man had and more viciously. I begged her to stop, but she just laughed and said that she'd known that I'd pretend to hate it. I told her over and over that I wasn't pretending, but she kept on switching and finally said, rather nastily: "All right, kid, don't overdo it." She was whipping me between my legs and I was sure I was bleeding, because I was all wet down there. I could feel the liquid all on my thighs.'

'Very interesting,' Garnett observed.

'The other woman was also watching. She seemed to be

getting very excited, and she kept saying over and over: "Don't tease the poor girl, satisfy her." Finally the girl stopped. She had taken off her skirt when she first came in, and now she ripped off her blouse and threw herself down on her stomach across the foot of the bed. "Do it to me while I watch her," she told one of the men, handing him her switch.

'He began to switch her buttocks while another man began to beat me with a bundle of three or four switches all tied together. The man who was switching the girl began hitting her very hard. I could hear the lashes whistling in the air. I don't know too much about what was happening to her because by now I was not thinking very clearly. Mostly I was just feeling the pain. But I do know that she suddenly rolled over next to me and put her arms around me. She pressed her stomach against me and pushed her thighs between mine. "Whip us," she cried. "Whip us both."

'Someone produced a whip, and one of the men began. I wouldn't have believed that anything could hurt more than the lash had, but this seemed to hurt a hundred times more. I screamed and screamed – as though, if I didn't, I would lose all contact with the little reality I had left.

' "Harder," cried the girl. "Oh, much harder!" She wiggled and squirmed, but she never once screamed. I could feel the liquid running out from between her legs and over mine. Finally she whispered in my ear: "Haven't you had enough?"

'I could hardly stop screaming to answer her, and my voice wouldn't seem to form the words at first, but I finally managed to say "yes." She sat up and said to the man: "I think our little friend here has had enough to keep her bottom warm tonight.' I could hardly believe it, but he stopped immediately and began unfastening my ankles.

'I was so weak I could hardly put my clothes on, but somehow I managed. While I was dressing, they strapped the girl down. She told them to strap her ankles, too, because she wanted them to beat her hard and she didn't know if she'd be able to stand it. Then, just as I was leaving, she said to me: "Don't you want to stay and watch? You can lie down in front of me and I'll suck you while I'm getting whipped – if you want me to."

'I said no, I had to meet someone, which made them laugh, and I finished dressing as quickly as I could and came right back here.'

While Clara had been finishing her account of her adventure, Garnett's fingers had not been idle, and, by this time, one of them had worked its way between her buttocks and was moving gently in and out of the rosette opening. Now, for the first time, the girl seemed to notice what was being done to her.

'Stop it!' she cried. 'What are you trying to do?'

Garnett poured a drop of lotion on the opening, which he had been so assiduously rubbing. He said: 'You said that the girl switched you here, didn't you?'

'You know very well that she couldn't have switched me there,' replied Clara, in an acid tone. 'Between my legs, I said.'

'Oh, here,' he said, gently caressing the petals of her rosebush.

'Yes, there. But it doesn't hurt any more. Not at all.'

'Oh, but it will if it isn't properly taken care of. Stop wiggling and let me rub some more of this oil on it.'

'I don't want you to. I don't care if it hurts a little. She didn't really switch me there very hard. Hardly at all, honestly. Now stop. I don't want you to massage me there!'

Garnett pushed her shoulders down firmly as she tried to sit up. 'But I'm going to anyway,' he told her. 'And, furthermore, I'm going to use what ought to be used for rubbing you there.'

He bent forward, undid his trousers and slid out his shaft. It came between her legs in one quick movement. 'Now don't try to struggle,' he said, 'because if you do, you might excite me so much that I won't be able to control myself and my member will slip all the way inside of you.'

She said nothing, and he proceeded to tickle several sensitive places between her legs with the end of his big pointer.

After awhile, he moved slightly forward. The oil-smeared tip of his hard organ touched the slit between her buttocks and rubbed at the orifice. He ran the tool back and forth over the opening for some minutes before moving it back to her Mount of Venus. Finally, he positioned himself so that he could rub her tiny petals with the base of his shaft while he nuzzled at her rear with its tip. He smiled down at her as he fancied he felt some movement in response to his efforts.

'Poor little girl,' he said with all the sympathetic commiseration of a hungry crocodile about to swallow a small fish. 'It must hurt terribly when I do this.'

'No, it doesn't hurt – much.'

'Does it make you feel better?'

'Oh, no! This never – uh, well, yes, it does, frankly. The oil, you know – '

'Of course. The oil. Certainly. Shall I rub harder?'

'No. It feels fine just like that.'

'Hold your legs tighter together.'

She did, and he rubbed more persistently until a spasm shook her body and she cried out, gripping his shoulders and bucking her whole body up and down. Then the spasm passed and she fell back, limp.

CHAPTER SIXTEEN

Garnett watched as Clara came out the small bathroom adjacent to her room and gingerly let herself down into a pink plush armchair. 'Is it painful?' he asked, smiling sardonically.

'No. It just feels awfully feverish, really. It makes me quite restless.'

'All that's wrong with you is a literal case of "hot pants." You know, Clara, I'm afraid you're simply incurably unfortunate. Wherever you turn, you seem to find yourself in the middle of an indelicate situation.'

'Don't make fun of me. You know very well that at least half the "indelicate situations" I get into are of your making. And, whatever I've done, I've done because I thought it would help you in your investigation.'

'I know,' said the devil's advocate soothingly. 'I was just teasing you. As a matter of fact, I don't think your efforts to help me have been in vain. Everything we learn about these people and this place will ultimately form a composite picture, which we can then study and analyse in terms of the causal factors of your sister's disappearance. And from this analysis we should be able to ascertain her current whereabouts.'

'That sounds like a lot more legalistic double-talk to me. And how can I help but be pessimistic when I see the horrible things that go on here? All those women going into a room to be whipped – wanting to be beaten, just like Ruth said she wanted to be.' She sat up with a start. 'Oh! Were you trying to suggest that because Ruth does seem to enjoy whipping, no matter how ghastly it seems to me, that we might find her in that horrible little room?'

'Well, it'd be a good idea for one of us to spot check the corridor every once in a while, just to see who goes in and out. There's no point in posting a perpetual guard, because that would ultimately draw attention to ourselves – and besides, it would waste time we can better use exploring the rest of this ever-fascinating entertainment palace.' He paused, then went on: 'But you know, Clara, you must be more tolerant of the things you see here. Who are you to say what's right or wrong, pleasant or horrible? If these people enjoy being whipped, and it doesn't disfigure them in any way, or mar their health, why should you think of them as perverts? Why, you yourself admitted that the whipping made you feel quite "restless." What you meant was sexually excited, didn't you? Well, that's why these people go to be lashed. To stir up their sexual appetites.'

'I don't want to hear such talk,' cried Clara. 'What I did just now, you made me do. You're just talking to hear yourself talk. You seem to forget that we're here to find my sister, not to see what dirty things you can make me do or like doing.'

'I haven't forgotten. You're the one who's delayed our investigation. What with getting yourself whipped, and then distracting, or should I say seducing, the investigator . . .'

'Oh . . . I never . . . how can you . . .?' Clara's apparent outrage at this suggestion left her seemingly unable to complete a coherent sentence.

Garnett, taking advantage of her sputtering, went on: 'I suggest we begin immediately to "case the joint," as I understand the saying goes, and waste no further time in this useless bickering.'

'And I suggest,' said Clara, who seemed to have recovered her powers of speech, 'that we ought to meet as many people as we can. We won't get anywhere staying in corners by ourselves.'

'Excellent,' said Garnett. 'And I'd especially like to meet your lesbian friend with the brand on her belly.'

They left the room and started down the stairs.

'Shall we begin with wine or something stronger?' he asked.

When she looked at him with apparent bewilderment, he explained: 'It's my theory that the people you meet at parties are determined by what you drink. So, shall we begin with wine or something else?'

'But if we start with such a mild drink, we're bound to meet mild people. And it seems to me that the people who were instrumental in Ruth's disappearance are more forceful than wine drinkers – more the scotch or bourbon type.'

'Theoretically, yes, but wine is a mocker. Red wine is especially deceitful.' By now they were standing near a large sideboard, and he poured them two glasses of Burgundy from one of the decanters among the vast assortment arrayed there. Then he took Clara by the elbow and propelled her through the crowd, keeping up a running commentary as they walked. 'Here, for instance,' he said, indicating the object of his attention with a nod of his head, 'is an excellent example of what I mean. The sizzling brunette in the red velvet gown. She looks pretty forceful to me. And she's sipping a good, red wine. And here – '

'Is something even better,' interjected Clara. 'The lady with the tattoo on her stomach.'

Alice Burton smiled and stood up as they crossed the room to join her. 'I'm so glad to see you, my dear,' she told Clara. 'I've missed you this evening.'

'Oh,' said Clara. 'I've just been showing my friend around the grounds. Mrs Burton, this is Mr Douglas.'

Alice smiled at Garnett and extended her hand. 'I'm very pleased to meet you. Your name is familiar to me, you know. I'm sure I know Douglasses somewhere. . . . Oh, yes, the aeroplane people. That wouldn't be you, would it?'

Garnett smiled and said no, that wouldn't be him. He

did not say what line he was in, and she did not press him. Instead, she asked: 'How do you like it here, Mr Douglas?'

'Very much, so far. Of course, we've just arrived, you know, but the grounds are lovely. At the moment, Miss Ree – Miss Morrow and I were speculating on the possibility of some formal entertainment.'

Mrs Burton did not appear to notice Garnett's slip of the tongue. 'What did you have in mind? A poetry recital? A pantomime? A record concert?'

'Something on the order of a Roman circus. Our minds have been stimulated for too long; right now we're looking for something to tickle the libido.'

'I believe they're throwing some male poets to the lesbians,' quipped Alice. 'But are you serious?'

'Completely.'

'Then we go this way,' she said, linking one arm through Garnett's, the other through Clara's.

As they walked towards the north wing of the house, Mrs Burton said to Garnett, *sotto voce*: 'I hope I'm doing the right thing. This is no puppet show, you know.'

'We've seen the puppets at Coney Island,' Garnett replied. 'Very silly and squeaky, with people batting each other about for no apparent reason... Dash it all...' He stopped. 'We must have some more wine. You wait here, I'll get some. Clara, give me your glass. Mrs Burton, we're drinking Burgundy. What's your brand of poison?'

'Burgundy will be fine,' smiled Alice. Then, as Garnett hastened off, she said to Clara: 'Your friend is charming. I suppose he's your lover.' She sat down on a nearby settee and drew Clara to her. 'Quick,' she whispered loudly, 'raise your dress!'

'Not here,' cried Clara. 'You can't.'

'I must!' She lifted Clara's skirts to her thighs. 'Just for one moment. It'll taste so nice with the wine.'

'He'll be right back,' warned Clara.

'He will be if you keep arguing about it.' She drew Clara's skirt all the way up and laid her hand against the bare stomach. 'No panties,' she said. 'You *are* progressing!

Or is this in honour of your friend? If that's the way it is, then you must let me know, for he'll have you all night and I'll have to be content with only the memory of a stolen moment. Don't begrudge me such a small pleasure, Clara.' As she spoke, she pushed the younger girl's legs apart and kissed the soft moss that grew between them. The tip of her tongue curled around and down into the slit. Clara shuddered. 'Rub against my tongue,' Alice whispered. 'I won't get off my knees until you do, not if everyone in the house comes by.'

Clara spread her knees, sunk her hips into a semi-squat and rubbed herself back and forth against the woman's mouth. Soon, Alice's lips and Clara's little flower-patch were both as wet and slippery as a peeled plum. 'Please let me stop,' begged Clara, continuing to rub. 'He'll be back any second . . . listen, someone's coming now!'

Alice ducked her head and brought her nose up through the petals of Clara's rosebud in a gesture of farewell.

When Garnett entered the room moments later, the older woman was primly seated on the settee while Clara languidly reclined on a nearby sofa. But the roseate hue of Clara's cheeks and the heavy feminine odour which hung in the air were enough to enlighten Garnett as to how the two women had occupied themselves in his absence. He pinched Clara's fingertips as he handed her a glass and smiled knowingly at her before extending the other glass to Mrs Burton.

Alice smiled her thanks as she accepted the Burgundy. 'This way,' she said as she rose. She led Clara and Garnett through a door in a shadowy corner of the alcove in which they had been waiting and up a tiny, twisting flight of stairs. At the top of the stairs they turned sharply through another door and down a narrow, unlighted hall which led to another tiny flight of stairs. At the top of these stairs, Alice opened a door and shepherded the attorney and the younger girl into a small private theatre.

At one time there had been two rooms here, one above the other, but the flooring between them had been broken through and had been replaced by a narrow balcony with a low railing. The balcony ran around the entire room and was furnished with chairs, couches, hassocks and countless, multi-coloured cushions, all of which were drawn close to the railing for the convenience of the spectators. At each corner of the balcony was a stairway leading down to the stage, and the hanging pillars that supported the balcony divided it into facsimiles of theatre boxes.

The balcony was submerged in darkness. One could see only by the soft glow of the lights underneath it which focused on the oval dais in the centre of the stage. Blue and diffused, this illumination was sufficient to light everything onstage with detailed clarity but soft enough to create an atmosphere of compelling intimacy, an atmosphere which was reinforced by the delicate romantic strains of a Chopin 'Impromptu' flowing through the theatre from hidden amplifiers.

The dais was covered with a huge, diamond-shaped, white angora rug. On the rug were over-sized satin cushions, some blue, some green, some black and some white, and a heavily smoking incense burner set into a dull brass stand.

The entrance of Alice, Clara and Garnett evoked no interest among the persons who were already in the theatre. Smoking and conversing in intimate tones, no person among the score or so of spectators so much as glanced up at the two women and the man who now stood near the entrance, adjusting their eyes to the dim light.

'We can still leave,' murmured Alice, glancing towards Clara and then looking intently at Garnett. But, if Garnett heard her, he gave no sign of having done so, for he said: 'Let's be seated, shall we?' He then sat on a small couch in an unoccupied loge, and motioned to Clara and Mrs Burton to take places on either side of him. They did so as he observed: 'Our hosts provide handsomely for their guest's entertainment, I must say.'

'The guests provide for one another,' Mrs Burton corrected. 'The hosts merely supply the opportunity.'

The throaty tone of an unseen gong, melting into the liquid quaver of a vibraharp, now cast a hush over the audience, putting an end to all conversation. Suddenly a girl materialised out of the darkness. She ran lightly to the centre of the stage and up onto the dais, flinging herself down on the cushions. Her red hair glowed like flame in the semi-darkness, providing a vivid contrast to the stark whiteness of her naked body. There was a pause, while the audience absorbed the picture before them. Then two men in their early twenties entered the stage. They approached the dais from opposite sides.

'The artistic touch,' whispered Alice Burton. 'Colour combinations: a blonde, a brunette and a redhead.'

The two men mounted the dais at the same moment, and the audience was now able to perceive that one was blonde, deeply tanned and muscular, while the other was black-haired, sallow and angular. Together they approached the cushions over which the girl sprawled.

Clara bowed her head and covered her eyes as the men sank down on the pillows surrounding the girl. Garnett leaned towards Clara and stroked the hair on the back of her neck, murmuring into her ear: 'Don't look away!' She pulled her head away from his grasp, but he persisted. 'I want you to look,' he hissed, taking her hand and holding it tightly in his.

The two men were sharing the girl, caressing her thighs and her belly, exploring between her legs with their fingers. Her clenched fists dug into the cushions around her, and she arched her body, rubbing her thighs against the men. Then she turned and rubbed her breasts – the nipples grown sharply erect – against the shoulder of the muscular blonde, at the same time rotating her buttocks against the crotch of the brunette.

Next, she bent over the blonde, swaying her shoulders and brushing her nipples against his chest. Then, jutting her breast forward, she rubbed them against his chest and belly, at the same time slipping her hands under the waistband of his trousers. He turned her over on her stomach, and she lay between his legs, probing inside his pants with frantic fingers as he began rubbing his hand between her thighs. She began to slide one hand up his trouser leg as Clara whispered: 'Please, let's go now.'

'No. Drink your wine.' Garnett pulled her hand across his lap and pressed it against the bulge in his trousers. He held it there, curling her fingers around his shaft as the girl on the dais opened the fly of the blonde man.

Now the girl pulled the trousers down over the man's smoothly tanned hips and along his strong, muscular legs. She ran her fingers through the blonde curls over his already erect organ, bending over him and taking the organ itself wholly into her mouth. While she did so, the other man stripped off his bathing trunks and lay down at her side, stroking her breasts and her belly. She removed the shaft from her mouth and turned towards the dark-haired man, arching her body as she did so. She licked his member for a short while, then rolled over on her back and began to rub the testicles and organs of both men simultaneously.

Almost immediately, the blonde mounted her. Supporting himself with one hand, he held his shaft with the other and pressed it between her legs, rubbing it back and forth for a moment before pushing it upward into her gaping love nest. He drew it back and then pushed it forward again, and the girl exclaimed loudly: 'Harder.'

The thrust that followed seemed to knock the breath out of her, but a moment later she murmured the word again. She fell silent as he began pumping rhythmically in and out of her, then once again cried: 'Harder!' She drew up her legs, bicycling them up and down in the air, lifting them higher and higher until at last they were practically straight up and down.

She now worked her hips violently against her partner's slow but unremitting strokes. After a moment, she turned her head and stretched out her hand towards the sallow man. He approached her, and she took his organ in her hand and moved it towards her mouth.

Clara, her hand trembling, gulped down the last of her

wine. Garnett quickly refilled her glass with some wine from his own. Then he removed her hand from his lap and put his own hand on her thigh, underneath her dress. He stroked the smooth flesh for a moment, then allowed his fingers to stray between her legs, gently probing and tickling the soft, fleshy lips of her nether-mouth.

Clara slid forward in her seat, allowing his hand more freedom to roam, as the girl on the dais rubbed the organ of the darker man against her lips. Suddenly, she took the whole rigid shaft into her mouth. The blonde man shuddered convulsively, then lay motionless atop her. She clawed the thighs of the sallow man, and the blonde rolled off her, to be replaced almost instantaneously by the other.

'Here,' whispered Garnett, 'give me your hand.' When Clara did not respond, he reached for her hand and placed it on his member, which protruded boldly from his trousers. He put his hand over hers and showed her how to move the skin of his shaft up and down. Then he put his hand back between her legs. He slid one finger into her now-warm oven and rubbed his thumb around the oven door.

The men on the dais were taking turns with the redhead, the sallow one making love to her while the other one allowed her to gratify him orally.

'Are you enjoying yourself?' whispered Garnett.

'No!' hissed Clara. 'This is horrible! Filthy! I don't see how she can let herself do such things. And with all these people watching!'

'Friends and enemies,' said Alice Burton's voice out of the darkness. 'Which do you think would be more trying?'

Clara did not reply, and the voice continued casually: 'And there's her husband. On the other side of the balcony.'

'She must be a monster,' whispered Clara, 'to do this with her husband watching.'

'Oh, he doesn't mind,' laughed Alice. 'He knows she married him for his money and not his sexual prowess. It gives him great pleasure to watch her sex workouts. You see, he loves her, and he wants to see her satisfied in every respect. And she has come to love him, because of his understanding and tolerance.'

The subject of their discussion was now laying on her stomach between the two men, each of her legs thrown over one of each man's legs. She took the blonde's sex in her hand, placed the other's member in her mouth and wriggled her toes as though she were in ecstasy.

Garnett gently removed Clara's hand from his shaft, which she had been pumping vigorously up and down. 'Oh . . .' she whispered. 'I didn't realise . . . that is, I didn't notice . . .'

' . . . that you were about to bring my organ to a state of erection which it would be impossible to sustain for any lengthy period of time – say, no more than fifty seconds?' Garnett's words seemed to add to her confusion, and she wrung her hands together in her lap, whispering over and over: 'I'm so ashamed . . . so ashamed.'

She squirmed and wriggled away from his fingers, but they would not release their hold. 'My bottom is starting to burn again,' she informed him suddenly. 'From the switching, you know. Strange, how restless it makes me feel. Or maybe it's the wine that's making me so restless. And you, too. With your finger wiggling up and down. That makes me restless. Do stop, Conrad. Or I'll make you stop. If I press my legs together hard enough, your hand won't be able to move and then you'll have to stop!'

She seemed very pleased with herself for having figured this out, but she did not suit the deed to the word. Perhaps she thought she did. Perhaps the unaccustomed amount of wine she had consumed so confused her that she thought she was pressing her legs together when, in reality, she allowed them to relax and spread even farther apart. Perhaps.

'It's cold in here,' she said suddenly. She began chafing her wrists, imitating the up and down motion Garnett had taught her to use to stimulate his love instrument.

On the dais, the darker man removed his organ from the girl's mouth and stood up. She turned to him on her knees and he thrust the shaft back into her mouth. She threw her arms around his legs and began sucking his member passionately and in such a way that it was apparent that she meant to bring him to a climax. Clara leaned forward in her seat.

Suddenly, the girl on the dais jerked the man's knees to her breasts with all her strength. He thrust forward with a savagery which almost sent her toppling backwards, with him on top of her. He staggered, and Clara pressed clenched knuckles against her lips.

The man recovered his balance. He then moved away from the redhead, who began to crawl on her knees towards the blonde. She approached him and tried to take his member in her mouth, but he made her lick it instead.

'More wine?' asked Garnett. He handed Clara his glass, and she downed the contents with one gulp. 'Slowly, slowly, or you'll get dizzy,' cautioned the attorney, raising her dress over her hips.

'Oh! Stop!' whispered Clara. 'I feel as though everyone is watching me – as though it's me on my knees down there . . .' Her voice faded as the redhead arched her torso and stretched, cupping one of her breasts in her hand and lustfully smearing the roseate nipple with the dark and fevered tip of the love instrument she had been licking.

Clara stiffened. Slowly she raised her hand to her own breasts and touched the nipples through the silk of her dress. 'Perhaps I should have worn a brassiere,' she said aloud, swaying her own hips in what seemed to be an unconscious imitation of the motions the girl on the dais was now making as she bent her head towards the blonde's manhood.

He drew sharply away from her. The theatre was totally silent – the music had stopped when the gong sounded – and the girl's heavy breathing could be heard in every corner of the balcony.

The man began to move away. The girl held onto his

member and crept after him on her knees, following him as he stepped backward across the furry rug. She stretched her neck forward, trying desperately to reach the object of her desire with her lips. 'Please...' she whispered loudly. 'Please...'

'Oh!' gasped Clara, 'I'm so ashamed... so ashamed... for her... to lower herself like that...'

The redhead bent forward again, and Clara's lips silently formed the word as the girl repeated: 'Please.'

The tanned, sleekly muscular body stopped its backward progress, and the blonde Adonis allowed the supplicant to touch his organ with her lips. Soon she had thrust the length of the coveted shaft into her mouth and was sucking it even more passionately than she had sucked that of the sallow man. She tossed her head from side to side as she moved the love instrument in and almost out of her mouth. Her hair fell over her face, but she didn't even stop to fling it back, only brushing away the strands that strayed between her lips.

Clara ran her hand through her own hair and pressed forward against Garnett's hand. Her thighs tensed, her belly shuddered, her breath came quickly and her fingers clenched tightly. Garnett moved his hand faster and faster, harder and harder.

The redhead drew back, then savagely plunged forward again. The blonde grasped her shoulders, digging his fingers into her flesh. He threw back his head, his face ecstatically convulsed, as his splendid body bucked uncontrollably. The redhead sucked and swallowed.

Clara gasped: 'Oh... I'm... I'm... going to... I'm... *Ahhhhhhh*! Her own body jerked spasmodically for several seconds before relaxing into limpness, and she murmured: 'Oh... what gorgeous fireworks!' Her eyes were tightly closed, and her lips smiled dreamily. 'So bright and green. And such interesting shapes... Oh! They're fading now. What a pity.' She slumped back against the couch cushions and opened her eyes.

A match flared suddenly in the darkness, revealing Alice

Burton with her face buried in Garnett's lap while his hand worked vigorously under her skirt, which was pushed high above her thighs. The brief illumination flickered out just as the attorney threw back his head, his face contorted. Tiny sucking sounds pierced the newly-fallen darkness.

Clara sprang out of her seat. She yanked down her skirt and adjusted the waistline. Almost immediately, Garnett was standing also, calmly buttoning his fly and taking Clara's arm.

'Shall we leave now?' he asked. He turned to Alice, who was lying back in her seat limply, licking her lips and working her hand violently up and down under her dress. 'Later,' she said.

Garnett took Clara's arm and escorted her out of the theatre. As they reached the bottom of the little staircase, Clara suddenly exclaimed. 'Oh, darn! I've left my purse upstairs.' She turned and Garnett prepared to follow her.

'You needn't bother,' she said. 'I can see very well in the dark. I'll find it myself.'

Garnett chuckled. 'In other words, you didn't need that lighted match to tell you what was happening.'

'I have nothing to say to you,' retorted Clara.

'You understand, of course, that I was merely trying to find the mark on her stomach.'

'Of course,' echoed Clara. 'And she was merely trying to bite the same mark into yours.'

'What she did was her own idea. I didn't ask her to, but I didn't see any reason to stop her either. You hadn't made a better offer.'

'Oh!' gasped Clara. She turned on her heel and ran quickly back up the stairs.

Three minutes later she reappeared. Her face was white and she looked as though she had just had a terrible shock.

'Is something wrong?' asked Garnett as she pelted down the stairs towards him. Clara nodded dumbly. He took her by the shoulders and shook her lightly. 'Pull yourself together,' he said, 'and tell me.'

Clara raised her head. 'On the stage,' she whispered breathlessly. 'Rita . . . my sister!'

CHAPTER SEVENTEEN

Clara crumpled against Garnett's chest. She swayed against him, and he clasped her tightly in his arms to keep her from falling. 'Pull yourself together,' he repeated. 'Now that you know she's alive and safe, there's no reason to fall apart.'

These words seemed to produce a steadying effect on Clara, for she lifted her head and pulled it slightly away from the attorney. 'I guess you're right,' she said, 'it's just the shock...'

'Yes, I know,' said Garnett quickly. 'But if you want to see Rita again, you'd better get hold of yourself. I'm not going to carry you up those stairs, you know.'

She nodded assent and took his arm. 'All right,' she said. 'I'm ready.'

When they were back inside the theatre, Garnett steered Clara towards their former seats. Alice had vanished, and they now had the couch to themselves. Garnett peered over the railing of the balcony into blackness. The blue light had dimmed and nothing could be seen on the stage but the red, unwinking eye of the incense burner. Then a greenish light suffused the dais, and two girls were revealed, lying languorously among the pillows with their heads nestled between each other's legs. Clara leaned forward.

'Which one is Rita?' whispered Garnett.

'Neither.' Clara sounded bemused. 'I... I... never saw either one of them before in my life. But she was there – honestly she was. I tell you I saw her...'

'I think we'd better leave and go someplace where we can talk privately.'

'But what about Rita? Maybe she's behind stage. Or maybe we could find someone who knows her – and knows where she is now.'

'Okay.' Garnett stood up. 'I'll go and ask around. Does she look like you?'

'Oh, yes. She's a little taller, and she wears her hair in a very sophisticated upsweep, but we do look a lot alike. In fact, people sometimes ask if we're twins.'

'Then I shouldn't have any trouble recognising her. Or describing her, either. You sit here and don't move until I come back, no matter what happens. Even if you should see Rita again. I don't want to have to investigate your disappearance too.'

'All right. I won't move, I promise.'

Garnett turned and disappeared into the blackness. Clara sighed, leaned back against the sofa cushions and closed her eyes.

She was still reclining, eyes closed, when Garnett returned some five minutes later. 'Come on,' he hissed, 'let's get out of here.' He took her roughly by the arm and propelled her down the narrow stairway. Clara tried to ask what had happened, but he silenced her. 'Wait till we get back to your room,' he said. 'Then we'll talk.'

When they arrived, Garnett shoved the girl gently down into the pink plush armchair. Then he stood in front of her, his arms folded across his chest. 'Well?' he said, his annoyance obvious.

'Well, what?' queried the girl innocently.

'Look here, Clara,' he asked, 'exactly how much do you feel the wine you had? Are you drunk?'

She looked startled. 'I suppose I'm pretty high,' she admitted. 'On the edge, you know? But I'm sober enough to go anywhere we've got to go – or to take any bad news you have to give me.'

'There's no bad news, and we're not going anywhere.

Just tell me: are you certain you saw your sister on the stage?'

Clara sprang from the chair, eyes wide, mouth agape. Garnett pushed her back down. 'Now take it easy,' he said. 'You say you saw Rita, and I'm sure you believe you did. You *saw* Rita, but she wasn't there. She certainly wasn't there when I looked.'

'But the time lapse . . . It was several minutes before we went back upstairs. She had plenty of time to leave.'

'Yes. And it was several minutes between the time we left the theatre and the time you went back for your purse. Several minutes, Clara. Maybe five in all. Do you really think Rita would have remained on the dais for only five minutes? And alone. She was alone, wasn't she?'

'Oh, yes. There was no one else. I would have told you if there had been.'

'So. She performed a five minute solo. Do you honestly imagine that that audience wants to watch a woman playing with herself, even for five minutes? Why, if they want that, they can go to a burlesque show. Practically the same thing . . . No Clara, it just won't wash.'

'You're being ridiculous! I wasn't having an hallucination, if that's what you're implying.'

'How can you be sure? An hallucination has all the appearance of reality. That's what makes it an hallucination. You were in a state of mental excitement. You'd been drinking an abnormal amount of wine on an empty stomach. Rita's on your mind constantly. What could be more natural than for you to imagine that you saw her?'

'And I suppose this conversation is an hallucination too, perhaps this whole party is an hallucination.'

'Now you're being irrational. Please try to calm down. You know, I haven't told you yet what happened when I went down to the stage.'

'No. You didn't. What did happen?'

'Nothing. Nothing at all. There was no sign of your sister, or anyone who looked like you or who answered to the name of Rita Reeves. And I couldn't find a single soul who could tell me exactly what did happen in the interval between the end of the act which we watched and the beginning of the lesbians' performance. Everyone I spoke to had either just gone out for a smoke, or hadn't been paying attention, or had just arrived, or something! No one saw anything, no one knew anything, no one had ever heard of your sister. I even tried checking with the man who works the lights. I was sure he'd be able to tell me who had been on the dais during the interim . . .'

'What did he say?'

'Not a thing! There is no man who works the lights. They're automatically rigged to go on and off at timed intervals.'

'Oh.' Clara seemed deflated. 'But you didn't prove that I didn't see her . . . that she wasn't there . . . And I was so sure . . .'

'Yes, Clara, I know you were sure. We won't argue about it, any more. Let's suppose for a moment that you did see Rita. What could you do about it?'

'You should know about that better than I do. You're the lawyer! We should go to the district attorney and have him arrest Mrs Mason for kidnapping, and have the police search for this mysterious husband of hers. I wouldn't be in the least surprised to find out that he's the "Scorpion." '

'In the first place,' said Garnett, 'if I went to the police now and asked them to arrest Mrs Mason, I'd be the laughing stock of the bar association. Even the greenest law student knows you can't accuse a party of any crime without having evidence to back up your accusation. Sure, you can prove, with the bookplates, that your sister had some association, either with the Scorpion or with some unknown third party who had an association with the Scorpion. But that's all you can prove. You don't even have the ring any more. You have absolutely no way of knowing for certain that Rita is here. And, in the second place, even if you swear up and down that you saw Rita on the dais, you'll have a pretty tough time convincing the D.A. that she wasn't in there of her own free will. Which brings us to another point. You don't suppose that if she was on the stage she was there against her will, do you? She could have screamed and tried to get away. And remember, she was alone there – so you said. I just don't understand your sudden hysteria, Clara. If you did see Rita, you know she's safe. If you didn't see her, then you have no reason to be any more concerned about her than you have been all along. I think that rather than talking nonsense about arresting Mrs Mason you should be much more interested in continuing to track down Rita.'

'Well,' said Clara, 'perhaps you're right. Perhaps I'm just overwrought. What do you think we should do now?'

'I think I should do a little more investigating. And the best place to start would be with your Mrs Burton. After all, she did remain in the theatre after we left. Perhaps she can tell us who, if anyone, was on the dais during that interval. Was she there when you went back?'

'Why, yes, she was!' answered Clara. 'How convenient for you!'

Garnett grinned. 'Don't be catty, little girl. It doesn't become you.' He pulled her to her feet. 'Come on, it's time for you to get some sleep. You've had quite a day.'

'That may be, but I have no intention of going to sleep. While you're having your little *tete-a-tete* with Alice Burton, I'm going to find my sister.'

'Do I have to put you to bed by force?' asked Garnett wearily.

'You don't have to put me to bed at all. And it's time you understood that I don't like this overbearing attitude of yours!'

'Disgusting, isn't it?' He chuckled. 'Nevertheless, you are going to bed.'

He picked her up and carried her to the bed. The instant he put her down, she rolled over to the edge and would have gone off the side if he had not caught her around the waist and dragged her back. Silently he pulled her dress over her head, imprisoning her arms. Then he slipped her shoes off and removed her stockings. Bare-legged, Clara writhed inside the confinement of her dress and spat out unintelligible insults.

'If you aren't quiet,' said Garnett, 'I am going to give your beswitched little bottom a spanking.' He turned her over and tapped her bare buttocks oh-so-lightly with his hand. Then he unfastened her garter belt. 'You don't want me to do that, do you?' he asked, gently stroking her thigh.

'What are you doing?' asked Clara's voice, muffled by the folds of the dress.

'Looking at you,' Garnett replied. 'What else would I be doing?' He let his hand fall on her hip and slither between her legs.

'Don't!' said Clara. 'Let me sit up! I don't like you to look at me when I can't see you. Let me up!'

'Not yet. I like you this way.' Garnett took a tuft of pubic hair in his fingers and gently tugged it. 'Very soft and nice,' he said.

'I can't breathe,' Clara objected. 'I'm smothering.'

'I'll let you up,' promised Garnett. 'But not just yet.' He moved his hand forward, spreading her legs farther apart. His eyes widened appreciatively. 'If you were any riper, you'd burst and spill all over my fingers, wouldn't you?'

There was a muffled protest from inside the dress, indicating, Garnett assumed, that the young lady did not agree with his estimate of her condition. Unruffled by this lack of encouragement, he asked: 'Can you guess what I'm looking at now?'

Clara jerked her legs together and squeezed the fleshy parts of her thighs against each other.

'You're clairvoyant,' Garnett told her, 'but I can still see it. In fact . . .'

'What did you do?' exclaimed Clara suddenly. She rolled away from him and thrashed about wildly inside her improvised prison.

Garnett pulled the dress over her soft white shoulders.

'What did you do?' she repeated.

'I kissed it,' he said coolly. 'Here, lie back and let me do it again from the front. It's easier that way.'

'I think I'll sleep now,' she replied hurriedly, slipping away from him.

'You change your mind so quickly!' Garnett clutched her around the waist and hips with one arm. 'I'm beginning to believe that you have absolutely no convictions.' He smiled. 'You don't really want to go to sleep, Clara. You want to lie here on the bed and let me play with you for a little while, and kiss you ... all over.' He arranged the pillows under her in such a manner that her shoulders were raised and she could look down at him as he bent his head towards her thighs.

'Why can't you leave me alone?' she whispered feebly. 'Just for a little while – until I get my bearings and – '

'Your mirror will tell you why I don't leave you alone,' he answered softly, brushing his lips across the hair which shielded her love-nest.

Immediately she placed her hands between her legs, guarding her treasure against further intrusion. 'Please don't do that again,' she begged.

Garnett propped himself up on one elbow and gently but firmly pulled one of her sweet dimpled knees away from its mate. 'Didn't you like it when Alice Burton did it?' he asked, reaching between her thighs and plucking at the hair which grew over the lips of her love-mouth. The little lips parted with a tiny, audible kiss. Garnett went on: 'I won't insist that you answer that question, but I do insist on the same privilege you allowed Alice.' He kissed her just above the knee and squeezed the flesh tenderly.

'Don't – please don't!' Clara murmured. She put her hand on his head to push him away, but the strength seemed to ebb from her fingers as his breath stirred the hair on her Mount of Venus. Her fingers curled in his hair as his lips slipped up over her thighs. 'No – no further,' she whispered.

With his ear pressed against her thigh, Garnett peered over her belly and the points of her heaving breasts. He took a bit of the flesh of her thigh between his teeth and nipped, evoking a surprised 'eep' from her. He spread her legs further and further apart, and carefully examined the glowing ruby treasure which now lay completely exposed to his sight and touch.

'Don't look at me down there,' the girl whispered. 'It makes me feel like an animal.'

'And what a lovely animal you are!' He kept his eyes fixed between her legs. 'And what a wonderful little treasure you carry with you!'

Clara slipped one hand between her legs to cover the object of his interest. 'Don't come any nearer,' she pleaded.

He brushed the hand away. 'Only near enough to kiss it,' he said. He stroked upward towards her crotch with his lips, dragging the inside of his lower lip over her now-warm thighs, leaving a wet and moist trail along the upper part of her leg.

Clara twisted and writhed as though the bed had suddenly turned into a briar patch. 'No nearer,' she begged, 'Oh – no! Conrad! The room is spinning! The bed is going around and around – like a – ' She tangled her fingers in his hair and clutched the strands tightly. 'Ohhhhh' she moaned. 'My bones feel so heavy!'

Garnett's lips now touched her dark crown of pubic hair. She shivered.

'I'm so ashamed – ' she whispered. 'So ashamed of myself for lying here without any clothes on and letting you do anything you want to me. For letting you look at me like this. I know what you want. I can feel it in your fingers. I can feel it in my own legs, in my thighs, even . . . down there, inside me . . . And now,' she continued, her voice barely audible, 'I'm ashamed because I can't control my body . . . because my body wants your mouth to press against me as much as my mind wants it to stop.'

Garnett kissed her welted slit, urging the lips open by turning his head from side to side. The tiny, fleshy lips pressed and swelled against the lips of his mouth. They were hotly wet and brightly flushed. He kissed them with a loud sound, then kissed them again, moving his mouth across the wet open area towards her buttocks.

Clara moaned. 'I can't move,' she whispered. 'I want to, but I can't move.'

He slid his arms under her hips and raised them so that he could kiss her solidly between the legs. He shut his eyes as he pressed his face into the thick tangle of her pubic hair and the soft mound of her flesh. He flicked his tongue across the throbbing lips of her sex. Clara shut her eyes and rolled her head from side to side on the pillow.

She began to press herself against him, spreading her thighs and drawing up her knees, allowing his tongue access to every part of her. 'How can you?' she murmured. 'How . . . can . . . you . . . do . . . that . . . oh . . . *do that*!' She rubbed vigorously against his chin, and he licked harder, curling his tongue, probing the extra-sensitive head with the very tip of his tongue.

Suddenly, he stabbed his tongue into her now-gaping love-well. She cried out, and pressed her hips forward, driving the welcome intruder further inside her. She appeared to be completely consumed with passion, and she stretched out blindly to touch his hard male body. Her hands encountered his trouser buttons, and she began fumbling with them wildly, seemingly desperate to open them and to unsheath the manhood which the cloth kept from her grasping fingers. At last she succeeded and was able to clutch triumphantly at his love instrument. Her hands slipped down to the sides of his crotch. She raked her fingers through the sweaty warmth of his pubic hair, then slipped them into the incredibly soft grooves of his thighs. She kept them there for a short while, just stroking the flesh and making small moaning noises in her throat. Then she moved them back up to cover his swollen organ.

In response to her touch, Garnett pulled his hips back and manoeuvred his organ out of his trousers as she began rubbing her hands up and down on it. He then made a muffled, glubbery sound – by which he meant that he wished her to unsheath the rest of his maleness. She plunged her hands back into his trousers and fished out the fleshy sacs. He ran his finger slowly along the crease between her buttocks and into her love cavern alongside his busily working tongue.

She hugged his body to her, pressing her breasts against the swollen organ she was holding. He inched his hips around towards her shoulders. Suddenly, her body went rigid. 'No,' she whispered. 'Oh . . . *no*!!!' Her hands froze around the shaft which she had been rubbing against her nipple. 'I'm doing the same thing that . . . that . . . redhead in the theatre . . . was doing. Oh! No more . . . please. . . .'

She pushed him away from her, but to no avail. He took his shaft in one hand and rubbed it across her face. 'Kiss it,' he said, pulling his mouth away from its task. 'Lick it if you want me to go on licking you.'

Clara grimaced as the hot bud seared her lips. 'But . . . I don't want . . . I told you I'm afraid to . . . Ohhh.' She moaned as his tongue curled back against that least-resistant part of her. She kissed the tip of the member and began to rub it with the flat of her tongue. She licked its length and breadth, taking it into her own hands and pushing his away. She licked it from top to bottom and back again, letting her tongue lap up the moisture that sprang from the tip. Her hips rocked back and forth under the gentle guidance of his hands.

It was not long before he took his organ out of her hands again. Her tongue lapped over his fingers in an effort to reclaim the newfound treasure she had so recently begun to lick. She probed between his fingers and under them and around them. 'No,' he chuckled, 'you can't have it. Not unless you're ready to suck it.' He pushed the spongy gland against her lips. She turned her head away sharply. 'Suck it, Clara,' he demanded. 'Suck it!'

She shook her head and whispered. 'Let's just go on as we were . . .' He did not reply.

She was silent for a moment. Then she said 'You know, I feel as though I'm watching myself, lying there on the bed . . . naked . . . squirming around in the arms of a man . . . doing unspeakable, unthinkable things. And she horrified me ... that girl on the bed ... she's lascivious and disgusting ...'

Garnett was not at all interested in the horrified and shocked Clara; only in the lascivious, squirming one to whose lips he now held his warm, ripely swelling engine. 'You must do it to me,' he whispered as he caressed her warm, succulent buttocks. 'Before you do it to someone else,' he added.

'I won't ever do it to someone else. Or to you, either.'

'I think you will.' He touched her mouth with the tip of the shaft. 'Lick it. Go on. You like to lick it, don't you?'

In response, her tongue slipped out and lightly brushed the tight-skinned organ. It was as though she didn't want to, but somehow couldn't help herself. She rubbed her tongue over it, and when it pressed into her lips, she did not stop. She kept licking it until it had pressed so deeply between her lips that she could no longer deny the fact that she had the tip inside her mouth.

But when Garnett slowly pushed the totality of the shaft into her mouth, she did protest. Pushing him away with all her strength, she said in a quavering voice: 'I can hear the voice of that girl – the redheaded one – pleading to those men to let her do what I'm doing to you. If I give in now, someday, maybe, I'll be on my knees, pleading ... like that ... please ... please.' Somehow, a note of supplication crept into her voice, and she bent her head to take the erect member back into her mouth. Garnett moved forward until it met her lips and slid easily between them.

She flung her arms around his back and hugged him close. He slid his tongue back into her slit and began lapping at her savagely, shaking his head wildly from side to side and licking fiercely. His hips pumped passionately as he drew his stout weapon in and out of her mouth, and she curled her tongue around the tip and licked each time he drew it outward. His movements grew faster and faster.

She tensed her body and rubbed wildly against his tongue. Her body began bucking uncontrollably as her mouth filled with hot liquid. His lips held her head on one side and the pillow held it on the other side. There was nothing she could do but swallow.

CHAPTER EIGHTEEN

For more than an hour after Garnett had left her room, Clara lay on the bed, tossing and turning. Finally, she rose and began to dress. Less than ten minutes later, she had completed a modest toilette and was making her way downstairs.

The usually crowded hallway at the foot of the staircase was almost deserted. Clara, in her high-heeled evening pumps, tip-tapped quickly through it into the large room with the sideboard where she and the devil's advocate had begun their 'investigation' earlier in the evening. There were not too many more people in here than there had been in the hallway.

She lingered in the doorway for a moment, and a tall, young man approached her carrying a glass of white wine. He offered it to her gravely. She accepted it with thanks, then fled while he was still deciding how to phrase his next offer.

She now slowly toured the ground floor of the house, wandering in and out of alcoves, libraries, nooks, conservatories, drawing rooms and a maze of hallways. Several of the rooms had bars or sideboards in them, and, by the end of a half an hour, she had quaffed *Liebfraumilch* from a bright blue goblet, sipped *Soave* from a cut crystal wine glass and gulped *Chablis* from a large brandy sniffer.

It was the brandy sniffer which she clutched as she made her way through the passageway which led to the discreetly hidden theatre. About halfway along the corridor she stopped and sipped from the sniffer, as a girl came careening down the hallway, practically knocking her over.

'I'm so sorry,' said the girl, who was tall and slender, with very prominent breasts and sensual lips. She helped Clara to steady herself, saying: 'It was all my fault. I wasn't watching where I was going.'

'No,' argued Clara, her words just slightly blurred, 'I shouldn't a been standing there ... in the middle like that.'

The girl laughed. 'Well, there's no point in bickering about who's fault it was. Let's just go on together, shall we?'

'Have some wine, first,' said Clara, graciously extending the sniffer.

'No thanks. Never touch the stuff.'

'Well, I will, if you don't mind.' Clara polished off the rest of the *Chablis*. She set the glass down on a small carved table. 'Verry nice wine,' she slurred, smiling at the girl, who now linked her arm through Clara's as naturally as if they had been old friends.

Clara's new companion said: 'I saw you several times today. I envied your escort.'

'Why ... why, thank you,' said Clara, apparently embarrassed by this forthright statement. 'I ... I've noticed you, too. Yesterday, I think it was. In a pink bathing suit.'

'Yes, that was me. Have you tried the pool yet?'

'No. I've been wanting to ever since I arrived, but it seems like every time I get near liquid, it's in a glass! I don't think I'll ever get to the pool.'

The girl laughed, tossing her pale blonde hair back from her shoulders. 'But you must! And you ought to play tennis, too. You can't live this sort of life without some kind of antidote. You have to eat a lot and sleep late and get a lot of exercise if you want to go on being sinful.' She smiled. 'I do a great deal of sinning, so I have to pay a lot of attention to the antidote.'

'You've never been on stage, have you?' the blonde asked casually as they slid together into a love seat.

'Oh, no!' exclaimed Clara. She seemed shocked that

anyone could even ask her such a question. The girl offered her a cigarette, and she accepted it. 'Have you?' she asked in return.

'Have I what?' asked the girl, lighting Clara's cigarette with the lighted tip of her own. 'Oh you mean have I ever been on stage? Yes. Once. I wanted to see what it was like to perform for a less intimate audience than I was accustomed to.'

'You mean that you'd had people watch you before?' Clara seemed incredulous.

'Oh,' said the girl lightly, 'you know how it is. The first time, you're in an alcoholic fog, and, when someone suggests it, it seems like a grand idea. Then, the second time, you just pretend to be drunk, and you watch everybody else out of the corner of your eye. After that, you don't bother to pretend anything – you don't need an excuse for liking to have people watch you. But I'd never done it in front of more than three or four other people until I gave my little performance here.' She smiled reminiscently, then asked: 'You've never had an audience?'

'Well,' replied Clara. 'Just once. But then I was forced into it. And I didn't find it a bit exciting. I thought it was just horrible. I don't see how you can enjoy it.' By now the blurriness had gone out of her voice and her sentences were more coherent than when she had first met the blonde. 'What was it like . . . down there?' she asked.

'Fun enough that I'll probably do it again. There was one other girl and four men. We took them two at a time, then three and finally four. It was fun, but it was hard, too. You have to be a contortionist to manage the positions.'

'But didn't you feel awfully ashamed?'

'Of course I did. That's part of the thrill. And, of course, it pays to advertise. When my act was over, two men came up to me and said that they'd watched my performance and had been very impressed by it. One of them was a sexologist, with a degree from some University in Vienna. He complimented me on my ensemble work and didn't believe me when I said that this had been my first time.

The two men asked me to join them for the evening and I accepted. Then they took me to a room and we just worked out all night along. They even rigged up a whirling basket with no bottom, which they hooked up to a pulley on the ceiling with three cords. They dumped me into it and took turns lying underneath and spun me around on their shafts while the basket went up and down as the cords twisted and untwisted. It was a scream.'

Clara appeared completely bewildered, but the other girl did not seem to notice. 'And just look' she went on, extending her hand, on which a diamond flashed and winked, 'I'm going to marry one of them next month.'

'Which one? The sex-what-did-you-call-him?'

'Sexologist. No. His beard tickled. And his shaft wasn't as big as the other one's.'

Clara shook her head. She still seemed bewildered. 'You mean that man is going to marry you after seeing you down there? Doing all those things . . .?'

'Why not?' asked the girl breezily. 'This is the twentieth century, you know. Men nowadays want a sample of your brand of sex before they marry you and promise to cherish you for the rest of their life. And references won't do. It has to be a sample.' She looked at Clara intently for a moment. 'Don't you think I'll make a good wife?'

'Why, why . . . I don't know . . .'

'Well, I think I will. I can cook and sew and make beds, and I can make love all night without tiring — or tiring of it. And I know enough little tricks to keep my husband happily at home for quite a while before he starts wanting some variety in his sex life. And I'm in wonderful shape to have babies. And I'm relatively well-informed about politics and litreature and things like that. And I'm easy to get along with. That's what makes a marriage stick — compatability, both sexual and intellectual. Not all this garbage you see in the movies about undying love. Believe me, if a wife can't keep her house clean and attractive, and feed her husband well, and satisfy him in bed, then no matter how undying she thought their love was, she's going to find her husband spending "late nights" in the office and taking frequent weekend trips "out of town." '

Clara sighed, seemingly dazzled.

'Now, don't misunderstand me,' the blonde went on. 'I don't mean that you have to be as much of a trollop as I am to be successfully married. But, contrary to popular belief, if you are, it won't hurt a thing – and sometimes it even helps.'

The blonde began to stroke Clara's arm and press her thigh. 'You know,' she whispered very softly, 'I like you. As naive and silly as you are. I like you. Maybe I even like you because you're so *jejeune*.'

Even in the stillness, Clara's reply was barely audible. 'I like you, too,' she breathed, making no motion to remove the blonde's hand, which by now had crept slowly over her breast.

Then the lights began to seep through the darkness and swell into an almost dazzling brilliance. Clara sat up suddenly, recoiling from the girl's hand as though it had bitten her. The girl seemed amused by Clara's reaction, but she made no reference to it. Instead, she stood up and said: 'I think I'll go and find out if my fiancée has got here yet.'

'So late?' asked Clara.

'He was supposed to drive out tonight after he finished work. But it's a good six-hour trip, so I didn't expect him to arrive before one this morning.' Then since Clara remained seated, she asked: 'Are you staying here?'

'No. I'm going too. I don't want to see any more.' She rose and the two girls walked out of the theatre arm-in-arm.

'Why don't you come to the pool tomorrow?' asked the blonde. 'It'll really do you a lot of good.'

'Yes, I know. I probably will,' Clara acquiesed.

'I'll tell you what. Why don't you come to my room about one o'clock. Then we can go down to the pool together.'

'Why I'd like that very much. Where is your room?'

'It's the second door to the left after the staircase, on the first floor.'

'That's easy enough to remember. I'm sure I can find it. But do tell me your name, just in case I can't.'

'I thought you wouldn't want to trade names.' The girl smiled. 'Mine is Bess Lynd. And I lied to you before. I already know who you are.' As she said this, a peculiarly knowing expression came over her face.

'You know who I am?' asked Clara. 'How? Oh! You mentioned knowing Alice Burton. Did she tell you about me?'

'That would be telling,' said the girl softly. She hastily flung her arms around Clara, lightly brushing the girl's cheek with her lips, then turned into a side passageway. She smiled back over her shoulder as she sprinted off, saying: 'Goodnight, Clara. I'll see you tomorrow. Sleep well.'

CHAPTER NINETEEN

Clara sat up in bed abruptly. The room was dark. The thick curtains were drawn, shutting out the outside world so that it was impossible to tell what time of day it was. Only the murky greyness, in which shapes without colour or design were barely discernible, indicated that it was no longer night.

At the foot of the bed sat Garnett, the glowing tip of his cigarette brightly visible in the darkness. 'Good morning,' he said with a note of sarcasm in his voice.

'Oh!' said Clara, starting violently. 'You scared me! How long have you been here, spying on me like that?'

'This long,' he said, indicating a fairly lengthy ash on his cigarette. 'Do you always sleep so soundly?'

'I sleep a lot more soundly when I don't wake up to find someone staring at me. Were you making faces at me while I was asleep?'

'My dear girl,' he said with deliberate pompousness, 'I am not in the habit of making faces at people — not even at bone-lazy young ladies whose sole aim in life seems to be to sleep through it.'

Clara glowered. 'First you tell me when to go to bed, and now you tell me when to get up. I suppose that next you'll be telling me to go brush my teeth. And not to forget to scrub behind my ears. And undoubtedly you've already decided what I'm going to eat for breakfast.'

'Undoubtedly,' echoed the Devil's Advocate, rising and stubbing out his cigarette in the ash tray on Clara's night table. 'Orange juice, a mushroom omelette, cinnamon toast and coffee. He crossed the room to the vanity table near the door and returned with a covered tray. 'Hardly breakfast,' he remarked, as with one hand he propped up the pillows under Clara's back and shoulders. Then he placed the tray across her knees and removed the white linen napkin wih a flourish. 'More like brunch,' he said. 'It's nearly one-thirty, you know.'

The expression of pleased surprise which had lighted Clara's face when she saw the tray and its contents now faded into one of dismay. 'One-thirty!' she echoed. 'Oh dear! And I was supposed to meet Bess Lynd half an hour ago!'

'Bess Lynd?' Garnett's eyebrows lifted questioningly.

'Yes. She's a girl I met last in the the – uh – hallway. She's very nice and friendly, and she invited me to go swimming with her this afternoon. I promised to be in her room at one o'clock. I don't know how I could've overslept. I usually wake up by noon, no matter what time I go to bed.'

Garnett smirked. 'Even if it's not until seven or eight in the morning?'

'You've been spying on me!'

'Not exactly.' Garnett poured some coffee into her cup. 'Milk and sugar?'

'Yes, please. Two lumps, spy.'

'Actually, Clara, I didn't spy. All I did was drop by about three a.m. to see that you were all right. And, when you weren't here at three, I checked again at four . . . and five . . . and six . . .'

'I don't know what time it was when I got back. Of course, if I'd known you were coming, I'd have made it a point to be here,' she said, her voice heavy with sarcasm. 'But I assumed you'd be too busy "investigating" Alice Burton to think about me.'

'My pet,' laughed Garnett, 'you underestimate me. I'm a man of many talents and abilities, and I'm perfectly capable of thinking about you while doing a number of other things.'

'If this is all such a big joke to you,' Clara pouted. 'Why don't you just forget it! All you seem to care about is making fun of me and displaying your cheap wit. You should have become a comedian instead of a lawyer!'

Garnett smiled unpleasantly. 'You seem to be very anxious to get me out of the legal profession. First you come to me and ask me to emulate Perry Mason – counsellor-cum-sleuth. Then, after I spend a great deal of my other clients' time sleuthing on your behalf, you announce that you don't think I'm suited to this kind of work – that in your eminently qualified opinion I'd be better off in another field altogether.' Malice was evident in his acid tone and in his icy gaze.

Clara's eyes widened, and her cheeks paled. 'Oh, Conrad,' she said, 'I didn't mean . . .'

'Look, Clara,' he interrupted her, the malice gone as quickly as it had appeared. Suddenly he was totally in earnest: 'Please believe me when I say that I take the Scorpion more seriously than I have ever taken anybody else in my life.'

'You really mean that, don't you?' she asked so softly that she appeared to be thinking out loud.

'Yes. I mean it. You see, Clara, when you grow up a little more, when you learn a little more about human nature, you'll learn that people very often make light of the things which matter the most to them. It's a defence mechanism, a way of protecting themselves against ridicule . . . and sometimes against danger.'

'Danger?' Clara's eyes widened once more. 'Are you trying to tell me something, Conrad? Did you learn something last night? Something that makes you think Rita's in danger?'

Garnett smiled and patted Clara's hand reassuringly. 'Yes and no,' he said. 'I did learn something last night. But nothing that led me to believe your sister's in danger. In fact . . . well, never mind that now. Suffice it to say that since the last time we talked, I've acquired quite a bit of knowledge of the internal workings of this little sex-mecca –

and of the powers-that-be here. And, if all goes according to plan, I'll reveal to you the identity of the Scorpion before midnight tomorrow.'

Clara gasped. 'Oh, Conrad! I feel like such a rat for not trusting you and for saying all those nasty things about your lack of interest in finding the Scorpion! But tell me all about it, I'm just dying to know!'

'All in good time, my child, all in good time. And speaking of time, it's now thirteen minutes before two. What were you planning to do about this Bess Lynd you were supposed to meet?'

'Oh dear, I'd forgotten about her. Well, I don't suppose she's still waiting for me. I guess I could find her at the pool, though I really ought to apologise. And I do want to take a dip.'

'An excellent suggestion. Why don't you hustle into your bathing suit while I take the tray back to the kitchen and change into my trunks. I'll meet you at the pool in twenty minutes.'

'That's fine. I'm sure Bess'll be delighted to meet you. She told me she'd seen you and me together. She thinks you're really sharp.'

'She does, eh? How very complimentary.'

'Yes, I think so . . . Would you hand me my robe, please? And look that other way.'

'Look the other way? Great scott, Clara, I've seen you completely nude. How can you possibly be embarrassed about letting me see you in a nightgown?'

'I'm not wearing a nightgown. And besides, our days of intimacy are over. I've decided that I'm not going to do any more sexing around. Now that you've found the Scorpion, I don't have to.'

Garnett studied her face gravely. 'I'm afraid you're wrong. You see, the Scorpion hasn't been found. We're going to have to set a trap for him – with you as bait. Now don't be afraid. You won't be in any danger. But you *will* have to do quite a little "sexing around," as you so quaintly put it.'

'Oh, Conrad. You didn't say anything about that before!'

'I know. And I'm sorry I brought it up now. I was planning on telling you when we came back from the pool, when we'd have plenty of time. I don't want to waste this lovely sunlight. Come on now, get up. I'll explain everything to you very soon.'

'All right, whatever you say. But please hand me my robe.'

'I think you'd better come and get it,' Garnett grinned. 'That way I'll know you're up and not planning on going back to sleep the minute I walk out.'

'I'll get up. Once I have my robe on... honestly, Conrad, I don't see how you managed to uncover the identity of the Scorpion. You're always so busy trying to uncover me.' On cue, she clutched the covers more tightly around her.

Garnett's grin broadened. 'Now who's trying to be a comedian? And stop hiding like that, you'll smother yourself.'

'Perhaps I prefer to smother than to have you ogling my body.'

'All right, you win.' He held the robe in front of him and advanced towards the bed. 'Here,' he said, 'take the robe. I'll keep my head turned.' But, as she reached for the robe, he dropped it and snatched the bedclothes away.

'Sometimes,' hissed Clara, covering herself with her hands, 'I hate you. You know, you can be so nice. But you don't want to be nice. Sometimes I think you just want to humiliate me. Sometimes I get the feeling that you make me do all those terrible, dirty things not because you enjoy them so much but because you enjoy seeing me do things that you know make me ashamed of myself. Am I right, Conrad? Do you want to humiliate me, to see me grovelling before you? Is that it?'

Garnett's face had lost its almost perpetual sardonic smile, and the mocking gleam was gone from his eyes. He looked at Clara almost tenderly. Then he said very gently: 'Let me teach you something, kid. Never ask a question if you won't be able to understand the answer.' With that, he lightly kissed the top of her head, gently tweaked one of her nipples and walked out of the room. Almost immediately he reappeared in the doorway. 'It is now one: fifty-three and thirty seconds,' he announced. 'You have exactly fourteen minutes and thirty seconds left. If you're late, I'll duck you.' He winked broadly and disappeared.

CHAPTER TWENTY

'Whew!' gasped Clara, flinging herself across the bed, 'I'm bushed! Why, what with the swimming and the tennis, I must have had more exercise than I usually get in a month. But it was fun, wasn't it?' Without waiting for his reply she went on: 'And isn't Bess a doll? Not minding about my being so late, then spending so much time with us and inviting us to play doubles with her and her fiancé. He's sweet, isn't he? She told me about him yesterday. She just met him, you know. Here. And wasn't it lovely of her to invite us to that private party tonight? She said she was sure that I'd enjoy myself. And . . .'

Garnett chuckled. 'Slow down, baby. I know you had a great time. But if you lie around in that wet bathing suit much longer, you'll probably catch pneumonia.'

'It's not very wet,' objected Clara. 'It dried out a lot on the tennis court.'

'That may be, but it's still damp. Besides, you want to take a shower, don't you? Why don't you take it now. Then, when you're finished and dry and comfortable, we can talk about my plan for tomorrow night. In fact, I think I'll take a shower, too.'

'Here?' Clara's eyebrows arched sharply.

'Sure, why not? I've got a pair of trousers and a sport shirt in my satchel.' He motioned towards a small canvas bag he had brought with him.

'All right. Do you want to go first, or shall I?'

'Why don't we just go together.'

'Take a shower *together*?' gasped Clara, apparently aghast at the idea.

'Well, a bath would be more fun, but for the time being a shower will suffice . . .'

'No, Conrad. I most certainly do not intend to take a shower with you. Not now, and not at any other time.'

'Why not? You certainly can't say it's a "dirty thing to do". And it's very economical – saves your hostess water.'

'No. I don't want to. I don't need a reason or an excuse. I just don't want to.'

'Come on, Clara,' said Garnett, dropping his bantering tone. 'Stop playing the prude. I've seen you without your clothes on and you've seen me without most of mine. We've brought each other to the heights of sexual ecstasy. If you think I've forgotten that, you're wrong. And you can't convince me that you've forgotten, because I know you haven't. So don't start pretending you're as pure and virginal as you were when you first came into my office. You aren't, and deep down inside you're glad that you aren't. Now when are you going to grow up and start acting like a woman instead of a silly little girl?'

She didn't reply.

He went on: 'All right, Clara, you have a choice. You can do things your way, or mine. If you want to act like an adult, you can follow me into the shower room. But if you insist on acting like a child, we'll play childish games. I'm going to go in and turn on the shower. If you're not there once I adjust the water to the right temperature I'll come back and carry you in – and strip the bathing suit off you, too.'

He turned and walked into the bathroom, not even glancing at the girl who stood stock-still in the middle of the room. She remained there, as if rooted to the spot, until the hissing sound of running water assailed her ears. Then she slowly walked towards the bathroom.

'You might take your bathing suit off,' suggested Garnett as she entered the room and headed wordlessly towards the shower stall.

'I might. But I won't. It needs to be rinsed out anyway.'

'Okay,' grinned the Devil's Advocate. 'Shall I strip you?'

'Don't bother!' She pulled her suit down roughly and stepped under the rushing water. Garnett had already shed his trunks and now followed Clara into the shower.

'The nicest part about taking a shower with someone else is that you don't have to stand on your head trying to reach inaccessible places on yourself,' he told her as he worked a cake of soap in his hands until he raised a fine froth. Then he pulled Clara out from under the spray, saying: 'I don't want the soap to wash away before I'm half finished.'

'But I don't need you to soap me,' protested Clara as he took one of her arms and began to suds it. 'I don't have any inaccessible places, truly I don't.'

'And that's the truth,' he laughed.

'Oh!' Clara gasped. 'But I didn't mean . . . darn it, you always twist everything around!'

Garnett merely laughed and devoted himself to the task of rubbing up foaming bubbles of soap so large that they fell in great white blobs from her arms and shoulders. Clara reached for the soap bar, but he held it away from her. 'You'll like it better as I go along,' he told her. 'Just hold still, now.' He covered her breasts with his hands and rubbed the cake of soap on her nipples.

'My breasts don't need that much attention,' declared Clara. 'They're not at all dirty.'

'Well, I don't suppose that I'd want to give a bath to a girl who really needed one,' said Garnett. He slid his hands down to her belly and rotated the soap against the taut flesh. He moved the soap in increasing circles outward, and soon he was soaping her delta and between her thighs, lathering the hairy triangle as though he were shampooing it. He then slipped his fingers between her thighs and rubbed soap gently into her slit. 'And I certainly wouldn't want to wash you here if I thought it was really necessary,' he added.

He dropped to one knee and began rubbing Clara's

calves and knees and ankles and feet. Then he dropped the soap and hugged her knees, rubbing his cheek against her soapy belly and the sudsy hair between her legs.

'Please get up,' said Clara.

But he stayed where he was. He picked up the soap again and rubbed the backs of her legs, then slid the cake between her buttocks and slowly over the small fleshy globes themselves. He moved his hands up to soap the small of her back, then down again, and reached through her legs to soap her delicate treasure. His fingers tickled and rubbed back and forth for several minutes. Then, at last, he stood and began to soap her shoulder blades. When he had finished that self-set task, he drew back and said: 'Don't wash it off yet, I want you to lather me first.'

He handed her the soap, but Clara shook her head. 'I'll lather your back,' she said. 'That's the only place that's hard to reach. You're perfectly capable of doing the rest yourself.'

'You'll lather all of me,' Garnett replied in a voice that brooked no argument. 'And you'll do just as thorough job on me as I did on you.'

He placed the hand with the bar of soap in it on his chest and set it in motion, working a small patch of lather into a large one in the mat of hair on his chest. Then he released the hand, and she continued to soap his chest, surprising him by rubbing quite firmly and with considerable gusto. She lathered his armpits vigorously and then slipped her hands down his sides to his hips. He quivered slightly, and she brought her hands back up and then ran them down his sides again, this time using her fingernails very, very lightly. He twitched once more and looked down at her with considerable surprise, but remained silent as she began soaping his belly with firm, circular strokes. She soaped and soaped until Garnett smiled and asked: 'Are you going to soap my belly all afternoon?'

'Oh!' Clara started. 'I must have been day dreaming.'

Garnett touched her wrist and moved her hand down

over his soft virility. 'Try down here if you want to kill time,' he suggested.

Clara closed her fingers gently around his manhood and began sudsing it by running her hand up and down on it. Not surprisingly, it soon began to grow under her touch until it had attained the size to which she was more accustomed. 'Ooooh,' she squealed, 'how funny . . . to watch it grow like that.' She rubbed the soap into the curly hair of his pubis until she had created a white cloud of suds from which black, curling tufts protruded. Then she buried the bulbs of his manly plant in lather, and, as she rubbed them between her palms, the stalk swelled even more proudly than before.

Suddenly she stopped, as if she had just realised what she was doing. She moved her hands away and with clinical impersonality rubbed them on Garnett's thighs.

'Kneel down,' said the attorney. 'You haven't finished yet.'

She knelt obediently and began lathering his knees and rubbing the soap slowly down to his feet. He pulled her gently to him by her hair, gripping it through the bathing cap she still wore, and pressed his now fully-stiffened member into the groove between her breasts. She lifted her face to his, her eyes wide and innocent. 'Is this part of taking a shower?' she asked.

'Of course it is,' he said. 'One of the nicest parts.'

Clara lifted her breasts together with both hands, pressing them around his rigid organ. He twisted his hips up and down while she bagpiped her soft globes together and apart, the soap from them leaving his organ. He let her continue for awhile; then he shoved her very gently away from him and turned around. She covered the backs of his thighs with soap, then ran her slippery hands over his buttocks. Between his slightly-spread legs, parts of his manhood peeped pinkly; strands of lather-dripping hair clung to the innermost parts of his thighs.

Clara finished sudsing his buttocks and started to get to her feet. 'Wait,' said Garnett, 'haven't you missed one place?" He turned around to face her again, and she put her hands between his legs, sliding one whole arm through and soaping the inside of his thighs, and, after a while, his anus and its hair.

'Strange,' she said, half aloud, 'I don't feel ashamed at all.'

She continued to rub him there until he pulled her to her feet. Then he asked her to soap his back while facing him. She put her arms around him and began to rub the soap on the hard, broad expanse of flesh. Their bellies slipped soapily together, and Garnett rubbed his stomach slowly back and forth across hers. His love instrument brushed against her thighs, bouncing each time he moved, and her nipples rose to erection as they rubbed against his chest.

'Don't you like to take showers *a deux*?' he asked. 'Isn't it fun?' He slid one knee between hers and moved his thigh back and forth against that most delicate and sensitive part of her. She leaned closer to him, saying faintly: 'We're doing more than taking a shower. I really shouldn't let you do this, you know.'

Wordlessly, he moved his swollen shaft to her belly and rubbed it against her navel. Then he pushed the cake of soap into her hand again and placed her hands on his organ. She lathered it, then let the soap fall to the tiles, taking hold of the shaft with both hands, pushing her curled fingers up and down and tangling them in his hair until there was a great ball of lather at his crotch, half-hiding her hands from Garnett's sight.

Suddenly he scooped up several gobs of foam from his own groin and slipped his fingers into Clara's welted slit, covering her Mount of Venus with huge white bubbles. 'Does it sting?' he asked while he pressed the raised lips of her love vessel apart and squeezed the lather between them.

'No . . . oh, yes . . . just a tiny bit,' replied Clara. 'It feels slippery and tickly, mostly.' She pressed her thighs tightly together on his hand.

Garnett faced her squarely, bending his knees just

slightly. He took his shaft in his hand and rubbed the plum-shaped tip on the girl's soapy pubic hair. Then he pushed the organ lower and between her thighs. Clara yelped as its hard tip slid back and forth over the lips of her sex. It pressed so hard against her that it seemed determined to enter her. But, just as it slipped up to the entrance, Garnett drew it away. He rubbed the whole shaft quickly up and down between her legs for a minute, then stepped back. He led Clara, who seemed rather weak, under the stinging hot shower, and the soap slid instantly from most of their bodies. Suddenly, Clara laughed.

'What's so funny?' asked Garnett.

'You are,' she replied. 'You said that taking a shower together would be more economical. And then we let the water run for close to half an hour without using more than a few drops.'

Garnett laughed, too. 'Do you always listen so closely to what I say?'

'Uh huh.'

'Okay, I'll just tell Blanca to send me the water bill for the month. Then we won't have to feel guilty about using up the water supply and costing the lady money.' He reached out and turned on the hot water tap full blast for a moment, then turned it off completely.

Clara seemed terribly weak at the knees. He led her out of the shower alcove and began to dry her off with a big, woolly Turkish towel. He towelled himself, too, and, when the first towel was wet, he picked up another, with which he wiped his and her sexual parts on it at the same time. Then he dried her breasts and reached down to lift up her legs and dry them, too. On the way down, however, his hands got sidetracked and ended up between her thighs, where they lingered for quite some time. Then he remembered about the legs and wiped them cursorily. This done, he rose, and they took turns wiping each other's back. Finally, he towelled her hair dry and fluffed it out with his fingers. 'You can comb it out later,' he said. 'Right now, why don't you run along into the bedroom and lie down. I'll be in in a moment.'

But Clara didn't move. She just stood, as motionless as a statue. She seemed to have lost her power of self-volition.

'Go on, Clara,' he repeated, 'lie down.'

She walked out of the bathroom like a person hypnotised, as the water in the bathroom sink began to run. It ran intermittently for the next few minutes, then it stopped, and Garnett came out of the bathroom, still nude, a shaving kit in his hand. He knelt and put the kit into his satchel, then crossed the room to the bed where Clara lay, face down. Gently, he turned her over and lifted her onto the pillows, stripping away the spread and blanket so that she was lying naked on the cool, white sheet.

She opened her eyes. 'Were you shaving?'

He nodded affirmatively.

She stretched out her hand and stroked his cheek. 'Very soft,' she smiled.

He lay down beside her and rubbed his cheek against her breast. 'This is why I shaved,' he said, his voice imbued with its customary sardonic tone. 'I don't want to irritate your tender skin.' He lay for a moment with his head against her breast, his hand lightly caressing her belly and her thighs. Then he rose and repositioned himself on his knees in a spot just near her shoulders. He knelt there for a while, studying her, letting his gaze travel dispassionately up and down her body. His eyes, cold as steel, travelled over every inch of her, over every curve and every plane, over every subtle swelling and every soft recession, over all the fine and private places. Then, with the same cold deliberation, he straddled her breasts. His organ had begun to stiffen of its own accord, but it was nowhere near the full blown thing of beauty it had been in the shower.

Unbidden, Clara ran her fingers along the instrument, causing it to start swelling and hardening. She closed her eyes, then opened them again. And she put her mouth a little closer to the long and sturdy shaft. Soon, and as if of its own volition, her tongue snaked out of her mouth and flicked across the utmost tip of the blue-veined shaft. Then the tip of her tongue encountered the hot, hair-flecked base of the member and began to work its way back up towards the tip. Up and down, back and forth her tongue travelled, running its own rhythmic shuttle service from tip to base and from base to tip. Then the tongue stopped. The mouth hovered around the plum-red tip. The lips puckered against it in a delicate kiss, then parted to admit the whole organ into the moist warmth of the mouth.

Clara began to suck the monstruous machine passionately. She worked her mouth and her lips up and down on it, and it swelled with pride at being so uninhibtedly caressed. It swelled until it would no longer fit whole into her mouth. Then she stopped. Putting her hands against Garnett's belly, she pushed him away. 'I – I can't do it,' she stuttered. 'I'm too, too ashamed.'

'Then why did you start?' he asked quietly, watching her as she covered her face with her hands. 'I didn't ask you to, you know.'

'I know you didn't. I just felt that you wanted me to.'

'And you want to do the things I want done?'

'Yes.' Clara whispered in an almost inaudible voice. 'Yes.'

'Always?'

'Yes.'

'Even things you've never done before? Things that make you so ashamed you want to die? Will you do those things if I tell you I want you to do them?'

He had been speaking in a low monotone, and the effect of his almost-chanted questions seemed to be hypnotic. Clara, as if in a trance, answered: 'Yes, Conrad, I will.'

'Good.' He snapped, thrusting his shaft back into her mouth savagely.

Clara resumed sucking it again, and within seconds, Garnett's hips were pumping in rhythm with the movements of her tongue. After a while, she began to roll her head around on his member as he thrust in and out, tonguing the tip every time he stroked out, sucking fiercely every time he plunged in. He threw his head back, and his motions grew more frenzied. 'Play with me,' he whispered, his voice constricted with passion. 'Play . . . with . . . me.'

Clara placed her hand under the shaft which she was so avidly sucking and began squeezing and fondling the two fleshy sacs which nestled at its base.

'And . . . put your finger . . . into my . . .' He did not finish, for he felt Clara's finger already obeying his command, moving towards and then entering his rear passageway. As it entered, her nail scraped the lining of the canal, but the pain it caused soon melted into the wild, spiralling ecstasy that engulfed him as she rammed her mouth onto his shaft and then scraped it fleshily back again, only to ravish it once more, while at the same time she jammed her finger in and out, in and out. Garnett gasped, and his whole body began jerking spasmodically. He almost fell forward with the force of the spasm which shook him, but he grabbed Clara's shoulders and dug his fingers into them, clinging insanely to the whiteness of her and moaning without making any conscious effort to do so. The moan crescendoed upward and twisted abruptly into a long, almost inhuman, scream as Clara's mouth filled.

He waited until he knew that he was empty, then rolled heavily to her side and lay there, immobilised.

When Clara awoke, it was night and Garnett was asleep at her side, breathing the slow, deep breaths of one whose slumber is wholly untroubled. She began running her finger along his sides, gently, softly stirring him awake. He moaned, then struggled upward, out of the black abyss in which he had been floating, 'Wha . . . what time izzit?' he asked, his voice fuzzy with sleep.

'I don't know,' she replied. 'Late, I think.'

He fumbled around on the dressing table until he found a match, which he struck and held up in front of his wrist watch. 'Nine o'clock. Time for us to get up and find ourselves some dinner.' The first match had flickered out, and he struck another, lighting two cigarettes from it before he shook it out. 'But first,' he said, taking an ashtray and balancing it on the flat, hard surface of his naked belly, 'I want to explain my plan for tomorrow night.' He paused for a moment, dragging on his cigarette and watching the tip flare redly in the blackness. Then he asked: 'Have you ever heard of a "Black Mass?"'

'A "Black Mass"?' echoed Clara. 'Why no, I don't think so. What is it?'

'A Black Mass is an inversion of the traditional Catholic Mass. Instead of honouring some diety, it is held in honour of the Devil.'

'What?' gasped Clara.

'Yes, in honour of the Devil, who is known to his devotees as his Satanic Majesty. Every part of the Mass is inverted so that each sacrament becomes a desecration, each holy rite a sacrilege. The celebrants burn black candles, they turn the cross upside down and spit upon it, they parody the *Ave Maria* so that it becomes practically a catalogue of obscenities, they recite the *Pater Noster* backwards, and so on, ad nauseum.'

In the darkness, Clara drew in her breath sharply. 'People must believe in God very sincerely to go to so much trouble to spite him,' she said.

'Oh, yes,' responded Garnett, 'they believe in him sincerely, all right. You see, the Black Mass was originated by a group of Catholics who were united by one of the strongest common bonds there is, the bond of fear. They believed in God, sure enough, but they couldn't quite manage to keep his commandments. So they decided that, since they were unquestioningly going to hell, they might as well start scoring points with the Devil while they were still here on earth. Thus the development of the Black Mass.'

'I can't believe it,' Clara murmured. 'I've never heard of anything so base in my entire life.'

'You'd better believe it,' said Garnett grimly, 'because you're going to see one – participate in one, that is – tomorrow night!'

'What?' Clara's voice was practically a shriek.

'That's right. There's going to be a Black Mass here, tomorrow night, and you – we – are going to take part in it. Now listen, Clara, I know you're not going to like this; you're going to want to refuse. But remember two things: first, remember the fear and the revulsion and the agony that your sister's absence has caused you; second, remember that your presence at and participation in the Black Mass may be our only means of rescuing her. Why? I can't explain why. You'll just have to take my word for it. And also, remember your promise to me this afternoon. Remember that you said you would do whatever I asked you to do, because I want you to do it.'

'But,' interrupted Clara. 'Conrad . . .'

'Wait,' he said, 'I'm not finished. I want you to promise me now, before I explain what you have to do, that you will do it – with no arguments, no questions asked; that no matter how repulsive it may seem to you, you will consent, because I want you to.'

There was dead silence, then the softest of whispers: 'I promise, Conrad.'

'Good. I knew you would. Now listen. There's one part of the Black Mass that I didn't tell you about. As you probably know, the Catholic Mass is celebrated on an altar. Well, so is the Black Mass: on a human altar. And at each Solemn High Black Mass a virgin is used as an altar – which is one reason why Black Masses are held so rarely these days; there are very few qualified altars on which to celebrate them. Anyway, once a virgin has been brought in to the Black Priest's service, holy wine, stolen from a church, is poured into her navel or sometimes into her vagina, and then drunk from there, by the priest.'

'Oh no,' whispered Clara, 'Oh no.'

Garnett went on as though he hadn't heard her. 'And then, the altar itself is desecrated; the virgin is deflowered.'

'Not that!' gasped Clara. 'Anything but that!'

'Yes. That. You and I are actually very lucky I think, to be invited to participate in the mass in such an important capacity. For the first time, I find myself really thankful that you're a virgin. That's why I was approached, you see. It's a chance in a million, Clara, a chance to unmask the Scorpion, to see how he operates, and' – he paused dramatically – 'to find your sister.'

'My sister? Rita! I don't understand.'

'You don't have to understand. Just take my word for it.'

'All right, Conrad. But tell me one thing: who . . . who . . . will . . . do it to me?'

'You mean who will deflower you?'

'Yes.'

'I will.'

'You?!' But . . . but . . . Conrad? Do you believe in the Black Mass? Are you one of those people who worship the Devil? Is that why you're going to do it?'

'My dear, silly child, when will you learn that I believe that nothing is sacred, that I worship no one but myself?' He stopped for a moment, then went on: 'But aren't you pleased? That's the real reason why I'm going to do it. I thought you'd want me to.'

'Yes, Conrad, you were right,' she said softly. 'I want you to.'

'Good,' Garnett said, turning on the bedside lamp. 'Good. Now, let's get up and get dressed. I don't know about you, but I'm starving. I'll give you all the details of the Black Mass tomorrow. Tonight, let's forget about everything but enjoying ourselves. In fact, after dinner, would you like to go to that party Bess invited us to?'

'Oh, yes, very much.'

'Good. Then get up and put on your prettiest dress. I'll go back to my room and change into evening clothes, and I'll meet you downstairs in half an hour. All right, sweetie?'

'All right, Conrad. Anything you say.'

CHAPTER TWENTY-ONE

A slim intense Javanese youth was seated at the piano, his long, slender fingers creating a symphony in movement which was more pleasing to the eye than were the dissonances he was now creating pleasing to the ear. Clara stood, leaning on the broad top of the baby grand, waiting for Garnett, who had gone to change into evening clothes A florid, bulbous-nosed man of about fifty seated himself on the piano bench beside the young Javanese, after first bowing ceremoniously to Clara. The youth at the piano smiled and nodded happily, apparently not in the least disturbed by his uninvited bench-mate. The newcomer must have taken this cordial reception as an invitation to join in the music-making, for he soon began picking merrily at the keys in the treble registers. The youth opened his mouth and began to laugh hilariously, the sound mingling with the raucous keyboard noises. To the uncritical ear, the additional tinkling of the intruder's contribution to the score did little to alter the quality of the piece.

Suddenly, a voice murmured in Clara's ear: 'Poor Kimmi. He'll never learn that he has to take his work seriously before he can expect the critics to. And he has such enormous musical genius!'

Clara turned with a start. Alice Burton, to whom the voice belonged, was standing just behind her. 'I'm so sorry,' said the older woman, 'I didn't mean to startle you. I thought you saw me before, when I was standing in the doorway.'

'No,' said Clara, 'I didn't. I was so absorbed trying to

discern the melody in this piece that I haven't been noticing much of anything.' She laughed brittly.

'Melody?' cackled Alice in reply. 'Why, there's no melody in this music. That's what makes it so marvellous. Kimmi's music talks to us through dissonance and discordance, not melody. He believes that the – quote – civilised – end quote – world is in a state of disintegration, and he says this through his compositions.'

'Oh,' observed Clara, looking thoroughly bewildered, 'I see.'

'Conrad asked me to look for you,' continued Alice. 'I met him just now in the anteroom, dressed to kill. He was carrying two heaping plates of roast chicken and potato salad. He said to tell you that he'll meet you out on the terrace.'

Clara picked up her evening bag from the top of the piano, saying rather stiffly: 'Thank you for telling me. It was very good of you.'

She began to walk away, but Alice laid a hand on her arm. 'You're still upset about what happened in the theatre last evening, aren't you?'

Clara shook her head. 'No – that is, I don't think so.'

'Then why are you so cool towards me today? Aren't we friends any more?'

'I don't know,' replied the girl with apparent honesty. 'I don't know if I'm sophisticated enough to remain friends with you any more.'

Alice laughed heartily. 'Bless you child, bless you. But don't underestimate yourself. And don't go fishing for compliments, either. We both know that you're as clever as you appear naive. And that's saying a lot.'

Clara smiled shyly, then extended her hand. 'Then I guess we're still friends.'

Alice took the proffered hand and pressed it firmly between her own. 'I'm so glad,' she said softly. 'I'm very fond of you, you know.' She paused a moment, giving Clara a look which spoke volumes about the exact nature of her fondness. 'But I'm keeping you from Conrad and your dinner – which seems to be a habit of mine. Run along now. Shall we see each other again soon? We still have a great many things to learn about each other.'

'Yes,' answered Clara in a very low tone, 'a great many things. Why don't you come to my room tomorrow morning, around noon, and bring your bathing suit? Perhaps we can go to the pool together.'

'Why, Clara, that sounds like a marvellous suggestion! I'll see you tomorrow, then.' Alice relinquished Clara's hand, which she had been holding all this time, and kissed the girl softly on each cheek. 'Till tomorrow,' she smiled.

* * *

The next day, promptly at noon, Alice Burton knocked on Clara's door. There was no response, and, after waiting a moment or two, she knocked again. When she still received no answer, she tried the knob. The door was unlocked, and she opened it slowly and entered the room, which was shrouded in darkness. She stood in the open doorway for a moment, allowing the light to filter in from the hallway so that she could see more clearly. Then she slowly crossed the room to the bed. As she approached, she could make out Clara's figure, huddled into a ball under the bedclothes. She reached out and gently pulled down the blankets over the girl's head and shoulders. 'Clara,' she said softly, 'are you awake?'

There was no direct response, but the slender figure began to shudder spasmodically, and choked sobs burst from the girl's throat.

'Clara, Clara, what is it, darling? Whatever has happened?' asked Alice, reaching out to embrace the girl.

But as soon as Alice's fingertips touched Clara's shoulder, the girl recoiled and rolled away, saying in a broken voice: 'Oh, go away. Go away and leave me alone. I'm no good. I'm miserable and filthy and I don't want to talk to anybody. Please go away.'

Alice rose. 'I *shall* go away, Clara but only for a moment or so. And when I return, I want to see you acting more sensibly. You know, whatever happened, I shan't think any the less of you for it, and neither will anybody else who is truly fond of you. And I think you'll feel much better if you tell me all about it. So dry your eyes, love, and get ready to tell me exactly what happened.' She bent over, kissed the top of Clara's head and went out.

True to her word, she returned a moment or two later. Clara was still huddled in the middle of the bed exactly as she had been. Her sobs, however, had ceased, and her body no longer shook.

Alice said nothing, but crossed to the windows and pulled back the thick drapes just enough so that the bright, harsh glare of sun was kept out while sufficient light filtered in to allow the occupants of the room to see without turning on a lamp. Then she flung the windows open wide, admitting a gust of clean, fragrant, country air. 'There,' she said cheerily, 'that's better. You just can't mope well in an airy, lightened room. So you might as well sit up, Clara, and stop pretending that you can't. You must admit that half the fun of feeling miserable was swept out of the window with the musty, stuffy smell.'

A muffled sob from the bed was her only answer.

'Really, Clara,' pressed Alice, 'you're being very silly. I wish you'd stop.' She crossed from the window into the little bathroom and turned on the tap of the sink. In a little while she returned to Clara's bedside, wearing a towel across her shoulder like a white, terry-cloth serape. She set down an oldfashioned washbasin, containing a bar of soap and a face sponge floating in luke-warm, scented water. 'All right,' she said, as though in response to a statement of Clara's, 'If that's the way you want it . . .'

'Want what?' sniffed the motionless figure huddled in the bed.

'If you want to act like an invalid, I'm going to treat you like one.'

Again there was no response. Alice reached over and rolled Clara to the far edge of the bed. She pulled the bedcovers all the way down, ignoring Clara's protests, and began to smooth out the bottom sheet and retuck it, saying as she did so: 'I always knew that the practical nursing course I took during the Depression would come in handy.' She then proceeded to remake the entire bed, rolling Clara back to the side she had first made, in order to smooth out and tuck in the sheet on the second side. When she had smoothed out every crease and every wrinkle, she gently removed Clara's head from the pillows. This action evoked further protest from the girl, but Alice merely replied: 'If you want the pillows back you'll have to sit up.' She thereupon plumped the pillows out briskly and propped them up against the headboard, adding several satin cushions from a long bench which graced one wall of the chamber. 'It's time to sit up now anyway,' she added. Clara did not respond, but neither did she protest when Alice reached out and drew her curled-up body towards the head of the bed. 'Now sit up, Clara,' said Alice. 'It's bad enough to have to treat you like an invalid, but it's ridiculous to have to treat you like a child.'

'Then go away,' said Clara, sounding exactly like a peeved six-year-old.

'You'd like that, wouldn't you? You'd like me to leave – so you could get up and close the windows and the curtains and go back to bed and wallow in your misery in the darkness. Well, I'm sorry, my pet, but you shan't get the chance. The sadist in me refuses to allow the masochist in you to enjoy itself. Now sit up, before I drag you up.'

Surprisingly, Clara obeyed, revealing for the first time that morning her pale, tear-streaked face. 'Well, good morning,' said Alice. 'How nice to see you again.'

'Please,' begged Clara in a tiny, strained voice, 'no sarcasm. I couldn't bear it.'

'All right, I'll make a deal with you. No sarcasm from me, no tears and no self-pity from you. Okay?'

'Okay.'

Alice glanced at Clara wryly, but said nothing. Instead she began to sponge the girl's face. 'You can do your hands yourself,' she said, handing Clara the freshly lathered sponge. Then she crossed to the vanity table and came back with an apothecary jar of talcum, a big powder puff, a hairbrush and comb, a bottle of *eau de cologne* and a vial of lip-rouge. She placed these items on the night table, removing the washbasin to make room for them. Then she handed Clara the towel and carried the basin back into the bathroom. On her way back to the bed, she stopped for a moment to rummage in the closet and returned carrying a golden, quilted bed-jacket.

Within minutes she had Clara powdered, scented, brushed and combed. She applied a dab of lip-rouge to the girl's mouth, saying: 'You need just a drop of colour.' Then she deftly helped her into the bed-jacket. She was just in the act of pulling up the counterpane over the girl's knees and lap when there was a knock at the door.

'Just a minute,' called Alice, smoothing out the covers. Then she rose to admit a boy who was standing in front of the door holding a covered breakfast tray. 'Thank you so much, darling,' said Alice, taking the tray from him and dropping a kiss on his head.

'Anytime, Mrs Burton,' said the boy politely. He went out, closing the door behind him.

Alice brought the tray to the bed. 'Nothing fancy,' she said, removing the napkin. 'Just orange juice, coddled eggs, toast and hot chocolate.'

For the first time that morning, Clara smiled. 'Thank you,' she said. She looked somewhat sheepish. 'This is my second breakfast-in-bed in a row,' she confessed. 'I'll be getting used to it soon.'

'Oh?' asked Alice. 'Who else is bringing you breakfast in bed these days? Conrad?'

'Yes,' admitted Clara, downing her orange juice. She smiled. 'That juice feels good. The taste in my mouth was just awful.'

'Did you drink too much last night?'

'No,' answered Clara, busily attacking her eggs and acting as though she wished she hadn't said anything about the bad taste.

'What caused the bad taste, then?'

'Oh, nothing... well, maybe... I smoked a lot, I guess... that's all.'

'What else did you do last night, Clara? Besides smoking a lot?' asked Alice, not fooled.

'Nothing. Nothing much, that is.'

'Then why are you so upset this morning?'

'Because... because... I would just as soon not talk about it, Alice. I'm all right, now, really I am. You can see that, can't you? And I'm very grateful to you for being so nice and understanding and coaxing me out of my sulks. All it was was a case of nerves. I'm not used to so much partying, you know. And I think that I mentioned I have a sister whom I'm a little worried about. So, between the two things...' Her voice trailed off, and she put a piece of toast into her mouth in the ensuing silence.

'I don't believe you, Clara,' said Alice bluntly. 'I don't believe you one little bit. Something happened last night – something far worse than anything that has happened to you so far. And until you can talk about it – until you can tell someone the whole story – then it'll continue to haunt you, to stalk you daily and to confront you nightly. I know what I'm talking about, Clara, believe me. Only by talking about it can you lay bare the spectre of this ghastly thing. And then it'll be gone, lingering only in the outer reaches of your memory, the way a nightmare lingers.'

'It was true,' said Clara, her voice little more than a whisper, 'that the bad taste came from smoking. I didn't say what it was that I smoked.' She paused to sip her hot chocolate.

'And what *was* it that you smoked?' prompted Alice.

'Opium.'

Alice's eyebrows lifted, but in no other way did she betray surprise or shock. 'Tell me about it,' she said gently. 'And start at the beginning. Do you remember everything?'

'Oh yes!' cried Clara. 'That's what's so awful. I remember every single thing perfectly. It's like having a motion picture machine in my brain – and the movie keeps playing over and over again.'

'Very well,' said Alice, 'start with the first reel. Only this time, add sound to your silent movie. As the events flash through your brain, begin describing them. Just tell me what you see yourself saying and thinking and doing. Forget my presence and just start talking. Once you begin, it'll be easy, you'll see.'

'Well,' said Clara, taking another sip of chocolate, 'yesterday afternoon, Bess Lynd invited us – Conrad and me – to a private party. So, after dinner, we went upstairs to where Bess had said the party would be.' She popped the last morsel of toast into her mouth and daintily wiped her fingers on the napkin. 'We entered a dimly lit vestibule,' she continued, 'with a small door at one side. Conrad closed the outer door and escorted me through the small one, which led into a room lighted by blue lamps. That is, the colour of the lights inside the lamps were blue. There was a funny smell in the air, like nothing I'd ever smelled before. I asked Conrad what it was, but he told me to be quiet. Then he took me by the wrist and led me to a corner where several cushions were heaped on the floor. He motioned me down on the cushions, and he sat down beside me.

'At first, I could see nothing but the lamps with the blue lights, but by the time we had sat down, my eyes had adjusted to the darkness and I could see that we were in a very large room with huge pier-glass mirrors where I would have expected to see windows. There were no windows there at all. In fact, there was very little in the room in the way of furnishings except for four or five couches and lots and lots of pillows. The corners of the room were made into alcoves by diagonal arches, and I could now see that we had entered through one of these alcoves which had been closed up to make a tiny room. There were about a dozen people sitting around, conversing in very low voices, and some of them held short thick pipes with tiny bowls which they frequently lighted and puffed with loud, sucking noises.

'Conrad told me to keep my voice very low. Then he reached into his pocket and took out a small silver box. I asked him what was in it and he said: "Opium." Of course, I was terribly shocked at that, for I had heard about the terrible things that people do when they smoke opium, and I knew that you could become addicted to it. "Are we going to smoke it?" I asked. "Is that what these other people are smoking?"

' "We are, and it is," he answered.

' "But it's dope," I said.

' "Of course it's dope," he whispered, "and you can become addicted to it if you're not careful. Do you want to leave?"

' "No," I whispered, "I'll stay." I don't quite know why I said that, why I didn't just get up and leave. But I didn't. And then it was too late. Conrad handed me one of the small pipes, lighted it and took another out of his pocket for himself. For some reason, it didn't occur to me to be surprised that he had the pipes and the opium with him. Perhaps the half bottle of white wine we had had with dinner made me a little more light-headed than I realised. At any rate, when Conrad told me to drag on the pipe as deeply as I could, I did so. Of course, I almost choked. But I didn't want to attract any attention, so I stifled my coughs as best I could. The stuff tasted awful, and the coughing made my eyes water. I was hardly enjoying myself, but Conrad insisted on my trying it again. I did so, and found it easier. I puffed on the pipe for several minutes. Nothing happened and finally it burned out.

'I handed the pipe back to Conrad. "Nothing happened," I said. He refilled and relighted it and gave it back to me, saying: "Just wait, you'll know when it starts."

'I began puffing again, more deeply this time, and suddenly I handed the pipe back. "I don't want any more," I said, speaking much more loudly than I had meant to. But no one seemed to notice, although everyone was speaking in whispers. A peculiar feeling came over me, and I would have been frightened if Conrad had not been sitting there so placidly beside me, puffing contentedly away. He looked like an Indian, sitting there so impassively, smoking his peace pipe. But the feeling that had come over me wasn't a peaceful feeling, and I leaned to one side trying to get away from it. I clutched Conrad's arm, thinking that I should have refused to smoke the second pipe, just as I should have refused to do every single thing he ever told me to do, starting from taking off my clothes and reading from my sister's diary! I also told myself that what I needed was a new backbone, and that I'd go out and buy one as soon as I got back to the city. I wondered if you could get one at a corset shop. Like whalebone, you see.'

'Buy a new backbone?' asked Alice, her eyebrows arched quizzically.

'I'm only telling you what I thought while I was under the influence of the opium,' replied Clara. 'Anyway, after that, I began to feel a little dizzy, as though I were going around in half-circles. Then I wondered how I could go around in only half-circles. What was happening to the other halves? I felt like Alice-in-Wonderland, and I glanced around for the white rabbit, but I couldn't see him.

'Suddenly Conrad said: 'Listen!' His voice was soft and oval-shaped. I thought that it was funny that I'd never before noticed what a lovely, oval-shaped voice he had. And such pretty colours, too: maroon in the middle, with a brown rim.

' "Do you hear the music downstairs?" he asked, and the oval rolled over and over, leaving the words behind like tracks from a wheel. I sat up very straight and tried to listen, but the floor seemed to be slanting, so I bent all the way over to one side to stay up straight. I suppose if anyone had been watching me they would have thought I looked rather peculiar, but, of course, everyone was too absorbed in his own pipe dream to even notice me.

'I looked around at the other people, who were all too busy to notice me. There seemed to be twice as many as there had been before. And they all appeared to be twins. It seemed funny to see so many twins at one time.

'They now seemed to be talking louder than they had been before, and all of a sudden I thought I could hear everything they were saying. But they all seemed to be saying such silly things that I began to laugh at how silly they were. My laugh seemed to go up and down like carillon bells, and I thought that one bell was off pitch. I laughed back up to it and laughed that note over a couple of times. It still seemed off. I gave it up and laughed back down the scale again. At the bottom I seemed to hear Kimmi's piano again. And I was sure that I could hear every note. I even seemed to be able to hear farther down the scale than he was playing. Also, I imagined I could hear the piano's foot pedal softly working up and down.

'My face felt very dry, and I passed my hand across it. It was as though there were several large cracks in it. The gesture seemed to take ages, and I had a feeling that I had flung my arm halfway across the room. "I ought to throw my other arm after it to pick it up," I thought, and that seemed so ridiculous that I began giggling again. This time the giggle came out as loud braying laughter, and I thought: "I'm making a jackass of myself." The picture of myself with long ears and a tail was so funny that I laughed once more, this time so loudly that I wondered why the walls didn't come tumbling down like the ones at Jericho.

'Suddenly, I realised that I was terribly thirsty. I whispered as much to Conrad, who now appeared to be straight up and down in the middle, like a barber-pole, while I seemed to be going around him in a circle on a merry-go-round. I reached out for what looked like a brass ring, but it turned into Conrad's hand. "I'm thirsty," I said again, thinking that I should keep my voice down to a shout. My throat felt as if it were filling up with sand. "Somebody," I thought, "has mistaken me for a sandbox."

'Conrad handed me a glass, which he seemed to have picked out of the air. I swallowed some of the contents, and, as the liquid ran down my throat, it seemed that I could hear it rumbling its way down, rumbling so loud that it sounded like a miniature Niagara Falls.

'I looked at the glass to see how large it was. I felt as though I were drinking quarts and quarts, and that I was spending ten or twenty days in the process. But when I had finished, Conrad was still sitting in the same place, and I thought that it was very nice of him to wait so long for me. "He must need a shave by now," I thought. "Funny, how men have things growing out of their faces that they have to cut off with razors."

'Suddenly I asked: "Why did you give me lemonade? Did I want lemonade?"

' "No," said Conrad, "you didn't want lemonade, and I didn't give you any. That was wine. How do you feel?"

' "I don't know," I said, "I never felt this way before." Suddenly the walls snapped up straighter and I felt much saner. And my eyesight seemed to have improved enormously. I looked across the room and saw a girl sitting across from me. "My goodness, she has one million, eight hundred seventy-one thousand and three hairs on her head," I thought. "And I can see every one of them." It seemed as if I had been able to count them all in one millionth of a second, and this made me feel very intelligent.

'I looked at the girl again and saw that she was sprawling across some pillows, just as I was, with a man seated beside her on the floor. However, although there was no one else sitting beside me but Conrad, there was a man sitting in a chair on the other side of the girl. I could see that her hand was in the lap of the man in the chair and that she was moving her hand slowly up and down. At the same time, I watched the man on the floor slowly running his hand up and down her thigh, raising her dress just one and one-three-thousandths of an inch – no more and no less, I was sure – each time his hand went up, but never lowering it at all when his hand came back down.

' "Watch them" I whispered to Conrad, and then I was ashamed for having said such a thing. I began to blush and I could feel the corpuscles of my blood rushing through my veins. I thought to myself that if I had the time I might count the corpuscles. I began and got to about nine thousand when I started imagining that I was being consumed by a raging flame. It felt so painful that I opened my mouth to scream, as, as soon as I did, the too-intense heat turned into a glow which I could feel seeping out of my skin and into the air around me.

'I turned my attention back to the girl across the room, and it seemed as though I could feel just which muscles worked to move my eyeballs, and I was sure that I could direct each muscle individually. But I forgot all about that when I saw the girl opening the pants of the man on the chair, while the other man stroked her hips, which by now were bare. I was suddenly filled with tremendous excitement. I could feel it running from some place in the back of my brain down my loins. From there it radiated out to all my limbs and gradually filled up my whole body. I could feel the excitement as though it were a real thing rather than a feeling, and I could especially feel it between my legs. I was getting so wet down there that I was afraid I was going to float away. I buried my fists in the pillow beside me to anchor myself down, as I watched the girl take the man's ... the man's ...'

Here Clara faltered for the first time since she had begun her narrative, and Alice Burton softly supplied: 'Cock?'

Clara then went on as though she had never stopped: 'cock ... of the man in the chair, and watched her stroking the man's ... thing. She put her fingers tightly around it and moved her hand up and down. Suddenly I thought: "Why, her hand is beating out Morse Code." I tried to read the message she was sending, but it seemed to be in a Scandinavian language. Then the girl turned her hips, letting the man on the floor pull her dress all the way up her waist. She wasn't wearing anything under the dress, and her buttocks were very white in the blue light. The man squeezed and patted one. The other seemed to be winking and glowing at me, and I thought: "Oh, it's the full moon! That means I'll be unwell next week. And blood will pour out."

'Now go on dear,' Alice prodded, 'tell me the rest of your storey.'

Dutifully, Clara went on: 'Suddenly, I seemed to snap out of my daze. I was horrified and I looked around the room, wondering which person wouldn't mind too much if I allowed the horror to seep out of my body and into his. Everyone seemed to be watching the two men and the girl, and I realised that every person in that room was participating in some way in what the trio was doing. It seemed as if we were all playing a much greater part in what was happening than we ordinarily would have. It seemed as if each of our thoughts was radiating towards the men and the girl, and each thought seemed to add to their excitement so that it was no longer the excitement of three people, but of twelve or thirteen people.

' "Take my dress all the way off," said the girl, and her voice rang in my ear, like the bells in a fire station. "I want them all to see me completely naked." Then she leaned back to let one of the men lift the dress over her head. She brought her hands down from her shoulders slowly, rubbing them over her breasts and belly and thighs. Then she pressed them one over the other between her legs, rubbing her fingers in her pubic hair and spreading and closing her knees slowly, again and again, showing herself to everyone in the room. And, it seemed, especially to me. I suppose I should have been dreadfully embarrassed for her, the way I was embarrassed for the redhead in the theatre, but I wasn't. I could feel the excitement between my legs more intensely and wetly than ever, and it even seemed as though I could feel every hair down there, as if each one had a separate identity.

'I became unbearably aware of my . . . my sex. The lips were squeezed together, and suddenly the sensation seemed too uncomfortable to stand. I spread my knees wide enough apart to separate the flesh down there, and, as I did, I noticed that the lips seemed to be swelling, although I couldn't ever remember their having done so before, and that, as they swelled, their odour became more and more powerful, so I could smell it quite clearly.

'Then the girl across the room turned towards the man on the chair and faced him, kneeling. She shook her head, and her hair fell over her shoulders like rain. It was so much like rain that I was sure I could hear the gentle hiss that it made. She began to rub and handle the man's pr ... thing, and she pressed herself in between his knees and leaned close to him. He stroked her shoulders and slipped his hands under her armpits, bringing her even closer to him.

'Suddenly, the girl pulled his thing towards her, as if it were a handle, and then she bent her head towards it and sucked it into her mouth. As soon as she did that, I felt as though I were going to choke. I looked sideways at Conrad, and for the first time I realised that his was the only face in the room that I could not read. He seemed to know that I was looking at him, although his face was turned away from me, for he handed me the glass he was holding. I drank it, noticing that it smelled like ether, and I thought: "I must be unconscious, and they are going to take out my appendix." I realised that I had already had my appendix removed, and then I thought: "Oh, well, this time they can take it out of the left side, I don't care."

'I was still drinking. The liquid tasted like wine mixed with iced coffee. It was a very interesting taste, and I wondered if Conrad had mixed it specially for me, or if it was one of those new instant drinks, and if it was, whether it was called "wiffee," or "cowine." I looked back across the room. The girl was still sucking the man's thing. I was horrified, because she was jerking her head from side to side as she sucked, and I was sure she was going to rip the thing from the man's body. She began to fling her own body about wildly, clinging to the man's knees as though she were afraid that she would go flying across the room if she didn't have something to hold on to. Then, still holding on to him, she lay down, with his thing still in her mouth, and her arms and legs sticking out in all directions. She looked like a huge broken insect as she lay there, and, for a moment, she seemed to turn into a gigantic dragonfly, which somehow or other had died from an overdose of human fluid. Finally she turned back into a girl again, a girl swallowing heavily as she pushed herself away from the man to whom she anchored herself.

'She now rolled to the centre of the floor, and the man who had undressed her began taking off his own clothes. When he was completely naked except for one sock, which he didn't seem to notice, he walked towards her and she got up on her knees again to clasp him around the hips and kiss his ... little ... sex-thing. She ducked her head between his legs, and those soft things down there bobbed up and down like bells and kept banging into her face as she rubbed her cheek against them. She looked very funny as she knelt there, licking the man with those things dangling down on her forehead, and I began to laugh. I laughed three notes up, and then the fourth note turned into a little gong, which I knew came from having gasped very suddenly, and I imagined that it was I out there, in the middle of the room, and that all those people were looking at me. I made myself gasp again, then I reached through the gasp and pulled myself back into my own body. Then I reached for Conrad's hand. He turned to me inquiringly, and I whispered: "I was looking for something familiar." He nodded, and I felt very relieved that he understood. His face seemed very drawn, and his eyebrows turned up at the outer corners, like a Chinaman's.

' "Don't try to hold anything back" he whispered, in a metallic voice. "Even if you lose yourself, you can always find the way again."

' "Yes," I replied, "especially if I leave markers to show me how I came."

'I turned back towards the girl and watched her hugging a pillow to her belly as she bent over double on her knees, her breasts brushing the floor. Her bottom rose, round and soft, like two moons. "Of course!" I told myself. "Have you already forgotten about the full moon?"

'I looked at the moon again, but all I could see was the nude man, who now was also on his knees. I noticed that he had a tiny moustache and a very big . . . thing. I wondered how a man could have such a tiny moustache and such a big thing, and then I remembered that American Indians never grow moustaches or beards. I was very curious as to whether they all had little things. It seemed like an interesting research project.

'I turned my attention thirty-eight degrees to the left, back to the man and girl. He had placed his hands on the small of her back and was inching his way forward. "No," I corrected myself precisely, "nine-tenths-of-an-inching his way forward," and she was reaching in back of her and clutching his sex thing. She began wiggling her behind and brushing her breasts against the rug.

'I felt as if the room were airless and I were going to choke. I took several deep breaths. Then I felt my fingers sink deep into the coarse pile of the rug. Its roughness made me shudder. I crossed my hands over my breasts and rubbed the nipples, which seemed to ache from the roughness of the rug.

'I rubbed the nipples gently, rubbing myself off the rug and back to my own body. "It must be very lonely for my body when I'm not wearing it," I thought, "and it's very rude of me to desert it for someone else's body."

'When I felt myself, in my own skin, sitting next to Conrad, I decided that it would be safe to watch the man and the girl again. They were now so close that there seemed to be no space between them. The man's thing was rubbing between the girl's legs, and she jerked her head to one side and arched her back sharply. She clutched the pillow tightly to her belly and wriggled her bottom ecstatically.

'Suddenly, I heard the sound of Kimmi's piano being played downstairs. It seemed that I had heard it before, but I couldn't remember when. Each note seemed to travel upward, clear and unmuffled, and I found that I could hear better if I leaned back against the wall, so that the vibrations could enter through the base of my skull. It felt, I thought, as though the tones were being tapped out by an iron mallet in my head. As I listened, I decided that I now understood exactly what the pianist was trying to say. The music no longer sounded garbled and disjointed. It unfolded before me, I thought, like an oriental blossom, revealing intricate patterns and forms, delicate blendings of subtle rhythmic designs.

'I was very pleased with myself for understanding the music so well, and even more pleased that I could describe it in such poetic language. I liked being able to analyse music with musical words, and I went on to think that the melody was now developing poignantly into several swirling threads, laid one on top of the other to form a lacy filigree of sound. Now, I knew, Kimmi was speaking of the Far East. I could hear the clashing of war cymbals of a young and barbarous land. I thought that people who could make music such as this couldn't possibly be uncivilised like it said in the schoolbooks I had read. Perhaps, I thought the men who write the school books haven't been to the countries they were writing about. I decided that I should leave soon on a sojourn to the Far East and write new school books about the new, civilised Orient.

'I glanced at Conrad, wishing that he'd help me move into the shelter of his arms. Then my glance froze into a stare. His eyebrows seemed to stretch way up into his hairline, and his face was expressionless. He had become, I seemed to realise with a jolt, a Chinaman. He looked deep into my eyes, and I suddenly thought that I now had no place left to hide. I imagined that he could look into my mind and that everything I was thinking was as apparent to him as if he were reading my thoughts in a book. He covered my hand with his, and my hand trembled. I let myself be drawn to him, and his arms went around my waist. And now I was glad that he had read my mind, for it seemed to take too much of an effort to speak out loud.

'He ran his fingers down the groove between my buttocks, creasing the fabric of my dress into the fold, and he said in Chinese: "It could just as well be you, couldn't it?"

' "What does . . . how do you mean?" I stammered. I was rather confused, because I hadn't realised that Conrad spoke Chinese or that I could understand it. My senses seemed to be reeling as he ran his fingers up and down my bottom. "What could just as well be me?" I asked again.

' "I don't have to tell you," he murmured. "You understand."

'And I did understand. I looked at the girl, and Conrad began to raise my own skirt along my thigh. The girl was so excited that it was frightening to watch her. I wanted to close my eyes and shut her out, but my eyes wouldn't close. The girl tickled her nipples wildly against the rug. Then she ground them into the rough mesh savagely, burying the pink tips into the pile. The girl moaned.

'Suddenly I gasped in horror, for the girl, it now appeared, was trying to impale herself, rear first, on a dagger. "Oh God," I thought, "what a ghastly way to die." I made a desperate effort and finally managed to close my eyes. When I opened them again, I could see that the girl was still very much alive, and that what she was trying so frantically to force into herself was not a dagger at all but the man's big, swollen shaft.

'While I was watching what was going on in the centre of the room. Conrad pulled my dress all the way up to my hips. Now he whispered into my ear: "I want you to take your panties off for me."

' "Not now," I replied. "In my room. Later. Or we can go now, if you want to."

' "No," said Conrad. "Not in your room and not later. Here! Now!"

'I knew that I should be ashamed, and therefore I kept protesting. "Wait." I whispered. "Wait until no one is looking."

'I reached under my dress in the back and lifted my hips.

Very cautiously, or so I thought, I drew my panties down over my bottom. Inch by inch I got them down to my knees. Now they seemed to travel much faster. I told myself that was because I had shaved my legs and therefore the silk could slide over them faster than if they were unshaven. I gave the panties a shove, and they went whizzing down my legs as though they were on a ski slope. They landed on the floor with a plop, which, I was sure, echoed around the entire room, but no one seemed to notice. Quickly, I grabbed them and shoved them under one of the cushions.

'Without my panties on, and with my dress hiked up to the waist, I felt entirely nude. I shivered with embarrassment. "Please," I begged Conrad, "tell me what you're going to do to me."

' "Watch," he replied, nodding towards the naked couple.

'The man was now bending closer to the girl, and his hands were caressing her bottom. His fingers slipped down the back of her thighs to her knees, then up between her thighs and into her anus. He twisted his finger around inside her while he continued to press his thing against her backside. Then it seemed as though I could feel that big thing tickling *me* back there.

' "Oh no," I whispered urgently to Conrad, tugging at his coat as though I were begging him to interfere. "Oh, no! He mustn't do that!"

' "To you or to her?" asked Conrad. He ran his fingers along the small of my back and lightly began stroking my behind. "To me . . . to her . . . oh, dear! I don't know which of us is which."

'Conrad said nothing. He merely continued to stroke my bottom, hugging the cheeks gently to him and raising my hips slightly. Then he slipped his hand underneath me and touched the under-part of my thighs and buttocks.

' "It's too real," I pleaded. "It's exactly as though it were happening to me."

' "It is happening to you . . . if you let it," said Conrad. I noticed that he was speaking English again, and his face no longer had an Oriental cast to it. "You see," he went on, "how easy it is to sin without sinning?" His finger slid between my legs and inside me. He rubbed my pubic hair and tickled my privates. He pressed the lips together to spread the wetness all around, then parted them by running his middle finger through them. He kept on like that, rubbing and tickling that little twig thing down there, which feels so good when you rub it. Then, suddenly, he rammed his finger all the way into me.

'I covered my mouth to keep from screaming, for just at that moment, the naked man unexpectedly drove his thing into the girl's front sex-place. She screamed, and I was sure the cry had come from my own throat. The man began doing it to the girl, holding her by the waist and lifting her hips while his thing went in and out of her. At the same time, Conrad's finger was going in and out of me, but it seemed as though it was not a finger that was invading me but something much larger. It stretched and furiously pumped in and out, and it seemed as though even the soft hairs on the backs of Conrad's fingers had turned into long curling bristles, pressing between my thighs and rubbing inside of me.

' "You're doing it to me," I whispered. "You shouldn't be doing it. You know that. You know you weren't going to do it until . . . until later."

'He didn't say anything, and I, to my own surprise, suddenly flung my arms around him and kissed him on the mouth, licking his lips with my tongue, forcing my hips against him, wiggling my bottom from side to side. I drew my mouth away from him and whispered: "Don't let anybody see you doing it to me."

'The naked girl across from us now slipped through the man's arms, out of his grasp. Then, turning, she grasped his thing and threw herself headlong on the floor in front of him. She took the sex organ into her mouth and sucked it. "Oh," I whispered. "She's sucking him! And he was doing it to her. She's sucking him after his thing was inside her. I wonder how it tastes. Your own self, I mean!" I said with a giggle.

' "Close your eyes," said Conrad, "and do exactly as I say."

'I closed my eyes, and he said; "Put out your tongue."

'I slipped the tip of my tongue out through my lips and held my breath, and I could smell the finger hovering near. Then I felt the wet fingertip touch my tongue and rub over it. The sweetish taste surprised me. I decided that it had a nicer taste than smell, and I wondered if that were true of all women. I opened my eyes, but Conrad gently closed them again with his other hand. Then he rubbed his finger back and forth across my tongue several times. It felt exactly as though a large, hard sex organ was being drawn over my tongue. Suddenly, Conrad pressed the tip of his finger against, then between, my lips. It was sticky with that stuff from between my legs, and it slipped right into my mouth. I was so surprised by that that I closed my mouth on it.

'Conrad laughed – and said: "It isn't to eat, you know. It's to suck, like a lollypop – or a man's organ." He moved his finger gently around in my mouth and whispered: "Suck it, Clara."

'I obediently began to do what he had ordered. I told my mind to take a vacation, that I didn't want to think about what I was doing, or why. I just wanted to sit there and suck on my lovely lollypop. "You'll never be able to watch a child sucking a lollypop again," said one half of my mind – the half which hadn't gone on vacation. Suddenly I began giggling, and I pulled my mouth away from Conrad's finger to tell him that I couldn't help laughing. "It's so funny." I giggled upscale, "to suck a man's thing and find that it tastes like a woman!"

' "I'll let you suck one that doesn't taste like a woman," offered Conrad, but I was very happy with the one I had and refused to give it up. After awhile, however, I tired of it, and turned towards the nude couple, just as the man was once again kneeling behind the girl. Suddenly, the girl on the floor uttered a quick gasp and her eyes rolled up like the eyes of a dead fish. The man had pushed forward and he was finally entering her. He went deeper, and the girl clutched at the rug, clawing like a cat, while she arched her back and pressed against her partner to force his whole thing into her. I was sure that I was out there on the floor, that I was the girl who was wriggling and twisting, arching and grinding my hips in that disgustingly obscene display. I watched myself cry out, clutch at my breasts, pull at my nipples, roll my head wildly. Then, while I – or was it she? – was being ravished in this manner, the second man left his chair and, without removing his clothes, sat on the floor facing her – or was it me? – his legs out in front of him, spread wide, his fly open.

'The girl – I could tell now that it was she – plunged her hands into his pubic hair through his open fly and hauled his sex out into the open. His organ was already very hard, and she put her mouth on it and began to suck it. I clutched Conrad's hand, nervously separating his fingers and squeezing them together. Suddenly I pulled his hand to my mouth and began to suck on his fingers and thumb, one after the other. In my mind, each finger seemed to be the organ of a man, and each one was a different colour. "And six different flavours," I thought. I would have giggled, but I was too busy sampling the different men.

'As I sucked on the purple one – black raspberry, it was – my eyes fluttered open and flickered over the girl on the rug. She had sucked the head of the second man's thing into her mouth and had thrown her arms around his waist, supporting herself on his thighs. He slipped his hands under her breasts and began to press them and fondle them and pinch her nipples while he fed her more and more of his thing until it was entirely in her mouth. Then he started jerking his hips back and forth.

'The girl suddenly clutched at the man's knees, then at his thing, and I saw that her mouth was filling up with that liquid stuff, and that she was swallowing it. Almost immediately the other man started jerking as though he had convulsions. The girl also seemed to be going into convulsions, and the first man's hands fell to his sides. At the same time, Conrad slipped his thumb inside my ... my privates, and I was shaken by spasms greater than any I had ever felt before. When I opened my eyes again, Conrad had taken both his thumb and finger out of me. "Come on," he said, "Get up."

' "Why?" I asked "where are we going?"

' "To look for Bess Lynd," he replied. "We were supposed to meet her here, remember?"

' "No," I said. "That is, yes. I mean, I remember now, but I didn't before you said anything."

' "Well," he said patiently, "now that you remember again, why don't you stand up and we'll go and look for her."

' "Because," I said, "it's so nice here. I don't want to go anywhere, Conrad. Can't you go and look for her by yourself? Then, when you find her, bring her back."

' "All right," said Conrad, "if that's what you want. Here."

'He handed me the little silver box, saying, "I'll leave you this box of dreams. Smoke your way into heaven if you want to, but, if anything happens and you seem to be heading in the other direction – not that I imagine anything will – and especially if you get frightened, try a change of atmosphere and go back to your room. Nowhere else, though – do you understand? Either stay in the rooms with the blue lights or go straight down the hall to the left, turn left again to the end of the hallway and you'll see your door. Okay?"

' "Okay, Conrad," I said brightly.

'And he disappeared into the blue lights. So now you see,' said Clara, acknowledging Alice's presence for the first time in over twenty minutes, 'how terrible it was.'

'Well,' said Alice, 'to tell the truth, no, I don't see. Granted that you had a new and rather frightening experience, but I don't think it was a really dreadful one.'

'But all those things that I thought . . . you don't know how awful they seem now. Or how scary and spooky it is to think you can feel your blood running through your veins, or to believe you've been changed into someone else.'

'But I do know, Clara. I don't smoke opium any more, but I tried it several times when I was younger. While it is a very strange experience, it's hardly one to get suicidal over.'

'But,' said Clara, 'I haven't told you everything.'

'Oh?' said Alice inquiringly.

'No,' said Clara. 'That was only the beginning.'

CHAPTER TWENTY-TWO

'After Conrad left,' said Clara to Alice Burton, 'I leaned back and closed my eyes. I felt pleasantly drowsy, and all I wanted to do was sit and wait for Conrad and Bess. I relaxed and let my mind wander. Kimmi had stopped playing the piano, and I could hear what must have been a phonograph record of African tribal music. The drum beats sounded clearly in my ears, and it even seemed that I could hear the words of the rhythmic chants. I was sure that I remembered a river, dark and slow with silt, and suddenly I laughed. "I didn't remember that they smoked opium in Africa," I said aloud.

' "Of course, they do," said a masculine voice right in my ear. It was so close that I practically leapt off the cushions, so startled was I.

' "In fact, it was in Africa that I first made my acquaintance with the stuff," the voice went on. "I'll grant that it's rather hard to come by there; it's so much easier, and cheaper, to get *kif* – that's the Berber name for hashish." My new-found companion smiled in a friendly way. He struck a match and looked at me. May I?" he asked.

' "May you what? I replied. Then I realised that he was looking at the pipe Conrad had pressed into my hand. "Oh," I said. "It's empty again. Do you think I should fill it?"

' "By all means, if you have something to fill it with." He blew out the match and watched me as I opened the silver box and began stuffing the contents into the pipe. Of course, I had no idea of how much to put in, so I filled it as full as I could, hoping that I looked like I knew what I was doing. Then I leant towards the second match, which the man was now holding out in front of the pipe. I watched the tobacco, or whatever you call the stuff, burst in a beautiful bonfire, and then I took several very deep drags and puffed out in what I hoped was a casual and nonchalant manner.

' "Do you always smoke such heavy loads?" asked my new neighbour.

' "No . . . n-not always," I replied nervously. I glanced sideways at the man and decided that I like the way he looked, although, frankly, it was very hard to tell exactly how he looked, since I was only able to see him out of the corner of my eye.

'I now remembered that most of the people I had watched smoking opium had handed their pipes to their companions, and, not wanting to appear lacking in manners, I offered the pipe to him. Apparently he had been expecting me to do exactly that, for he didn't even thank me, but merely took it and began puffing away. After a while he handed it back to me, and we went on like that for some time, smoking and passing the pipe back and forth between us.

'Then, the man moved some of the pillows so that he could sit closer to me, and, in doing so, he uncovered the panties which I had hastily buried under one of them. He held them up, pursing his lips and of course, I could see his face perfectly, but I was so embarrassed by his discovery that I completely forgot to notice the features. I snatched the panties from his hand and hastily thrust them under the cushions on which I was sitting. "I . . . I . . . was with someone," I explained, and then realised that it was not exactly the right thing to say.

' "So I see," the man said. He suddenly took me into his arms, kissing me hard on the mouth and running his hands across my body. I didn't resist. Oh, I wanted to – I wanted to push him away and tell him that it was wrong to do that to me, but somehow I couldn't. My hands wouldn't respond to my brain's order to push, my lips wouldn't respond to the order to pull away from his lips, nor would my voice respond to the order to protest his violation of my body and mouth. The flesh, I realised, is not always as one with the spirit. My flesh obviously had a mind of its own, for, much to my horror, my body was responding to the man's caresses, rubbing up and down against his hands. My hands were stroking the back of his neck, my lips were clinging to his lips. Even when he began to push me back down into the pillows, I couldn't cry out in protest. My voice stuck in my throat, and I was helpless to resist as he pressed himself against me, putting his hand under my dress and raising it several inches.

'He stroked my bare thigh, then slid his hand between my knees, pushing them apart. "Now lift your dress," he whispered, "I want you to show yourself to me."

'At last my voice responded to my urgent command. "No," I made it whisper. "No, no, no! There are . . . other people . . . they might . . . see." I felt as though I were wrenching each word forcibly from my reluctant throat. But I might as well have saved myself the tremendous effort, for the man merely said: "All right, then, we'll go into an alcove."

' "But," said my voice, this time without any prompting from me, "it's miles away. We'd never get there before morning."

'The man laughed humourlessly and pulled me to my feet. I couldn't stand very well, and he had to hold on to my arm very tightly to keep me from falling. I took one step and I felt as though I were caught in a short length of movie film whose ends had been joined together. I seemed to be forever taking the same step and yet forever remaining exactly where I was. I kept my eyes fixed on the opposite side of the room, but no matter how far or how fast we walked, the alcove remained as far away as when we had started. At last I stopped. "I'm exhausted," I said, "I can't walk another step."

' "But you've only taken three steps," said the man,

looking at me rather peculiarly. "That's something a novice would say."

' "I was only joking," my voice said. It seemed very important to whoever was running my body that no one should know that I had never before smoked opium. Suddenly I seemed to be sitting in a large hammock which was under the water in a lily pond. I was watching a movie of Clara and the man, through a periscope. Suddenly the film jumped several frames and the man and Clara were across the room, just entering one of the alcoves. I saw that it had a curtain which was made to close it off partially, but not completely, from the rest of the room. That was good, I thought, because if the curtain closed the alcove off completely, I wouldn't be able to see what I was going to do.

'Suddenly the lily pond seemed to turn upside down and I imagined that it wasn't a lily pond at all, but the moon, and that my periscope was really a telescope. How silly, I thought, not to know the difference between a lily pond and the moon – especially, I thought, because the moon was so obviously made out of cheese. I could smell it. It smelled like the smell of my sex, which I had smelled on Conrad's fingers.

'I now noticed that there was one very deep chair in the alcove. I looked at it so hard through my telescope that I was nearly pulled through the lens and into the chair. I saw myself standing there, crossing my arms over my breasts and squeezing them. I looked around, and my head went all the way from front to back and back to front again.

' "Okay," said the man, "now nobody can see us. Get out of your clothes. Quickly."

'I wanted to shout that he was wrong, that *I* could see him and myself through my telescope on the moon, but I thought: "He won't hear me until five million weeks from now, since that's how long it takes sound to travel from the moon."

'I watched myself undress, dropping my clothes in a puddle at my feet. Then, barefoot up to my neck, I stood in the dim blue light, letting the man look hungrily at me. "Put on your shoes again," he said. And I watched as I obediently stepped into my satin pumps.

'With the shoes on, I could see I was almost as tall as the man was. He came close to me and made me put my arms around him. Then he pressed his belly close to mine, squeezed himself against my bare thighs and rubbed my pubic hair with his trousered leg. Next he made me turn around, pressed his thighs against my bottom and told me to wriggle around while he pulled at my breasts with one hand and felt my stomach and sex organs with the other.

' "Now," he said, "go over to that chair and kneel in front of it."

'I watched myself kneel, and I imagined that I, at the end of my telescope, was taking a piece of notepaper and writing: "Clara is that thing in the *Reader's Digest* article..."'

'How's that?' interposed Alice Burton quizzically.

'That "thing," explained Clara, 'was something called a massoh ... massa ...'

'Masochist,' supplied Alice helpfully.

'Yes,' agreed Clara, 'that's it. How did you know?'

'I read a lot.'

'Oh. Well, anyway, it was in this article in the *Reader's Digest* about analysing yourself on your own living room couch. Is that where you read it?'

'No,' answered Alice, with only the faintest hint of a smile at the corners of her mouth.

'Oh,' said Clara again. 'Now where was I?'

'On the moon, looking through your telescope and making a note about being a masochist.'

'Yes,' said Clara. 'I thought that, by kneeling, the Clara in the alcove had committed a monstrous indecency, although the man was not touching her and was not even near her. I watched her looking meekly at him over her shoulder. Then, all of a sudden, I imagined that my telescope had turned into a cannon, into which I stepped, pulling the lid down tightly and sealing myself in. Then I lit a match and I shot out of the cannon, off the moon, through a million light years of space and back into my own body.

'A terrible shame swept over me as I knelt, nude, in front of the strange man. I seemed to be kneeling on hot coals, while hot flames licked at my bare body and singed the hair on my head and between my legs. The flames slithered along my thighs and danced over my belly to strike at my breasts. They washed over my buttocks in waves and darted their stinging, forked tongues between my thighs and deep inside of me. I could feel them making my skin blacken and bubble. I was sure that my blood was boiling in my veins and that my eyeballs were about to explode out of their sockets.

'Then the man spoke, and I forgot about the fire. "If I were sitting there," he said, "what would you do?"

'I couldn't answer. I just stayed there, feeling once again the raging fire of hell licking at my charred flesh.

' "Show me,' said the man. He spoke softly, but there seemed to be an authority in his voice which could not be disobeyed.

' "Show me," he said again, "exactly what you would do if I were sitting there. Lean forward, put out your hand..."

'I think his voice trailed off about that point, but I'm not sure. It's possible that he continued to speak, guiding my hands with his voice, urging me to act out the obscene pantomime. I honestly don't know. I don't think I knew then. But I do know that something compelled me to lean forward, as though there really were a man in the chair. Some force stronger than myself lifted my hands to tug at buttons that weren't there, some force moved my fingers into a pantomime of unzipping a zipper, pushing open imaginary underwear shorts, lifting out an invisible male organ. Almost as though I were in a trance, I watched my hands go through the motions of stroking and rubbing, curling around the air, moving up and down with swiftly-measured movements. As though I had been hypnotised, I then cupped my hands and moved my mouth close to them. I dropped my head and began to lick and suck the invisible organ in my cupped hands. It was at that point, I think, that fantasy took over completely, and it seemed as though there really was a man's thing in my hands and between my lips. I sucked and sucked for what seemed to be hours. At last I looked up at the chair and discovered with a shock that the man had somehow sat down when I wasn't looking and that the imaginary thing in my mouth was quite real after all.

' "Stop sucking it," said the man, "and lick it for a while. You must do that very well."

'Again, that force that was stronger than my own will took over, and I obediently slid the organ out of my mouth, putting the tip of it against the tip of my tongue and then rubbing the organ slowly around and around. Then I held the skin forward over the tip of my tongue, while I ran my tongue around underneath it, along the ridge of the thing. He seemed to like that, for he began to twist and turn vigorously. I turned my head to one side and ran my lips up and down one side of the thing, then up and down the other side, and over and over the tip. My cheek brushed the hair above his organ, and I found myself turning and kissing the wiry curls, running my mouth down the line of his thigh, tasting the salt of his skin as I caressed his manhood with my tongue. Then I put one of those things – the ones that hang down – into my mouth, and sucked on it for awhile, and then I put the other one in my mouth and sucked it along with the first one.

'I heard a step behind me, and I started, practically biting off the man's things. I jerked my head away and turned, to find another man standing behind me, staring down at me from what seemed an incredible height. Suddenly, I felt utterly unrestrained and wholly degraded. It was as though I had fallen as low as I could, and now nothing that I did could make my shame any worse or my degradation more complete. I turned back to the man in the chair and once more took his sex-thing in my hands. I licked it from base to tip, pressing the soft, rubbery tip between my lips. I licked off the juice which had risen to the top, and tried to put the tip into my mouth again. But the man pulled away. "Beg for it," he said.

'I opened my mouth to say "no." Once again, my voice betrayed me. "Please . . ." it said. "Please."

'After a while, he gave it to me. It felt so large in my mouth that for a moment I thought I was going to choke. I put my hands on his belly and tried to push him away. But, now that I had started, he wouldn't let me stop. He grasped my ears and held them so tightly that I couldn't move my head. My hands moved upward from his belly, and my fingers entwined themselves in the mat of hair on his chest.

'My sense of taste seemed much more acute than usual, and the taste of his thing seemed overpowering, almost as overpowering as the intense smell which rose from the organ. At first I tried holding my breath, but, after a while, my nostrils and tastebuds got used to the smell and taste, and I stopped feeling as though I was about to gag.

'After I had sucked and sucked for some time, I even began to enjoy the taste. I stretched the skin away from the tip of the thing with both hands and licked and sucked up the taste from the newly uncovered places. Then I tried to suck more of the taste from the entire length of the organ, dropping my mouth heavily on it and driving it deep into my throat until I almost gagged.

' "What do you like most about sucking me?" asked the man, roughly jerking my head back by the hair and staring brutally into my eyes. My mind told me that I should be terrified by the savagery of this stranger, but I felt completely calm.

' "It's the taste," I said. "It's the taste I like the best."

' "I'll give you something you can really taste," said the man, thrusting his thing back into my mouth. "Get down on it hard," he rasped, "and don't pick up your head for even an instant."

'I obediently held my mouth tight around his thing and

sucked in strongly. Instantly my mouth filled with something hot and liquid. I thought I was going to faint, but the feeling of weakness passed, and I swallowed, and swallowed again.

'Then I heard a noise behind me, and I remembered for the first time that there was a man standing there watching my lewd and disgraceful performance.

'Suddenly the full impact of my behaviour struck me. Once again I imagined that the fires of hell were lapping against my flesh. "This time," I thought, "I'll be roasted to a crisp. There'll be nothing left of me but ashes."

' "Turn around," said the man behind of me.

' "No," I whispered. "No. I'm sinful – too sinful for you to look at me."

' "That doesn't matter," said a voice just behind my left ear – a new voice, deeper than the first.

'I whirled around, and found that there were, indeed, two men standing there. I recognised one of them as one of those who had whipped me in that awful little room, and I knew that I had seen the other one, a tall and very thin Negro, several times about the house, but I had never come into contact with him before now.

' "What have you done" asked the white man, "that is so sinful?"

'I couldn't answer. I merely hung my head and lowered my eyes.

'The man who had asked me the question then reached out, grabbed my hair and pulled it so hard that I was forced to stand up. Smiling evilly, he put his fist under my chin, viciously forcing my head upward so that my eyes looked into his. "Answer me," he commanded. "Why are you so sinful?"

' "Because," I whispered, trying to force my head from his grip. "I did something to him."

' "To whom?" he asked, releasing my chin at long last.

' "Him," I replied, pointing at the man who had been sitting in the chair. Now, for the first time since I had turned, I saw that he was no longer seated but rather was standing near the chair, quietly observing my conversation with the newcomer.

' "What did you do to him?" asked the Negro.

' "I won't tell you," I said.

'Without the slightest change of expression, the Negro hauled off and slapped me across the face. The man who had been standing beside the chair then walked up to us and punched the Negro on the jaw. The Negro didn't move, but his arms leapt out like two terrible cats, swift and graceful. One arm hit my defender in the stomach, the other clipped him ferociously on the point of the jaw. He crumpled, and the other white man dragged him out of the alcove by his heels.

'I was completely dazed by this rapid succession of bizarre events. My jaw still ached from the blow it had received, and my head seemed to be swimming several inches above my body in a murky pool of water.

'At this point my thoughts were interrupted by the voice of the Negro. "Now," he was saying, "will you tell me what it was you did to the man I just laid out. If you don't," he said, in the same bland, uninflected tone "I'll slap you again."

' "I . . . sucked him," I whispered.

' "What did you suck?"

' "His . . . his sex organ."

' "Say it. Say the name for it."

' "I sucked his . . . his . . . p . . ." The word stuck in my throat. It felt as large and uncomfortable in my mouth as had the organ itself.

' "Go ahead," prompted the Negro.

' "Isuckedhispenis," I said, running all the words together so that the one unutterable one wouldn't stand out so much.

' "And you think that was sinful?" asked my interrogator.

' "Oh, yes," I replied. "Very, very sinful."

' "So sinful," asked the white man, who had returned without my noticing him, "that you deserve to be beaten?"

' "Oh, yes," I answered. "I do deserve to be beaten."

' "Very well, then," said the Negro, "we shall beat you."

'He turned and went into a corner of the alcove, where, I noticed, there was a large cedar chest. He bent over the chest as the white man took my arm and said: "Come on." He then began to walk me out of the alcove and back into the large room with the blue lights. So confused and muddled was I that I made no protest but allowed myself to be led out through the curtain into the middle of the room.

'I looked around. There seemed to be twice as many people as before. I could see them wherever I turned, staring at me from all sides, reflected in the mirrors that lined the walls.

' "I feel like a slave brought out before the Romans," I whispered, half to myself and half to my jailer. "To be beaten," I added.

' "You are going to be beaten," he said. At that moment, the Negro returned, dragging with him a heavy chair and clutching one of those hateful little whips. "You are going to be beaten," repeated the white man, this time with a look of ghoulish delight on his face. My blood froze.

'The two men forced me to lie over the softly padded arm of a chair. I raised my head and looked around the room again. Everywhere eyes seemed to be watching, expectantly, lustfully. The eyes swarmed over my body like flies until my flesh crept. The white man put his hand on my bottom and lovingly stroked my cheeks. The surprise of the blow which landed seconds later was as great as the pain. I shrieked and writhed in torment. The man continued to switch my buttocks methodically. Then, suddenly, the Negro also began to beat me, with monotonous and frightening regularity. This also surprised me, for I had seen only one switch in his hand, but I suppose he could have been carrying two, or had gone and fetched another while I wasn't looking.

'The white man concentrated his blows on my bottom, but the Negro beat me everywhere, from my shoulders to my calves, always with the same biting force. I was amazed at his natural sense of rhythm. My back seemed to be covered with ferocious little ants, which nipped and picked at my burning skin. They seemed to have burrowed under the skin and now were trying to eat their way out again. It hurt unbearably, but I still felt that I deserved greater punishment. "Harder!" I cried, "Harder!"

' "Why?" asked the white man.

' "Because I'm wicked and deserve to be punished!"

'The lash fell on my buttocks harder than before. A voice suddenly cried from somewhere in the room: "Bind her! Bind her and use whips on her."

' "Oh, no," I cried. "Oh, no! Please don't tie me up! Please don't."

'But I could have saved my breath. The two men seemed to have no intention of tying me up. In fact, they seemed unaware of the request, and of my pleas. They were oblivious to everything except the beating which they were administering.

'The pain grew and grew until it seemed truly unbearable. I begged them to stop, but once more my pleas fell on seemingly-deaf ears. I glanced around the room through tear-blurred eyes, seeking deliverance. And suddenly one of the faces wavered into a recognisable and familiar set of features.

' "Bess," I cried, "Oh, Bess. Do help me. Make them stop. Please make them stop."

' "As soon as I called her name, Bess Lynd rose and came towards me. She whispered a few words into the Negro's ear, then into the ear of the white man. Almost immediately, the lashing stopped. I allowed myself to roll off the chair. I fell to the floor, overcome with pain and exhaustion.

' "Come, Clara," said Bess gently, "get up. Where are your clothes?"

'For the first time, I realised that I was stark naked. But I felt no additional shame. I think I was already as ashamed as I was going to get. "They're in the alcove," I said, rising to my feet unsteadily. "That one, over there."

' "Well, go get them and get dressed, and we'll leave," said Bess. "I imagine that you're ready to go by now."

' "Oh, yes," I answered. "I'm ready to go now." I started towards the alcove, then stopped. "Bess," I asked, "where's Conrad?"

' "Conrad? Why, I don't know," she replied. "I thought he was with you."

' "No. He was, before, but then he went to look for you."

' "Oh," said Bess, "well, our paths must have diverged, then. But don't worry. I'm sure Conrad can take care of himself. He'll turn up sooner or later."

' "I'm sure he will," I said, and went on towards the alcove.

'Crossing the room alone was like walking through a rain of machine gun bullets. I kept my eyes glued to the floor and walked as fast as I could, which seemed to be at about the rate of one step every twelve and one-quarter minutes. By the time I arrived at the curtain to the alcove I felt sure that I had been walking for at least four days.

'I found my clothes, still in a heap on the floor, and began putting on my stockings. Suddenly a voice said: "Wait. Don't dress yet." It was the voice of the man who had wanted me bound and whipped. I turned to face him and found that he was a rather medium-size man with a blank, almost moronic face and pale, grey eyes. I hadn't liked his sentiments, and now that I saw his face, I decided that I didn't like him, either.

' "He came closer to me and seized my wrist, and said harshly: "Come to my room with me."

' "No," I said. "Why should I?"

'In answer, he began to stroke my buttocks and then to caress my thighs and my privates. I felt as though a snake were crawling over me. I wanted to scream out, to run away, but I was paralysed with fear.

' "If you come to my room," he said, now in a wheedling tone which terrified me even more than the harsh one had, "I'll whip you. Not with a little switch. With leather. With whips with iron nails tied into the knots." He still had his hand between my legs, and he rubbed it there, sending an involuntary shiver of excitement through my body. "I'll whip you as you've never been whipped," he whispered, "until you faint from it, and I'll put my . . ."

'Suddenly I found my voice. "No," I cried, interrupting his ravings. "I don't want to go with you. Now let go of me." I began backing away from him, but his hands were still on me and I couldn't shake free of them.

' "You don't have to be afraid of me," he whispered.

' "I'm not afraid," I said.

'And I wasn't afraid. I was terrified.

' "I can see that you are," said the man, "and, of course, since you've been smoking opium, there's no point in even trying to reason with you. But there's really no need to be frightened."

'With that, he threw his arms around me and held my arms so that I couldn't fight him off. Then he forced my legs apart with his knee. He raised my arms over my head, holding them by the wrists with one hand. He had my back to the wall and his knees between mine. He pressed his stomach against my bare belly and suddenly I felt the hot thrust of his sex between my legs. He rubbed it against me, trying to push the tip of it down and back far enough to enter me. He bent his knees to try to get into me from underneath, but each time I felt the head of the organ probing at the entrance, I'd jerk my hips so that he couldn't get in.

' "I know how to punish you for sucking off that man," he said. "I know you need to be punished. And you want to be punished. Come with me and let me give you the punishment you deserve. Oh, I'll be cruel, I promise you that!"

'It was then that I managed to free one of my hands, and I tried to snatch his thing from between my legs. But as I stretched out my hand, I felt the liquid spurt out of his thing, splattering my hand and the flesh between my legs. It clung to the hairs between my thighs and mashed stickily over my skin as I struggled to free myself.

'Then, of his own accord, the man stepped away from me, smiling wryly. "I almost had you," he said. "Perhaps I'll have you yet." Abruptly, he took my hand and rubbed the palm across his thing. Then he forced the hand to my face and smeared the liquid on my mouth and cheek. "That," he said in a conversational tone, "is so you'll recognise me if we meet again."

'He disappeared as abruptly as he appeared, leaving me so confused and bewildered that I wasn't quite sure if I had imagined him, as I'd imagined so many other strange things this evening. Then I ran my tongue over my lips, and I knew that he, at least, had been quite real.

'After that, I got dressed and went out to find Bess. I was quite ready to leave at once, but she suggested that we sit down and smoke one more pipe before we left. It seemed impolite to refuse, so I agreed with as much enthusiasm as I could muster. I had found both the pipe and the silver box laying among my clothes in the alcove, and I now filled the pipe for the fourth time that evening and began puffing away with what I hoped was the aplomb of a veteran smoker. As I smoked, I glanced around the room and found that several pairs of eyes were watching me expectantly. "What do they expect me to do now," I wondered. "Take on a Bengal tiger?" The thought amused me, and I giggled. Across the room, a man smiled at me, obviously mistaking my giggling for a sign of encouragement, since, without really seeing him. I had been staring right at him when I began to laugh. Now he raised his eyebrows in a gesture of invitation. But I was in no mood for accepting invitations. "Can't we go now?" I asked Bess. Haven't you smoked enough?"

' "Why, yes," said Bess. "I guess I have." She stood up and offered her hand to me, for I was still rather unsteady on my feet. "Just hand your pipe to somebody," she said, "and we'll go."

'I hesitated a moment. Then, indicating the man who was still smiling at me, I said: "Would you give it to him? Tell him . . . tell him it's my way of giving him . . . what he wants." I handed her the pipe and slowly made my way towards the alcove through which we had entered, not caring about what the man would say or do when Bess handed him the pipe.'

Here, Clara paused in her narrative. She was silent for so long that at last Alice prompted gently: 'What happened after that, Clara?'

'Do you remember,' asked Clara, 'what I said about being able to see perfectly clearly everything that happened last night, as though I were watching a movie?'

'Yes,' replied Alice, 'I remember.'

'Well, at this point, it's like somebody cut the film and then pieced it together again, because I don't remember anything about actually leaving the room or waiting in the outside corridor for Bess. The next thing I do remember is walking arm in arm with Bess, down what I imagined to be a broad avenue lined with trees. All the people we passed were dressed in the style of the eighteen hundreds, and, as we walked by, the men would bow very politely and the women would smile and flutter their fans.

'Suddenly I stopped and clapped my hands. "I'm so happy because everyone is so friendly. Don't you get happy when people are friendly?"

'But Bess didn't answer. Instead, she asked: "You smoke a very large dose of the stuff, don't you?"

' "What stuff?" I asked.

' "The stuff that you were smoking inside just now."

' "Oh, yes!" I tried to be very nonchalant. "Yes, I do smoke quite a large amount. That way you don't have to fill the pipe so often."

' "And how long have you been kicking the gong around?" asked Bess.

'Of course, I had no idea what that meant, but it seemed to me that it would be a very grave tactical error to admit it, so I replied: "Oh, for years and years, I think. Probably before you were born."

' "This made Bess laugh, and her laughter made me laugh. We arrived at her bedroom door in hysterics."

' "Wait a minute," said Bess, "it used to be my room when I was a little girl." This also seemed terribly funny and we started to laugh again.

'Bess opened the door, and I went in, quite forgetting to ask her why we had come back to her room, since mine was closer to the room with the blue lights and I would now have to walk all the way back by myself. Bess turned on all the lights, saying: "Take off your clothes and lie down. Make yourself comfortable."

' "Without questioning this rather unusual invitation, I began stripping – for the second time that evening. The brilliance of the lights was torture, and I began bouncing around the room, making a little game out of turning them off. Then I bounced back onto the bed and began singing a wordless little song, which, if I remember correctly, involved the imitation of a big bell and a little bell.

' "Turn around," said Bess's voice, interrupting my bell-song, "I want you to look at me."

'I turned ... and gasped. For a moment I was completely speechless. Then I said: "Oh, it's only rubber, isn't it? For a minute I thought ... I didn't know what to think. And you with breasts and everything!"

' "Everything is right," said Bess. She was wearing an artificial male sex organ, which was strapped to her waist and thighs with harness which blended so well with her skin that, in the dim light, I couldn't tell where the harness left off and where Bess began. "I've never seen a better one," said Bess, proudly stroking its erect head. "It does look just like a real one, but it's better than any real one because it doesn't ever get soft." She curled her fingers around it and squeezed it. Her palm slipped down and touched the large balloon at its base. "I've made love to lots of girls with it," she said casually, "including myself, and it's still as good as the day I got it."

' "But where did you get such a thing?" I asked. To tell the truth, I was rather embarrassed by it and wished that she would take it off, but I didn't dare say so.

' "This one was made for me by a Russian doctor, who

died just last year. He made one for a friend of mine with a vibrating motor attachment that's really wild, but this one is fine for me. In fact, I like it better when you have to work a little. The motorised one does the whole job for you ... takes the fun out of it, if you ask me. Of course, you can't buy one like this one, you know. It's even better than the Oriental ones. I was very lucky to have got it when I did."

'I nodded in what I hoped was an intelligent manner. Naturally, I had no idea of what she was talking about. I had only seen something like what she was wearing once before, and that one wasn't half as realistic as this, nor did it have straps attached to it. So my acquaintance with this sort of thing was very limited. But Bess didn't seem to notice my bewilderment. She was too proud of showing off her toy to really notice much of anything. She sat down next to me on the bed and started stroking my arm. For a while I was very confused. I wasn't quite sure whether Bess was a man with breasts or a woman with a penis. I was so muddled that I made no protest as she began to fondle my breasts, squeezing my nipples between two fingers and pulling on them gently.

'I was lying on my side, with my head almost level with the artificial penis. I tried to look away from it, but it seemed to hold a certain obscene fascination for me and I had trouble wrenching my eyes away. At last, however, I did lift my eyes, to be confronted by something which startled me even more than the whatchamacallit had. It was a scorpion, right on Bess's stomach, in the exact same place as yours.

'At first, I didn't believe it. I thought it must be the opium playing tricks on me again. So I closed my eyes. But when I opened them again, it was still there. Of course, you can imagine how surprised I was. After all, I had never seen a woman branded before, and to find two women, in the same house, branded in exactly the same manner — with the same brand — is rather shocking.

' "I see you have one, too," I said to Bess.

' "One what?" she asked, too absorbed in teasing my nipples to pay much attention.

' "A scorpion," I replied.

'I felt Bess's fingers freeze on my breasts. Quickly she rolled me over on my back and looked at my belly. "What do you mean, 'too'?" she asked.

' "Someone else I know has one," I said. I didn't want to say who, because I thought that perhaps you wouldn't want Bess to know. You see, I didn't quite understand what they were for. But Bess said, and it seemed to me that there was relief in her voice: "Oh, you mean Alice! Yes, I'd forgotten that you would have seen hers, too."

' "It's sort of a fad here, isn't it?" I asked.

' "Well," said Bess, "not exactly. It's more like a sorority?"

' "Oh?" I said. "What kind of sorority?"

' "A secret one," said Bess. "We're really not allowed to talk about it."

'Naturally, I couldn't say anything else after that, because it would have been rude. But I was very confused. You didn't say anything about a secret sorority, Alice.'

'No, Clara, I didn't. Some day I'll explain it to you. But not now. One long storey at a time is quite enough. And you haven't finished yours, you know.'

'There isn't too much more to tell. Bess obviously regarded the subject of the scorpion as a touchy one, and she seemed to want to distract my mind from it completely. She began teasing my nipples again, and tried to draw me into her arms. I pulled away, but she rolled over almost on top of me and held me close. After the whippings and the brutality of that horrible little man in the alcove, her soft warmth felt good. I wanted to stay in her arms forever, never moving, always feeling the same warm, mildly-exciting feeling running through my body.

'But then, the rubber thing began pushing against my stomach, and I tried to push away again. "It's so funny feeling that," I said, "when you feel so soft and feminine everywhere else."

' "And I'm soft and feminine under it," said Bess, guiding my hand along her thigh and between her legs.

'As my hand touched her ... there ... it suddenly occurred to me that I was doing something wrong, that I shouldn't be here at all. How had I got here in the first place? ... I wondered, but somehow I couldn't remember.

'I tried to explain to Bess that I must have made a mistake, or perhaps she had made a mistake. At any rate, someone had made a mistake, and if she would be so kind as to get my clothes, I would leave.

'Bess seemed to think that was very funny. She laughed and laughed until one of the notes of her laughter bounced off the wall and, or so it seemed to me, boomeranged into my throat. Then I too began to laugh.

'When we had both laughed ourselves silly, Bess said: "You don't really want to go, do you, Clara?"

' "I don't know," I said. "I really don't know what I want." I noticed that my hand was still between her legs. I tried to withdraw it, but she pressed her thighs together so that I couldn't. So I left my hand there, and Bess slipped hers between my legs and began gently rubbing me there, whispering softly: "You want to stay here with me. You want me to make love to you and you want to make love to me. That's what you want, Clara. That's what you want."

'So gentle and soothing was her voice in my ear that I actually believed it was my own voice I was listening to, the voice of my conscience, telling me to stay here where it was quiet and warm, where no one would whip me or make me do nasty things or watch me degrade myself, here where there was only softness and love. I began to respond to Bess's probing fingers, letting the warmth spread from them into my own body. I spread my legs wide, so that she could see everything there was to see, so that she could fondle and touch every part of me. At the same time, her own thighs relaxed, and I began to imitate her tickling and touching, doing to her what she was doing to me.

'After a while, Bess withdrew her hand. "I want to kiss

you there," she whispered, sliding off the bed. "Move over into the middle," she said. "Raise your knees and spread your legs as wide as you can." I did so, and she came back onto the bed, curling up between my legs. She began running her tongue up the inside of my thigh, snaking it in and out of my you-know-what as her hands reached up to pet and stroke my breasts and belly. She continued in that manner for quite some time; then she whispered: "You must feel my dildo! Put your hand on it and make it grow big and strong." She took one of my hands and clasped it to her buttocks and put the other hand on the artificial penis.

' "It's real," I gasped. "I can feel it moving." I touched it gingerly, and then I slipped my hand underneath the thing to assure myself that it was truly rubber. My hand encountered the soft, moist warmth of Bess' privates, and I was convinced of her true femininity.

'At my touch, Bess rolled over on her side, then onto her back. I sat up, holding the rubber thing in one hand and rubbing Bess between the legs with the other. "You're a man-woman," I said delightedly. "You have everything you need to go to bed with yourself."

'Bess laughed, and the laugh seemed to bounce off the walls with a wild echo. It frightened me, and a shiver ran down my spine. Bess sat up and flung her legs over the side of the bed.

' "Get down on the floor," she suggested, "and lick my thing."

' "Oh, no," I said. "I couldn't."

' "Sure you can, go ahead. Try it. If you don't like it, you can stop."

' "All right," I said. I slipped off the bed and knelt between her legs. I began to lick the dildo very cautiously. It had no taste, but it was so realistic that I kept having to look up at Bess to remind myself that it wasn't a man's flesh and muscle that I was licking.

' "You should suck it, too," Bess insisted, and I allowed

her to place the tip of it between my lips. Then I put my head forward and sucked more of it into my mouth.

'"Did you ever have a feeling that you wanted to bite a man's shaft as hard as you could?" she asked. "I get it sometimes," she said. "Sometimes I want to set my teeth into the thing and chew it like a dog chews a bone. She smiled down at me as she rhythmically pushed the false organ in and out of my mouth exactly like a man would have. "You can bite this one if you want to," she said. "Please bite it. I want to see your face when you do it."

'I drew my lips back from my teeth and tried to get myself to bite the realistic looking organ, but my jaws refused to close. "I can't," I said. "It looks too real, and I just can't bite it."

'"Sure you can," said Bess in a very matter-of-fact-way. "If you bite it just once, you'll like it – and after that you won't think you can't any more."

'I forced myself not to think about what I was going to do. Suddenly I sank my teeth into the thing, biting deeply and as hard as I could. It made my jaw ache. "Chew it," urged Bess's voice – or perhaps it was my own. "Chew it as hard as you like."

'I tore at the thing until a low growl, emanating from my own throat, startled me. Then I began sucking it again, afraid of my own instincts. Suddenly some sweet and lukewarm liquid spurted into my mouth. "I've spent," sighed Bess. She moved her thighs, and again the sweetish fluid trickled into my mouth. Without thinking, I swallowed, and then, as the full impact of what had happened hit me, I tore my mouth away and looked up at Bess. She began to laugh as she saw how worried I looked. She laughed and laughed, but this time I couldn't laugh with her, and her laughter only pricked my curiosity more.

'Finally her last giggle sputtered out, and, wiping the tears from her eyes, she said: "It was wine . . . just wine . . . but you should have seen the look on your face." She went off into more gales of laughter.

'This time, when she had stopped laughing, I asked:

"But how do you do it? I mean, how do you control the flow?"

'"Oh, that's easy. The balls are filled with it. When I squeeze my legs together, the pressure forced the liquid into the organ and out the tip. Clever, isn't it?"

'"Very clever," I agreed. "I've never beeen so bewildered in all my life.

'"I can believe it," said Bess, "judging from that look on your face." She was silent for a moment. Then she said: "Lie down now, Clara, and I'll make love to you. Then you'll really see how lifelike it is."

'"Oh, no," I said. "Thanks anyway, but I'm already convinced that it's very realistic. I don't need any more demonstrations."

'"But don't you want me to make love to you?" asked Bess. "It's just like having a man inside of you."

'"But . . . but . . . but . . ." I blurted, "I've never had a man inside of me."

'"What?" cried Bess, looking really startled for the first time since I had met her. "Are you joking?"

'"It's true," I said. "Really."

'A red tinge spread across Bess's tan face. "I'm blushing," she said incredulously. "I haven't blushed in years. Whatever is wrong with that man you're with? Let's go find him and I'll remind him of his duties. Why, I just can't believe it!" She looked me up and down for a while, as if looking for something which would confirm my statement. Then she patted my bottom and said: "I didn't know girls could be so nice and bitchy while they were still virgins. To do all the things you've done and see all the things you've seen and still be a virgin, that's quite a trick. No wonder you seem so embarrassed and squeamish about things. Why, I'd been getting it regularly for nearly a year before I let a man put his thing in my mouth. She looked at me again and asked: "Are you two-way?"

'"Two way?" I asked.

'"You know," she said. "In the mouth and between the breasts?"

'Now I could feel myself blushing, "Yes," I confessed, hanging my head.

'Bess laughed heartily. "And still a virgin! What a storey! Just wait until you've had a man between the soles of your feet or in your ear. And you haven't really lived until you've done it for a man by taking out your glass eye and winking him off."

' "I haven't got a glass eye," I said, and this sent us both off into fresh spasms of laughter.

' "Well," said Bess a little while later, "if you're a virgin, I certainly don't want to be the one to deflower you. But you can make love to me. I'll show you just what to do."

'She strapped the dildo into place and said: "Now you're a man."

'I stared down at myself. The erect organ stuck out obscenely. I went to the vanity table and looked at myself in the mirror. "It makes me feel funny," I said, "as though I'm not a woman any more."

' "Then come over here," said Bess, "and I'll teach you how to act like a man."

'I went to her. I felt somewhat ashamed, but also very excited by the newness of the experience. She was lying on the bed with her legs spread far apart. As I approached her, she reached up and pulled me down on top of her. She took the dildo in her hands and pushed it in between her legs, rubbing it around and around. Then she moved it back and down between her buttocks and pushed it inside her. She showed me how to support myself with my arms and wrists, and how to brace myself with my feet. Then she showed me how to move my hips and pelvis so that the organ moved in and out of her.

'At first it felt very strange, but after a while I got used to it. "I feel as though part of me is really in you," I whispered in her ear. In response she pressed her body closer to mine and rubbed her breasts against my own. I closed my eyes. The shield of rubber that held the dildo in place against me pressed against my privates. As it rubbed up and down, it excited my nether-lips, and I could almost believe that the sensation was in the organ that I now moved even faster in and out of my girl friend.

'Once more I lost my sense of reality and I imagined that I really was a man. The bed melted away into a mossy bank by a river. It was a bright summer afternoon, the sun was blazing through the trees and there wasn't a cloud in the sky. Bess was a young, pretty dairy-maid whom I had found near the river-bank. She had just taken a swim, and her clothes were scattered beside her. I had embraced her, and she had fought me, more out of a belief that she should resist than out of distaste for my caresses. But at last she had given in, and now she was giving me everything she had.

' "Will you let me do this again, you pretty thing?" I whispered, completely lost in my fantasy. "Will you come here from the dairy every day and let me do it to you?"

'I don't know whether Bess was as lost as I was, or whether she was just humouring me, but she promptly responded: "Oh, yes. You can do it to me every day. Maybe we can even climb up a tree and do it in the crotch between the big branches. I'd be afraid of falling, but the danger would excite me."

'We went on like that for some time. Then, finally, Bess gently pushed me away from her. "Let's lick each other now," she whispered, unbuckling the dildo. As she did, the last shred of the fantasy drifted away, and I was once more a girl.

' "We'll be two little Greek girls," said Bess. "You can be a flute player, and I'll be an acrobat." She kissed my breasts wetly, tickling the nipples with her tongue. Then she showed me how to lie head-to-heels with her so that we were both on our sides with our heads on each other's thighs and bellies.

'In a moment we were kissing and licking each other's thighs, but almost immediately our lips moved simultaneously to each other's privates, and we pressed the lips of our mouths to the lips of the others sex. We tickled each other with our fingers, excited each other with our tongues and with our lips. Oh, Alice! . . . ' Clara broke off suddenly, 'I'm so embarrassed! I never thought I could do that with any other woman. And here I am telling you all about it. I *am* an awful bitch.'

'Don't be silly,' said Alice Burton firmly. 'You should know well enough by now that I'm not at all a jealous person. It makes me very happy to know that you enjoyed yourself with another woman. Only if she treated you badly or didn't satisfy you would I be upset. And it makes me feel good to know that if I hadn't been good for you, you never would have gone with Bess. So don't be ashamed. And do tell me the rest of the storey.'

'Well,' said Clara doubtfully, 'all right. We went on to do all the things you taught me to do. We kissed and licked and lapped and sucked. We rubbed our bellies together and rolled back and forth across the bed. Sometimes I felt as though I were going to explode, and I think Bess felt the same way. I don't know how many climaxes we had. It seemed like hundreds. We went on like that for hours, until finally we were both so exhausted we couldn't move any more. We lay there and rested for a while, and then got up and went around the room, collecting my clothing.

' "Won't you come downstairs with me?" I asked Bess. "It must be wonderful downstairs."

' "Later, maybe," she replied. "Right now I just want to rest. You nearly knocked the life out of me. You virgins are too much for us sex-crobats. And besides, I promised some people I'd go back to the party and smoke some more with them."

' "You're going to tell them what you did with me, aren't you?" I asked. "Well," I went on without waiting for the answer, "tell them I was a wicked, wicked little girl," I went to the door.

' "Aren't you going to put your clothes on?" asked Bess.

'I laughed, blew her a kiss and skipped out the door with my clothes under my arm. I meant to go downstairs, but I stopped as I passed the door to my room. I thought of the long curved staircase down to the parlour, and I pictured those steps, stretching for miles and miles. Then I seemed to remember that there were several complicated turns to make . . . to the right, to the left, to the left, back to the right. The journey began to take on the importance of a long trek, requiring, it seemed to me, the equipment of a safari, and the natural fortitude of an explorer with a pith helmet and three days' growth of beard. "It would be foolish," I said to myself, "to go so far, when I can be so happy right here!"

'I went into the room, undressed, climbed into bed and closed my eyes. When I opened them again, you were in the room with me.'

CHAPTER TWENTY-THREE

Alice Burton smiled reassuringly as Clara finished her story. 'Well, my dear,' said the older woman, 'you've had quite a night of it. But I wouldn't worry if I were you. You may feel terribly ashamed now, but in a few days your memory of the opium party should be no worse than the memory of a bad dream. Meanwhile, you've had some very interesting and valuable experiences – experiences which will contribute greatly to your development as a sensual human being, and as a woman. I'm especially pleased to learn that you rediscovered on your own some of the pleasures of lesbian love which I first introduced to you. And now' – she smiled enticingly – 'if you'd like to explore some of these pleasures a bit further, I'd be more than happy to serve as your guide. I just happen to have in my room a dildo very much like the one Bess showed you. I fancy that I know a few tricks she doesn't. Why don't you come with me and – '

'Oh, no,' Clara interrupted, her facial expression testifying to her apparent alarm. 'I'd never do those things again.' Then, as if realising that Alice might take offence at her refusal, she added quickly: 'I mean, Alice, I'm not quite ready for any more sex right now. I feel much too ashamed and embarrassed. But perhaps later – ' She let the sentence trail off.

'Of course,' said Alice knowingly. 'I understand completely.' She got up from the bed. 'Still, we can spend the rest of the day together if you like. That is, unless you've made plans to pass your time with someone else. . . .'

'As a matter of fact,' replied Clara quickly 'I'm expecting a visit from Conrad. He's taking me to the Black Mass tonight, and we're supposed to have a part in the ceremony. I think he might want to rehearse.'

'Of course.' Alice's smile was pained. 'Perhaps I should leave now, then. Or would you like me to stay with you until he gets here?'

'I'd like very much for you to stay. But I do expect him soon. . . .'

As if on cue, Garnett pounded a shave-and-a-haircut rhythm on the door, then poked his head inside. 'Ah, what a lovely afternoon!' he beamed enthusiastically. 'And here you two are missing the best part of it! Or should I say that you've found something better than weather to gratify your senses?'

'Don't be so *gauche*, Conrad,' scolded Alice Burton. 'All we were doing is talking.'

'In bed, of course,' observed the devil's advocate.

'If I've learned to spend most of my time in bed, Conrad, it's because you taught me to,' said Clara tartly. 'And why didn't you wait for me to answer your knock before you barged in? Your manners are abominable.'

'Oh well,' mused Garnett, 'here at La Casa Blanca, amenities aren't always observed.'

'Isn't he so gallant,' said Alice dryly.

Garnett flopped into an armchair and lighted a cigarette. 'Gallantry, shmallantry. Clara's *my* date, Alice.'

'How bitchy. How absolutely bitchy.'

'She's right, Conrad,' said Clara. 'You're a total demon this afternoon.'

Garnett smiled. 'Ah, yes. Oh my, yes. Oh-my-ass.' He blew a thin stream of smoke towards the ceiling. 'But I didn't come here to swap insults, ladies. I came to invite you to poolside for a little sun and a little water. What say you both slip into your bathing suits and join me?'

Alice got up from the bed. 'That's a hint if I ever heard

one – seeing as how I'll have to go to my room to put my bathing suit on. But I'll overlook your impoliteness this afternoon, Conrad, because frankly I'd like nothing more than a little sun right now.' She crossed the room to the door. 'I'll meet you both at the pool in ten minutes. And, if you're a second late, I'll think the worst of both of you.' Smiling lasciviously, she made her exit.

'You really are a boor, Conrad,' said Clara when the door was shut behind Alice. 'You made Alice feel very badly.'

Garnett took another drag on his cigarette. 'So much the worse for her. We've got business to discuss. And it's important enough that I'm not even going to try to feel you up while I tell you about it.'

'Well, well, well!' said Clara. 'It must really be important.'

'It is.' Garnett ground out his cigarette in an ash tray and leaned forward in his chair. 'Everything's all set for the Black Mass tonight. You're going to serve as the altar on which the Mass will be celebrated. And, after the High Priest has annointed you with wine, I, as the Deacon, will devirginate you.'

'What does this have to do with our trapping The Scorpion?'

'You'll see. As for now, all I can say is this: follow my instructions and leave everything to me. I'm the only one who'll tell you what to do. If anyone else gives you an order or a command, don't obey or answer. Just remain silent. Speak only if and when I tell you to. But let me warn you: if you don't cooperate fully in everything I say, I won't be responsible for the consequences. I want you to understand, Clara, that this will not be a dangerous undertaking if you obey me fully. But if you disobey, the experience could be disastrous. Do I make myself clear?'

'Quite clear, Conrad.'

'Good. Now, as concerns the details: after dinner tonight, I want you to return here to your room. At ten o'clock, a woman will come for you. She'll be gowned in black, and she'll be wearing a black mask. She'll bring you everything you'll need for the ceremony, including underwear and shoes as well as your outer wearing apparel. I took the liberty of checking your dress and shoe sizes yesterday morning while you were asleep, so the garments will all fit.'

'You're really very thorough, aren't you?'

'I try to be. Anyway, I suggest that you wear a dressing gown with nothing under it when the woman arrives. That way you won't have to waste time undressing. You must be ready to leave here at 11:30 at the very latest, and you'll need all of an hour and a half to prepare yourself. The Black Mass is scheduled to start at precisely twelve, and delays will not be tolerated.'

'Where do you fit into the picture?' Clara asked. 'I mean, when will I see you? And what will we do together?'

'You'll get the answers to those questions in due time. As for now, all I can tell you is to follow the instructions of the woman who comes to dress you. More than that you don't need to know.' He got up from his chair. 'Now, get your bathing suit on and let's go to the pool. I want to mingle with some of the people I'm spying on, and every minute we waste here is a minute we could use to much better advantage elsewhere.'

Clara got out of bed, fished her bathing suit from a dresser drawer and withdrew to the bathroom to change. Garnett watched the tantalising movements of her lithe young body as she moved about the room, but he made no attempt to follow her into the bathroom. When she emerged dressed in the bathing suit, he beamed approvingly at her and ran his palm appreciatively across her firm, round buttocks. Then he led her down the stairs to the pool.

At poolside, he and she joined Alice Burton for a round of drinks. They chatted a while, then Garnett wandered off with Blanca Mason. Alice and Clara spent the rest of the afternoon together, discussing Alice's ideas about sex and sensuality. Then it was dinner time, and Conrad returned to escort the two ladies to the dining room. Soon the meal was over and Clara returned alone to her room. The time was 9:30. The big moment was rapidly drawing near.

CHAPTER TWENTY-FOUR

At exactly ten o'clock, there was a knock on Clara's door. Clara, wearing nothing but a wrap-around dressing gown and a pair of satin slippers, admitted her caller – a slender, black-clad figure who stood at the threshold clutching a large cardboard box.

The caller entered the room and closed the door behind her. She was enveloped in an enormous hooded cloak of black satin which concealed both her figure and her hair. Her mask, woven of jet beads, allowed her to see and breathe with complete freedom, while at the same time it completely obscured features.

The apparition – or so she seemed to be, so silent was she – now glided to the vanity table and laid her parcel on it. She opened the box carefully, beckoning to Clara with one black-gloved finger to join her. Clara crossed to the table as bidden. Her visitor withdrew from the box an array of vials, tubes, bottles and brushes. Then she proceeded to make up the young girl's face, lavishly enhancing her eyes with black mascara and glossy white eyeshadow, rouging her cheeks and lips heavily.

Next the mysterious woman took a small green bottle with an atomiser head and began to spray a peculiarly musky perfume over Clara, litreally from head to toe, paying particular attention to the ripe red berries which crowned her two snow-white breasts and to the ruby treasure nestled beneath the silky locks curling delicately between her legs. Then, putting the atomiser aside, she lightly rouged the nipples and the lips of the welted slit, crimsoning to perfection their already-rosy complexion.

Now the silent chambermaid began to manicure Clara's nails, completing the process of applying several coats of white, frosty enamel to each shell-like oval. While the polish dried, she sprayed Clara's hair with lacquer. Clara sat silently, her hands on the table, fingers slightly spread, seemingly awed by her mute visitor, who now swept all the toilet articles back into the box.

Next the woman took from the box an armful of white, lacy lingerie. She motioned to Clara to stand up. Then she fastened a fine white garter about the girl's alabaster loins. The garter was followed by a lacy brassiere, custom-made to clasp in front. After that were stockings, gossamer-sheer, and a pair of white lace step-ins.

Now the black-clad figure drew from the seemingly bottomless box a tissuepaper-wrapped garment, which she placed on the bed. Carefully, she folded back the protective wrapping and lifted out a white, silk-brocade, floor-length sheath. She held it out to Clara, and the young girl gasped with delight. 'Oh,' she cried, speaking for the first time since the visitor had entered the room, 'Oh, it's gorgeous.'

It was obviously a hand-made garment, one with which the designer and the dress-maker had apparently taken great pains – for unlike most evening gowns of the day, it did not fasten at the back, but rather, in the front, by means of a zipper which ran the entire length of the gown. The zipper was cleverly concealed by a panel of fabric which blended so perfectly into the rest of the material that it was completely unnoticeable. The style of the gown was starkly simple. It had fitted, full-length sleeves and a high mandarin neck. The only decorative touch lay in the long side slits, which were ornamented with seed pearls.

Clara hastily slipped her arms into the sleeves of the magnificent creation, and her mysterious maid knelt and zipped the zipper up to the neck. She motioned Clara before the mirror. Once again the girl gasped. 'Why, it fits as though it were made for me!' she cried. 'As though it were moulded to my body.'

And indeed it did. The rich fabric clung to every curve of the supple young body, displaying every nuance, betraying every subtlety. The side slits rose to the lower part of Clara's luscious thighs, parting temptingly each time the girl took a step, revealing glimpses of flesh smooth and white as marble. The black-cloaked apparition nodded her approval, then delved back into the box to produce a pair of white lace wrist-length gloves, a pair of white brocade sling-back pumps and a white florist's box. The pumps were handed to Clara, the gloves and box placed on the vanity table. Then the silent figure took from the box a hood of chantilly lace, set with seed pearls. This she slipped over Clara's head. It looked rather like a bridal veil: from under its heavy crown of pearls, lace billowed prettily, falling to Clara's chin, where it was tucked and pleated so that it ballooned out at the hem, creating a bubble-like effect.

The mute aide now applied the finishing touches to Clara's toilette. Once more she took the green atomiser and sprayed the young girl head to foot, innundating the fabric of both the gown and veil with a sweetly heavy odour. Next, she handed Clara the gloves. Then back she plunged into the box for another tissuepaper-wrapped package, this time a white satin, floor-length cape with a mandarin collar, white pearl buttons and slits for the arms. This she helped Clara into, leaving the girl to button it herself, as she returned to the florist's box and produced a large and extraordinarily beautiful camellia.

The silent figure pinned the flower to the cape, then stapped back to examine her work. Nodding approval, she beckoned Clara to follow her.

'I'm sorry,' said Clara, 'but, before we go, could I . . . I mean . . . I guess I should have gone before, but . . . the excitement and everything . . .' She indicated the bathroom with a wave of her hand. Her chaperone nodded consent, and Clara, handing her gloves to the masked figure, hastened through the bathroom door.

When Clara returned, her silent companion led her down the hallway and out of the house. She then guided her along a path which led through a nearby wood to a large cabin, built in the style of a Swiss chalet. The thick, oak door to the cabin was decorated with a wrought iron knocker in the shape of a scorpion.

Now the black-cloaked figure lifted the scorpion and let it fall, producing a crash which resounded loudly in the soft stillness of the night. Almost immediately the door opened and the two cloaked figures were admitted into the dark, candle-lit interior of the chalet. The thick door closed heavily behind them.

Clara found herself in a large, wood-pannelled room, the only furnishings of which were ten oak benches, arranged haphazardly, and four, gigantic carved candelabra, each of which held six, three-foot-high black candles. On the far wall was a door. Clara's masked companion led her through it. A moment passed, then the door opened again, and Garnett, magnificent in a flowing black cape, came striding into the room.

The Devil's Advocate glanced at his watch, then at the two cloaked figures. 'Good,' he said, 'it's only 11:15. You're early. That gives us plenty of time.' He took Clara by the shoulders and peered appreciatively into her sparkling blue eyes. 'Well,' he smiled, 'let's look at you.' He put his arm around her, then drew back and surveyed her with a pleased expression. 'Very nice,' he beamed. 'Especially on such short notice. Well, kitten, are you happy with your outfit?'

'Oh, yes, Conrad, very happy. It's just beautiful. Why, I feel amlost like a bride . . .'

Garnett looked from Clara to her black-clad chaperone, then back again, an ironic smile on his lips. 'Very pretty,' he murmured. 'Very pretty indeed. The black and the white. I trust, Clara, that the significance of the two colours has not escaped you. Black and white; evil and good – impurity and purity. You do get it, don't you, Clara?'

'Why, yes, Conrad, I get it. Why do you ask?'

He ignored the question. 'Ah, black and white,' he went on, appearing almost to be talking to himself. 'It seems almost a shame to spoil it – to sully the pure, to stain the whiteness. Yes it seems almost a shame. And such a lovely contrast. The black and the white, the virtuous and the debauched.' Suddenly his tone sharpened, and he seemed to snap out of the reverie. 'The young lady seated next to you, Clara,' he said, 'is my acolyte. She will assist in every step of your defloration. Just as she robed you tonight, she will also disrobe you. She will stand by me throughout the entire act. It is she who will hold you down if you show the slightest signs of resistance, and it is she who will prepare the way for the ultimate penetration.'

Clara turned towards the black masked figure, who remained deathly silent.

'Don't you think you should thank her, Clara?' asked Garnett.

'Thank her?' echoed Clara.

'Yes, thank her. For acting as my acolyte, for assisting me tonight. Go ahead, Clara, thank her.'

'Th . . . thank you,' stammered Clara.

The masked head acknowledged the expression of gratitude with a brief nod.

'And now,' said Garnett, 'Aren't you curious about the identity of this acolyte? Haven't you wondered what face lurks under that mask? Is it perhaps the face of someone you know? An acquaintance? Maybe your charming hostess, Blanca Mason? Or the delightful Miss Lynd. Or perhaps a more intimate friend? Maybe Alice Burton?' His eyes took on a glazed look, and his right hand began stroking the bulge in his robe. 'Or perhaps an even more intimate acquaintance?' He raised his left hand almost imperceptibly. The girl's black-gloved fingers lifted the mask just as he said: 'Your sister, perhaps!'

Clara, whirled towards the figure. 'Rita!' she shrieked.

'Rita!!!' She fell on the other girl's neck and kissed her hysterically. 'Oh, my God' she whispered. 'Oh, my God!' She drew back then, seemingly in horror. 'What have they done to you, Rita? What have they done to you that you can do this to me? To help . . . to watch . . oh, God! What have they done to you?'

Rita leaned forward and took Clara's hand in hers. Then, for the first time, she spoke.

'Listen to me, Clara,' she said. Her voice was gentle, almost compassionate. 'I want you to understand that I didn't want to do it. Believe me I didn't.' She spoke slowly and coolly, her calmness contrasting as sharply with Clara's hysteria as her black garments contrasted with the younger girl's white ones. The sincerity in her voice was unmistakable as she went on: 'But I had to do it. He forced me to do it, Clara. I tried to refuse. I tried to argue, even to bargain, but I couldn't. He insisted. He said he'd never touch me again if I didn't assist in your defloration. You know.' she added in a clinically impersonal tone, 'I love you. You're my sister. You're the only family I've got. I wouldn't hurt you for the world. But if he insisted on it, I'd kill you. That's how much he means to me. I'll do anything he tells me to. Just as long as he loves me, just as long as he keeps on making love to me, I'll do anything he wants.'

Clara seemed totally stunned. 'Who are you talking about?' she asked. 'Who is this man who can make you say such evil things?'

Rita looked surprised. 'Why, the Scorpion,' she replied.

'The Scorpion!' Clara gasped. 'Who is he, Rita? You must tell me.'

Now Rita looked incredulous. 'You mean you don't know?' She glanced towards Garnett for confirmation. 'She really doesn't know?' she asked him.

'No, she doesn't know,' he replied. 'But I think that now is as good a time as any to tell her. Clara, what would you say if I told you that in one hour from now you'll be deflowered by . . . the Scorpion?'

A tiny shriek rose from Clara's throat. 'No!' she whispered. 'Oh, no, Conrad. You promised. You said it would be you. Nobody else! You promised!'

'Precisely. And I never break a promise.'

'But . . . you said . . . but . . . I don't understand . . .' Clara stammered. 'If you're going to do it, how can the Scor . . .' She broke off suddenly. 'Oh, no. *No! You!* I don't believe it. You're lying to me. You're making a joke. I don't believe it. I won't. I won't.'

Rita put her arms around her sister's shaking shoulders and hugged the younger girl close. 'It's true, Clara,' she said. 'Conrad *is* the Scorpion.'

'No!' wailed Clara. 'No! No! I won't believe it. She sobbed wildly for several minutes. Then, suddenly, she grew still. She raised her head from Rita's breast and turned to Garnett. 'You tell me,' she said. 'I want to hear you say it.'

'It's true,' he said.

'No. Say the whole thing. Go ahead. Say it. Say: "I, Conrad Garnett, attorney-at-law, am the Scorpion. Go on, say it.'

'Clara,' chuckled Garnett, 'this is foolishness.'

'I don't care. I won't move until you say it. If you want me out there, you'll have to carry me. And rape me. And the whole time I'll scream. I'll scream until you'll have to knock me unconscious, because you won't be able to stand it any more. Believe me, Conrad. I mean it.'

'All right,' said the Devil's advocate wearily, 'I, Conrad Garnett, attorney-at-law, am the Scorpion. Are you happy now?'

'Yes,' said Clara with surprising steadiness, 'very happy.' She gave Garnett an almost radiant smile. 'You did everything I asked you to. You found my sister, and you uncovered the Scorpion. Of course, it was a great shock, all coming at once like this. But, now that I think of it, how can I really be angry with you, when all you did was what I asked you to do?' She smiled at Rita and kissed her soundly. Then she ran lightly to Garnett and kissed him, too. 'My sister loves you.' she said. 'And I love her. If it'll make her happy, then I'll do anything you ask.'

'Including being branded with a scorpion?' asked Rita.

Clara's eyes widened, but she answered sombrely: 'Yes, including being branded with a scorpion.'

Garnett shook his head incredulously. 'Women! he said. Then he glanced at his watch. 'But the hour grows late. The ceremony is about to begin. Put on your mask, Rita. And come with me, both of you.' He opened the door and extended his arms sideways. Each sister linked one of her arms through one of his, and the trio made its way back to the main chamber.

Several changes had taken place in the large room during the three quarters of an hour that Garnett and the two girls had been away. For one thing, the benches were now arranged in neat rows, resembling church pews, and there were about thirty people, all in evening dress, seated on them. Also, in the space between the two inner doors, there had been constructed a high platform, with a movable stairway pushed up against it. The platform was draped in black velvet. On it was a small lectern, holding a heavy, Bible-like book and a gigantic crucifix, positioned upside down. A similar crucifix, also inverted, stood at the door.

Garnett ushered the sisters to a bench in the first row, directly in front of the platform. The trio seated itself just as a chime sounded, then another and another until twelve chimes had rung. As the twelfth one died out, an organ resounded through the chamber.

A hush now came over the assemblage as the door at the left of the room opened, admitting a procession of black-robed and masked men. The men carried slim, black, lighted tapers and paraded silently about the room, positioning themselves at regularly spaced intervals.

Garnett looked up with a start.

'What is it?' whispered Rita.

'This wasn't planned,' he whispered back. 'I didn't tell Blanca anything about bringing in any guys with candles. Something's funny.'

'Don't be silly,' hissed Rita. 'Maybe she just forgot to tell you. Who's the priest, anyway?'

Garnett grinned and looked at Clara. 'An old friend of your sister's,' he said to Rita. It was Clara's turn to start. 'Who?' she gasped.

'Can't you guess?'

'No. Tell me.'

'John Webster.'

'Oh.' Clara grinned mirthlessly, but she seemed somehow relieved. 'Some friend he is.'

'And there he is,' whispered Garnett, momentarily distracted from his worries over the unexpected change in procedure as the door on the left once again swung open and a tall figure, clad in richly-jewelled black velvet, a cowl over his features, walked through the doorway and mounted the stairs to the platform.

The organ swelled to a crescendo, then fell silent as the Black Priest raised his hand. As if on cue, the hooded men around the room snuffed out their candles.

'Okay, don't anybody move,' said the man on the platform. 'My men are armed, and they've got you covered. This is a raid.'

CHAPTER TWENTY-FIVE

The corridor is long and dark. It leads to a cell. The guard ushers you into the cell, then slams the door shut. You're alone.

Yes Garnett, you're alone.

Alone.

And under arrest.

You never thought it'd come to that, did you?

But it did, didn't it?

And now here you are.

So what do you have to say for yourself?

Not much, huh?

No, not much.

You won't say anything, because you know that anything you say will be held against you.

And you don't have to say anything.

They really have the goods on you.

They can put you away for the rest of your life.

And all because you pushed things a little too far.

Sure, it was fun while it lasted.

But now it's over.

The chickens have come home to roost.

And you're at the end of the line.

What was it the D.A. said?

Crimes against nature . . .

Unlawful possession of narcotics . . .

Indecent displays . . .

Running a house of prostitution . . .

Yep.

They really threw the book at you.

And you couldn't even duck, because the evidence was overwhelming.

What you need is a real good lawyer – the best lawyer in the business.

Unfortunately, he's indisposed . . .

Roman Orgy

CHAPTER ONE

The slim fingers of the Egyptian slave girl trembled lightly as she guided the penis of her master, Lucius Crispus, into the bronze urn. She pulled back the skin to make it easier for him. She wanted to look away but she didn't for fear she would make a mistake which might cost her a lashing.

Senator Crispus, whose banquet it was, lay drunkenly on his side on the couch and relieved himself noisily into the urn. His hand wavered up and fondled the buttocks of the girl as she bent over her task. The long stola which she wore to indicate she was not just any slave, but the slave of Lucius Crispus, did nothing to hide the sleek bulges of her flesh from his caressing fingers. His long, white member thickened slightly in her hand, but then she had drawn the urn away and was gliding quietly away herself. Lucius Crispus turned his attention wistfully towards his guests.

They numbered a good thirty including the few women which his wife Clodia had insisted on inviting for company. Looking around at them where they chatted animatedly on their couches, stuffing themselves with his best wine, Crispus could not repress a smirk of satisfaction. They were drawn from some of the oldest and best patrician families of Rome and they had all come to the fine house of their fellow senator, he who had started life as a small, ambitious farmer, he who could still hardly believe that he was hob-nobbing socially with the descendants of the aristocrats who had ruled Rome since its earliest days.

It was true that some he had hoped might come had sent their apologies or had simply not turned up. Before the wine had mellowed him, Crispus had suffered agonies at the thought that they might still not consider him to be of the proper clay. But now he didn't give a damn. His guests had enjoyed themselves, he knew. And why not? His wine was of the very best. His slaves, male and female, of the most comely. On the tables from which the guests took their fill were panniers of olives, dormice rolled in honey, a ram's head, crab, lobster, wild pig, truffles, succulent mushrooms, a goose —no table in Rome could have looked better. And as a special treat a boiled calf had been brought in, followed by a slave in hunting clothes.

Crispus peered hazily through the welter of sprawling bodies and what seemed like a solid din of voices until he could make out his wife chatting, calmly, with a group of people on the far side of the heavily draped room.

Clodia was one of the most beautiful women in Rome. Her reputation, unlike that of so many of her time, remained unsullied. Crispus knew he had her to thank for his rise in the world. But then, although her wealth had introduced him to new worlds, it was true that it was his good looks and clever, smooth tongue which had ensnared her. He could feel no gratitude towards her. In fact, now that the settlement was made on him, she could have gone, as far as his emotions were concerned. It was simply that his position and vanity demanded the retention of a beautiful and virtuous woman by his side. He had to admit he'd found her very cold of late.

"Well, Lucius, at the risk of being indiscreet, I say here and now that I've never known a better feast."

Crispus felt his heart warming, his face flushing with pleasure. This was the sort of confirmation he loved to hear. He twisted awkwardly towards the speaker, who was sitting behind him on the same couch. He had quite forgotten the presence of Tullius Canus.

"Could have been better, could have been better," he said with hypocritical modesty.

"Well, of course, we've yet to see the dancing girls—but if there were a better feast I'd like to be there."

"Ah-ha. You liked the dinner? Wait until you see these dancing girls. They're real, full-blooded barbarians from the province of Spain."

Tullius Canus raised his eyebrows, eyes gleaming with voluptuous anticipation. He reached out a pudgy hand and whisked a few olives from the nearest table.

"Nothing better than a bit of barbarian flesh," he wheezed with a wink at his nearest companions.

Crispus took another long draught of wine from a silver goblet; a long, satisfied draught. Tullius Canus, one of the most powerful and influential orators in the Senate, was notorious for his attendance at many of the orgiastic banquets of the city. His appetite was well-known. If he was pleased then there was good reason for the host to be pleased.

Crispus clapped his hands and several more huge vats of wine from the hills of Alba were brought in by his slaves. Goblets were filled and re-filled throughout the room.

"Now for the barbarians," Crispus whispered to Tullius Canus.

When he clapped his hands a second time most of his guests were too drunk, or too steeped in argument, to pay any attention. The noise of voices and laughter droned on, along with the noise of clinking goblets and the clatter of dishes. But when the Spanish maidens danced into the room, there was an immediate hush. They were completely nude.

The fame of the dancers from Spain had spread to Rome, but few had been seen up to now. It was joked that they so excited the governors of the Spanish provinces that they could not let even one out of their sight.

Crispus had, indeed, had to pull strings to obtain the two specimens now moving under the flushed eyes of the company. And he'd had to pay a stiff price as well.

The two girls weaved sensuous patterns in the central space before the couches and tables. Their long black hair swished around their shoulders and the little ebony castanets with which they clacked out a fast rhythm seemed to add a mysterious lustre to their taut, brown skins.

Watching them, Crispus unconsciously passed his tongue over his lips. Behind him he heard Tullius Canus shift his bulk, wheezing, to get a better view.

The girls were slim, but their breasts were

enormous. Their pubic hair had been shaven and their strong, slim thighs ran straight into the soft, brown flesh of their bodies.

"Did you ever see such breasts?" Tullius Canus' voice was soft, almost awed in Crispus' ear. "I've seen a few on my campaigns. I remember the woman I raped in Gaul on Caesar's last expedition. She was a wild one—and well made too. But these . . ." Words failed him and his eyes bulged.

Crispus forced his hot eyes from the supple movements of his dancers for a moment to steal a swift glance around the room. Everywhere eyes were riveted on the extraordinary proportions of the Spanish girls. His gaze swept back to them with renewed satisfaction. This was going to make him the talk of aristocratic Rome. And the younger Cato was the only one who would disapprove.

The dancers kept time with each other, clacking their castanets above their heads in gestures which raised their breasts upward, then sweeping their arms down in a windmill action to a level with their hips. Their feet pattered on the marble floor which Crispus had had specially laid for the further glory of his name.

"Beautiful . . . beautiful," Tullius breathed. And Crispus clamped his thighs eagerly together under his toga on the couch.

The dances became more and more lascivious with each of the girls weaving her hips from side to side, pushing out her breasts with a backward movement of the arms towards the guests. Their skins began to glisten with perspiration, giving a sensual oiliness to their bodies. Their buttocks brushed the food tables as they whirled and the guests, some of them laughing and making lewd gestures, others deadly serious with hot, hard eyes, began to clap in time with the castanets.

Face shining with lust and triumph, Crispus leaned forward on the couch. They were well worth the price, he told himself. It was true he had wavered, even though it was Clodia's money—but now he knew they were well worth the price.

Big, bulbous breasts swaying from side to side, seeming about to swing away from contact with their bodies, the girls bent slowly at the knees until they were half squatting, buttocks a couple of feet from the floor. In that position they began a last wild convulsive dance in which their hips seemed to undulate apart from them, describing incredible circles in the air. With every fifth circling they would plunge their rumps down to within a few inches of the cold marble as if running themselves onto a phallus. Every man in the room wished he could have been lying there on the cool marble beneath those plunging thighs to skewer up inside the warm, soft depths of the brown bodies with each descent they made to the floor.

Breathing was heavy in all parts of the room, faces flushed with wine and desire, bodies moving, shuffling uneasily on the luxurious couches.

Clodia must hate this use being made of her wealth, Crispus thought with a chuckle, and involuntarily he raised his eyes to where Clodia reclined on one of the far couches. He was surprised to see she was not looking at the dancers at all. Her glance was directed at the darker extremities of the room. There was a curious expression on her face which he could not fathom. He tried to follow her gaze, but all he could see were guests, with slaves waiting on them. Nobody was looking at Clodia.

The Spanish maidens were now making a last tour of the room, hips weaving a sinuous pattern in the hot air. Their castanets had fallen from their fingers and now dangled from their wrists on slender gold chains. Their hands clasped the underside of their breasts and offered the full globes with their lush, ripe nipples to the choking aristocrats of Rome. Their hips thrust forward suggestively, thighs wide apart and offering. A single movement would have taken any man they passed right between those lovely legs which promised such delight. But no man moved to break the voluptuous spell which had been cast.

When the girls disappeared, with a final backside quiver at the eyes which followed them right to one of the entrances to the room, there was a momentary hush. All eyes turned to Crispus and suddenly the room echoed with clapping and wild applause.

"Bravo, bravo," Tullius Canus chuckled behind Crispus. "That little spectacle alone is worth any man's place in the Senate."

"I should bring them back for another dance?" Crispus suggested, his bloodshot eyes warm with delight.

"Ah—no." Tullius lowered his voice. "That would be a mistake. Don't overdo it. Bring them out every time you have a dinner and your name will go down through the centuries and be remembered even longer than Sulla's. By Jupiter I can see you ruling political decisions of the Senate with your offers to show the beauty of Spanish flesh." Tullius broke into a roar of deep, contagious laughter which soon had one side of the room rocking. Taking cover of the din, he bent towards Crispus and whispered:

"Give me but one of your beauties tonight and I'll boost your name as the finest host in Imperial Rome—and give my allegiance in the Senate into the bargain."

"Done!" Crispus whispered back.

The two men sat grinning at each other for a few seconds until Crispus became aware of the hot tension at his loins.

"Excuse me," he said, and looked around for the Egyptian slave girl.

She was standing with averted eyes close to one of the doors. She took badly to slavery. It was said she had been snatched from the Egyptian court, a girl of noble blood.

Crispus clapped his hands and through the resumed babble of voices and laughter the girl turned her face toward her new master and slid quietly through the couches with the urn clasped in her hand.

"This is a beauty of a different sort," Tullius said behind him. "A timid deer. What is she like with a man between her legs?"

"I had cause to give her a lashing soon after her arrival and she squirmed nicely," Crispus replied. "But as to how she wriggles with a staff in her body I couldn't say."

"What!" Tullius' voice was a bellow, which

he controlled with difficulty. "You mean to say you've not yet given her the pleasure of a Roman rod in her cranny—an aristocrat's at that?"

Crispus felt his heart beat in gratitude at his alignment with the aristocracy.

The slave girl reached him and fumbled under his toga, pulling it awry to find him. Yes, it had been an oversight, he admitted to himself. But even now there was something which made him wary of raping his slaves—but perhaps it was the noble blood in the girl. And then he scorned the idea. Was he not, himself, accepted as nobility? Had Tullius not just referred to him as such?

The girl's fingers had found the thick tower of flesh and were delicately performing their unaccustomed task of pulling it into view. It was stiff as a Roman sword.

Trembling, the girl held the great erection over the urn. She had vivid, painful memories of the similar weapons with which she had been violated by two Roman centurions, one after the other. She wanted to run away, but her back still smarted from the whipping she'd received for refusing to perform this function a few days ago. She was very frightened.

The hot flesh moved in her hand, seeming to expand. She held up the urn a little while Crispus and the great pig-like man behind him talked in a language she didn't understand and roved hot, drunken eyes over her. Crispus did not relieve himself and she was forced to stand, bending over, holding his sweating organ in her hand—waiting.

"Difficult to see her under that stola," Tullius was saying. "You should dress her in a tunic, Lucius."

Crispus was looking at the girl, at her huge dark eyes, her small, slightly flattened nose, full, crimson lips and that long dark hair which had been torn out from its neat bun by Roman hands and now cascaded around her shoulders like that of the Spanish dancers.

She was quite small. When she walked towards him he could see the slightly outlined mounds of her breasts under the loose-fitting stola, he could see the lines of her thighs as she moved, and now as she bent sideways before him, he could see where the cloth indented slightly between her buttocks, billowing out on either side, tracing the ovals of her rump. His flesh throbbed in her hand.

"You like her? She's quite a beauty, too, in her way," he said over his shoulder.

"Well I know, by Jupiter, that I'd have been athwart her by now," Tullius said, shuffling. "Why don't you strip her, Lucius, and let's see the quality of your latest slave."

As the slave girl felt Crispus' hands pulling at her stola she was tempted to resist. But she was completely in his power. She had no recourse to justice. Her mind sank into bewildered submission. Only recently, it was said, a slave had broken his master's favorite vase and half the slave household had been killed and beaten as a punishment.

All those around Crispus' couch drew closer as they saw the slave girl's stola being pulled over her head. Her calves were slim and shapely as they came into view, her thighs slim and strong and then her hips, with creases in the flesh following the bones, dark hair lightly covering the jut of flesh above her mound. Her buttocks were firm and oval, dimpled and seeming to squirm away from the light which suddenly, rudely revealed them.

Forcing her to bend before him, hearing Tullius' approving clucks and wheezing behind him, Crispus pulled the stola over her head and flung it to the marble floor.

The girl tried to cover her breasts with her hands, but Crispus knocked them away with a threatening gesture and the firm, pointed orbs swayed before the lustful eyes of the company.

"Jupiter, she is a sweet little beauty," Tullius hissed. "She must have been at pains to hide that from you."

Crispus felt a little irked. He felt slightly foolish in the eyes of his guests that he had not taken advantage of the sexual splendors of his new slave before this.

Frightened and bewildered, the girl had risen to her feet and taken Crispus' penis once more to direct it at the urn. Crispus felt it pulsating at her touch. He wriggled slightly on the couch and her hand slipped on the flesh. His face flamed and his heart thumped loudly.

"If you don't ram her now instead of trying to piddle in that pot, I shall beg leave to," Tullius said hoarsely.

Crispus became aware that the whole company was now watching, amused and lustful. He could see Clodia, too, watching him with expressionless eyes from among the women.

"Go on, have her, have her," Tullius urged,

"and give a lead to your guests. Hospitality demands that you show your guests the way and then offer them like facilities."

"Go on Lucius—and then pass her over." The cry was taken up by all near the host.

Crispus was sweating with desire. After all, this sort of thing was not uncommon in the very best houses. It should never be said that he was lacking in one iota of hospitality . . .

He made an indication to the girl and she began to move her hand gently up and down his staff.

Feeling terribly helpless in her nudity, the girl obeyed her master's instructions, revolting though she found them. The presence of dozens of pairs of eyes all ransacking her nakedness, leering at her body and her actions, filled her with a further undefined terror so that she tried to forget the room, the lewd faces and just concentrate on the gentle massage of the horrible organ in her hand.

She cringed with fright as she felt Crispus' large hand stroke up her thigh and fondle her buttocks. The touch of his flesh on hers was a physical shock which almost robbed her of breath. His hand was holding her bottom, squeezing it, fingers probing lecherously between her buttocks.

All around loud, coarse voices were talking, with eyes which never left her body. Her knowledge of Latin was increasing with each day that passed but she recognized none of the words which filled the hot air around her.

And now the fat, piggish man was moving off the couch and Crispus was pulling her towards it to the lustful cheers of his guests. She pulled back in sheer, blind terror, but he jerked her savagely onto the couch beside him, muttering something furiously, daring her with his bloodshot eyes to disobey him.

She lay on her back on the couch with a ring of faces pressing around and glaring down on her and Crispus' hand fumbling over her breasts which jutted helplessly toward the eyes above. He was degrading her; he didn't care what he did in front of all these men—and women too. He was sucking on her nipples so that sharp pains shot down in her chest. He was squeezing the plump flesh of her bosom, tweaking it, pressing it. She would rather have been buried alive.

And now he was forcing her legs wide and his vile fingers were exposing her sex, revealing it to all the world which seemed to be contained in the circle of obscene, salacious faces above her. Crispus' hands were running, trembling, all over her body, roughly as if he wanted to tear her into pieces. His breath jerked as his fingers squeezed the flesh of her belly and she could feel the stark, hot mass of him on her thigh.

She felt lost in a horror from which no god could save her. All these bawdy faces were evil gods, too powerful for anyone to help her; she was descending into the bowels of the earth. And then she cried out in horror, and pain shot through her belly. Her breath constricted under her breasts as the rigid flesh of Crispus seared into her. He drove into her mercilessly, every thrust feeling as if it were doing her some horrible internal injury. He forced her legs wide, abandoning her channel and his surging, violating member to the gaze of the eyes which seemed to dance and laugh, become pink and green, around them. His mouth descended on hers, sucking it, containing it in his; his hands grasped her waist in a vice, pawed her breasts, slid under her buttocks and strained them to his shaggy belly. She was degraded forever.

"Oooh, what a punishment! What delight!"

It was the voice of Tullius which penetrated Crispus' ears as he jerked in tight, tingling fury into the violated passage of his slave. Crispus' body, as he bucked on the soft flesh beneath him, was a mass of strains and gaspings. Her body was unworldly delight. It was the first time he'd had a woman obviously against her will and he gained a sadistic thrill from forcing her into extreme positions, from ramming into her with teeth-gritting brutality.

Under him she was moaning. Her eyes were screwed tight with pain. Her slim legs were pressed wide, flat against the couch on either side of him.

Flinging his hips at her crotch, he grasped her slim, warm shoulders, and fixed his mouth like a leech on hers. He forced her lips apart, biting them, and pushed his tongue into her mouth. His hands trembled over the sleek bulges of her breasts, gripped the flesh-covered bones of her hips. He took long, slow strokes deep into her body. He didn't want it to end. It was such pain, delight, pain, delight, on and on.

He could hear the drone of coarse, jocular, lustful remarks around him, but he heard nothing specifically, just an accompaniment of noise to the pressure in his groin. And the pressure was growing and growing, his breath gasping hoarsely and dryly, his whole body shuddering —and then the shuddering was a great furious convulsion of hot, burning liquid fire.

Crispus lay on her, body heaving with effort, heart thumping.

He heard the voice of Tullius Canus:

"Come on Lucius. Don't faint on the job. Move over."

CHAPTER TWO

Among the many pairs of eyes which had witnessed the using of the Egyptian slave girl by Lucius Crispus, was a pair of cool grey. At the moment they were hard eyes, very hard eyes.

They belonged in a face which any Emperor would have been proud of: a broad, strong face with a square jutting chin, a straight fine mouth and a broad forehead from which the eyes looked deeply out, hard and unafraid. A face which could have made a kingdom into an Empire, a face which was going to lead ten thousand men to their doom. The face of a slave.

It was during the lecherous performance of Lucius Crispus that the slave became aware of Clodia's eyes upon him—as they had so often been upon him of late. As Crispus was urged to greater efforts by the licentious crew of Rome's aristocracy, she finally called his name.

"Spartacus!"

He turned his grey eyes toward her and walked over to her side.

As he walked, the muscles in his calves below the tunic bulged; long lengths of muscle stirred in his arms. In spite of his height—he was slightly taller than any other man present—his body radiated a potential dynamism. It seemed unlikely that he could be taken off his guard.

He bent towards his mistress and the cloth of his tunic stretched in wrinkles across his shoulders.

Clodia's eyes held his with a look he could not understand as she said quietly:

"I'm tired of this. I'm going to bathe. I shall need you to stand guard over the door."

She bade goodnight to her women guests who watched her sympathetically as she left. It was very hard on her, her husband acting like this in public, and Clodia such a beautiful woman and not one man noticing her leave. It was a wonder she didn't divorce him—or get herself a lover.

Spartacus strode silently after her, leaving the noise of the banquet behind, through the portico flanking the huge quadrilateral, which in turn enclosed the gardens with their walks and arbors and the baths which Crispus had had specially built to the pattern and proportions of the huge public thermae.

It was not unusual for Spartacus to be asked to accompany his mistress. He was the head of the several hundred slaves which Crispus boasted as his entourage and he occupied a comparatively privileged position. Descended from the Thracian princes, he could boast at least as much culture as his master—which he had to admit was not saying an awful lot—and he knew himself to be more of a man.

But lately, it seemed, Clodia had been singling him out to be with her in nearly everything she did, everywhere she went. He had become, virtually, her personal bodyguard.

Watching her walk before him through the torch-lit porticos, Spartacus wondered why she stayed in Crispus' house. It was well known— even among the slaves—that he treated her badly. There was nothing to stop her leaving.

Spartacus' lips tightened as his mind dwelt on Crispus. His master treated nobody well, in fact, except those he considered of superior rank and birth on whom he fawned his attentions or whom he tried desperately to impress — not without success.

Spartacus was aware that Crispus regarded him with a certain reluctant respect, which he felt sometimes bordered on hatred. For a long time he had been at a loss to understand this, but eventually it had dawned on him that, to his master, he represented the threat of enslaved but superior classes who in different circumstances would have thought him nothing but an ignorant upstart. There were many such slaves; cultured Greeks and Egyptians, many of them.

He wondered why Crispus did not put him in the slave market at times, to be rid of him, but then again it had dawned on him that he represented a challenge. If Crispus got rid of him, he would have admitted his inability to dominate, admitted defeat.

Following Clodia into the bath buildings, Spartacus wondered why she should require him to accompany her. Was she afraid one of her guests might wander away from the banquet and try to take liberties with her?—nobody would dare. Was she afraid of her slaves? They wouldn't dare—besides he was a slave. Spartacus became suddenly aware of the intimacy of leaving the bright, noisy company and disappearing through the grounds with his mistress to guard her while she bathed.

"Wait here."

Clodia left him with this command and disappeared into one of the dressing rooms just inside the building.

Spartacus stared around him in the flickering torchlight. Beyond was a large vaulted hall, its walls of blue and white stone mosaic. The center of the roof was taken up by a large space in the vaulting through which the sun poured at noon and the stars glittered at night. In the middle of the floor was the great bronze basin of water, water which steamed now from the heat of the hypocausta beneath.

The slaves were never allowed to use these baths, which had separate hours—like the public baths—for men and women. It was still permissible in the public baths for mixed bathing, but it was never seen. No woman cared to sully her reputation. There had been so many scandals in the past.

In the past . . . How many years had Spartacus been here in Rome, in the great town house of Lucius Crispus? How many years had he listened to the suffering and indignities of the slaves? How many years since he had seen his Thracian hills, those beautiful, free, Thracian hills? How long would it go on?...

His thoughts were suddenly stopped dead by the appearance of his mistress. Without a glance at him she ran across the marble floor and disappeared down the stone steps into the warm water of the sunken bronze basin. Spartacus was dumbstruck, a hundred times more so than when he had seen the Spanish maidens dance into the banquet room. Clodia had been quite naked!

He gazed incredulously through the ill-lit gloom of the bathing room. It was so. Through the gloom and the rising vapors he could see her white body floating lazily on the surface of the greenish water. Even now he could make out—how anguishingly vague—the lines of her pale breasts, breaking the surface.

Spartacus' mind wouldn't function for some seconds. This had never been known. A Roman patrician woman undressing before a male slave! He turned and peered back through the gloom of the grounds, half afraid that he might be struck down for the sacrilege of having seen what had been paraded before him.

In that fleeting glimpse he had seen the body of one of the most beautiful women of Rome; a body which he knew many noble Romans would have given a fortune to see. Cold virtue in a beautiful woman always increased desire for her.

How could she have been so indiscreet? Why?

She could have slipped on her stola and then bathed in one of the smaller baths out of sight. It was as if she had paraded herself intentionally.

Spartacus stood, undecided, at the entrance to the building. He felt he should withdraw to the grounds just outside, but hesitated to disobey his mistress' explicit command. It seemed further sacrilege to remain where he was, particularly as Clodia was making no effort to escape his view, seemed, in fact, to be parading herself quite unconcernedly.

As he watched her misty outline, she turned on her stomach and floated, face down in the water, her long, unloosened hair streaming over her wet shoulders, rounded tips of buttocks showing like some ghostly half-submerged fish.

Spartacus folded his arms. Under his hands he felt the smooth, tight bulging of his biceps and the feeling reassured him. This was Clodia's fault. He would stay where he was.

From time to time, as he watched her leisurely lolling in the warm water, he saw her raise her head, or simply turn it, towards where he stood in the shadow of the entrance. Perhaps she was afraid he would go and leave her unprotected. Although why she should was unthinkable. To disobey an order!

Reflecting, with the image of her nudity in his head, Spartacus began to remember little incidents of the past few weeks: the way her eyes were so often upon him, the fact she had asked his advice upon some Thracian vase she had considered buying, that once her hand had rested on his arm, as if absently, when she gave him an order. Spartacus reflected on these things and gazed with his cool, grey eyes through the steam at the bronze basin.

* * *

Time passed. To Spartacus it seemed an eternity, at any moment of which he expected some guest to stray away from the noise of the banquet which he could no longer hear, and find him standing his lonely guard over the senator's naked wife.

But when at last the silent worry of his thoughts was interrupted, it was such an interruption as to fill his head with an even darker cloud of anxiety.

From the bronze basin, Clodia's cultured voice reached him. There was a trace of nervousness in the usually firm, imperious tones.

"Spartacus. A cloth and my robe are in the dressing room."

He hesitated a second or two for her to add something, but she lay back in the water, waiting.

His heart was beating a little faster than normal as he went into the dressing room. There on a wooden seat were strewn her clothes. His face flushed as his eyes passed, in the gloom, from her stola to the under tunic, the brassiere which clasped those proud breasts, the loincloth which contained those virtuous hips.

He picked up the woollen napkin and the blue robe made of the still rare silk from the mysterious Orient.

As he strode towards the pool, muscles flexing and unflexing in his powerful legs, he was filled with the foreboding of strange things. This was no ordinary night. This was no ordinary duty he was performing.

He reached the pool's edge and stood looking down into the opaque green waters where Clodia, still unconcernedly, floated. She seemed to ignore him as he gazed down at the parts of her body which showed through the steam.

Spartacus waited, while Clodia paddled. He could see the smooth slope of her white shoulders, the deep cleft of the upper part of her breast. Half lying in the water, she turned her eyes toward him.

Her face was radiant with the pale beauty, the clear-cut lines of a Roman aristocrat. Her hazel eyes were bright with a peculiar fire.

"You dislike your master, Spartacus," she said. Her voice had regained its old, firm tones.

Spartacus said nothing.

Clodia laughed. One of the few times he'd ever heard her laugh.

"Your silence condemns you. He dislikes you, too."

She hesitated and still Spartacus said nothing.

"Today he finally admitted defeat. He decided to get rid of you, sell you in the slave market."

Spartacus stared at her. So at last it had happened. But her next words astonished him.

"He wanted to sell you, but I put my foot down. Because I want to keep you."

"My lady is kind," Spartacus said softly.

"No, not kind," she said, "just self-indulgent."

Giving Spartacus no time to ponder her words, she began to raise herself to the marble floor of the baths.

He stared at her, unable to avert his eyes as she came, like a nymph, out of the water. First her breasts stunned his eyes, large, firm and white with the red smudges of nipples a startling contrast to the color of the skin. And then her belly, flat, smooth, white; and then her abdomen, with the two pink creases in the soft flesh and the black down of hair reaching to a point between her legs; and the long thighs, themselves like marble, supple, cold and beautiful.

She stood dripping in front of him. Her eyes were those of the sphinx. His lips opened slightly.

"Rub me down," she said quietly. "Have you forgotten yourself?"

The whole of Spartacus' skin all over his body seemed to be pulsating as he bent to his task. Clodia stood quietly watching the bunching of his powerful arm muscles as he wiped the moisture from her arms, her breasts, her belly, her back, her buttocks. Spartacus hesitated. Her buttocks were full, contained firmly in long sweeping lines. His hands trembled as he felt their shape and texture through the woollen napkin.

"Go on," Clodia's voice commanded from above as he knelt. Her voice sounded firm but there was a hollow undertone as if she were steeling herself. He realized suddenly that she was trembling.

His big hands moved down the backs of her thighs, shaping the almost imperceptible down into a slim arrow. His hand contained the rounded calves in the napkin and he swivelled round and rubbed up her legs in the front.

He was more aware of her trembling. Clodia shifted her legs apart, moving on the balls of her small, bare feet. Spartacus looked up at her. Her lips were parted as she looked down on him. Her eyes pierced his with a look which was command and desire and not without a tremulous undercurrent of fear.

"Go on," she said softly. There was a tremble in her voice as well as her limbs.

Spartacus hollowed his hands around the napkin and moved them up her leg. Astonishment had now given place to a masculine certainty and strength. There was no doubt in his mind, only a deep, luxurious wonder.

His hands moved up over the knee, soaking the moisture from the skin into the napkin. Through it he could feel the solidity of the thigh. He wanted to touch the thigh without the napkin, but he continued pulling the napkin, like a broken glove, up the leg to where it broadened into its fullness and his eyes were on a level with the crease of flesh between her thighs.

Once more he hesitated.

"Go on." The voice above him was a controlled Vesuvius.

Spartacus held the napkin in the flat of his right hand. With the other he boldly grasped

Clodia's thigh, his fingers denting the buttery flesh and with a long, slow movement, he wiped the napkin between her legs, dabbing it into the intimate places of her crotch.

As he felt the soft yielding flesh under the napkin flatten out against the inside of the thighs, Clodia's hand moved uncontrollably down to his head and her fingers grasped his long, fair hair and pressed his face to her lower belly.

Spartacus rose slowly up her body, his lips tracing a path up over her navel, the taut flesh of her ribs, resting on the beautiful pearl hills of her breasts, brushing the rich, hard protrusion of nipples, sucking in the hollow of her shoulder, on up the white, slender neck, until they found her lips and fastened there, his lips on those of Clodia, famed in Rome for her beauty, Clodia whose slim, smooth tongue now forced its way between his lips, between his teeth and snaked in his mouth, the mouth of her slave.

After a moment she drew away from him, trembling violently.

"Give me my robe," she said. "We must not be seen here."

Spartacus put her robe over her trembling shoulders, she pulled it tightly around her and, bidding him follow her, walked quickly away from the baths.

Walking behind her once again, Spartacus was filled with a joy of incredible discovery, an emotional power which was overwhelming. Here he was following her as he had so often followed her before—but now what a difference! Now he knew those breasts which had vaguely excited him before as they pressed through her stola. Breasts which had excited so many men in Rome; breasts so inaccessible and far away. Now he knew that slender back which shaped into the girdle of the robe as she hurried before him, knew those buttocks which were outlined by the clinging silk, those thighs over which the silk hung loosely from its swelling over the rump. Now he understood the looks which Clodia had cast toward him. Now he understood the touch on his arm. Soon she would be his, unbelievably his.

Hurrying before Spartacus, Clodia was aware that his eyes were on the tension of her buttocks under the robe. She pulled the robe tightly around her to give him a more exciting spectacle.

Now they were going to her room and she would seduce him. It was no sudden decision Clodia had made. It had been developing in her mind for months.

She was well aware of Lucius' lack of interest in her. She was no longer terribly interested in him. She had in fact made up her mind at one time to divorce him.

But then she had become suddenly aware of the slave, Spartacus. There was some magnetism in him, some superior strength of character which made her, even now, half afraid of her fascination for him.

She had seen Lucius' recognition of the same quality, had watched the battle Lucius, who could not bear to find himself in competition with a stronger man, had fought with himself. She had watched the indifference of the slave to the attempts of an inferior being to degrade him.

It was a fascination, a very physical fascination, which had kept her in Lucius' house. She would sit and watch Spartacus, his big muscles tensing in his big body as he performed his tasks; she would watch the calm, handsome face and if the cool, grey eyes alighted on her she would look quickly away lest he should notice her interest.

The desire had grown in her to touch that athletic, muscular body. A desire which had finally found its outlet a few days before when she had allowed her fingers to rest lightly on his arm while directing him to some duty.

And then she had wanted that touch, that physical communion returned. Had wanted to give, to yield under the superior power which she sensed in the man.

Even now it was a desire completely physical which drove her on. The unheard of, forbidden liaison with a slave. That taboo which gave such an emotional desperation and glory to the act.

Although, it was true, a slave could eventually become a freedman—and perhaps rise to office—there was no denying the fact that a slave, as a slave, was the scum of the Empire. Such a liaison would have the whole of Rome howling for the blood of both parties; such a liaison would resound beyond the boundaries of the peninsula to the very outposts of the Empire.

It was partly the knowledge of this that had

driven Clodia on in her desire rather than deterred her. She had a will the equal of most in the city and Spartacus, all unwittingly, had driven her towards the inevitable with every movement of his body, every look in his eyes, every one of the few words he ever uttered.

The noise of the banquet, still in progress, reached them as they walked in the shadow of the portico and mounted the steps to the upper story. Without a word, Clodia led the way through Crispus' room to her own. Starlight shone in through a window which looked out onto the quadrilateral. Spartacus moved uncertainly in the poor light and stood silent and still, while Clodia pulled a heavy shutter into place across the window. She lit torches in their brackets on the walls, and while she moved quietly to the door to close it, Spartacus looked with quick curiosity around her room, which he was seeing for the first time.

The room was dominated by Clodia's bed, the bed in which she must have spent so many lonely nights, listening perhaps to the breathing of her husband in the next room. It was a huge bed of oak. The woodwork was inlaid with tortoise-shell, the feet were made of ivory. All three materials shone with a lustre which bespoke much labor from Clodia's female slaves. There were two divans also, strewn with exotically colored cushions, and in a corner near the window space was a tripod table on which lay Clodia's mirrors of silver and a few adornments.

The furniture, as was customary in the grand houses, was sparse but superb.

After Clodia had shut the door she and Spartacus stood looking at each other for a few moments. Her beautiful face was slightly flushed; there was a tint of fear in her eyes which she tried vainly to conceal.

The interval of walking had made Spartacus wary. He was well aware of the penalty for this sort of thing and, although his length of rigidity had itched against his loincloth from the moment he'd seen Clodia run from her dressing room, he now remained where he was, making no move towards her.

Looking at him, Clodia, too, felt the slight embarrassment that the interval had built. She had a sudden, fleeting fear that she might be scorned.

She brushed past Spartacus and stretched out on the counterpane and cushions of the bed.

"My bones ache with all that sitting in the banquet room," she said, holding his eyes again with her own. "I want to be massaged."

Spartacus moved towards her, his sandaled feet rustling lightly on the floor. She saw in his eyes the deep unwavering purposefulness that so many were to see and it filled her with a shuddering anticipation.

"Have you seen the women wrestlers being massaged in the palaestrae?" she asked softly. And as he nodded, she added, slipping from her robe: "Well I am just one of them waiting for the masseur. Clodia does not exist."

As his fingers began to move over her body and her breath fluttered in her throat, she thought, "Perhaps this is the *only* time that Clodia exists."

Once again her full, beautiful white body was

exposed to her slave. But Spartacus, running his hands over the beautiful tapering arms, the slim shoulders, the glossy swelling of her breasts, knew that he was no longer her slave but her master.

His strong fingers kneaded the firm flesh of her belly, drawing it in little ridges, flattening it with his palms. He stroked the sinuous lengths of her thighs, his chest palpitating, an aching pressure under his loincloth.

His hands rifled her body, knowing the virtuous flesh, all the more sensual for its virtuousness. As his fingers moved between her legs she gave a muffled squeal and jerked over onto her stomach, burying her face in a cushion. Her back heaved as his hands caressed her bare bottom. The white skin of the firm mounds was so smooth it seemed glazed. The hips flowed out from her slim waist, full and receptive; her feet twitched and her thighs rubbed convulsively together as his hands made bold love to her.

Spartacus gazed down, from his ascendant and intimate proximity, on the beautiful rounded lines of her body and choked with a desire to flop his hips down on that filled-out cushion of a bottom and nuzzle his loaded cudgel between the warm, downy pressure of her thighs where they joined her buttocks.

He worked his fingers up between the tight challenge of her thighs, with the flesh giving before his hand, running in ripples up to the arch in which the moist lips nestled.

His hand trembled as he reached his goal, trembled as he was about to touch the intimate secret of Clodia, cold, unfathomable Clodia whose beauty was the talk of Rome. And then his hand, unrestricted now by any napkin, ran along the soft flanges of flesh, savoring their warmth, their heat, their moistness of gentle perspiration.

Clodia gave a sharp intake of breath as his fingers explored, and she slid up the bed overcome with desire. His hand followed and this time she lay still, breathing wildly as his fingers parted the lips.

As he caressed the little clitoris she gave a squeal into the cushion and the squeal became a gasp as his fingers plunged up through the elastic brim of flesh into the warm depths of her passage.

"Spartacus . . . Spartacus!"

She uttered his name as if in delirium and rolled onto her back. Her hands seized his arms, digging fiercely into their strands of muscle and pulled him down to her. Her lips pressed onto his, working on them as if she were trying to eat them; her tongue jerked into his mouth, gliding like quicksilver.

Spartacus dropped onto her, her body taking his weight as if she were some complementary part of him, giving in places, resisting in others.

"Spartacus, Spartacus," her mouth breathed incessantly, as if she had been saying the name to herself for months and it was a relief to say it aloud at last.

He shifted on her, hips grinding on hers, feeling, even through his tunic, the flesh of her belly billowing and swelling under him. The rigidity of his penis hurt him in its confinement.

Her hands moved round his back, arms locking him to her, legs twining with his. Her eyes were closed, mouth open. She seemed more beautiful in her passion than he had ever thought her before.

"Spartacus," she breathed. "Don't torment me. You are the master."

Feverishly, yet with the same sure glint in his eyes, Spartacus raised his hips off her and slithered out of his loincloth. He didn't bother to remove his tunic; it pulled up to his waist. From the foot of the bed his sandals dropped with a thud to the floor.

Her long fingers came down between his thighs and grasped him, making it throb. Then she was stroking his small, tight buttocks, urging them at her and her thighs had opened wide.

Spartacus slithered down her. He wrapped his strong arms around her body—and with a swift, full stroke, he shot into her like a Roman legion cutting through the tangled brushwood of a forest in Gaul.

Clodia gave a strangled gasp as she felt the dull pain of his entry. He seemed to split her in all directions. He was bigger by far than Crispus.

He thrust into her, splitting her farther and farther as his thickening organ coursed up into the core of her body. She wanted him to fill her; she wanted him to make her ache, make her sore, make her cry with the sweet tears of exquisite pain. At last this man, this silent, magnetic man, was hers, was alone with her in the world, his mind focused only on her and the superb satisfaction of her body.

Spartacus, soaring into her with an unleashed ferocity, felt a tingling in every pore of his body where it touched her. His chest against her sleek, bolstering breasts, his belly against hers, his hairy thighs brushing her columns of marble-smoothness—above all his great, uncovered tool, hot and bursting with sensation, moving tightly, excruciatingly into her lower mouth.

He gasped out his breath, crushing his lips over her face, over all those beautiful features.

Writhing under him, moaning her ecstasy, the cold, virtuous Clodia was in a bitch-heat of passion, pulling her thighs back to her breasts, almost to her shoulders even, wriggling her buttocks so that the counterpane crinkled and dampened under the sweating movement. Spartacus exulted in his raging lust.

His hand roamed over her skin, holding the flesh which belonged to him, doing what he liked with the beautiful body which all Rome would have given its eyes to see.

Gripping her shoulders, squeezing until the white skin turned red, grasping the breasts as they overflowed from under him, holding the waist, cradling the buttocks in his big palms, feeling them overflow from his fingers, so that his fingers dug into them as if they were soft, silken cushions.

Clodia groaned and panted as his hands reached under her buttocks, caressing the soft, sensitive skin, moving down to the source of their liaison.

She spread her thighs to the limit, forcing herself to endure the pain which accompanied the ecstasy, moaning with a masochistic pleasure under his rough impalement of her. His crushing, aggressive weight seemed to be forcing her through the bed, which creaked under the furious rhythm of their intercourse. She felt inside her belly, as in her throat, a sort of growing restriction of breath, a bubble of sensation which seemed to grow and grow until she knew she could contain it little longer.

The heavy staff which surged in the wetness of Clodia's channel was the only part of himself that Spartacus could now feel. His knees slipped on the silken counterpane as he moved up to try to shove more of his length into the passage.

Her chin was on his shoulder. He could feel the heat of her normally cold cheek on his own hot flesh. Her mouth was fluttering over his face. His own name, Spartacus, seemed to mix with the animal noises of her moans. She strained toward him as he felt a heat in his belly move down to his loins. She panted and the gasps became a continuous low-pitched moan which suddenly choked off into a staccato spluttering and screaming as she pushed her belly up at him.

She was still groaning as the tide of lifegiving fluid swept through Spartacus making him cry out with the unbelievable ecstasy of it, making him want to destroy this beautiful creature whose body he was wildly ravaging, whose hips still squirmed slightly under his, whose cheek was still against his, whose arms clasped his shoulders tightly, whose buttocks still tensed in his hands.

He wanted to destroy, to make this woman completely his. Passion made his head swim, his eyes glaze. But to his astonishment, Clodia suddenly began to struggle under him, scratching at him with her nails so that thin weals of pain stung in his arms.

"Beast, beast!" she cried. Tears were suddenly in her eyes. Spartacus fought down her arms, held them to her sides as her body writhed to escape. Bewildered he recoiled.

It was as he stumbled from the bed, confused and distracted that he heard a gasp from behind him. He whirled around in horror.

In the doorway, a look of shocked disbelief on his face, stood Lucius Crispus.

CHAPTER THREE

After his gratification on the slim, brown body of the Egyptian slave, Crispus had passed her on for the pleasure of the others in his company. Other female slaves had been seized and a general slaking of sexual appetites had begun.

This sort of behavior was more or less the accepted thing in libertine circles—which, after all, comprised most of the aristocracy—and Crispus was not terribly concerned about the effect his public copulation would have on his wife, Clodia—nor any of the other women. After all, they had all seen a penis before—even if they hadn't seen the nook of an Egyptian girl.

When Crispus looked blearily around the room he was hardly surprised to see that Clodia had left. A few women remained—those whose husbands had not yet given way to the temptation of the helpless flesh ready to do their bidding. But Clodia, sensitive soul—he sneered to himself—had left, doubtless to escape from the bawdy atmosphere.

Anyway, she'd done her bit. She cut a fine figure amongst the women and the reputation of her virtue was flattering for him.

Crispus straightened his toga and slipped his feet into his sandals. He felt hot and rather weary. He needed a bath to round off the evening.

A glance around the room satisfied him that his guests were well taken care of in everything their appetites might demand. He could safely leave them for half an hour.

Carefully he picked his way through the couches on which patrician masculinity throbbed out its passion in the feminine softness of the slaves. He passed through the door into the gloomy cool night air of the portico with the grounds and the baths beyond.

It was as he strolled noiselessly in the dimness of the portico's columns that he saw the two figures pass and disappear up a stairway into the house. He stood still for a moment in surprise. The first one had been Clodia, the second Spartacus, the slave.

After a minute or two, Crispus walked on towards the baths. For a second he had thought the slave was creeping after his wife, unobserved. But in a moment he dismissed this thought as an absurdity. It was simply that Clodia had been for a walk in the grounds and now she was going to her room, taking Spartacus with her to shut the shutters and ensure that everything was safe. The number of robbers and cut-throats had been growing of late in Rome. One had to be careful—even in one's own home.

Bathing in the warm, soothing water of the bronze basin, Crispus allowed his mind to dwell on the slave, Spartacus. He knew he had acted stupidly that day in suggesting that the Thracian should be sold in the slave market. Clodia, quite rightly, had refused anything of the sort. He was one of their best workers and he had a natural power of command over his fellow slaves that Crispus secretly envied. He was afraid that Clodia might have seen through his demand. The idea that he was half afraid of the big slave was one that he hardly admitted to himself.

There was something about the man on which he couldn't quite put his finger. It was hardly any one thing, but a combination of several: his fine physique combined with that strong face— but above all, perhaps, that strange, deep, unafraid look in his eyes. Crispus cursed his own feeling of helplessness when he looked into those eyes.

He climbed out of the bath and towelled himself absently. He'd have to find some way of getting rid of the man eventually. It was too wounding to his self-esteem to have him around.

Crispus walked back through the grounds, pausing to watch the twinkling jets of the fountains. Thinking of Spartacus had made him uneasy.

Back in the banquet room the guests were still eating and drinking. Others were still doing all sorts of things to the slaves and yet others were lolling in drunken stupors.

Standing unobserved in the doorway, Crispus noticed that Clodia had not returned. His eyes searched among the couches and tables. Nor had Spartacus. A feeling of uneasiness continued to grow in him. He told himself not to be a fool, but, nonetheless, he turned sharply and strode along the portico to the stairway leading to the rooms above.

His heart pounded as he mounted. This was ridiculous, he told himself. But they had been gone a long time.

Reaching the door of his room, Crispus heard muffled sounds from Clodia's room. Sounds of gasps and movement. His face blanched. He pushed quickly and clumsily through the darkened room, crashing against a table on his way. As he flung open Clodia's door he heard the words, "Beast, beast," spat into the air and an incredible sight met his eyes.

There, pinned down on her bed, struggling, was Clodia, naked. On her was the slave, Spartacus, his great organ still in her, his hips still wedged between her thrown-back thighs. The slave was breathing heavily and in a shattering instant it was clear to Crispus that this scum, this slave, had just achieved the rape of his wife.

He stood stock-still in astonishment and disbelief as Spartacus stumbled from the bed. The slave wheeled around and the next minute his eyes, those cool, grey eyes, which now contained something close to bewilderment, had fastened on him.

In spite of the extra seconds he'd had, Crispus' reaction, due to the wine, perhaps, was much slower than the slave's. He tried to jump aside as the big body lunged towards him, but the great fist caught him on the side of the face, knocking him back through the door and sprawling onto the floor of his own room.

As Spartacus' brawny legs sped past his eyes, Crispus cried out at the top of his voice: "Help, help! Slave revolt!"

Clodia had, with her passion spent, her senses returning to normal, heard the sound of Crispus as he knocked over the table in his room. She had understood immediately, with a clarity of mind which was her strength, that she would have to pretend she had been raped.

The alternative was attempted flight with Spartacus, inevitable capture, almost certain death for her, and very certain ostracism from the society which she held dear. The alternative was out of the question.

Likewise, Spartacus had immediately realized her game when he saw her husband standing in the doorway. The stinging weals from her nails impressed on him the fact that he could expect no quarter from the woman who had just joined with him in the act of love. The penalty for rape was death. The penalty for a look of insubordination could be death! To flee was the only possibility.

Had it not been for the lecherous capacity of Tullius Canus, Spartacus might well have escaped into the grounds and from there to the dark streets of Rome where he could easily have evaded the pursuit of the night patrols.

But Tullius Cañus, who, in an adjoining

room, had just enjoyed the exquisite rapture of one of the Spanish maidens, heard the cry of his friend, Crispus, and waddled out into the passage, nudely obese.

The first thing he saw was the slave, Spartacus, whom he'd noticed before, bearing down on him.

"What's up?" he began to say when the voice of Crispus rang out from behind Spartacus.

"Stop him, stop him! He's assaulted my wife."

Tullius Canus took one further look at the big frame which was almost on him, realized he had no time to get out of the way, and flung himself at Spartacus' legs.

The two men crashed to the ground, Tullius clinging to the slave's ankles. Crispus hurled himself on the Thracian's back and fastened his arms around his neck. Both he and Tullius began to call for help.

Spartacus was filled with fury. His considerable strength was augmented from the desperation which knowledge of his fate if taken captive instilled in him. He lashed out with a foot, heard the thud of a hard heel against Tullius' face, felt his ankles immediately released. He pried open the encircling arms of Crispus, staggering to his feet, dragging Crispus with him in the process—and then flung him back on top of Tullius.

He descended the stone steps four at a time —straight into the hands of a group of several guests who had heard the noise of the cries above the dying hubbub of the banquet.

Arms seized him at all levels. He was pulled

to the ground, but fought his way to his feet again. One aristocrat's head he split against the stone wall, another he knocked into oblivion with a blow of his fist.

From behind, Crispus and Tullius joined the fracas, dragging him to his knees. Again he got to his feet, using fists, elbows, head, knees, the whole of his body as a weapon.

Despite their numbers, the Romans fell away all around him, slow and clumsy from the night they'd had. Later Crispus was to remember that not one slave of his household came to his aid, and to exact a terrible toll.

Spartacus, breathing heavily from his effort, body running with sweat, saw the patrician ranks draw back, saw his chance to make his escape through their midst when, as if from nowhere, an outer ring of men, broadswords in hand, closed in on him. They were another group of guests, who, at the first cries, had stayed to collect their swords. One of their number had gone out to call the patrols.

Trapped, Spartacus stood where he was, not taking his eyes from the group of men who surrounded him with steel.

"Clodia will say that I raped her," he said woodenly to the company. "But it is a lie. She had me watch while she bathed and then invited me to make love to her. How, otherwise, would nobody have heard her cries?"

Spartacus knew as he spoke that he was simply adding to his crime if that were possible. The fact that he should slander her after raping her would simply add to his infamy in the eyes of the Romans. Nobody would think of believing him.

"What a vile lie!"

The voice, trembling with emotion, was that of Clodia. Spartacus turned and saw her slowly descending the steps as if she had been injured. Her whole being was the picture of violated virtue. He hated her in that moment.

"How could you add so vilely to your wickedness?" She appealed to him, with a voice that shook, pulling her stola protectively against her. The heart of every man in the portico inflamed against Spartacus with a rage that was half jealousy.

Sword in hand now, Crispus confronted Spartacus. His face was livid with rage and Spartacus wondered why he did not cut him down immediately.

"You scum!" he snarled. "Death by the sword or the cross is too good for you. I have another way to make you suffer."

"He should be lashed! Let's lash him!"

The cry was taken up on all sides.

"No, gentlemen." Crispus' lips drew back from his teeth as he spoke. "I have an acquaintance who'll make good use of him, an acquaintance who'll give him such a life that he'll never know which day he's going to die. I'll give him to Larcius Priscus for the gladiators' school."

Crispus had had to think hard. His first inclination had been to have Spartacus tortured and executed. But one could not, even in these days, execute or torture without people knowing about it. And if they knew, they wanted to know why. If it got around that Clodia, his unsullied Clodia, had actually been forced to yield under the ravishing of a slave, her reputation would be torn to tatters and he in turn would feel the weight of the derision of his fellows; his dignity and position would be ruined forever. Only a score of men now remained in his house. He would have to throw himself on their charity.

"How will you enjoy facing death afresh every day?" Crispus snarled, jabbing Spartacus in the chest with the sword. "Kill or be killed, that's what it'll be and the longer you stay alive the more torment you go through."

Spartacus' hard, grey eyes held his, and Crispus stepped back a pace. He looked around at the reassuring ring of swords. He was not concerned about Clodia. It was the thought of the reflection of this act on himself that terrified him.

He dropped his voice to a tone which he hoped appealed to the decency in the men around him.

"This has been a terrible blow," he murmured. "If the story gets abroad, my wife will suffer agonies of the mind. I trust you gentlemen will find it in your noble characters not to mention the night's events—or at least to ascribe some other crime to this filthy swine."

"Aye, aye, aye."

The confirmation came from every mouth.

"You have our word on it," Tullius Canus said quietly.

His penis dangled lewdly from below his fat belly.

CHAPTER FOUR

It was the day of Spartacus' first fight in the arena. He had had precious little training. His fellows in the prison-like barracks, where Larcius Priscus, the contractor—Death's middleman as the slaves called him—kept them meagerly, were all slaves, men condemned to death for crimes, prisoners of war, all those whose lives were considered to be worth less than the street dogs'.

Spartacus had talked to some of them in spite of the strict discipline under which they were kept. The majority, he found, had committed crimes that only their masters would consider to be so, others had been bought straight from the slave market to fill the program of butchery on which their new owner grew rich.

An atmosphere of jocular mournfulness hung over the gladiators. They accepted their fate, living from day to day. They knew that sooner or later they would die.

"Your first fight today?"

Spartacus turned on the rough wooden bench in the cold, stone dining room and saw Marcellus, the Samnite.

"Yes. For you, too?"

Marcellus nodded. As a Samnite he would fight with the sword and shield. Spartacus, as a Thracian, would battle with the round buckler and the dagger.

Marcellus was in the school because, underfed, he had stolen some of his patrician master's fruit and been caught in the act. He had an athletic build to vie with Spartacus' although he was a head shorter. His eyes were brown and his mouth twisted often into a bitter smile.

"Are you afraid?" Spartacus asked.

"No. I am only sad that my opponent will not be Marcus Sallust, my ex-lord and master." Marcellus spat on the floor.

"A wish that many here could echo," Spartacus said.

Later they were divided into pairs. The pairs in which they would fight in the amphitheatre.

When they were marched out through the streets of the town to the arena, Spartacus strode beside a big Gaul who had been given the net and the trident for his protection.

Today's Game was to be a big one with fighting in pairs. The survivors would then be let into the arena two at a time, each conqueror being set upon by another opponent. A sacrifice of some score of men would have taken place before the dusk.

Spartacus and the Gaul did not talk nor look at each other as they marched. Spartacus did not relish the thought of the senseless slaughter, but the instinct to survive was as strong in him as in anyone.

Dressed in their chlamys of different colors, all embroidered with gold, the gladiators made an almost gay procession. Only their faces did nothing to add to the gaiety of the scene.

Soon the amphitheatre, its superimposed tiers of stone arcades resplendent in the sun, could be seen by the parade marching to their death through the busy streets of Rome. People gathered at the roadsides to watch the procession pass.

When they were met by valets, who came to carry their arms, and marched through the ground-floor colonnade and one of the arcades which led into the arena, the gladiators really felt the shadow of fear fall on their hearts.

Marching in step on the loose sand which covered the beaten earth of the arena, they heard the hubbub of tens of thousands of people sitting happily on the terraces waiting to watch the carnage which would follow.

The lowest terrace was nearly twenty feet above the arena and inside it and running around the whole circumference of the amphitheatre was the metal grating—also twenty feet high—a grim reminder of the horrors of men fighting beasts.

All over the terraces bets were being laid on known gladiators and as the men reached the end of the shorter axis of the arena and raised their hands in salute to the balustrade-protected terrace of the Consuls, the tens of thousands of voices hushed and the tens of thousands of eyes stared, weighing up the possibilities of the newcomers.

Marched off like animals, the gladiators were grouped in one of the enclosed arcades at the end of the longer axis of the amphitheatre. It was here they would wait their turn. They could watch the death of their fellows, if they so chose, through a heavy iron grating, which was slammed shut after each man entered the vast expanse to meet his adversary.

Most of the gladiators watched, fascinated,

as the first pair came to grips to the accompaniment of the strident tones of a band, and the fever which seized the amphitheatre.

The duel lasted some ten minutes before the first body of the day sprawled into the dust and the first blood mingled with the yellow sand. The victor walked, pale and thankful, to rejoin his fellows; the loser was dragged unceremoniously to another exit by the attendants.

In the arena as the day wore on and the battling shadows of the gladiators became shorter, Spartacus lost interest in the gory, repititive spectacle. He was aware that Marcellus had won. That simply meant that Marcellus would have to fight again later in the day.

It was some time after the sun had passed its zenith that Spartacus and the Gaul were let out into the huge oval of ground, alone, and deadly enemies under the eyes of the bloodlusting citizens of Rome.

The terraces, right up to the highest point where the women sat just inside the outermost wall, seemed huge and far away. Spartacus wondered where Crispus was sitting—and if Clodia had come to witness the slaughter which she had created.

He and the Gaul walked out to the center of the arena opposite the places of the Consuls and then separated. Neither had spoken a word.

Then, they circled each other. The hint of nervousness Spartacus felt at this strange new entertainment he was providing did not show in his eyes. The Gaul was an old hand.

Spartacus kept on his toes. He knew he had nothing to fear from the trident. It was the net which his adversary held loosely in his left hand that he had to be wary of. The thought of being suddenly ensnared in its coils, jerked off his feet and then helplessly to await his slaughter, sent a cold shiver up the Thracian's spine.

Shouts of impatience came from the crowd.

"Get to it! Kill him! Strike!"

They reached Spartacus with startling clarity and he felt a surge of disgust against the swarms gathered on the terraces to watch and bet on their favorite sport.

And then the big Gaul lunged out with the trident.

Spartacus took the blow on his buckler. The buckler slewed slightly in his hand from the force of the blow and he gripped it more tightly as he backed away and took a second blow.

His dagger seemed small and useless against the long-range weapon of his opponent. He found himself moving around the arena taking blow after blow on his buckler. All the time he watched the burly arm of the Gaul on which the net jerked in a feint from time to time.

The yelling of the crowd had reached a fever pitch, but both men were now oblivious to the din. Sweat stood out on their brows, their muscles were tensed for the other's slightest reaction.

Suddenly the Gaul's net snaked out. Spartacus saw it coming, swayed aside as the trident crashed once more towards his chest to be taken on the buckler. He thanked the gods he'd had a little training at the school.

All the time Spartacus retreated. It was impossible for him to get to grips with his opponent without the risk of being enmeshed in the net.

The noise in the terraces had reached fever pitch. The Gaul was well-known. On his fate depended the wager earnings of a vast portion of the crowd.

Spartacus retreated still, parrying the continual rain of blows. His eyes watched every move his opponent made, but he could see no way of attack.

The close quarters came quite unexpectedly. The Gaul feinted a blow toward Spartacus' chest and with a great deftness of wrist swept the trident down to the ground. Had Spartacus witnessed the Gaul in action before he would have known of the trick he employed.

The side of the trident smashed against his ankle, knocking his feet from under him. He landed on his back, and as the Gaul leapt in, the crowd yelled in a homicidal frenzy.

"Slay! Slay! Slay!"

Spartacus' mind reacted with the cool urgency which came to him in desperate moments.

On the ground, unable to get up, he would tire, inevitably, under the hammer blows of the Gaul. He threw caution to the winds. As the Gaul's sweating face, grim above his black beard, loomed over him, he flung his buckler, with a force which few could have summoned, at the man's legs.

On the verge of victory, the Gaul felt his knees crumple under him as the buckler hit them. He was flung forward on his face and twisted over immediately, whirling his trident round at his opponent in the same movement.

The crowd, delighted at the rapid action, the incredible fluctuation in fortunes of the two gladiators, saw the trident catch Spartacus' arm a heavy, glancing blow as he in turn sprang in for the kill, saw the dagger drop from his hand to the glistening sand.

Down at the ringside terrace, Senator Crispus beamed his satisfaction. Sitting with the women in the outer heights of the amphitheatre, Clodia bit her lips and then glanced guiltily at her companions for fear they should have noticed.

Spartacus' lunge took him with a thud onto the prostrate body. His smarting wrist grasped the trident just above the spot where it was held by the Gaul.

The Gaul's free hand came up to Spartacus' face, fingers reaching for his eyes and the Thracian grasped the wrist as it came.

For several seconds they lay as they were, the slow strain on their muscles the only indication of their struggle.

The eyes of the Gaul were frightened. He was suddenly aware of the greater physical strength of his opponent. He looked into hard, grey eyes and experienced a chill of horror.

On the terraces, the shouting had died. There was a hush; everyone was straining to see.

The trident bent outwards from the Gaul as Spartacus' wrist slowly twisted it away. The Gaul gritted his teeth. His wrist was giving, slowly giving. There was nothing he could do. With his last trick he suddenly let go. The sudden relaxation took Spartacus by surprise. The trident spun out of his hand and thumped to the ground some feet from the two men. The crowd began to scream again.

A desperate relief flashed in the Gaul's eyes. His suddenly freed fist smashed into Spartacus' belly. The Thracian, cursing the folly which had taken victory from him, fell off his opponent, gasping for breath, still clutching at a wrist.

The big body of the Gaul flopped onto him. The hands came to his throat. Above him the face was creased in effort, the teeth bared.

Spartacus caught the man's little fingers and jerked. The fingers cracked and broke and the Gaul cried out with pain. He struggled still as Spartacus twisted from under him, fastening one arm around the man's neck, pinning his arms with the other.

The Gaul's pain-wracked eyes stared up to the clear, blue sky as under him Spartacus tightened the pressure of his arms. The Gaul struggled furiously. It was no good.

Tightening his arm around the man's neck, Spartacus gritted his teeth as he heard the gasps of his adversary.

"Kill or be killed." That was all there was to it. One could have no pity.

The Gaul choked, heavy upon him. His struggles were weakening. The tens of thousands of voices were yelling. An instructor had come into the arena to make sure there was no prearranged trickery between the two gladiators— no relaxing on the winner's part in the hope that a long match would earn a second chance for both men.

Spartacus heard the Gaul wheezing. After a

little more tightening, his struggles came to an end. Spartacus continued to squeeze his neck until he saw the sign from the instructor.

He pushed the Gaul's body from him, got to his feet, collected his dagger and his buckler and walked slowly from the arena to the tumultuous cheers of the crowd. He felt slightly sick.

On the terraces Crispus watched the broad back disappear with a malicious glare.

"He'll lose next time," Tullius Canus said softly, beside him.

Higher up in the terraces, Clodia found her palms were sweating. She felt relief mixed with a strange foreboding as she watched the broad shoulders disappear from the shadow of death into the gladiator's arcade.

* * *

There was no repetition during the afternoon of the first time within memory that a man had been strangled to death in the gladiator's arena.

Body after body was dragged from the amphitheatre; the attendants raked and re-raked the sand.

In the gladiator's arcade, Spartacus sat beside Marcellus.

"One of each pair comes back," he said, more to himself than the Samnite. "One of each pair comes back until later in the day when he'll join his victim. Later in the day or maybe tomorrow or maybe three weeks."

He looked at Marcellus, whose sad eyes regarded him sympathetically.

"If I were in the Senate, I would stop this slaughter," he said.

Marcellus smiled sadly.

"If you were in the Senate you'd be betting and getting richer—or maybe you'd be hiring us to perform and add to your prestige."

He shook his head mournfully. "It's only those who've actually experienced the suffering and slaughter who'd put a stop to it—and not all of *them*."

From outside the cheers of the crowd heralded yet another death and victory.

"One of us will die later today," Spartacus mused. "Inevitably one of us will die. Two men in the prime of body and mind, and inevitably with the chain fight one of us will die."

Marcellus was silent. He looked at Spartacus and then up at the new victor just returned from the hot arena with the cheers of the crowd still ringing in his ears.

"It does happen," he said, "that for a very good fight both men earn their lives."

"Until the next time," said Spartacus.

"Who knows."

"Then if we meet we must fight well—and hope?" Spartacus said with a wry grin.

"Who knows," Marcellus repeated quietly, his sad brown eyes speculating.

It was more inevitable than it might have appeared that Spartacus and Marcellus should eventually face each other in the grim loneliness of death's arena. They were probably the strongest and most intelligent of the remaining gladiators.

When the chain fight began, in which each

victor had a new opponent unleashed upon him of those remaining in the arcade, it was Spartacus who was first to leave the shade for the hot desert of the arena.

Learning all the time with his dagger and his buckler, using his great strength and his cool brain, he survived three fights in a row to the overwhelming enthusiasm of the crowd. Wagers were laid as to how long he would last. He won two more in a row and then Larcius Priscus, fearful lest the Senate should think it a put-up job and lest the crowd should eventually grow impatient with the domination of one man, looked around the remainder of his men and picked Marcellus as the most likely to test the big Thracian and perhaps bring his reign of killing to an end.

When Marcellus was chosen he picked up his long shield and sword and sadly bade farewell to his fellows. There was nothing in his eyes but a resignation to kill or be killed.

Spartacus, waiting in the sun for his next opponent, wondered how long it would go on. Already he felt the first traces of weariness. As he saw Marcellus stride through the iron gateway he felt a curious disgust that he should have to fight this man with whom he'd felt a certain sympathy during the few days past. "Kill or be killed." Marcellus, too, was fresh and strong.

The two men began the procedure of circling each other, feet shuffling softly in the sand.

The yells of the crowd wafted over the amphitheatre:

"Don't be frightened of him—he's only killed

six today." ... "Slay the superman." ... "Kill!"

Marcellus launched into the attack, cutting at Spartacus with his sword, stabbing at him in the way the Roman legionaries were taught. Everywhere he stabbed, Spartacus' buckler moved as if by magic, always there to take the blow.

Spartacus waited, waited for Marcellus to expend some strength, grasped his short dagger firmly, biding his time.

With Marcellus' first energy fading, Spartacus began to advance, pushing the buckler before him, forcing his opponent to keep cutting at him, to be always on his toes.

Spartacus had, by now, learned to use his buckler as a weapon, and it was as Marcellus made a defensive thrust, that the Thracian sprang in, forcing the Samnite's sword arm up over his head, taking him slightly off balance. His dagger sliced Marcellus' short sleeve and at the same time he dropped his buckler and grasped the sword arm. He had already learned to take only the chances which would allow his short dagger to be an aggressive weapon. At all costs he had to get to close quarters.

Marcellus' shield, also used as a weapon, crashed against his shoulder and then Spartacus' leg had tripped him and they were both struggling on the ground.

Their eyes, gleaming, fighting eyes, met as they struggled.

"If we can make it look good, we'll be granted a draw," Marcellus said softly.

Spartacus said nothing. Could he trust this

man? He recalled the old gladiator's maxim: No quarter for the fallen. His eyes hardened again.

Marcellus, too, had dropped his shield, not to be encumbered with its weight now that he was down. His grip was still comparatively fresh and strong on Spartacus' dagger-wrist.

They writhed together, rolling over on the sand. From the terraces the crowds strained once more to try and see.

"In a moment I shall drop my sword as a token of trust." Once again, Marcellus' lips hardly moved. "If then you will fall away as I heave, we can recover our shields and start again."

"What if I prefer not to accept your token?" Spartacus muttered.

"I have nothing to lose," Marcellus muttered back. "I covet no titles. I'll take that chance."

Spartacus did not relax his grip on Marcellus' wrist and as they rolled and struggled, the Samnite's sword suddenly dropped from his hand.

A tumult broke out on the terraces. Those who had bet on Spartacus rubbed their hands and shuffled on their seats for joy.

Spartacus was startled. His grip had not changed. There was no reason why Marcellus should have dropped his sword and put himself in mortal danger. Marcellus' eyes looked into his as their muscles bulged. It was the look of a man who has made a big gamble on another's character and hopes he is not wrong. Spartacus' eyes answered the look.

Violent shouts and urgings were sweeping down from the terraces as Marcellus gave a desperate heave with his hips. It was a strong heave, a heave which might almost have succeeded anyway. Spartacus rolled away, sprawled on the sand and then grabbed for his buckler.

As Marcellus, too, sprang to his feet seizing his sword with one hand and reaching for his shield with the other, Spartacus was on him. If this was to succeed, Spartacus decided, it must look real. He gave Marcellus no time to recover his shield.

Forced back under the advance of the Thracian's shield, Marcellus lashed out wildly with his sword. His eyes were desperate. He had been tricked, they proclaimed.

Again Spartacus swept his sword-arm aside with a blow of his buckler. When his dagger tore a fresh rent in Marcellus' tunic, inflicting a light flesh wound, Marcellus breathed with relief. He realized only too well that Spartacus with his speed could have plunged the dagger into his chest.

They fought on. At one stage Spartacus allowed the sword to catch him a glancing blow on the wrist to send his dagger spinning across the arena and let the blood flow on his arm.

As he parried strenuously, dancing and weaving under the rapid blows of his opponent, he backed to where his dagger lay. Whereupon, Marcellus left him to hurl himself at the spot where his shield had rested, bronze surface shimmering in the sun for a large part of the fight.

Muscles bulged, bodies sweated and bled as the two men fought. The crowd yelled now for one, now for the other and eventually, after the fight had lasted for close on half an hour, began to call for a draw.

Hearing the cries, Spartacus and Marcellus redoubled their activity, slashing and stabbing, advancing, retreating, neither giving the other too obvious an advantage.

The roars of the crowd grew. The men were equally matched, had fought a magnificent duel. Handkerchiefs fluttered on the terraces, the Consuls looked at the public signal, looked at the two men still battling in the arena, consulted each other and waited.

All around the terraces the crowds had risen to their feet, a chant of "Let them go!" . . . "Draw—draw!" rumbled around the amphitheatre. The Consuls consulted each other again, brought in a few of the Senate, nodded wisely and raised their hands for silence.

The great crowd hushed and one of the Consuls called out in a clear voice for the men to stop fighting. A draw had been proclaimed, he said. Both men had fought magnificently and would be rewarded with silver plate.

Breathing heavily, bowing before the Consul, the two men in the arena did not exchange a glance.

Next to Tullius Canus, Crispus was furious. "Silver plate!" he spat, almost in tears.

"He can't last," Tullius said reassuringly.

Up in the summit of the amphitheatre, Clodia touched her lips with a hand which trembled slightly. She was not sure why she trembled.

CHAPTER FIVE

After days of smarting, Lucius Crispus was now pleased with himself. He had paid heavily for another little spectacle which was to take place on the morrow. True, it had cost him dearly, but it was well worth the money.

Tomorrow a certain number of men were to be killed in the arena. Most of them were freshly convicted criminals but a fair sprinkling were gladiators. They were to be killed partly for their crimes, partly for the amusement of the crowds who would again fill the terraces to watch the blood bath. The method would be the usual one in such circumstances—pitting a man clad only in a tunic against an adversary armed to the teeth. After the unarmed man had been—inevitably—slain, his opponent would be disarmed and made to face an adversary as heavily armed as he had been.

Crispus chuckled to himself as he pictured Larcius Priscus standing before him weighing up the advantage to himself of keeping Spartacus as a crowd draw or selling him into the butchery and accepting the considerable sum Crispus was offering him. Few men could withstand the desire for immediate gain—and a gladiator was always a gamble. Crispus made his way to the Senate with a smile of pleasure on his face.

Lying on her couch in her room—the room in which Spartacus had enjoyed her body to the full—Clodia was disturbed. In the first place rumors had somehow spread that something had happened between herself and her former slave, rumors which were ill-defined and uncertain, but nonetheless creating an atmosphere. Secondly, and in a curious way more important, she could not feel at ease as long as Spartacus remained alive.

She recalled how, watching him in the arena, she had simultaneously prayed for his life and his death in a strange prayer which seemed to struggle with itself just as Spartacus struggled with his opponent down there in the sandy enclosure. In another society things might have been different. But Spartacus was a slave and a gladiator; she a Roman patrician. There was no compromise. So she must continue in her listless existence from day to day, wanting him to live, fearing the continuance of his life.

* * *

The moment Spartacus had learned of his fate he had begun to plan his escape. From such butchery there was no reprieve. It was a question of "Kill and be killed" this time.

He had told his plan to Marcellus and the latter, with a band of some thirty, had thrown in his hand with Spartacus.

"We have nothing to lose," Spartacus had said. With a wry grin he had added: "And we have an empire to gain."

There was little opportunity for planning, but little was needed. Nobody ever thought of a break by the gladiators. Where would they go? How would they live? Many, in fact, preferred to remain and take their chance in the only job they knew and the only one in which they might make a fortune before they lost their lives.

It was just a question of killing the guards.

On the evening that Crispus went home from the Senate, well pleased with himself and looking forward to the bloody day in the amphitheatre tomorrow, Spartacus and his band fell on the guards who watched over their dormitory quarters and then sped silently across the courtyard to the outer gates of the barracks. It was easier than had been expected. They took the gate guards from behind, thrust their daggers deep and left their bodies in the shadow of the inside wall.

Out into the unlit streets of Rome they swarmed, a motley crew in their colored, gold-embroidered tunics with their strange assembly of weapons. Down the narrow stone-paved streets they sped like ghosts—a soft thudding of sandals, a passing of darker shadows and then silence.

Rome was silent at night. Doors of the dark apartment houses were barricaded against robbers, shutters were drawn, safety chains pulled across the doors of the shops. Occasionally an upstairs shutter would open in a narrow street and a chute of urine would cascade to the stones below. The shutter would close again and fresh silence follow.

All the gladiators had to watch for were the squads of night-watchmen, the armed patrols who, torches in hand, tramped the night streets, cutting the city into sections in their vigilance for housebreakers and footpads.

At the corner of a large square, Spartacus

stopped and waited for his companions to reach him.

"We'll head south," he said, "out on the Appian Way. There's some wild forest south and we can get food from the farms."

They continued silently and carefully, flattening themselves in a dark alley to watch one of the patrols pass by, flitting on when it had passed.

It was near the outskirts of the city that a rich man's cortege turned suddenly into the street along which they were running. The torches of the man's slaves lit up the band of gladiators and the man immediately let out a cry for assistance.

His slaves, seeing what appeared to be a large band of armed robbers, immediately drew their swords.

There was little time for thought.

"Join us, friends," Spartacus called. "All here are former slaves."

The slaves hesitated and the approaching gladiators saw there were two women with the rich man.

"They're robbers," the rich man, a moneylender, bellowed to his slaves. "They'll slice you to pieces."

"No they're not, I saw the big one in the arena—they're gladiators," shouted one of the slaves.

His voice acted as a signal. The moneylender was struck down by one of his slaves and sank groaning to the roadway. Spartacus and his band joined in the ensuing melee, telling the slaves to keep quiet or the patrols would be on them.

The women screamed and were slaughtered, and the whole band—now some fifty strong—raced on through the night, leaving the bodies of their victims sprawled across the street and a crowd of frightened listeners behind the closed shutters of the nearby houses.

By the time the patrols arrived on the scene there was no sign of the gladiators. And when the people opened their doors to see, they found the road was stained with Roman blood.

CHAPTER SIX

By the time the whole of Rome knew of the escape and the atrocities, the following day, the gladiators were far south of the city on the Appian Way.

A hasty meeting of the Senate was convened. A small army was voted to march in pursuit of the fugitives, regrets on the moneylender's family were expressed, security arrangements in gladiator schools were discussed.

In the late afternoon a cohort—some 300-400 soldiers—began the march south beneath the silver eagles.

On hearing the news, Crispus had immediately considered arming all his slaves, immediately reconsidered the wisdom of such action and over all had cursed his folly at not having Spartacus put to death when he'd had him in his power. He then made a special plea to the Consuls, who eventually allowed him a small band of soldiers to guard his house in view of the bad blood between him and Spartacus. They also said there was really no fear of the gladiator's returning to the city and assured Crispus that the whole band would be in chains by the following day.

Walking in the grounds, Clodia glanced uneasily around and drew her stola closer to her shivering body.

Far to the south, a mile inland off the Appian Way, the gladiators and their new slave recruits moved quietly through the trees towards the big country house of a patrician. They were hungry. They had eaten nothing since lunchtime of the previous day.

"The only trouble is the slaves," Marcellus whispered to Spartacus, as the big stone house became clearer through the dwindling foliage. "You can never be absolutely sure whether they're going to be for you or against you."

"A small matter," said Spartacus softly. "How often are they armed?"

"If they're well treated by their owners he arms them and they protect him willingly," Marcellus whispered back.

"And how often does their owner treat them well?" asked Spartacus.

Marcellus fell silent.

At the fringe of the trees the party stopped. Beyond them was a space and then a stone wall surrounding the well-kept grounds of the house. The house itself, with its brick and concrete walls embedded with stones and pebbles, rose majestically above the marble entrance steps and the fountains of the gardens. As the gladiators watched they saw a couple of armed slaves standing guard on the big iron entrance gate.

Spartacus grinned at Marcellus, who grinned back.

"One place where they're well treated," he said.

Splitting up under Spartacus' orders, the gladiators skirted the front wall, scaled the side ones and dropped into the grounds. It was the work of seconds to deal with the surprised guards and then the band streamed up the marble steps and into the house.

The household slaves were taken by surprise and overpowered. The owner, a senator, was in Rome, they said, his wife and daughter were in the grounds.

Streaming through the quadrilateral, through the other side of the house and into the grounds at the back, the gladiators took the women completely by surprise.

The mother was a handsome woman with a long nose and imperious features, her daughter a haughty, attractive, pouting girl, a spoiled girl, a girl who would whip the slaves if they were slow in their work.

Both women tried to run and then to struggle, but they were caught up and dragged kicking and screaming into the house. Rough, hard hands held their kicking legs and felt their bodies, lewd laughs and cries assailed their ears, lustful eyes glared into theirs.

Inside the house the overpowered slaves were talking to the men who guarded them.

One of the gladiators turned to Spartacus as he entered.

"This is a house where they have a class system amongst the slaves," he said with a guffaw. "They give some weapons and allow them to beat the others and keep them in order."

Spartacus' grey eyes swept over the slaves, herded together in a corner of the room. Many had weals across their naked shoulders, some had chains hobbling their ankles so that they could take only small steps.

"Appearances are deceptive," Spartacus said to Marcellus, his eyes hardening.

"Were these given you by another slave?" he asked a young male slave, whose weals across the back and shoulders were fresh looking.

"No. It was the young mistress." The slave's eyes blazed and he spat in the direction of the young girl, whose haughty face was still trying to maintain an air of superiority.

"What would you like to do to her?" Spartacus asked.

The slave gave a short, bitter laugh.

"What would I like to do to her? I'd like to stuff her until she couldn't bear it. I'd like to lash her all over until she bled and then I'd like to rip her from her hole to her tits with the master's sword."

Spartacus looked at the girl. There was disgust and fear in her face. She looked at Spartacus, hatred and an appeal for pity fighting in her eyes.

"So you shall," he said slowly to the slave. "So you shall—and the mother will watch before the same is done to her."

The mother gave a little scream. Had she been able she would have dropped on her knees before Spartacus and begged for mercy. As it was, her only thought was that these wretches, these dregs of humanity, this scum, wouldn't dare to defy her, to touch her daughter.

"Another word and I'll see you whipped through the streets of Rome and crucified in the forum," she snapped.

Spartacus smiled. And there was something in his eyes which robbed her of all confidence in her power. He turned to the slave.

"If you care to join us she's yours," he said. "But if you want to continue in this miserable existence then you'd better be careful what you say and do."

The slave's eyes lit up with a fire which Spartacus was to see in the eyes of many within the next few weeks. It was a light that indicated joy at a change of action, a readiness to move from fetters and misery to whatever else might be in store. It could be no worse.

"I'm with you," he said.

Spartacus signalled to the gladiators to bar the doors.

"Well, take her," he said to the slave.

"Don't you dare touch her!"

The mother's voice was harsh as she moved to protect her daughter. She was seized in strong arms and hauled fighting and screaming to the edge of the room. The daughter stood for a moment, a picture of scared defiance, and then tried to run to her mother.

Hairy arms pushed her back to the middle of the room, sandalled feet smacked her squarely on her pretty buttocks.

Seeing his former mistress treated thus, the

slave, who had not moved, seemed to come to a realization of the reality of the situation.

He walked warily towards the girl, his eyes bright with feverish desire and anticipation of revenge.

The girl backed away, trying to repel him with her look. Only too clearly did she remember the casual beating she'd given him a few days before. She could not remember exactly why she had beaten him, the reason was confused with the reason for so many other beatings she'd inflicted on the household staff.

"Father will have you killed!" she cried desperately, as the distance between them lessened. There was a roar of guffaws from the gladiators.

"He'll have all of you whipped and killed," she flared, glaring round at them with tear-filled eyes.

The slave stopped, tensed, a few feet from her.

"How does it feel not to have a whip in your hand," he snarled with acid in his voice. "How do you feel now that I'm going to tear your clothes off and have you? Virgin, are you? Well you're not worth being made into a woman. So you'll get it in your behind."

The mother tore her mouth free from the hand which covered it.

"You beast, you beast!" she cried. "Don't touch her, don't touch her." Her voice rose to an hysterical scream which choked off as a big hand clapped over her mouth again.

"And after you've had it, no doubt your

mother'll have it," the slave said slowly, with gloating satisfaction.

He moved slowly towards her again.

"How does it feel for you, for once, to be subject to me?" he asked. "I'm going to repay you for every lash you've ever given me." He laughed grimly and as he seized her arms the girl began to scream.

Crying hysterically, with her mother echoing the sounds, she struggled like a fury. Privation had weakened the slave from his original robust state and she managed to break away from him, her stola ripping down almost to her girdle and baring a quivering, naked breast. Arms flying, nails scratching, feet kicking, she rushed at the gladiators guarding the door, in a lunatic attempt to push through them.

She was seized, twirled round and round and flung back sprawling on the rugs which covered the floor.

"Come on, come on," called Marcellus to the slave. "Not going to let her beat you again are you?"

The slave flung himself on the girl and they rolled, struggling violently, across the floor. Clawing and scratching, the girl drew blood from one of the fresh weals on the slave's back. Her stola had pushed back up her thighs bringing roars of appreciation from the watching gladiators.

Stung to fury by the smarting wound and the blood which splashed to the floor, the slave caught the girl around the throat and lashed his hand across her face again and again. Her face rocked from side to side with the blows, blood ran from a split lip.

"Come on, come on. Get in the bitch," the gladiators began to roar. Once again the mother pulled her head free and her screams mixed for a few seconds with the whimpering of the girl.

When the slave began to tear her loincloth from her hips, the girl's struggles were too weak to provide much resistance. Her haughty face lolled helplessly on the rug. The fleshy display of her helpless hips seemed far removed from imperious command.

The slave ripped the stola right up to her uncovered breasts, so that it formed a useless girdle around her ribs.

"There," he called, in false mockery to his fellow slaves. "She has a hole just like every other woman although we didn't think so."

The other slaves shuffled nearer, eyes roaming over the strangely defenseless nudity of their mistress. Those were the taut proud breasts which had heaved as she whipped them, those were the thighs that had swayed under the effort.

Yet again the mother bit the hand that held her, struggled ferociously and screamed at everyone in the room.

The screams seemed to revive the girl and she, too, began to struggle once more, her naked skin rubbing against the naked legs and arms of the slave.

Astride her, he lashed his hand across her breasts until the white skin glowed almost as pink as the young nipples.

"How does it feel, how does it feel?" he muttered savagely, lowering his face close to hers.

"Get in her, get in her," chanted the gladiators.

The slave caught her arm and twisted her sharply over onto her stomach. With her face muffled in the rug, the girl tried weakly to kick her tormentor. He sat across the loose swelling of her rump.

"The cow," he thought. "The little cow. Now she knows what it's like to be helpless under punishment." He looked down at her slim, well-tapered body, at the way the hips flowed out like a loose skirt from the tight little waist. They could keep themselves well fed and beautiful, these patrician women. On the sweated labor of slaves they did it. He pulled off his loincloth—the only garment the slaves wore in the house. She'd had enough fun with his body. Now he'd have a little with hers.

The gladiators roared their approval.

The girl made a last vain effort to get away, turning her haughty face, cowed now, from side to side on the rug, trying to raise her bottom and throw him off her.

The slave pushed her roughly flat. He slapped her head with his fist until she whimpered into a sobbing stillness and then he drew her warm buttocks apart.

"No, no, no!" the girl sobbed. But that was the only resistance she could offer. The will to struggle had left her.

"Yes, yes, yes!" bawled the gladiators. Tears streamed down the mother's haggard face.

He kicked her legs apart and sank between them. Under him she sobbed, coughing, feeling his weight on her, crying at the thought of being bestially ravished, treated like a harlot by a man she'd always commanded, a man she'd never even considered a human being.

She felt the weight pressing hard upon her, felt the hot flesh of the male thing which she'd never seen or experienced. She felt its heat, its massiveness, its probing, pressing, painful forcing. She felt his fingers on her flesh. She groaned in shame and humiliation. And then her whole body seemed to split and throb in a sharp, unendurable spasm of pain and she jerked convulsively and bit into the rug.

The slave wriggled into her as if he were doing some sinuous dance with his hips. Prostrate under him, the girl wallowed in self-abasement. He heard her groan, felt her body shudder, her buttocks tighten together. He muttered coarse, sadistic words of encouragement to himself as he dug into her. This was what he'd been waiting for all these years. This was the slaves putting things to rights, showing women what happened to them when they treated a man like that.

Kneeling back on the rug, he pulled the girl with him.

"Come on you bitch," he muttered. "Let's bend you open."

The girl slid back onto her knees, in clear view of the whole company. From the side of the room, her gagged mother's horrified eyes watched the clutching, yielding, clutching, yielding rhythm of her daughter being raped by a slave. Her beautiful, virginal daughter who she'd hoped to marry to a senator, or maybe a general. Bitter tears stung in her eyes.

"Come on, come on. More room in her yet," yelled a gladiator.

The girl was moaning continuously. Her lips moved, forming words which, could they have been heard, begged for mercy. She felt dazed with the pain even to the extent of forgetting the degradation.

"Bitch, bitch, bitch, bitch!" muttered the slave as his teeth gritted with each thrust. He was sweating. He felt the moisture on his brow, on his neck, on his hands even. He panted over her, moving his chest back, giving his hips a final flick with each pumping stroke. He wanted to get right through her. Coarse thoughts, words, feelings, rushed through his brain. He wanted to hurt her, hurt her. He was coming, coming. He laughed wildly, savagely inside, grunting and panting.

His mouth opened with an explosion of breath. Hot sluices raced in his loins, tearing all feeling in his body with them. Now, now! He pushed, pushed with all his might.

The room thundered with the guffawing applause of the gladiators as his deflated organ slipped out of the stretched aperture. The girl collapsed, sobbing afresh, to the floor and the slave staggered to his feet.

Marcellus picked up a bowl from a table.

"Here, fellow. A bowl to wash away the stains," he laughed, and the room filled with laughter again.

The slaves who had watched, stared like hungry dogs at the naked girl sobbing face down on the floor in front of them. In their eyes was a hatred, a desire, a release of inhibition and envy of their comrade.

"First man to her has her as he likes," Spartacus said.

The rush at the girl was a wild stampede, a tearing and a quarreling, and the gladiators had to separate the men to decide who should take her first.

As the terrified girl was turned over, her legs pulled apart in preparation for the next assault, Marcellus surveyed the mother. He turned to Spartacus.

"Why should the slaves have all the fun?" he jested. "I'd like a fill of the mother myself."

"Go ahead," Spartacus said.

The mother, her eyes wide with horror that she was to suffer the same fate as her daughter, that she, wife of a senator, was to be debased, to be unclothed and raped, struggled to escape. She could hardly believe it.

Nonetheless she in turn was flung to the ground. Her clothes were torn from her body. Standing over her, gazing down on the ripe fullness of her breasts and hips, Marcellus grinned avidly.

"This is a better battle than the arena any day," he said, as he fell on her in a struggling sexual plunder.

Both women suffered considerable ravaging at the hands of the slaves and the gladiators. The girl suffered by far the most. Almost all of the house slaves wreaked vengeance on her body. Then she was forced to watch her mother abandoned to the gladiators, writhing and sobbing, trying to be brave for her daughter's sake as her nude body was crushed under the brawny frames.

Spartacus ransacked the house while his men ransacked the women. In the kitchens he found game and fruit, bread, garum paste, milk and fine wines. He noticed in the store cupboards supplies of wheat, potatoes, sugar, salt, figs, wine, beer, everything he and his men could possibly need to take with them. He pulled off the wing of a cooked chicken and munched it; he took a long draught of wine; and then he felt better.

When he returned to the room where he'd left the others, he found both women strung face down over two couches. The slave who had first had the girl was brandishing a horsewhip. He held it out to Spartacus as the Thracian entered.

"See here." He pointed at the length of thong. "That's my blood still on it. We're going to be blood brother and sister."

Spartacus nodded. "Don't be too long. We have to be on the move," he said.

The girl, who thought she'd taken so much that she was capable of feeling no more pain, no more degradation, cried out as the lash bit into her smooth white flesh. She cried out again and again, her voice rising in a wail so that the mother bit her lips so hard that they bled, and cut herself struggling against the ropes that bound her.

The lash rose and fell, curling viciously around the girl's back and buttocks, circling her waist like a lover, flicking the bulging overflow of her breasts on the couch.

When the slave finally stepped back, the girl

was no longer conscious. Her back was a mass of angry weals.

"That still doesn't make up for all she's done," he grunted.

When the same punishment was inflicted on the mother she begged for mercy, offering everyone pardons and riches, anything they wanted.

By the time they had finished with the mother, the girl had returned to a half-dazed lucidity. She groaned and winced as they untied her and held her face up on the couch.

The slave took a sword from one of the gladiators. His face was set as he held the sword in front of him.

"Open her legs," he said through clenched teeth.

His lips were drawn back, chin thrust out, a vein throbbed in his neck. As he thrust the sword into the girl's vagina and ripped upwards, the girl let out an unearthly scream and choked to silence. Spartacus turned away as she slipped to the floor. Every whip that fell on every slave would turn against the hand that held it.

When the slaves began to move south with the gladiators towards dusk, they left the two mutilated bodies hanging from the gateway.

CHAPTER SEVEN

During the next day, the band of gladiators grew to well over a hundred. Nearly every Roman villa they passed they raided and released the slaves. Often they had to break heavy chains to free those who had been brought to Rome from far-off lands.

From every villa they took supplies of arms until nearly every man had, if not a sword and shield, at least a couple of spears.

Towns they skirted, leaving the Appian Way and streaming through the inland forests to rejoin the road beyond.

Late in the day a few slaves who had escaped of their own accord, after the news of the gladiators had passed around, came to join them. It was from one of these that Spartacus learned of the cohort bearing down on them in pursuit.

The slave had heard it from his master. His master had said it should have been at least two cohorts as the gladiators were armed and desperate characters. Spartacus nodded. Indeed it should have been two.

The gladiators by-passed Tarracina and marched several miles south to a spot where the hills swept from the Appenines to within a short distance of the road. They were low hills, no more than a thousand feet above the level of the sea. Spartacus considered them ideal for his purpose.

In these woody hills, overlooking the road, he and his men waited for the arrival of the Roman troops.

* * *

Titus Philippus leaned forward on his horse, peering along the road in front of him. Behind him his troops marched wearily. He had hoped to catch the gladiators by nightfall. Already the moon had risen in the sky and the sun was sinking below the foothills.

The youngest member of the Senate, he was eager to bring back the gladiators in chains through the streets of Rome. The city had been shocked at the escape, horrified at the slaughter of noble families on the march south. Already the name Spartacus was passing from mouth to mouth in the city. Those who had seen him fight in the arena accepted him as the leader of the fugitive band. Slaves everywhere were becoming restless.

The young commander had been among those to witness Spartacus' skill in the amphitheatre, but to him the notoriety attached to the name was nonsense. Some people would glamorize anything. The man was an ignorant thug, a small blemish on the Roman countryside that should be stamped out immediately.

Titus Philippus did not overtake the gladiators before dusk. He knew they were heading south along the Appian Way; the witnesses had been numerous. He was annoyed that another day would have to be spent on their trail, but his men were tired. He gave the order and camp was made in the shadow of the foothills.

That night he could not sleep. He thought of the patrician families which, even now, might be powerless, reluctant hosts to the gladiators. He had been so sure he would have caught them by tonight. In a sense he felt as if he'd failed. But he'd make up for his slowness. When he caught them he'd have them beaten through the streets of Rome with sticks . . . he'd get the little children to beat them with sticks.

He was still working out refinements of their punishment when the gladiators fell on his camp and annihilated it.

* * *

Rome had been stunned by the fate of the troops it had sent in the wake of Spartacus. A handful of the 300-400 men had been the only survivors. Nobody knew whether the gladiators had suffered any casualties, so complete had been the surprise.

The bewilderment had been rapidly followed by rationalizations, explanations—excuses. The number of Roman soldiers had been too few in the beginning; the Senate should have authorized more. The gladiators had doubled their ranks with slaves. They had spies everywhere.

It was decreed that the two Consuls should themselves take the two legions—all that remained, with Pompeius in Spain and Caesar in Gaul—and put a peremptory and salutary end to the gladiators' antics.

While the wheels of organization slowly turned, Rome went about its business. Nobody was going to be put out by a handful of gladiators somewhere down near Capua.

Last of all to allow himself to appear put out was Lucius Crispus. Since the small band of soldiers allotted to his house had been withdrawn he'd been putting a bold face to the world and tonight he had hired some professional players to perform a play for an invited audience in his house.

The couches for his thirty guests were arranged in a semi-circle at one end of the banquet room, a large space for the players left at the other. A fair section of the aristocracy were present, a fact which pleased Crispus immensely. He looked around for Clodia. She should be here with him to receive the guests. It was very bad form for her to be missing.

Up in her room, Clodia smoothed her hands over the counterpane of her bed. She now knew that something was happening to her. She was not the woman she had been a few months ago. Something was going on inside her head leaving her listless, half afraid, almost dazed. Spartacus was still alive. It seemed that he had some god personally interested in his welfare. She did not think she was being illogical when she believed the odds had been all against him since the day she handed him over to patrician justice. She wished she could separate her conflicting feelings, wished she could decide, once and for all, if she wanted him to die. In some mystic way she felt that her willing him to die would bring it about, or that her willing him to live would bring it about. If only she could make a decision.

Suddenly she remembered the play, the guests. With a startled lift of her eyebrows she pulled her stola about her and tripped down the steps to the crowded banquet room below.

Away from the public theatres—even there performances were frequently designed almost purely to titillate the audience into an erotic response—productions reached a peak of sensuality.

The tale which unfolded before the fascinated eyes of Crispus and his guests was that of incest and the ravishing of a daughter, who, unlike her sisters, resisted the amorous advances of her father.

"How scandalous!" the patrician women tittered as realistic movements on a specially provided couch illustrated the ravishing. The actress was a doll-like creature, a mere accompaniment to the actor, who was one of the finest mimes and dancers in Rome.

Men and women in the audience felt themselves grow hot around the loins as the doll-like face assumed expressions of horror, sudden shock, pain and then abasement, as the actor's hips writhed beside her in the acme of suggestiveness. His hips actually jerked against hers in solid contact and it was clear that both achieved a considerable satisfaction from the intimate motion. The actor simulated a panting and the girl opened her mouth and screwed up her eyes in pretended passion.

Crispus' attentive eyes discreetly watched his guests' reactions. Another success. What a pity that business with Spartacus had happened just as he was really creating a name for himself with his lavish entertainment. All around, men and women had bright eyes glued on the actors. What a pity, he thought, that both Consuls had been too tied up with the organization of the legions to come. Still, everyone else was here with fewer exceptions than at even his banquet.

Clodia sat beside him, looking straight ahead. She didn't seem to be at all affected by the performance. He wondered if she were even noticing it and for the first time he felt a twinge of pity for her. She was probably still worrying about her rape. It must have been pretty grim for her as well as for him, he supposed. But it was always worse for the man to have something like that happen to his woman.

He looked back at the actors who were just gasping in climax. The auditorium was hushed, savoring every explosion of breath, when a louder commotion suddenly broke out at the back of the room.

Looking around in annoyance, Crispus was astonished to see that the room had suddenly filled with soldiers, fully armed, metal-covered leather tunics glinting in the light of the few torches.

Crispus stood up, others around him turned on their couches, the actors stopped and stared. Crispus was bewildered. What did this mean? Was there some emergency? He was about to call out demanding information when the soldiers who had surrounded the couches stood back to let a tall figure through.

Crispus gazed at the figure, at the face under the burnished helmet of a Roman commander. His stomach turned to ice. He was looking into the hard, smiling eyes of Spartacus.

Beside him, Crispus heard a gasp from Clodia.

"Spartacus!"

At the name a gasp of horror rippled through the room. Everybody seemed to cringe.

Spartacus stood before Crispus, his hand on his sword hilt.

"Did you not expect me back?" he asked in a

tone so soft that only those close to him heard the words.

Crispus' mouth opened but no sound came. The room was silent. The gladiators—a chosen score of them—almost unrecognizable in the uniforms of Titus Philippus' former army, were an impenetrable barrier around the room.

"Have you left your voice in the Senate?" Spartacus' tone rose and he took a step towards Crispus, his eyes sweeping over Clodia. "Have you no words of welcome for the man back from the death to which you condemned him?"

Clodia's mind clouded over as Spartacus' hard, bitter eyes bored into hers. She could hear his voice but she no longer made out the words. There was nothing but his eyes and the memory in them of her betrayal.

A senator moved forward, Claudius Laberius, a bold speaker, who was in the running for next year's Consulship. He seemed to have little understanding of the situation.

"How dare you force your way in here?" he snapped. "Don't you know, madman, that 10,000 men are preparing in this city to wipe you from the face of the earth?"

He walked close to Spartacus. No slave was going to command his patrician blood. He jutted his face towards the gladiator.

"You'd better get out and fast before—"

Spartacus' hand struck him flat in his face and Claudius Laberius staggered back several paces, tripped over a couch and crashed to the floor. When he started, spluttering, to get up, a Roman sword was held at his throat.

Spartacus turned back to Crispus. His eyes

looked past him to Clodia. His voice was controlled, almost conversational.

"We were watching the play for a while," he said. "We don't want to spoil the entertainment. But we think it would benefit from a change of actors."

Crispus could not fight down the nervousness in his chest, which betrayed him in a trembling of his lower lip. Spartacus' casualness was all the more ominous.

There was a slight gasp as Spartacus extended his sword and deftly slit Clodia's stola from neck to hem. But nobody moved to her aid. His sword ripped the short sleeves and the garment fell away from her, tumbling against her neighbor.

"Get up," Spartacus commanded.

Clodia stood up, her body swelling ripely under the thin coverings of brassiere and loincloth. It did not occur to her to disobey. Spartacus' eyes seemed to hypnotize her. Her large, shapely bosom rose and fell. All eyes were on her and Spartacus.

Another delicate slit with his sword and Spartacus had snapped her brassiere supports and torn the loincloth away from her hips. Her breasts, hips and buttocks emerged as if they had oozed from the coverings, splitting them of their own volition. Pale, beautiful and suddenly chilled, she was exhibited to the prying eyes of gladiators and patricians alike.

Crispus was horrified. This was degradation for him. His terror of the ruination of his esteem overcame his fear and he lunged towards Spartacus and gripped the short sleeves of his tunic. Two gladiators stepped quickly towards them, but Spartacus made no move to use his sword. He moved in towards Crispus' body and brought his knee sharply up between the patrician's legs. Crispus groaned, doubled up and sagged to the floor at the Thracian's feet. Nobody moved to help him.

Spartacus looked back at Clodia. She had not looked at Crispus. Her eyes never left his.

The rebel leader swept his sword in an all-embracing movement.

"Choose one from among my men and you and he will act in reality the part of the play we interrupted," he said.

There was an audible intake of breath all over the room. Looking at Clodia's lovely body, many of the patricians felt, mixed with their fear and disgust, a crumb of gratitude that this ex-slave had allowed them to see what they could never otherwise have hoped to see. Oh to see that voluptuous body, that body which made one's hands itch to hold its breasts, its perfect buttocks, those hips and thighs made to cushion and open under one's weight—oh to see it in any other circumstances!

"Choose!" Spartacus commanded.

Clodia felt numb, her eyes filled with tears which overflowed and coursed quietly down her pale cheeks. There was to be no pity. She saw it in his eyes.

"Kill me," she said. "I would rather die."

Spartacus looked at the gladiators and grinned. They were all staring at Clodia, eyes hot, trying, it seemed, to draw her eyes to them.

"See how eager they are." He turned back

to Clodia and the grin was gone. "Strange you should find them so little to your taste," he said savagely. "I remember when you had different desires."

He leaned slightly forward and traced a line with his sword point from her navel up between her breasts to her neck. His eyes followed the path of the sword and then bored into hers again.

"Choose," he said with controlled ferocity. "Or I shall choose for you."

There was no pity, no mercy. Clodia knew, suddenly, that things were coming to an end. Life for her as a Roman patrician was over. Even if life remained there was the shame, the impossible shame.

"I choose you," she said softly.

The room had been hushed. But the hush seemed to take on a deeper quality, as if the air itself were stunned into motionlessness. Spartacus glared at her, surprised and then strangely furious that she should try to ensnare him a second time.

"Marcellus!" he snapped. "Take her."

Spartacus watched them take Clodia at sword point to the couch; watched Marcellus, grinning lustfully, strip; saw the rampant penis boom out as they flung Clodia onto the couch; watched her legs pulled apart; noticed the patrician men leaning forward, seeming to forget their danger; watched while Marcellus, unabashed and unembarrassed, crammed into Clodia's still, unresponsive body.

Lying under Marcellus, Clodia felt almost no sensation—just a numbed disgust and a dull ache in her vagina where Marcellus bored cruelly into her dry, unawakened passage.

In her degradation, she also felt a deep bitterness that Spartacus had scorned her, had treated her desperate choice as if it were an impertinence. Seeing the end so near she had decided to succumb with this man between her legs—a last clinging to sharp life. But he had scorned her. In front of the noble blood of Rome he had scorned her. And now she had the double shame of the scorn and the unfeeling spectacle she was providing. She closed her eyes. The man on top of her was tearing her passage apart with his rough enthusiasm.

The male nobility of Rome could hardly believe their eyes. There on the couch in front of them, the noble, virtuous, beautiful, frigid Clodia was stripped, all her nude charms there under their eyes. That in itself was a sight to make the genitals tingle, the penis lurch from its slumber into a stiff awareness.

But to see her ravaged by a gladiator. That was something from wild dreams, something that would be remembered with awe in Roman history.

Their eyes bulged as Marcellus surged into the spread-eagled body. Her large breasts indented a little under him, her buttocks oozed outward on the couch, her drawn-up thighs were still, resigned.

Marcellus was bending her legs this way and that, raising her buttocks off the couch, leaning up from her for a deeper angle, panting and gasping. Clodia's passage, in spite of her, had lubricated and the entry was less painful for him. He forced her legs obscenely out so that her calves dropped, doll-like, over each side of the couch. Her thighs made the sides of a concave bowl for his hips.

Every man in the room made a mental note that if he—and she—got out of this alive he must do his utmost to possess Clodia during the days of life and strength remaining to him. Every woman felt a mixture of hysteria and hot fascination.

The spectacle did not last very long. Clodia's beauty, combined with her frigidity towards him, had so whetted Marcellus' appetite that he felt himself racing to a climax within a few minutes. He would have liked to stop and draw the whole thing out, but now he couldn't. His long powerful strokes swept up into her inner regions in regular, forcing intrusions. His breath panted in Clodia's face as he fastened his mouth on her cold, horrified lips. He swivelled his small hips in large vigorous grindings. Prostrate under him, suffocated under his weight, her face hot and flushed, her belly filled and hurting, Clodia opened her eyes and saw the scores of eyes feasting on her. In them she saw the thirsting, the lust which would always be there, remembering, when those eyes looked at her. She closed her eyes again. She felt sick and deadened.

With the darkness before her eyes, she felt his strokes grow feverish with speed and intensity. She heard his breath exploding. His lips clasped down on hers and she let her mouth fall slackly open against the fury of his efforts. Then she heard him choke. She felt the heat of liquid in her channel, half swooned under his final, brutal thrusts and lay with her eyes closed, sick and unmoving as he stretched his hot, sweating length on the cool softness of her flesh.

Spartacus had watched for a time. Something about Clodia's apathy touched him, made a small dent in the bitter animosity he felt towards her. He remembered how she had responded, led even, in his arms. He had intended to kill her tonight. But now he knew a better way. It would spare her life, but shame her in a way which would remain for her days a reminder of his vengeance. Watching Marcellus panting in passion, Spartacus felt a twinge of pity for the woman. Under different circumstances she would have made a fine woman for him. He felt a slight sickness of regret and walked out into the cool air of the quadrilateral, leaving his men to guard.

Much later, when the streets of Rome were quiet, the house of Lucius Crispus lay in darkness. The off-duty slaves had retired for the night before the play had begun. The remainder now lay trussed up with Crispus' guests in one of the upper rooms.

In another, Clodia lay, hands and ankles bound beside Crispus who was similarly secured. Their faces were lit up by a couple of torches which the gladiators held over them. In the shadow behind the torches, Spartacus stood with a branding iron in his hand.

The flames of a torch had flickered over the iron for a long time. Now it glowed redly in the darkness.

"Untie her ankles," Spartacus commanded.

His men bent and loosened the ropes. She was still naked. Her eyes were filled with a fresh terror. Beside her, a piece of cloth stuffed in his mouth, Crispus closed his eyes, but opened them again as if the closing had not rid him of an image of the scene.

"Pull her legs apart."

Eager, trembling hands grasped the smooth flesh of her thighs, drawing them wide, exposing the closed portals of her vagina. Spartacus bent towards her with the iron. The light from the torches lined his arms with shadows, enclosing the lengths of muscle as they bulged.

Crispus grunted, trying to raise his voice in horrified protest. Clodia slithered backwards on the floor, cringing from the red glow.

"Hold her."

Spartacus moved the iron down to her body, ranged it at a point high up on one of her thighs, aimed it at the soft fleshy fullness just before the inside of the thigh joined her crotch.

He looked at Clodia, gagged too.

"This is how a slave is made," he said. There were evil chuckles from his men in the half-darkness.

With a swift movement, the iron travelled the distance to the white flesh. There was a searing sound, the smell of burning flesh. Clodia writhed under the hands that held her, tore at the gag with her teeth.

When Spartacus stood back there was a little crescent-shaped burn deep in Clodia's thigh. He bent again to the other leg, and Clodia fainted as the branding iron withered her flesh once more.

Spartacus stood up. He looked at the scars with satisfaction. He turned to Crispus with a malicious grin.

"How does it feel to be married to a slave?" he asked.

* * *

Later still, there was a soft stirring from the house of Lucius Crispus. The master and the mistress went out into the dark night. She was still naked and she walked in difficulty as if with pain. They were surrounded by the gladiators.

Swiftly, silently, the gladiators hurried them through the stone-paved streets, with scouts going ahead to watch for the night patrols.

They reached the forum without meeting anyone.

A pale crescent of moon cast only a slight, ghostly light over the huge esplanade as Spartacus and the gladiators pulled their prisoners through the portico which was the public entrance on the south side. To left and right a double colonnade of pillars flanked the forum and opposite—more than a hundred yards off through the gloom—the raised buildings of library and law courts made darker shadows.

Spartacus knew the forum well. How often he had passed through it on the way to the market. He knew just where the bronze equestrian statue of Scipio Africanus glinted in the noon sun in the center of the forum. It was towards this statue of the vanquisher of the great Hannibal that the creeping shadows hurried.

At the base of the statue, rearing above its ten foot hight stone pedestal, Spartacus gave a few orders.

Working quietly and efficiently, the gladiators scaled the pedestal, that statue, and hauled Clodia up with them. There on the bronze rump of the horse they lay Clodia on her back, pulled her legs back to her head, spread them wide and tied them round the back of the horse to its bronze tail. Her womanhood and the slave scars on the insides of her thighs were thus presented to the market, to the throngs who would flock into the forum with the rising sun.

From behind the statue, Spartacus surveyed the obscene contortion into which Clodia was tied. In the darkness he could but vaguely make out of the whiteness of her upturned thighs. But in the morning those thighs would be struck by the first rays of the sun.

Thus, one of the most renowned and virtuous women in Rome would smart with shame under the gaze of rude crowds of peasants, under the eyes of the merchants coming to spread their wares, under the warm glances of the lawyers on their way to the courts, the soldiers, strolling senators, slaves brought for sale; the whole of Rome would view the offered intimacies of Clodia, wife of Senator Lucius Crispus. Spartacus smiled with grim satisfaction.

But the work was not yet complete. On Spartacus' command, his men stripped Crispus and flung him, bound and gagged, to the ground behind the statue. There he would lie to see his wife's and feel his own shame in the morning. So that he might not roll away to hide from the scene, his ankles were attached to the horse's tail with a long rope. Spartacus knew that Crispus would die a thousand deaths from the ignominy of his plight and Clodia's, he knew that Crispus would carry the stigma of that morning with him to his grave.

Spartacus bent beside Crispus' prostrate body. He saw the man's eyes gleam up at him in the slight moonlight.

"In the morning," he whispered, "you will know what it is like to be exhibited in the slave market."

Before they disappeared into the darkness, Spartacus and his small band left Crispus' purple-banded toga at the feet of Scipio Africanus' horse. They wrapped around it the broken chains of a slave.

In the morning, when the first merchants and the first shoppers found the two naked Romans, they were afraid to touch them in case in some strange way they should be associated with the crime and punished. By the time the authorities had been contacted and one of the Consuls with his cortege of lictors arrived in the forum, the word had spread over Rome and a large portion of the population was crowded into the esplanade, jostling to get a better view of Clodia's charms. Crispus, appealing with his eyes for release, was still tied to the horse's tail.

CHAPTER EIGHT

In the days that followed, while arguments about command and stores kept the legions waiting in Rome, Spartacus and his followers began a large-scale plunder of the countryside to the south of Rome. They appeared unexpectedly here and there, always in the place they were least expected, until even citizens in the northern town of Verona began to feel fear.

Spartacus' numbers grew and grew. More and more slaves flocked to his side. As the country houses were plundered, horses and a certain number of weapons were acquired. Soon Spartacus could muster a rabble army of some thousands. Nobody knew just how many he had under his command.

Behind his horde, a scattered trail of destruction and rape was left. His men were the terror of patrician women. Spartacus was the scourge of the land.

It was a symbolic act of rapine that finally forced the commanders of the legions into a settlement and launched the weight of existing Roman soldiery at the gladiators.

A Senator Catius, who had been a Praetor, a Pro-Consul in the distant province of Cicilia, had three attractive virgin daughters. Afraid for their safety in the country house he owned on the Campanian plain, he decided to send them to Rome.

Catius was one of the few people rich enough to own a carriage and it was in this, with a strong bodyguard of loyal slaves, that he dispatched them northwards along the Appian Way. He himself accompanied the carriage on horseback.

It was when the carriage was rumbling slowly along the cambered road only a few miles south of Rome and everyone was beginning to breathe with relief, that the little procession was suddenly intercepted by a band of Spartacus' scouts who had been sent north to watch for the departure of the legions.

The slaves fought valiantly, but were no match for wild men now well versed in the art of skirmishing. They were slaughtered and their bodies left in a straggling line across the road.

They had, however, managed to keep the gladiators at bay while the carriage and Senator Catius made a mad dash towards the capital city. A furious chase began in which the gladiators rode daringly close to Rome before they finally overtook the fleeing carriage.

Catius, twisted on his horse, tried vainly to fight off his enemies as they overtook him, and his daughters shot arrows from the carriage which killed a uple of their pursuers. But their father was cut down and the carriage brought to a standstill when, perhaps, another fifteen minutes of fierce driving would have seen them within sight of the walls of Rome.

There, so near to the Roman legions, the daughters were pulled from their carriage and mauled, struggling and screaming, to the grassy bank of a roadside tomb. They were rudely stripped and beaten and staked down to the tomb by their wrists and ankles. While a few men watched, the remainder raped the women in turn, ripping into their bodies without heed to their screams of pain, satisfying their laughing lust in virgin bellies, while the girls prayed for someone to ride south from Rome, prayed until pain and horror and disbelief filled their minds with a blankness which knew only the suffering of their senses.

After the seed of two dozen gladiators had been sown between their legs, their wrists were slashed and their blood gushed out over their bonds and the tomb of their ancestor. Broken chains were fastened around their necks, gladiators' nets enclosed them and their defiled flesh was stuffed with the great wooden clubs of some of their captors.

Thus they were left, dying on the roadside. Roman nobility was now the slave, bound in chains and nets and rendered sterile by the weapons of the rebels.

Rome, so used to the horrors sown in the wake of the gladiators, shuddered with a fresh chill of horror when the latest outrage was discovered and the legions were immediately marched south without further wrangling. Blood still darkly stained the roadside tomb as it shook to the passing thunder of their feet.

* * *

It was on the slopes of Vesuvius that Spartacus strode, organizing the barricades, encouraging his men, while the Roman legions marched to battle, helmets dazzling in the sun, the silver eagles proudly raised at their head.

Spartacus was well pleased with his position. Paths up the side of the volcano were few and elsewhere the mountain was so steep that the Romans would only be able to attack slowly and awkwardly. His only fear was a siege—the almost inevitable step for the Romans to take. For that contingency he had a trick in hand.

The gladiator chief's forces had now swollen, incredibly, to almost seven thousand men. To his Roman adversary his numbers were unknown and therein lay his advantage. For behind the barricades on Vesuvius, when the silver eagles fanned out in the valley below, crouched only half that number. The remainder were quietly ensconced on the far slopes of a neighboring wooded hill. Scouts in the wood would now be watching the legions' flank with keen eyes.

Spartacus joined Marcellus where he stood, higher up than the barricades, looking out over the thousands of Roman helmets and shields, marching and spreading in a solid wall in the valley. On their flank a few hundred horsemen pranced in controlled exhibitionism. At their head rode Consul Gellius who had finally been given sole command of the army by his colleagues. It was a deliberate show of strength. An eagle spreading its beautiful wings before swooping on the lamb. Spartacus grinned down on the might of Rome and seeing him grin Marcellus grinned too. Time would see who was the lamb.

Consul Gellius was slightly irritated as he rode at the head of his troops into the upland valley which Vesuvius dominated. The gladiators had chosen the most suitable spot to resist what he had hoped would have been a short and glorious mopping up of a scourge.

His eyes travelled up the steep, rocky sides of Vesuvius, right up to where he could see the barricades of the enemy—trees and boulders, shields and rubble. It might be that the barricades would crumble under the weight of his troops. Perhaps he could send wave after wave of men one after the other so that eventually some would scramble through the fire from above and swarm into the rebel camp. Anyway, and Gellius gave a grim chuckle at the thought of it, he could easily starve them out if everything else failed. Spartacus had been very foolish to overlook this obvious possibility. Reassured, he turned on his horse and stared back over the tightly packed regiment of his soldiers. The finest army in the world. He smiled at their solid weight of arms, their smart, efficient appearance.

The first assault began soon after the arrival of the Romans in the valley. The Consul wanted the whole business cleared up quickly. It would be an insult to his command if too much time were spent on what, in a military sense at least, was a small matter.

Shields high, swords drawn, the Romans swarmed quickly and solidly up the lower slopes. But as they climbed, the ascent became more and more difficult, slowing them down to half speed. Those on the paths also went slowly, waiting for their fellow-legionaries. Robbed of their usual cover from the archers, they held their shields above their heads as they advanced. But, eventually, even that became difficult as they needed both hands to clutch at shrubs and rocks in order to keep their footing.

Spartacus watched them come through one of the holes in the barricades. Twelve thousand Roman troops lusting for his blood—and here came the first of them. He could see their swords glinting. Occasionally one dropped a spear with the difficulty of the climb and it rolled and clattered down the side of the mountain. He saw the leather of their tunics swaying and flapping with their efforts. Soon he heard their breathing, watched their muscular arms grasping handholds. His grey eyes were cool. He looked along the barricades at his waiting men and smiled. Gaining strength from his strength, those who saw him smiled too and turned back to watch the Romans struggling towards them.

Spartacus bided his time. What a target. He wondered how they could approach so blindly, so uncovered. Maybe they thought he had only a couple of hundred men and that they would just push away the barricade with their shields and find their adversary cringing at the base of the trees.

Nearer they came, ever nearer. Spartacus waited, stiffening slowly and then, when some of his men were beginning to wonder if he would ever give the command, he uttered a sharp order. A hail of arrows flew down the mountainside, each carefully aimed, each carrying death.

Watching from far below, the Consul saw his first attack fall back. He muttered fiercely to himself as he watched his men crashing to their deaths. The arrows of the gladiators had taken a deadly toll, against which, in such conditions, his legionaries were no match.

As some crashed backwards, clutching their chests, they formed a human avalanche which swept with it those who came behind.

On the paths, after the arrows—less effective as they could be deflected by firmly held shields—the gladiators sent down a shower of boulders.

By the time the survivors reached the level of the valley, Consul Gellius had lost many hundreds of men and the gladiators had not suffered a single casualty.

The Roman commander swore to himself. But it was what he had half expected. He ordered another attack. He was not terribly concerned about the loss of life amongst his ranks. That was what soldiers were for—to lose their lives in the cause of duty. And it would irk him considerably to have to sit down in the valley for a two or three or perhaps even a four day siege.

This time he ordered a regiment of archers to take up positions as best they could behind the advancing legionaries and try to give them as much cover as possible by firing at and over the barricade. He increased the number of men to attack up the paths, ordering them to carry straight on in advance of the others to try to make breaks in the barricade and hold them until those climbing up the rough mountain reached them.

Watching the second attack begin, Spartacus

saw clearly the slight variation in strategy. He ordered his men to pile up the reserves of boulders at the paths, thickened his archery defense at these points and prepared to shoot arrows in a high falling mass on the Roman archers, before they dispersed, while they were still thick on the lower slopes.

The first flood of arrows fell short and fire was withheld. Spartacus waited, watching, judging how soon the Roman archers would have to split up to find niches from which to fire up at his men, judging how soon his own archers would be able to reach them. He judged well and the next flood of arrows hit the legionaries, finding them just in range before they began to split and thin their ranks with the awkwardness of the ascent.

But a fair portion of the Roman troops were able to scatter, lodging themselves in crevices, between boulders, any spot where they could fire over the heads of their advancing comrades and be reasonably safe themselves.

Arrows began to fall over the barricades, to search for and find the apertures through which the gladiators were preparing to fire.

Up the paths, the Romans, no more than two abreast, were making rapid progress, sandaled feet scraping on the rock, kicking up little clouds of dust.

Spartacus waited. The Romans were brave enough. They knew just what had happened last time, but still they came on. There was little hope for those in the early ranks. He looked around, along the barriers. His men crouched close in to the wall of trees and boulders. The Roman arrows flew too high to trouble them.

Up the paths, as they came, eyes looking ahead at the still barricades, he could see the sweat running on the brows of the legionaries above their shields. He gave a sharp order.

Another rain of arrows hurtled down the paths. As shields were raised in defense, the boulders were released and before many Romans had had time to look, a mass of stone was crashing down on them.

The front ranks were crushed, fell back. Those behind clambered off the paths, clinging to the craggy rocks at the side. When the avalanche had passed they climbed back and tried to rush the last distances which separated them from their goal, but the reserves of rock were awaiting them.

Again a mass of rock bowled down against them, again they clambered to safety—and again. And all the time as the back ranks leapt aside they were picked off with well-aimed arrows. They could get to within a certain point of the barricades, but no farther.

The Roman archers found their volleys ineffective. The trajectory of their arrows was too high in clearing the barricades to fall on the gladiators. Occasionally a clever piece of sniping reaped a reward in the apertures of the barrier, but that happened seldom. Meanwhile the rebels, well ensconced, loosed salvo after salvo of destruction into the legionaries crawling up the rock face.

By the time Consul Gellius called off the second attack his losses were already more than he had expected would be necessary in wiping out the gladiators to a man.

Reluctantly he ordered camp to be made, sentries to be posted. He would starve them from their hill.

Spartacus watched the legions settling with satisfaction. This was just what he had foreseen. He, too, posted sentries and ordered the remainder of his men to rest until nightfall.

It was well after midnight that the small fire glowed from a hill just across the valley from Vesuvius. It gave off a small light, small but important, low down on the slopes out of sight of the Roman camp. The light was seen by one of Spartacus' sentries who made haste to call his leader.

"We have an hour to wait," Spartacus said to Marcellus. "Then the way should be clear."

When, later, the gladiators began to descend in shifts of a few hundred at a time, the little fire had disappeared.

They went carefully, keeping to the paths and moving slowly, feeling their way for loose stones, guarding against the slightest noise. On the lower slopes where the descent became easier they came across the first group of Roman sentries, corpses now, throats slit from ear to ear. From the shadow of the trees, Spartacus' own men stepped out to greet him.

"The Roman camp is surrounded," reported Lucinius, whom Spartacus had left in charge of his forces on the far hill. "All the sentries are dead. We had no trouble. They were watching Vesuvius. We took them completely by surprise."

"Good." Spartacus spoke the word like a prophecy. This night was to see the most ignominious defeat the Roman legions had known since the plundering days of the Gauls and the Carthaginians.

In the trees and scrub at the foot of Vesuvius, he waited until all his men had come down from the rim of the volcano. Then he gave a number of quiet orders and they moved out quietly to thicken the ranks of their fellows already surrounding the tents of the legions.

Quietly they closed in, a tighter and tighter ring around the camp. Spartacus came to the very edge of the tents where they stretched away in neat rows in front of him. All was still; the remnants of twelve thousand Romans lying in a sleep from which many of them would never awaken.

Spartacus looked along the crouching ranks of his men as far as he could see them on this side of the camp. He strained his eyes between the tent rows. He could not see his men on the far side of the camp. For a moment he had an unreasonable fear that perhaps they were not there. Ten thousand men was an enormous number to have to kill even if one had the advantage of taking them unawares, in sleep. The eyes of his men were watching him, waiting for an order, motley weapons at the ready. Spartacus hesitated no longer. He gave a sharp cry, the short howl of a wolf. And from all sides his men attacked the tents.

Fewer than two to one were the odds against the gladiators. And many of the rebels had killed three before the alarm was given. The

Roman camp was thrown into confusion. Legionaries were murdered in their beds, others cut down before they had time to find their arms; tents collapsed, others were cut down to enmesh the struggling occupants before the slaughter.

Only in the very heart of the camp, the last portion to be reached, did the Romans have time to realize the emergency, to seize their arms and form themselves into any sort of organization.

Fighting desperately, with Consul Gellius at their head, losing men all the way, they managed to struggle to their horses. Even then some were hauled down, rider and horse crashing to the ground. But a few, the Consul among them, cut their way through the gladiators and made a desperate flight across the valley, pursued by a host of arrows.

The battle among the tents raged for a comparatively short time. Here and there little pockets of heroic resistance fought a glorious and short-lived action before they were overwhelmed by sheer weight of numbers. No prisoners were taken. For those who had not escaped it was a battle to the death—a battle in which the gladiators were well versed.

When the sun rose over Vesuvius, it lit up a scene of carnage the like of which had been seen on Roman soil only few times in its long history.

With the exhausted arrival of Consul Gellius and the other survivors in Rome, the city was dazed. The unbelievable had happened and Rome was defenseless. The whole of the peninsula was open prey for the gladiator chief and his horde.

In a desperate fear which was close to hysteria, messengers were dispatched by land and sea to Pompeius in Spain and Caesar in Gaul.

CHAPTER NINE

Losing no time, Spartacus began a march of destruction northwards from Vesuvius. He alone of his men realized the obvious and incredible possibility. He alone saw how near he was to becoming Emperor of Imperial Rome.

Before him stretched the Campanian plain, fertile and welcoming, with its rich little cities afraid and almost unarmed against him.

The first of them, he entered almost without opposition. At first he had considered leaving garrisons of his men behind and pressing on to Rome. But his men wanted plunder and luxury. Having lived their lives in chains they wanted a taste of what had been denied them. Spartacus gave way before their desires and in every town they pillaged and slaughtered, lived on its food, its women, its wine and then left it a burning ruin behind them. All up the peninsula, the perfume of the grapes and the olives was polluted with the heavy tang of smoke from the embers of what had once been towns.

As they moved north up the Appian Way, they found that greater resistance had been organized against them. Citizens had voluntarily formed themselves into small armies, gates had been barricaded, walls of the cities manned with makeshift weapons.

When they left the road to take Antitum on the coast, they were forced to besiege the city for a couple of days before they eventually broke its resistance.

Once inside the walls, they wreaked havoc as usual and it was while he was gazing with a reminiscent hatred at the amphitheatre that Spartacus thought of another way to avenge his men against the Romans.

A fresh horde of slaves had been released from their chains in the city and these, Spartacus decided, should gain their revenge for their years of servitude and give his men some entertainment at the same time.

Into the arena he had driven a crowd of patrician women clad only in their short undertunics. Into the terraces he and his men crowded, forcing with them the husbands and relatives of the women below. Then at a sign from Spartacus, the newly released slaves were let into the arena, naked.

The women, screaming and pleading for mercy, were chased all over the amphitheatre, thrown to the ground and forced to submit to whatever particular pleasure their captor desired. Some women, more attractive than others, were seized by more than one man. Those that were left tried vainly to climb the sheer wall to the terraces or to force open the grill into one of the arcades at the opposite ends of the amphitheatre. Many cried out to their loved ones watching from the terraces, imploring their aid. After the gladiators had cut off the head of one man who tried to rush to the aid of his wife who was groaning under the passionate impaling of a slave, the remainder just watched in dumb horror.

Particular rapes or perversions became focal points of attraction, according to their strangeness or ferocity, or according to the beauty of the woman involved or the fight she put up.

One such spectacle was the seizing of a woman whose figure, by its provocative proportions under the tunic, gave delight to every man who watched from the arena-side.

She was chased by three slaves at once and made a great effort to escape them, running blindly towards one of the bolted gates. Her tunic curved tautly around her hips as she ran, outlining the sinuous lines of the straining buttocks beneath. Her limbs were long, loose looking and well rounded. Her breasts jutted out from the tunic in sharp, uplifted convexities.

The men took her from behind before she reached the gate and she fell under them. Each one in his lust became almost a lunatic, rubbing his stiff member against any part of her bare skin he could find, feverishly clasping breasts and buttocks through the tunic.

The woman twisted and rolled, clawing and kicking. The tunic slithered tightly up and over her bottom, leaving it bare and beautiful in the sunlight. Her buttocks grazed against the sand, patches of dust streaking them.

Fighting over her, tearing the tunic, the slaves soon had it off her. They fought over her breasts, biting them, chewing the nipples so that she screamed with pain. One of them had an orgasm during the struggle and fell back on the sand.

The other two continued to maul and pummel her, each trying to force himself into the orifice between her legs. Spattered with dust, sand and sweat, the woman fought and fought until eventually they forced her onto her side and took her from either side.

The slave facing her pulled her legs around him and jammed into her with a gasp which was heard all over the amphitheatre. The woman cried out and began to weep profusely, whereupon the man behind her forced his weapon slowly but firmly into the same aperture.

The woman groaned hysterically. She felt as if her sex had been enlarged with a sword. The pain was excruciating. She felt as if she were just a huge vagina, nothing else, no other part of her existing.

To each of the men, too, the fit had been difficult and pleasantly painful. But now, their throbbing, splitting staffs wedged tightly together, they began to slip in slowly, farther and farther into the moistened passage between her legs.

They jerked in time with each other, ramming their hips into her from each side in a regular rhythm. Up in the terraces the woman's husband, one of their hated masters, was watching helplessly, making their fierce pleasure even greater.

The slave behind her ran his hands over her breasts, holding each, squeezing them, arms clasping her in a suffocating embrace. While the man behind bit her neck in his passion, bringing out little pink scars in her skin, the one performing the frontal attack put his tongue in her mouth and sucked the flood of tears from her tormented, lovely face.

While the two of them ground into her with increasing vigor, the third man, watching them, began to recover, to feel a weight of desire unfolding him again.

He crawled on his knees to the trio, locked in a fury of passion. He pulled the woman's face away from the lips of the panting slave who was kissing her. He pushed himself at her lips, spreading them apart, away from the white, even teeth. He slapped her face until the teeth parted and his cudgel had entered her mouth.

The woman's tear-stained face was blank-looking. The horror had gone so far she could no longer think. She was just in a terrible nightmare of degradation. That was all there was. A hot nightmare of sensation, of raping, of excruciating, painful horror.

On either side of her, the rapists were panting and wheezing. From behind the one clasped her breasts in a cruel pressure, his fingers digging mercilessly deep into the flesh. He couldn't help himself. He was hanging on, hanging on to something while the flood of passion left him defenseless in space.

He rammed and rammed, muttering, gasping, panting, groaning. The tide swelled and swelled. A great wave was rushing towards the shore and with a sudden, almighty drawing out of all the forces of his body, it was crashing onto the rocks of the shore, driving on and on and on in gasped-out passion until it was dwindling and receding and he slid out of her.

As he rolled away and lay on his back, gasping with satisfaction, the third man, pulling himself from the woman's mouth, scrambled round her, and thrust his member in.

The drubbing of her body was coming to an end. Pulling her legs higher around him, making more room for the other slave as he did so, the second slave finished, gasping.

As his passion broke from him, he barked, almost like a dog and pulled her hair with an involuntary viciousness.

When he came out of her, a trickle of blood dribbled after him and soaked into the sand. The woman lay drooping and beaten, her flickering eyelashes the only sign of the pain she felt where the third man was still working away.

After he had exploded behind her, so that she felt the final, hurting fury of his last strokes and the sudden sting of his teeth in her neck, she rolled over onto her stomach, uncaring of the thousands of eyes which watched her, and lay exhausted, physically and emotionally, on the floor of the arena.

All over the arena similar scenes of carnality were proceeding. The noblewomen were undergoing every kind of ravishment. All were filled with shame and degradation as they lay helpless, after the depravity which had been unleashed on them, in crumpled heaps of bare limbs and breasts.

On the terraces there were tears among their

men, tears of shame at the disgrace the women had suffered.

After the mass debauchery, Spartacus had the arena cleared of slaves, He had his gladiators enter, fully armed, bringing arms and shields for the women.

The raped, dazed creatures, formerly the pride of Antium, were then forced to fight each other. It was a case of kill or be killed. Those who were victorious kept their lives.

It was difficult, at first, to get them to fight. They stood, weeping, trident or sword dangling in their hands. The gladiators began to whip them, or beat their bare buttocks with the flat of their swords, until at last from sheer desperation to escape further pain one of the women swiped out at her opponent with her sword. The other nearly lost an arm, gathered her shield, crying abandonedly and began to fight back as if in a trance.

Up in the terrace, Spartacus' lips were set in a thin line. This was the final hard revenge. The revenge par excellence. Patrician women fighting like gladiators, like the uncouth beasts they considered such men to be.

When the first woman fell with her opponent's sword between her taut breasts, the victor stood for a moment with a look of dazed horror on her face, rocked back on her heels and passed out.

The slaves in the terraces were thoroughly enjoying the gruesome entertainment. They watched with delight, the female warrior's buttocks tensing and quivering as they lunged and withdrew, their breasts shaking like dainty jellies, their stomachs heaving with the unaccustomed effort.

"They look as if they were born to it," Marcellus shouted, and the amphitheatre shook with laughter.

At one point, two adversaries suddenly turned on the gladiator who was whipping them to greater efforts. But the man, grinning from ear to ear, knocked their weapons from their hands in quick succession and gave them a fresh beating before setting them at each other once more.

The long day's entertainment was drawing to a close when at last the arena was littered with the bloody bodies of the women of Antium. Those who had won were herded into an arcade while the bodies were dragged away. They were shaking with horror and disbelief. Some broke down completely under the strain of the most fantastic day of their lives and they were left to cry themselves into oblivion on the ground.

After the arena had been cleared and religiously raked in biting mockery of the usual gladiatorial shows, the women were driven back into its unfriendly confinement.

They gathered in the center lifting arms and faces to their menfolk who were still watching in horror. They were beginning to lose their reason.

A murmur began to ripple among the watching men. Their women were going to have to fight ad bestiarium, to be set upon by wild beasts. No sooner had the horrified rumor begun than a team of a dozen tigers was let into the arena.

The gate clanged shut behind them and they began to stalk slowly round the arena, lowered eyes on the women who backed away towards one of the walls.

Growling quietly, the tigers moved nearer, crouching low on thick, supple paws. Their teeth showed as they growled, their eyes were dark suns.

Some of the women had fainted, others collapsed, weeping, unable to believe in the reality of everything that was happening to them that day. Others again, aware of their weapons, formed a shivering barrier against the animals, trying to encourage their weeping friends to do likewise.

Their scalps tingled with horror. Even the gladiators watching from their safe heights were hushed.

The tigers circled and circled, watching the women whose tridents and swords jutted threateningly towards them, growling softly to themselves all the time, a sinister menace which filled the whole arena with a chill.

The first one to spring did so with a growl which became a full-throated roar of savage attack. He was impaled on a trident, but carried it under his weight and landed, clawing and writhing amongst the women, knocking several of them to the ground. One of them desperately plunged her sword into his back, but there was momentary terror and confusion, and amidst the disorder, the remaining eleven beasts launched themselves into the fray.

At this point, one of the patricians in the terraces uttered a cry of horror and ran amok at the gladiators who guarded the aisles and exits. Tears were streaming down his face and his voice yelled wild and incoherent abuse. He was cut down trying to grapple with three armed men with his bare hands.

His example was not without effect and another man suddenly sprang down the terraces and hurled himself the twenty feet from the ringside terrace down into the arena.

There he landed on his feet and was flung forward onto his face. A wild strength brought him almost immediately to his feet and, seizing a sword from one of the women, he lunged at the nearest tiger who was clawing a woman to pieces.

A gladiator raised his bow, but Spartacus gave a sharp order and the bow was reluctantly lowered.

In the arena terror was everywhere. A couple of tigers were dead, but now there was almost no opposition to them. They were simply stalking and killing terrified, cringing women.

Spartacus, watching the Roman who had sprung valiantly, but hopelessly to their rescue, wondered if any other Roman would follow him, but none moved. Some had covered their faces with their hands; others seemed transfixed with horror.

Cursing and shouting, even in the throes of struggle, the Roman tried to rally the women. He managed to push the tiger, whose belly he had ripped, from him and stumbled, bleeding badly, to his feet.

He called to the women to get back against the wall of the arena and face the animals with a wall of weapons, but nobody seemed to hear him. His voice was half drowned by the screams and the growls and the women's terror was too great.

In a final, gallant giving of his life, he leapt onto the back of a tiger, whose claws were ripping the breasts of a prostrate, unconscious woman. The tiger turned on him savagely, wounded once, and grasped his arm in its jaws. The sword fell from his hand.

Within a few more minutes not a soul was living in the arena. Only the remaining animals, tearing the corpses, snuffling the blood.

At a sign from Spartacus a shower of spears and arrows slashed down from the terraces. Struck down as if by magic, the tigers clawed vainly at their backs, roaring in anger. And one by one they collapsed beside the bodies of their victims.

CHAPTER TEN

News of the gladiatorial ignominy was the final bitter pill which pushed Rome into fresh and furious action. It was one of the richest men in the Empire, the banker Marcus Crassus, who financed the rebuilding of the legions. From his own pocket he offered to equip a new army of which he would retain command.

Rome, the Senate, agreed, from desperation and in some gratitude although they doubted the motives of Marcus Crassus. His love of power, which, so far, had shown itself only in the acquisition of his great wealth, was well known.

Marcus Crassus began immediately, methodically, and efficiently to set about his task. He had the advantage of the time the gladiator horde wasted in every city they took on their march towards Rome. Everybody knew that had the gladiators besieged Rome straight after their victory they would have taken it in a matter of days. Now it might be too late.

It was while he was bent on his organization that Marcus received Clodia Crispus into his house.

Since the day all Rome had seen her in the flesh, Clodia had hardly appeared in public. She had begun to divorce Crispus—which pleased him as he would never have been able to live in connection with her since such shame had been endured by him; apart from that she had stayed scheming in her own part of their house.

The degradation through which she had been forced weighed on her like a fever. During the day she went through fresh agonies of mind as she failed to keep her thoughts from picturing the obscene spectacle she had made that morning. At night she wept hot tears in her hatred for Spartacus who had done it to her.

As news of his latest victories and revenge on the Roman aristocracy filtered through to her, she developed an obsession for vengeance.

On her thighs the scars no longer burned, but they had left a permanent mark to remind her that Spartacus had branded her a slave. She would lie on her bed and stare at the marks until tears blinded her and she clawed at the counterpane in rage. She could not live unless she revenged herself on her former slave.

Marcus Crassus looked up with interest and hurried to meet Clodia as she arrived. He knew of her beauty and it was a source of envy to him that he had missed the spectacle she had provided on both occasions.

He had excused himself from Crispus' play performance and he had not had reason to go to the forum early on the following day. The desire-provoking beauty he had thus missed had been relayed to him together with rumors that Clodia had been having an affair with the handsome Thracian and he had revenged himself for her betrayal. Of course nobody knew the truth of these rumors and Crassus took them with a pinch of salt—without of course discarding their possibility—but that Clodia's renowned beauty had been twice paraded before Rome and that on one occasion she had provided half the spectacle in the sexual act were facts which brooked no denial.

"It is a pleasure to see you," he purred, leading the way into an inner room. She should not think that she had suffered any stigma in his eyes due to her misfortunes.

Settled in his inner sanctuary, to which he had wine and sweetmeats brought, Crassus regarded her while they exchanged pleasantries.

Yes, she was beautiful all right. Her breasts pushed her stola out at a sharp angle so that it pulled in a long slope down to her girdle. He found it difficult to take his eyes off the tilt of her breasts.

She seemed rather nervous—not surprising

after her experiences—but was at pains to disguise it. In spite of her nervousness, he read in her eyes a look which bode ill for somebody.

Even small talk these days ended on Spartacus and his gladiators. When Marcus Crassus remarked that he'd been rather busy lately fitting out his army and that it was coming along very well, Clodia looked him in the eyes and said: "It was that which I came to talk to you about."

Crassus raised his eyebrows in surprise.

"You've no doubt heard of the way I was treated by this beast," Clodia said, and giving no time for confirmation, continued: "You must also realize that he's ruined my life in Rome. People do not act towards me in the same way they used to. I'm some sort of circus."

"My dear lady—" Crassus began. Clodia cut him short.

"Thank you. But I'm afraid it's true. And I am no longer the same person. There is something which occupies me exclusively." She paused and Crassus wondered if he should prompt her, decided against it.

"What I want—in fact the only thing I want—is revenge."

She spat the last words in such a bitter tone that Crassus was startled. He wondered if she was like that when she made love. His eyes lowered to her breasts and fluttered guiltily away.

"I have thought about it a lot," Clodia went on relentlessly, "and the best way I can get revenge seems to be to help your army and you."

Crassus stared at her with a new interest.

"I have no idea what your plans are in a military sense," she continued. "But everybody realizes by now that Spartacus is a redoubtable enemy."

Crassus noticed that as she pronounced the name she seemed to hesitate and her lip quivered. He waited for her to go on talking. She obviously had something worked out.

Clodia's eyes still held his as she said: "You no doubt have also heard that I was branded with the marks of a slave. I may never be rid of those marks so it seems I might as well put them to some use." She paused. Crassus continued to regard her attentively.

"I believe the battle in which he routed the legions," she went on, "was won because of a ruse."

"That is so," Crassus said.

"Had there been a spy in his camp—someone who knew what the movements were going to be—I think Gellius need never have fallen into the trap."

"Very possibly."

"So all Rome needs is a spy—and I am willing to fill that role."

Crassus was taken aback.

"My dear lady, that is no job for—"

"I need my revenge," Clodia cut in fiercely. "This is the only thing I want to do—to see this man and his ruffians crushed."

"But for a noblewoman like yourself to attempt such a task would be suicide," Crassus said. "How could you possibly pass as a slave?"

"I have the proof burned into my legs," Clodia said bitterly.

Crassus' eyes dropped to her uncovered ankles on the divan wondering exactly where the brand was. Near her coveted treasure, he'd been told.

"But that would mean considerable embarrassment to you," he remonstrated. "And it's possible someone would recognize you in any case."

"Not if I went dressed as a slave, had my hair cut, made myself unkempt. What slave ever looks up from the ground in Rome, anyway? Nobody would recognize me, I'm sure. As for the others, I no longer care. They could see the scars for their proof."

Crassus licked his lips. He felt a flutter at his loins.

"They would kill you if you were discovered," he said. "That would be a ridiculous, shameful fate for such a beautiful woman."

"My fate doesn't worry me," Clodia said. "Only that of Spartacus. If they killed me I hope it would not be before I had the pleasure of seeing a dagger in his heart."

"You are a very brave woman," Crassus said. He felt a slight frustration. If her fate mattered so little to her, how could a night in his bed be refused him. But her cold beauty repelled any consideration of making advances to her and he contented himself with adding: "But I think such a plan would be madness."

"Well I offered my services," Clodia said coldly. "I am going anyway."

Crassus stood up from his couch and paced slowly to the window and back.

"If that is so," he murmured at last, "then naturally, in spite of my horror at the danger into which you put yourself, I should be foolish to refuse your help."

"Good," Clodia said, with finality. "Then if you'll give me a day to prepare, perhaps you'll then give me an escort to within a reasonable distance of the gladiators' camp and arrange for the safety of my passage when I return."

"Certainly," Crassus said. "I'll give instructions to specially trusted guards on the city walls. You'll have no difficulty."

Clodia rose. Her eyes had not left his throughout the interview.

"Finally," she said, "I would like you not to mention my plans to anyone at all apart from your special guards. I am leaving word with my slaves that I am going north. I'm sure everyone will understand why I should wish to leave the city."

"You may trust me implicitly," Crassus assured her. He had in fact the reputation of a man who could keep his mouth shut.

Walking with her towards the door of his house, Crassus cast sidelong glances at the soft swaying of her breasts. But in spite of what he considered her suicidal mission, he could not bring himself to suggest a last night of joy before she went. Perhaps he was afraid of refusal.

"Incidentally," he said as they walked. "It is my belief that this man Spartacus is becoming some sort of god among his rabble. With him out of the way I believe half the battle would be won."

"We shall see."

He watched the stola, pulled in at her slim waist, writhing gently around her bottom as she walked away.

CHAPTER ELEVEN

When Clodia rode out from the city with the two Roman centurions galloping on either side, her appearance had changed considerably. Her hair had been cropped much shorter and allowed to become unkempt; she wore none of the perfume and adornments of her class. Her lips were unrouged, she wore no powdered antimony around her eyes, no cream on her skin; she was dressed in the dirty tunic of a slave and her nails, even, had been cut and allowed to become impregnated with dirt.

In some strange way these preparations, while altering her appearance, seemed only to add to her beauty, giving her a wild, forest beauty in place of the refined, hothouse loveliness of before.

They rode hard in the darkness, towards the south, their horses' hooves clattering on the stones of the road until it became too risky for the escort to go farther.

At a point in the wilds, Clodia dismounted and watched silently while the men wheeled and disappeared back towards the safety of Rome, taking her horse with them.

Clodia shivered, unaccustomed to the short tunic. And then she began to walk. For some time she kept up a good pace, her sandled feet thudding steadily on the stones.

After an hour or two she was beginning to tire. She had been used to travelling by carriage or in a slave-borne litter. All around her was dark loneliness and she began to feel afraid. It occurred to her that she might not even get to Spartacus' camp, but might be struck down by robbers. She quickened her pace again.

Another hour passed and Clodia felt sure she must be in enemy territory. Antium had been the last town they'd wrecked. They must by now have moved farther north.

Her legs ached now and her shoulders responded to the ache with another. She sat down for a while on a roadside tomb, listening to the wind, the night noises of insects, hearing nothing besides. She nearly fell asleep, resisted and began to trudge south once more.

When she suddenly found herself surrounded by a small group of armed men she was startled that she had not heard the slightest sound before they were there.

"It's a woman," a voice shouted.

There were murmurs of curiosity.

"I am Marcia, slave of Lucius Crispus," she cried quickly. "I have come to join Spartacus."

The men moved in closer. Clodia was not afraid. Many slave women had fled, sometimes with male slaves, sometimes alone, to escape from the cruelty of their patrician masters.

Now she could see the men. They were armed with short swords and some had shields. They were clearly some advance guard of Spartacus' forces.

"Why should you want to join us?" The words had come from a big, bluff man, shaggy as a monkey, with a big moustache. He appeared to be the commander of the group.

"Because I hate the Roman overlords," Clodia said with a snarl in her voice. "I want freedom."

"And what did your overlord do to you, my pretty one?"

"He tried to rape me," Clodia said boldly.

There were hoots of laughter.

"Only tried!" someone yelled. "He must have been senile."

"Shut up! Do you want the Romans to hear us?" snapped the leader.

He came closer to Clodia, examining her in the gloom, from head to toe. His eyes were wary. They had not accepted her without question.

He put his hand on her breast and Clodia felt it there, warm and heavy for a few seconds.

"A beauty, all right," he said softly. He whistled quietly through his teeth.

"Will you take me back to your camp?" Clodia asked. "I've been walking from Rome and I'm exhausted."

"Let's exhaust her a little more, first," somebody said.

"Yes. I lay first claim," said another.

The big man turned savagely on them again.

"I said shut up," he snapped violently.

"What odds? There aren't any Roman soldiers left," one of his men said petulantly. A titter of laughter greeted his remark.

The big man left Clodia and pushed his way to the speaker. He hit him squarely on the jaw and the man fell backwards and lay holding his face.

Nobody else moved and the big man surveyed them.

"I'm in charge," he said. "If I say shut up, everybody shuts up."

"All right, all right," they growled around him.

He turned back to Clodia, who, now that she had actually stopped walking again, began to feel weak. She had a sense of anti-climax about the whole thing, a numbness in her head where there should have been fear, determination, some acute reaction to the situation.

The leader's eyes were on her again. She could still feel where he had held her breast as if weighing it.

"Turn around."

She almost hesitated—and then turned obediently, presenting him with her back.

"Lovely piece of flesh," someone said. There was a note of awe in the voice.

The big man suddenly gripped her tunic at the shoulder, ripping it across the back. Clodia stood still, trembling slightly. "Why haven't you any lash marks on your back?" the man snapped.

"He never lashed me," Clodia said. "He preferred to slap my face and try to rape me."

The man grunted and then she felt his hand move down her back and feel her bottom. He cupped his big hand around the buttocks and drew it across her whole rump. She heard the almost inaudible whistle through his teeth again.

"Where are your brand marks?" he asked roughly.

"On my legs."

"Where? Show them."

Clodia turned towards the watching men again and pulled up her tunic. Everybody pressed closer; the air resounded with suckings of lips, cluckings of tongues. The big man looked round and pushed them back. "Give her some room," he said unnecessarily.

Clodia edged up the hem of her loincloth, stopping short at the verge of her crotch. The little crescents made dark marks on the white skin.

The man nodded. He touched the marks with his finger tips. His fingers were moist on her skin. And then he ran his hand suddenly between her legs, brushing it along the thin curtain of cloth over her vagina.

Clodia breathed in sharply. The feeling of his rough fingers on the thinly-veiled flesh brought home to her what she had let herself in for, seemed to bring back sensation to her mind and body.

The big man chuckled, noticing her reaction.

"All right," he said. "Let's go."

"How about it chief. Let's stretch her out and give her a welcome."

Clodia was horrified now that she was confronted with the reality, even though she would have to submit to somebody. It was a thought she had hidden in the back of her mind, overwhelming it with her desire for revenge on Spartacus.

The leader seized her arm and turned to the others.

"Listen," he said. "This one is mine. I've been looking for something like this for a long time —and if anybody wants to quarrel with that then say so now."

There was a hostile silence.

"Maybe Spartacus would like to see her—or Marcellus," someone said threateningly. Clodia's heart fell.

The big man's lip curled savagely under his moustache.

"If anyone thinks that, he can come and take her."

He released Clodia's arm and stood in a posture of mock invitation. Again nobody moved.

"And if anyone tries to be funny later on," he added, "they tell me it's a pretty uninteresting existence in one of those things." He indicated the dim shape of one of the roadside tombs.

There was no more argument and Clodia was marched with them across the plain to the inland hills. The big man held her arm all the way. Her mind simply refused to react to the thought that she was his."

They were challenged by a number of lookouts on the way and finally passed by the sentries into the gladiators' camp.

The camp was set in a small valley in the foothills of the mountains, well-guarded to the west by the hills with their lookout posts, well-guarded on the other three sides by the height and steepness of the mountains. It was a big camp. It now housed close to ten thousand people. The tents were arranged in neat rows with here and there a clearing where a fire glowed and people sat talking and drinking in the flickering light.

A fresh patrol went out to replace the one which had just come in and the group of men dispersed.

The big man led Clodia through the ranks of tents, stopping finally in front of one. He bent and untied the flaps and stooped into the interior, dragging her with him. He released her while he fussed with something in the darkness. Then the light of a stolen lamp flared up and he fastened the tent flaps behind them.

Removing his helmet and his armor, then unstrapping his sandals, he looked at Clodia. He nodded towards the rough bed and she sat down on it. He continued to look at her as he drew off first one sandal then the other. His eyes lingered on the exposed portions of her legs and thighs. She was the most beautiful slave he'd ever seen.

"You eaten?" he asked.

Clodia shook her head and he indicated a leather pannier.

"Bread and cheese and wine in there," he said. She was to learn as she came to know him better how sudden flashes of kindness and humor would break through his usual domineering and sadistic attitude.

He never took his eyes from her while she ate. At last he stood up, his great, hairy body bulging mountainously from his loincloth, and took a draught of wine.

"Get undressed," he snapped.

Clodia sat there dumbly while he took off his loincloth. His big penis was in full erection, soaring out from his loins like a stiff, artificial fixture. Clodia felt sick. She had known this would have to happen, but somehow she hadn't faced the reality.

He turned towards her and his shaggy testicles swung under the organ which seemed to point accusingly at her.

"I said get your clothes off," he snapped viciously.

Mechanically, Clodia began to pull off the tunic.

The man sat and watched her, scratching his testicles.

As each article of clothing came off, he whistled through his teeth. Her breasts were so taut and big, the skin looked soft and flawless, different from so many of the women he'd had.

When she slipped out of the loincloth, her heart was thumping and her face was burning with shame. Revenge, revenge, she kept telling herself. This was the only way.

The man smacked his lips.

"Turn around," he said.

She turned around. He had her turn around several times, looking at her body in admiration and a desire which he increased by not seizing her immediately. He could hardly believe the perfection of the lines of buttocks and breasts, the skin pulled in tautly below the breasts so that the lines of the ribs were light shadows. Her hips! The breath wheezed through his teeth at her hips with their fleshy flowering into thighs and the tufts of central hair that gleamed in the flickering light . . .

"Jupiter, what a wonderful piece you're going to be," he muttered.

Clodia turned away, overcome by the coarseness of his tone.

"You have such a beautiful ass I'm going to take that first," he said. He laughed. "Ever had that before?"

Clodia's stomach was heaving in and out, her breasts rising and falling in a constricted pain.

"No," she said faintly.

He whistled in surprise.

"This lord of yours must have been a woman," he cracked.

He got heavily to his feet and came over to her. He pressed hard up against her and she could feel his great club hot against her buttocks. His big hands closed over her breasts as he pressed her back against him. He kissed her neck, his hot breath panting over into her face, his moustache tickling her.

In his arms, Clodia felt crushed. She had a peculiar revulsion in her loins which was half excitement. He was like an animal, a great hairy beast. She felt his hand wander down from her breasts, feeling her body, pressing on the stomach, the abdomen. And as he pressed on her lower belly, she felt his hips pushing into her, felt herself pulled back onto his penis.

"Lie down on the bed," he ordered thickly.

Clodia lay on the bed, her eyes closed.

"On your belly," he snarled impatiently.

Clodia's lips moved in a prayer as she rolled over onto her belly. She clutched the blankets with her hand, pushing her face into the rough sacking he used as a pillow.

She heard the breath whistle through his teeth again as he stood looking down on her for a moment. She heard a shuffle, sensed him bending towards her and then his great hairy body seemed to envelop her, crushing her into the rough blankets. He did not blow out the lamp.

Clodia tried to forget herself. She tried to imagine that perhaps it was Spartacus and that she no longer hated him. But the filthy wheezings would not allow her to forget that this was an animal, a great, uncouth, shaggy animal using her delicate body. She was afraid, too, of the pain of being used in this disgusting way. She wished she could faint.

She cringed under his shuffling hips. She could feel the thick, curly hair of his loins, brushing warmly on her bottom. She clasped her buttocks together, hopelessly.

His fingers tugged her hair so that she gave a little shriek, muffled in the blankets.

"Open your legs," he commanded.

He tugged her hair again, viciously, panting with a mixture of annoyance and passion. She squealed and spread her thighs automatically.

The man slithered between them. She forced herself to relax. It was no good fighting him.

She felt his fingers pressing, at last, against her tender flesh and she jerked her hips involuntarily into the blankets.

"Relax," he snarled.

She relaxed again and his fingers were prodding the tight, tender skin. She felt the blunt, hot hugeness of him there now as his hips jerked and shuffled on her.

He was muttering fiercely, wheezing through his teeth. He did not penetrate. His breath was a series of gasps. Suddenly he slithered up from her, kneeling between her thighs.

He pulled her hips off the blankets, up towards him.

"Kneel up, kneel up!" he cursed.

Reluctant and frightened, she kneeled up. She felt his knees pushing her knees further from each other. A tremor went through her body at being treated this way. It seemed unreal.

She felt his hands on her waist, pressing down, forcing her back to arch concavely. She flopped her hot face down on the sacking. Her bottom seemed to be something apart from her, right up in the air, exposed behind her.

Looking down on her, the big man was twisted with passion at the beauty of her body. He was aching to get in the small hole with a passion that shook his whole body.

As he pushed forward, he began to pull her bottom back as well, grasping her hips at the soft, creased flesh where her thighs joined them, feeling her soft belly trembling beneath his finger tips.

He undulated his hips, pushing, pushing, stabbing, and suddenly there was a give.

Crying noiselessly into the sacking, Clodia felt his thickness suddenly invade her with the sharp pain of a sword thrust. She couldn't bear it. She tried to struggle away, but he held her hips in a fury of passion and kept his knees between her thighs. Her breasts brushed against the blankets so that her aching nipples hurt against the rough texture.

She cried out, biting into the sacking, her hands twisting the blankets into ridges. She felt as if she wanted to be sick. Gradually she became used to the filling. It was just a terrible, degrading soreness, which flared into a new pain each time he thrust forward. Clodia cried abandonedly into the sacking. This was the final indignity.

The fact of her crying and clutching the blankets added to his passion. It was like a blind spot in his head. His head was passion. There was nothing else in it.

He grasped her hips so hard that his fingers dug deeply into the flesh. He pulled her hips back at him every time he jerked forward, so that she helplessly assisted in the further impalement. He had never known such exquisite pain.

He stabbed hard at her and she tried to jerk forward again. He could see her flaming cheeks, the tears spilling on the sacking, feel the stomach heaving like a mad thing. And then he rammed forward with all his might.

That was it. His lips pulled away from his teeth as he looked at her helpless body, writhing under him. A sadistic fury was in his loins. He pulled almost right out of her and then pushed stiffly in again the whole way.

Clodia was unable to think. She was just a great, gaping pit of pain in the secret depths of her behind. Her body was no longer hers.

It belonged to him and he was using it cruelly, abusing it, shattering it with pain.

At a time when the pain was at its worst, she wished she had not set out on this mad mission. She cried out inside herself, mouth working against the sacking, feeling the salt of her tears on her lips. She could no longer escape. She was held too firmly. She had to remain grotesquely positioned, to be skewered and skewered until he reached his finish and it was over.

His panting was faster, becoming uncontrolled. It filled the tent, resonating from the walls. His hips jerked with rapid fury. His heart was thumping so loudly in his chest that he could hear it. His loins were an inferno of sensation. The sensation seemed to swim round and round in them aimlessly while he gasped and screwed up his face in passion.

Round and round, jostling, flowing in his loins. And then he felt it gain direction. He pressed her waist down towards the blankets, and he heard her muffled gasping.

The hot, burning liquid was flowing now, coming to the outer world like an erupting volcano. He slowed to grinding thrusts, trying to savor the last delights. And then his mouth opened wide and he could no longer control, only yield, and the volcano had erupted.

Clodia had a spasm of horror as she felt him, felt the jagged punishment of his final thrust. When she felt him slip out of her she collapsed thankfully to the bed, crying softly, aware of an empty burning soreness inside her.

He lay on her, crushing her, breathing heavily and she kept still under his weight. Her body felt exhausted, emotionally she felt exhausted. She wanted badly to sleep and forget.

After a while he rolled off her and lay, face up, on the bed. Soon she heard him snoring and she breathed a sigh of relief; then she, too, relaxed and, in spite of everything, her mind sank into comforting oblivion.

She was awakened much later, by his big hands which were wandering over her body, up her back. She was forced to turn over and open her thighs to receive him again. She was having to pay dearly for her revenge.

CHAPTER TWELVE

Marcus Crassus sat thoughtfully on the lowest marble tier of the circus. It was the first time he had been to see the chariot races for some time. In fact lately he'd found himself doing a number of things he'd not been used to doing.

The legions were nearly ready now. He'd made good pay offers and managed so far to organize some five legions—close on 35,000 men.

Apart from this work of organization he'd been able to concentrate only on unimportant and rather frivolous happenings. The races fell under this category as far as he was concerned.

Crassus was well aware to what his restlessness was due. Always his thoughts returned to the same thing, the same image—Clodia. Many times he had cursed his cowardice in not making an open suggestion to her that they have a night of love. After all, with such a dangerous future she might have decided to give herself over to a last night of pleasure. It was highly probable that on arriving at the rebel camp she would have to submit to some coarse fellow and at least Crassus had breeding. He felt ridiculously jealous that some stupid slave should possess Clodia while the exquisite delight should be denied him. And then, at worst, she would simply have refused. Her life in Rome, as she herself had said, was finished. She could have made no difficulty for him.

At night he pictured her body, stripped her slowly of her clothes, imagined their first advances and then practically had an orgasm at the thought of her writhing and moaning beneath him. Again he pictured Spartacus having her—he was now convinced of the affair. How had she been? Enthusiastic, obviously. He tried to imagine her throwing the whole fervor of her beauty into their lovemaking. Then, in turn, he pictured Marcellus, having her on a couch in front of patrician Rome, with Clodia lying mute and motionless. He felt an itch at his loins and sighed.

He looked round the circus, up at the crowds balanced on their wooden tiers behind him, all shouting, betting, gossiping, flirting. He decided he would make a bet, otherwise he was afraid he'd see the stallions fade into a picture of Clodia as he watched.

The races today were the trial of some fresh horses from Spain. Crassus forced Clodia from his mind and allowed himself to be carried on the great surge of excitement which filled the circus.

Below him the track was neat, the sand freshly replenished and raked. On the embankment in the center, which joined the two posts around which the chariots would whirl, were the seven large wooden eggs. The attendant who would remove one as each lap was completed, was fussily arranging and rearranging them.

In the open boxes at the western end of the track, the twelve chariots glinted in the sun, and the horses jostled gently and whinnied. A soft breeze wafted through the circus.

Crassus had begun to drift off again into the rebel tents and the pictures of Clodia being ravished—perhaps, even, in more places than one—when he was brought back to the present by the white napkin, fluttering down into the arena from the hand of the Consul.

A trumpet sounded the start and the Consul sat down, draping his embroidered Tyrian toga over his scarlet tunic, while a slave steadied the heavy wreath of golden leaves on his head.

As the ropes, stretched between the marble Hermes on each side of the boxes, fell away, a wild excitement seized the scores of thousands of people in the circus. They could enjoy themselves now. The legions were almost ready to depart. They were estimated to outnumber the gladiators' forces by at least three to one.

The dust flew beneath the chariot wheels as the competitors raced for the first bend.

Crassus studied the horses. They were certainly fine animals. Their breast-plates studded with plaques and amulets, their manes starred with pearls, gave them a glorious appearance.

He searched for the red ribbons around the horses' necks. That was the color of the party he'd backed.

Crassus had always marvelled at these charioteers. These men, who, like the gladiators, often started from slaves. With success they became practically the playboys of Rome—although they were never invited to the houses of the noblemen. They were the heroes of the masses of the city.

Crassus had gained such power as he had by his scheming brain, his power of manipulation. He was not essentially a man of action, a public hero, a man whose physique and cool strength of mind made him an imposing figure. He wished he could have inherited the courage of a charioteer to go with his other useful qualities. Nothing could have stopped him then in his ambition to control men's lives.

His eyes flicked over the charioteers. He could make them out through the dust and swirling of horses. Their helmets shone, whips flashed, their colored tunics were cut in half by the binding reins which would be slashed by a dagger to release them from the horses if there was a crash.

The crowd was already shouting with excitement by the time one egg had been removed from the central embankment. A charioteer of the green faction was going neck and neck with the red. Their horses raced, snorting, nostrils flared side by side, the chariots swung towards each other and then away again. Behind them thundered the rest of the field in a fluid pattern.

Both chariots turned well. The two outside

horses, attached not to the shaft but by traces, had been well trained. The inside one acted as a vital pivot as the offside horse swung out.

Crassus felt his blood stirring. Women were screaming with excitement on the terraces. If he had the nerve of a charioteer he could have had Clodia before she left. He wouldn't have worried about being rebuffed. He wouldn't have laughed and made some coarse witticism without turning a hair. How he envied them that cool quality!

Another egg had gone down, and another.

The fluid pattern shifted. The green chariot swung out too far on a corner and a white one shot inside next to the red. They raced, three abreast, along the straight side below where the Consul watched; the wheels scraped as they wheeled around the far bend and then the white was firmly established beside the red and the green had fallen back.

Crassus began to take a partisan interest in the red. After all he had backed it. If it won, he told himself, he would have Clodia yet. Yet, this was the omen.

Four, five eggs down and still the red was there on the inside—a winning position if it could be maintained until the final bend.

And then disaster. Hugging the turning post too close at a bend, the red chariot crashed into it. The wheel caught and tipped in crashing. The crowds shrieked. There was the flash of the charioteer's dagger and the chariot had turned over, dragging half the horses with it.

The charioteer who had crashed off the back, lay where he was, arms over his head as the following chariots swerved to avoid the tangle.

As the last of the remainder swept around the bend, attendants rushed to right the frightened, but unharmed horses and drag them away to the boxes before the return of the throng.

The charioteer was helped to his feet and carried to the embankment. He was lucky to have escaped with only a broken leg.

Of course, there was always that, Crassus thought, in the disappointment of the wrecking of his omen. They came to grief. They were brave, their nerves and bodies were of iron, but these qualities which led them into such exciting and dangerous callings were so frequently their undoing. The death rate among charioteers was considerable. Often the most successful was killed in his prime, when his glory could not have been greater.

The chariots thundered on in a close mass, the white in the sole lead now.

Another egg down—a last circuit with its two bends to go.

And now, from the mass of flying hooves and wheels, surging out from the dust and the roar, the second red driver emerged.

Crassus had given him no chance. The man had been left at the start. But now he had moved up, lost in the middle of the throng, suddenly to leap forward.

The white chariot hugged the embankment as the red drew away by a fraction of a wheel from the remainder. The whip flew in the charioteer's hand, the horses panted and thundered.

At the last bend but one the red-ribboned

horses had drawn level with the chariot ahead and the crowds were shouting themselves hoarse.

The leading charioteer glanced sideways at the oncoming horses. He had thought himself well away. That glance took his eyes for a moment from his stallions and the track ahead. His wheel caught the embankment and the chariot rocked and skidded. The frightened horses, feeling the pull, slowed. The driver lashed them forward again as the chariot righted itself from the near disaster—but it was too late. His red opponent had shot smoothly ahead and taken the bend well, cutting in to the inside position.

The crowd rose to its feet as the red chariot raced along the inside and took the last bend with ease. The white chariot was a length behind. The result was a foregone conclusion.

As the leading chariot flashed past the winning line, cheers rocked the hills on which the terraces rose.

Crassus was astonished and pleased. He would have Clodia. And then he laughed at himself for such fantasies. But he was still pleased that the red had won.

Chattering broke out along the terraces, expert discussion of the qualities of the new horses and of the rider who had won so unexpectedly. Winnings were gathered and bets placed for the next race.

During the interval a program of acrobatic tricks was shown. This was almost as great an attraction as the races themselves. Jockeys guided two horses at once, leaping from one to the other with perfect control. Others snatched pieces of cloth from the track at full gallop; others, even more versed, seized swords without suffering a scratch. Yet others made mimic war on horseback with blunted weapons until one was toppled to the soft, sand-covered ground.

And finally the arena was cleared and the next race was ready to begin.

A dozen races were scheduled in all to cover the day. Some were simply horseback races, others chariot races with two, three or even ten horses taking the place of the more usual four.

Crassus thought of Clodia through the intervals, stretching his red-sandaled feet in the sun, adjusting his purple-striped toga. During the races he imagined that if his color won he would have her in this circumstance or that.

It was towards the end of the day when one of his trusted freedmen came to him and whispered that the lady, Clodia Crispus, had arrived at his house and was waiting to see him.

As if aroused from a dream to find that it was actually true, Crassus rose, adjusted his toga once again, and strode after his attendant, leaving the roar of the crowd behind him as yet another race came to a whirlwind close.

CHAPTER THIRTEEN

It had taken Clodia only a few days to learn that her owner in the gladiator's camp was one of Spartacus' minor lieutenants—which meant that he was kept well-abreast of future plans.

He had used her body in every imaginable way in that short time and then, under her encouragement, finding her interested and intelligent, he had begun to confide in her.

The gladiators had heard of Crassus' plans to organize an army to fight them and they intended to watch for its departure from Rome, attempt to skirt its southward march through the hills, leaving, perhaps, a minor contingent to maintain the illusion of the camp, and then take Rome.

The legions would return as soon as they realized the trick that had been played on them, her master, Martius, informed her, and then they could be beaten slowly and systematically while they attempted to besiege the newly-fallen city.

"A very clever idea," Clodia commented. "This is your leader, Spartacus' strategy?"

Martius' eyes took on a glint of respect and deference as he nodded.

"He is a great man," he said. "Without him we'd be a number of aimless, wandering parties —easy meat for the soldiers. Who'd ever have thought we could have taken Rome?"

"Who indeed?" said Clodia.

It had become clear to her, too, over the last few days, that Spartacus—whom she'd not seen—was treated more as a god than a human being among his men. He was the brains behind every move. His were the cool eyes which filled every member of his band who looked at him with an overwhelming confidence. As long as Spartacus was there, not only was there hope, but almost undoubted success, was the feeling.

Clodia remembered his big, muscular body

and that strong face. It seemed a long time since she'd seen him, but his image was still vivid in her memory. Her desire for revenge was still deep.

During the day, she worked with the other women, grinding corn, washing clothes in a stream, chatting, hiding successfully her birthright, learning about the future movements and the awe in which their leader was held.

During the night she submitted to the careless and violent intercourse of Martius—all in the cause of learning still more on her path of revenge.

On the day that Marcus Crassus was watching his red charioteer race to victory, Clodia learned that Martius was to go on night patrol.

That evening, taking her life in her hands, she crept from the camp with Martius' horse, rode like the wind across the plains below the foothills, eventually joining the road at what she considered a safe distance, and thundered up the Appian Way to Rome.

The sun was sinking towards dusk as she was received by one of Crassus' special guards who were kept permanently on duty to await her arrival.

She was escorted quietly through the back streets where small shops were still selling their wares and bawdy houses were rocking with laughter and song, to Marcus Crassus' house where she was made comfortable to await his arrival.

Hurrying towards his mansion in the wake of his attendant, Crassus felt a nervous excitement bubbling inside him. He was much less concerned about what news Clodia might bring than the possibility of possessing her—a fact which astonished him. He wondered if he had the choice whether he would be prepared to risk Rome before the gladiator horde if, in return, it meant that he might have the woman he so desired. He found no ready answer.

He found Clodia still in the unkempt, but wildly beautiful role of the slave. She looked tired and her eyes had taken on an unemotional, fatalistic expression. He wondered exactly what she'd been through the last few days.

She rose to greet him and he kissed her hand.

"My dear lady, I'm very happy to see you. I had fears that dreadful things might have befallen you."

"They have—but no matter," Clodia said without expression.

She was wrapped in a toga which had been found for her in the house. Crassus felt a twinge of excitement run through him at her words. He fought down a desire to beg her to tell him what had happened to her.

"You have news?" he asked. But before she could answer he recollected his duties as host.

"I beg your pardon—my excitement at learning the latest situation at the gladiators' camp got the better of me. Have you eaten? I will have a meal brought to you straight away."

Clodia dismissed his hospitality with a wave of her hand.

"Thanks. I have eaten," she said. "After I have given you what information I have, perhaps I might be allowed to bathe."

"Most certainly," Crassus said. "Anything at all you wish."

"When will the legions be ready?" Clodia asked.

"In two or three days. We are still trying to recruit . . ."

"Good. Well, at the time they pass through the gates of Rome, a band of Spartacus' scouts will be watching."

"That is to be expected," Crassus said. "I trust their report will make him feel a new respect for Rome."

Clodia cut him short, impatiently.

"Not at all," she said. "It will simply give him the signal to move quickly north through the foothills, leaving a small company in his camp.

"By this maneuver he hopes to outflank Rome and move in to the attack while the legions are hunting for the scattering remnants of the camp far to the south. He thinks he will be able to take Rome without too much difficulty and be well established by the time the legions return."

Crassus whistled.

"The man's audacity is astonishing," he said slowly. "How big are his forces?"

"He has close on ten thousand well armed men."

Crassus whistled again.

"We have been very badly served with information hitherto," he said. "I would have put the figure at half that and thought them badly armed into the bargain."

"Their army is a formidable one," Clodia

said. "Every day, the gladiators take cohorts of slaves and teach them how to fight. They give them instruction in how to deal with the special tactics and formation of the legions, too."

"And every man with everything to gain, nothing to lose," Crassus mused. "This is not a very pretty picture. This man Spartacus must have some spark of genius in him."

"How will you meet them, now?" Clodia asked.

Crassus thought for a moment.

"Naturally the details will need some attention," he said. "But in broad principle we'll send out only two of the legions we've organized. We're hoping to have seven by the time we're ready so that'll leave some 30,000 troops in the city—more than enough to surprise Spartacus and his crew. As for the other two, we'll dispatch a fast messenger as soon as the gladiators appear. They should be back in time for any possible hitches or—let us confidently hope—the last skirmishes."

"It won't be any simple matter even then," Clodia said. "So to achieve my aim, and perhaps spare a few Roman lives, I, too, have a plan which may be of some assistance."

"Pray go on," Crassus invited.

"I intend to kill Spartacus before his massed troops as he advances on the city," Clodia said.

Crassus was dumbstruck. The thought of the Thracian leader simply being struck down by a woman in the midst of his forces—after all the power and destruction he had wielded and wrought—was beyond his comprehension.

"But—but . . ." And then he smiled. "This is madness my dear. You have done wonderful work. You have almost undoubtedly saved Rome from this barbarian. All Rome shall honor you. But as for this plan, it really can't be considered. It's impossible. And even were it possible, it would be suicide."

He took her hand comfortingly, and a distracting cloud passed behind his eyes at the soft touch of her hand in his, her beautiful face so close.

"You have had a hard time," he said. "You must rest. Spartacus will meet his doom anyway. I offer you the hospitality of my house in all discretion if you wish to rest for some days."

Clodia did not bother to withdraw her hand. She let it rest in the pudgy fingers of the banker. His catching her hand had turned her attention to him for the moment. It was as if she saw for the first time the man who was going to defeat the army which Spartacus had built.

She looked into the gleaming eyes under their heavy lids, set in the gross, overfed face with its clean-shaven skull. This fat, wretched man was going to head five legions to the destruction of Spartacus' army. The thought made her slightly sick. She thought of Spartacus, strong and handsome and magnetic, his courage giving out confidence to his men and again she wished it could have been different.

"There is no difficulty," she said, with quiet resignation. "I shall muffle myself in the clothes of one of his minor lieutenants. That should enable me to get close to him. I shall strike him down with his lieutenant's sword, or perhaps with a dagger. After that I don't care. They will have no time to do more than kill me and I may even manage to escape to the Roman lines."

Crassus saw that she intended to carry out her plan. He hated the thought of such a beautiful woman walking into such certain death.

"You are too lovely a women to do this," he said passionately. "All Rome would abhor your decision."

"All Rome makes me sick," Clodia retorted. "Can't you see the additional advantage you would have from this. Spartacus is divine in the eyes of his men. He has become like the Pharaohs, only his divinity is augmented by the natural veneration they feel for him, the confidence his power gives them. Without him they will be thrown into confusion. They will fight. Oh, yes, they will fight. But they will lose the belief in their victory which they have when he is fighting at their head. They will be routed in half the time and with half the danger to the Roman troops."

Crassus had listened to her with further astonishment. Her insight was considerable. It was true that he also had heard that Spartacus was blessed with the protective hand of a god. It was easily believable that all she said was true. It would provide the final, shattering blow after the presence of the Roman legions.

"I think such a plan has small hope of success," he said. "Surely you will be noticed before you have time to strike. Surely they will see you are a woman."

"It will succeed. Don't worry," Clodia said.

"And how will you get the clothes and the horse of one of his lieutenants?"

"I shall kill him first," Clodia replied.

Crassus stared at her in growing astonishment. Truly this woman wanted her revenge more than anything else, more than anyone he'd ever known. He thought of the intrigues he'd known, political, military, commercial, politico-military, the jealousies, tricks, knaveries, vengeances. He could think of nothing to equal this for sheer, daring ruthlessness and fatalistic acceptance of one's own destruction.

He had let her hand drop in his surprise, but now he seized it again in both of his.

"I can't let you do this. It is a ridiculous sacrifice," he remonstrated.

"Why should you care?" she asked.

"Because it is a sin to deprive men of your beauty."

"Men have enjoyed my beauty enough in the last few weeks."

Still holding her hand in his, Crassus pressed it to his lips. With his heart thumping he took the plunge.

"Would you not share that beauty with me for a while before you go, if your mind is really made up?"

Clodia looked at the gross man, clutching her hand, the man who was going to try to cut a brave figure in front of Spartacus. She felt a twinge of pity for him in her loathing. She withdrew her hand.

"I no longer have the energy to be insulted," she said. "The answer is no."

To Marcus Crassus this seemed a ridiculous injustice, an unnecessary refusal to give him what would be such bliss. What difference could it make to her if she were determined to die in a few days anyway? He felt somehow robbed of his masculinity, another failure in the light of the courageous, conquering figure he would like to be.

"Very well," he said.

"I would like to bathe, now," Clodia said. "I haven't a lot of time."

"I'll show you the way," Crassus said.

He led her through the quadrilateral and into the bath building. As they reached it she slipped off her toga. He opened the door for her to pass through. Her breasts seemed to move under his very eyes, hillocks of tight tunic, pushing out from her body. He caught his breath.

"You'll find all you need in there," he said.

"Thank you," she replied.

He watched her for a second, with her buttocks pressing against the tunic, as she walked, in an impudent rippling. His eyes travelled quickly down her long, slim legs and back to the sinuous movement of the bottom. He closed the door quietly behind her and stood there trembling.

* * *

Inside the baths, Clodia removed her tunic, her brassiere, her loincloth, and walked down the steps into the warm water of the pool. The water moved up her body like a lover's hand, embracing her thighs, hips and at last her breasts. It was soothing, relaxing. She stood letting the steam soak into her pores. It seemed that all the horrors of the last few weeks—or was it months or years—were being gently, luxuriously washed away.

It was in the baths, she recalled, that the whole business had actually begun to take shape. But for her original desire, there may have been no escape of the gladiators, no raping of patricians, killing of their menfolk, no razing of cities.

She sighed. It was impossible to think that all of that had been her doing.

Clodia floated off on the water. This was luxury. Except for the ache in her loins, it washed away everything—all the dirt, lust, beastliness, shame of the last few days. The baths were a wonderful institution—as good as sleep.

She noticed the couches around the bath, the gold encrusted in the marble mosaic. Crassus was reputed to be the richest man in the Empire. He had virtually proven it with his equipping of the new legions.

What a nerve the man had! But then her anger dissipated, listlessly. How could she feel angry at his suggestion after what she'd been through. That was what every man wanted when he looked at her. Though she couldn't remember if Spartacus had so much as looked at her before she'd made advances to him.

Spartacus. She tried to remember his touch,

the way he had been that night in her room. That was the last sex she had enjoyed, had needed. She felt a slight gnawing in her stomach. She had to kill him. That was the only way. The only hope for her.

She climbed out of the bath and began to dry herself on a cloth. She dried her face, neck, shoulders, dabbed her breasts and belly, towelled her back and rubbed her buttocks. She put one foot on a couch to run the cloth down her thigh. A noise disturbed her. She looked up to see Crassus just inside the door, naked and in a state of obvious sexual excitement.

Crassus had started to leave the baths, but the desire to have Clodia was too excruciating. Across the quadrilateral he had stopped. Little drops of perspiration gathered on his forehead and on his upper lip. It was dark now. It was now or never, he told himself. A fresh image of Clodia formed in his mind, an image of her retreating into the bath, with the tunic outlining those firm buttocks.

Who would know? He could spread the word she had joined the rebels.

He looked at the building. Lights were on in the kitchen quarters. That was all.

He walked slowly back to the baths. His heart was thumping, his stomach trembling. Once he made the move he'd have to go through with it. The image of Clodia formed again, almost restricting his breathing.

Gently he pushed open the door of the baths and peered in to where the lamps glowed through the steam. Clodia had her back half towards him. Her leg was raised, foot resting on a couch while she dried herself.

He stared at the delicate sweep of buttocks, the long, well-shaped thighs and calves. The breast he could see was superbly tilted, crowned by a large, jutting nipple which would be hard under the fingers.

Crassus fingered his penis through the toga. He could feel its heat through the cloth. He never wore underclothes.

Crassus slipped inside the door, closing it softly. He couldn't help himself now. He was in sexual torment.

Standing just inside the door he pulled off his toga. As it rustled to the floor, Clodia turned and saw him. Her eyes were astonished and then cold.

"Get out of here,'" she said sharply.

Crassus walked towards her, his eyes roving over her naked body. His penis preceded his fat belly by several thick-fleshed inches. The steam mingled with the perspiration of desire on his forehead.

"You must, Clodia," he pleaded. "You must."

Clodia glared at him furiously.

"Don't you dare touch me," she snapped.

"This is the last time you may ever make love with a man," Crassus begged. "Surely you can't be so cruel."

Clodia felt a great tide of fury and indignation well up inside her.

"You fat, loathsome slug," she hissed. "For the last several days I've been raped, raped, you understand? I had to permit it because it was the only way to get what I wanted. But really it was rape. And not only what you understand by rape, but rape of my back passage, my mouth, everything." Her voice rose shrilly.

"And I'm tired of it, do you see? I want no more of it. So get out, you disgusting beast."

Crassus had stopped short at the beginning of her tirade. But the words had simply inflamed him. So that was what they'd done to her. They'd put it in her behind, put it in her mouth. A violent shiver ran through him and he came on towards her.

"Now that I've seen you, I can't live without having you," he said.

His pudgy hands reached out for her. Clodia pushed him away, turned to run around the bath and slipped on the marble floor.

In a moment his great fat body was on her, his fat flesh enveloping her.

Crassus felt like crying with delight. She struggled but he hardly noticed. His lips were on hers. He kissed her lips with a hard, moist pressure, smelling the soft bath smell of her skin, feeling her flesh wriggling under his.

"Clodia, Clodia," he panted. "You must, you must. Don't struggle."

"Oh, you beast." Clodia scratched and bit. The others she had allowed to happen. This was her rape by a fellow-patrician. He thought so little of her esteem, her dignity, that he, Marcus Crassus, whom she had helped, was trying to rape her. Was there no end to man's lust, his brutality?

She struggled out from under him, tried to break away again. But he clambered up after her, grabbing her thighs, rising to his feet, holding her from behind.

All the time he panted: "Clodia, Clodia. Oh Clodia!" like a maniac.

Weakened from the exhaustion of the preceding days, Clodia felt herself being pushed and half carried to one of the couches.

She tried to kick it away with her feet, but then he had forced her over it and was holding her on it face down.

Crassus was in a delirium. His belly was churned up with desire. He held Clodia down on the couch and half lay on her, half stood behind her. His great penis was on a level with her buttocks, and still breathing, "Clodia, Clodia," he forced her struggling legs apart, shuffled between them.

He saw before his blank, desire-filled eyes, the folds of flesh around her vagina, and a giant hand was squeezing his belly, nervous currents shivering all over his body.

He was so excited he could hardly direct his trembling penis. He ranged it, unable to believe that this was true. He was about to have Clodia. This was what he'd dreamed of for days. He breathed her name once again and then buried himself in her vagina.

Crassus moaned with delight and fulfillment on the very first entry. It was an unbelievable relief. All the time of wanting Clodia, picturing Clodia, was coming out now as he thrust into her.

She continued to struggle, but sheer fire, now, helped him to hold her down without effort, his hands on her shoulders, his weight on her back.

His great belly rolled on her buttocks as he

drove in and in again. His emotion seemed to sing in his head. There was a release of emotion in his loins as he stabbed and ground into her. It had to go on now to the climax, nothing could stop it. And he felt a wild, shattering thankfulness that it was so.

"Oh, Clodia. Oh, Clodia. Oh, oh, oh!" he continued to moan. His organ was well within her.

He moved his hands from her shoulders, which trembled now with indignation, and pushed them under her breasts on the couch. He ran them over the beautiful, glossy, budding globes as his thighs pressed her thighs wide and he rammed deeply into her body.

"Clodia," he begged. "It's too wonderful. Don't struggle, please. Please!"

Lying under him, stretched over the couch so that her face looked over one edge and her feet reached down almost to the floor on the other, Clodia found her struggles to be of no avail. She heard Crassus' words as he filled her with that heavy, pulsating slug between his legs. She hated him, loathed him. But suddenly her loathing took on a fury at his stupid pleadings. The dolt, she thought. Why didn't he rape her without trying to beg her forgiveness at the same time? Lying passive, feeling his penis worming in long, smooth strokes right up inside her so that it made her wriggle slightly with the sensation, she thought that after all what did it matter now? Who cared? The last time. Might as well let him have what he wanted.

She jerked her bottom furiously back at him as he moved into her channel once more.

Marcus Crassus kissed her neck as his passion grew. Then he leaned up from her, leaving only his hands on her waist, standing on the marble floor, his loins between her thighs. His hips jerked at her in a steady motion. He was transported to a heaven of delight.

She had stopped struggling. Something had happened to her. Now she was wriggling like a hundred snakes under him, pressing her bottom close against his belly, rubbing it against him as he speared into her moist depths.

He gasped with his excitement, tears stood in his eyes. "Clodia, Clodia," he uttered.

This was undreamed-of bliss. And she was undulating her hips in cooperation.

He felt the prickling in his loins and slowed. He didn't want to hurry.

He worked up slowly again in a burning delight. He intended to slow and start again for a long time. He would have liked to go on like this forever.

But this time, his passion was too much for him. He went beyond the stage where he could control it.

Clodia was lying there, squirming beneath him and her body was a waiting receptacle to give him relief, to accept the heavy load which was now an embarrassment to him in his desire to be released from it.

Clodia heard him gasping furiously, felt his strokes quicken and then slow, felt him shuffle in towards her so that even the couch moved forward slightly as he tried to get further into her. She pushed her hips back at him, feeling excited, but knowing that she would not reach a climax.

Crassus was on the verge of completion. This was the unbelievable moment. Clodia prostrate, he possessing her. He felt the confined forces trying to break through. He gasped and shouted her name in his passion. There was a moment while the walls held and then the confinement fell away and the sperm of years, it seemed, was flying into Clodia's belly in a flow of never-ending, red-hot shafts.

CHAPTER FOURTEEN

Clodia lay on the tent-bed watching Martius lace his sandals. He was off to the last conference the minor lieutenants would have with Spartacus before the attack. Word had come that the Roman legions were massing outside the gates of Rome in preparation for their march to the south. The camp was a bustle of activity.

"Wait here until I come back," Martius commanded. "Then you can ride with me to see the first fall of Rome."

"I'll wait," Clodia said.

She lay, relaxed, on the rough blankets thinking what a thin line divided the civilized man, the Crassus, from the barbarian, the Martius. Even if she kept her life, she could not, now, go back to Rome. In the desperate last moments of life what had happened between Crassus and herself had seemed unimportant. But she knew that if things returned to normal, she would never forgive herself, or him. She had no clear idea of what to do.

She had not seen Spartacus since she had joined the camp. It was eerie to think that Martius, who a few hours before had lain on her, possessing her as Spartacus had done, should now be standing before his leader, receiving final instructions.

Outside it was growing dark, the hour that the Romans would be expected to make a rapid march to the south to quell the rebels.

She began to roll the blankets and collect the few things that Martius would need. She was glad she was going with him to within sight of Rome. Otherwise she would have had to kill him now, increasing the chances of her detection.

Outside was the continual clinking of weapons, rustling of tents and clothes, whinnying of horses, buzzing of voices. Spartacus had decreed that women were to form the main force to stay behind. Only the lieutenants could take their women with them.

In charge of the women he would leave a few hundred men. Fires were to be built high as an indication of life and a few horsed sentries would shoot a few arrows at the vanguard of the Roman troops before making a get-away. For the rest, as the Roman troops began to cross the wooded plain to the foothills, those in the camp would flee north in the foosteps of the main body. It was thus hoped that by the following evening every man and woman would be safely barricaded behind the walls of Rome.

Clodia looked up as Martius returned. He smacked her happily across the rump. He was in a good mood.

"Well, we're off," he said. "And woe betide Pompeius when he returns from Spain."

Pulling down the tent with him, loading it onto the baggage horses, Clodia felt for a second that she was too small a thing to carry the responsibility for the betrayal of all these people. But the moment passed.

"Where is Spartacus?" she asked.

"Oh, he'll be ready. Don't worry. Do you want to go and kiss him good luck?" Martius guffawed at his own humor.

Spartacus, with Marcellus riding at his side, led the gladiators from the camp and north through the foothills. He had dispatched more scouts to watch the progress of the legions. His first observers had told him the Romans numbered only a couple of legions which had struck him as a rather weak effort. He had expected the sons of Rome to flock to the eagles in greater numbers. Marcellus had been all for waylaying the legions and entering pitched battle with them. But he had crushed that idea. It was pointless losing men in open battle when they could fight from the security of the city's walls.

Behind him, his army streamed, some riding, the majority marching. It was a difficult path through the foothills, a tiring one. But he had promised them all a rest within sight of Rome.

Now it was necessary to hurry. They should see Rome by daybreak.

His mouth set in a grim smile as he thought of Rome. What would it be like to live in Rome as its lord? How would it be to own the city? He would do away with the gladiator fights. He would try to encourage something on the style of the Grecian Olympic Games, which he'd heard about. Those who were the backbone of bloodlust in the masses would have to accustom themselves to another form of sport. He would do his best for the people, but the patricians would suffer. Some he would keep on the Senate, to guide him, but he would give no opportunity for corruption or revolt.

He pulled himself back to the present with a jerk. He was not yet inside the walls of Rome.

He wondered about Clodia who had started all this, who was going to bring about the downfall of Rome. He had hardly thought of her for some time. But now, with the entry into Rome at hand, he wondered how she had recovered from her shame, whether she had left Rome. Perhaps as lord of the city—and later of the Empire—he would seek her out and make her his woman. There would be few in the new city who would then regard her with anything but envy.

He looked back through the dusk at the thin lines of low torches. They were making good progress.

"We'll have a banquet in the forum tomorrow night," he said to Marcellus.

"I'll have roast senator," Marcellus grinned.

Riding on the back of Martius' horse, along

the flank of the scrambling, slipping body of men, Clodia could see ahead the torch borne by somebody in Spartacus' group. She could not see Spartacus, however, as the light the torches threw was dim, only sufficient to light up the few paces ahead of horses and men.

She clutched Martius around his leather Roman overtunic. In the sheath at his side was the sword with which she would kill him. She felt a smouldering pity for him for a few seconds. He was happy at the moment. He was going into the sort of activity he loved, the only sort of activity he really understood and felt for.

At intervals the horde was intercepted by scouts. The word got to the lieutenants that they were now parallel with the legions, separated only by darkness, a few miles of plain and a range of foothills.

Martius chuckled.

"Picture their faces when they find out," he roared. "I'd give my horse to see them."

"How is Rome to be taken?" Clodia asked, leaning forward, raising her voice against the clacking of the horses' hooves.

"Very straightforward," Martius replied over his shoulder. "At daybreak we'll just move forward in a mass, leaders in front, across the plain. There can't be more than a few score of soldiers left in charge of the walls. They'll be so terrified, they'll collapse over the top. Everyone who's not for us'll probably try to escape through the north gate. They can go." He laughed heartily.

"We'll be having a merry time tomorrow night," he guffawed.

They saw the lights of Rome before the day broke and they made a brief camp in the foothills opposite the city.

"Let me climb up with you to see the lights," Clodia said. "I want to see just how unsuspecting Rome appears."

"They're all sleeping like happy babies," Martius chortled.

They moved away from the camp, climbing through the trees and undergrowth to the summit of the low hills overlooking the plain.

"You see. Not a murmur. Every soldier forty miles to the south."

Clodia looked across the black plain to the flickering lights of the city. On the walls sentries would be watching this line of hills, waiting for the first sight of the attack. In the streets and squares, soldiers would be crammed together in their thousands waiting for the gates to open to march out at the startled enemy. But only she knew this.

"This is where you, the other women and the rear guard will watch us from," Martius told her. "You'll have to wait an hour before you have the pleasure of joining us—just to make sure there's no unexpected trouble."

"What trouble could there be?" asked Clodia.

"That's right," Martius said. "If I had my way, I wouldn't make you wait. But Spartacus is cautious. Never get him to make a false move."

Clodia felt Martius' arm move around her shoulder. Now was the time, she told herself.

"They say a satisfied man doesn't fight as well as the next," Martius was saying. "But I can't see that a quick fuck is going to do me any harm."

He pulled her over, hands fondling her breasts and she turned onto her back and slipped out of her loincloth.

Martius pulled off his loincloth and she felt his erect penis against her thighs as he rolled onto her.

"Take your sword out; it gets in my way," she said softly.

"Getting to like it, aren't you, you hot little bitch," Martius said good-humoredly.

He unsheathed his sword and laid it beside them on the grass.

Clodia put her arms around his neck and kissed him, feeling his moustache on her face as she shot her tongue into his mouth.

She opened her legs and he gave a grunt as he embedded his flesh in her.

Clodia moved her hand down his back, stroking, and then let it fall away, simulating a moan as if in abandon. Her fingers were on the sword at their side. Martius was thrusting into her, grunting heavily. He was oblivious to everything but his senses for the moment.

She moved her hand over the sword, finding the hilt, grasping it. She drew it gently nearer.

Martius gasped with passion as he buried himself completely in her passage.

The gasp became prolonged and grated into silence as the steel ran into his belly.

Trembling, Clodia slithered from under him, pushing him away from her. She looked at him.

He was dead. She wiped the blood from her belly and thighs with her loincloth. Quickly she began to pull Martius away from the hill summit, down into the trees. She dragged him over rocks and through bushes for some distance and then let him flop in the scrub. With trembling fingers she began to pull off his tunic. She was frightened, but a sense of urgency impelled her with a cool efficiency.

After fifteen minutes she straightened. In the darkness she was a man, dressed in a Roman helmet, tunic and arms. Everything was big for her, but that simply helped to hide her feminine body. Most of the arms and apparel of the horde were stolen. Strange fits were a common sight.

Clodia rubbed dirt into her legs and arms to hide their whiteness. She wished she had some gladiator's greaves. She rubbed dirt and the juice of berries into her face as well. By the time she had done, it was no longer Clodia who walked back towards the camp, but some nondescript soldier, who, if you looked very closely, had a handsome profile and a rather feminine delicacy.

She settled herself against a tree where Martius had left his horse on one flank of the main body. She thanked her stars that he was a lieutenant, keeping himself somewhat away from the body of his men. He was a surly character, too, and few sought his company, few would notice his absence at this tense hour.

Clodia stayed where she was waiting for the dawn. During those moments of time which remained to her, her thoughts went back into the past thinking of all the might-have-beens. Most of her life had been a series of might-have-beens. In spite of her advantages of beauty, wealth and upbringing, she had singularly failed in her personal relationships. She had made mistake after mistake until the final one had reduced her to this. She realized she no longer had any great desire to live. Spartacus was the one man who had really affected her deeply and that result, too, had been disastrous. Now she would kill him and probably die herself. She thought this as if she were another person, calmly. Her only fear was that she might not succeed in destroying the Thracian.

When the sun began to rise behind them, the sky to streak pale blue, green and then yellow-silver, and the whole heavens to lift and lighten, Spartacus rode up to the hill summit with Marcellus behind him.

He took a long look at Rome, at the light of morning glowing on its walls, enclosing the seven hills, and then he called to the lieutenants to follow him, to the men to begin the march.

From all directions the leaders galloped to join him. There was a great excitement as the men climbed the hillside and began the descent to the plain.

Spartacus galloped at the head of his few hundred lieutenants. He looked back at the thousands of his men marching across the plain and he felt a thrill quiver inside his calm exterior. What a moment!

Everybody's eyes were glued to the city's walls. Nobody spoke. Nobody noticed the young lieutenant on the flank, whose eyes never left Spartacus.

The gladiator chief reined in his horse to a slower pace. He did not want to get too far ahead of his men—although he saw no danger. What resistance could they possibly put up? They might bar the gates while they tried to escape from the northern gate, but it would take him only a few minutes to scale the high walls and open the city to the army behind.

Closer and closer the city came, glorious and never conquered. The plain trembled under the feet of the gladiators' march. The distance lessened.

Spartacus smiled to himself. What would Pompeius say?

And then his smile began to disappear.

The gates of Rome had opened and ranks of horsemen began to gallop out into the sun, arms and armor flashing in the morning rays.

The gladiators' march did not stop. At first Spartacus thought these were the men that remained, coming out on some ridiculous and brave suicidal defense. Then as the numbers swelled and the horsemen split, forming the flanks of a large body of foot soldiers, he realized that he had underestimated.

Even then he thought that perhaps a thousand men had been left to guard the city and the march continued.

But as, in the distance, the thousand men began to spread, turned into a legion, two legions, three legions—and still more poured from the city—he reined in, waved for his men to halt.

As all eyes gazed in startled disbelief at the Roman legions bristling out in defense of city and Empire, the young lieutenant on the flank moved in, weaving between the loose ranks of the lieutenants toward the leader.

The legions advanced. They seemed unending, spreading across the face of the seven hills, a great shining of helmets, a thunderous tramping of feet.

Spartacus sat on his horse, staring grimly into the Roman ranks. Somehow he had been tricked. Crassus would not have sent such a small force to the south, leaving such an enormous one in the city, had he not known what was afoot. Word had gotten to him somehow.

No time now to look for traitors, though.

"What do you think of that?" he said to Marcellus.

"Four or five legions," Marcellus said grimly. "Four to one at least."

"Do we run?" Spartacus asked.

Marcellus looked at his leader. He looked around at the still horde of gladiators and slaves. He looked back at the Romans and drew his sword.

Spartacus laughed.

"We'll still be in Rome tonight," he said.

Uneasily fingering their weapons, the horde watched their leader. They saw him turn on his horse towards them, a majestic figure. They saw his smile and were warmed by it.

"A gladiator is a better fighter than a Roman any day," he roared. "Four heads apiece and it'll be roast duck and wild boar tonight."

His words carried, were relayed from mouth to mouth across the horde. Every heart was strengthened. What were four Roman heads? Spartacus would claim forty.

A great cheer roared from the throats of his ten thousand men. Spartacus would lead them to victory. He had never failed. He would never fail.

Spartacus waved his sword and the cheer died in ten thousand throats.

From amongst those surrounding him, a figure had suddenly lunged forward, a sword had flashed and Spartacus had fallen forward on his horse, hands hanging limply down across the animal's neck. With his fall, the animal had leapt forward and begun to race towards the Roman ranks, carrying the gladiator chief toward the enemy ranks.

Watching from his vantage point at the flank of his troops, Crassus, who had left the command of the first assault to a young aristocrat, had been waiting for Spartacus' death.

He had been the leader on his black horse, cutting a finer figure than any Roman general. He had heard the cheer. And against all the indications his heart had sunk.

The gladiators and their trainees were a tough bunch who would fight to the death. He had the feeling there would be little left of his beautiful legions to cheer the victory that night.

Had Clodia failed? If only she had got this man out of the way.

And then his heart had spun as he saw the thrust of Clodia's sword and heard the shocked cries with which the spectacle was met. He had tried to see what happened to Clodia. But she was swallowed in the mass. With a sick feeling in the pit of his stomach he was aware she had made no effort to escape.

He had looked back to where the big black horse was racing towards his advancing troops and he saw another horseman racing after it. He shook his head in wonder. The mad courage of these men.

By the time Spartacus' body had slithered from his horse into Roman hands, Marcellus, galloping with a wild fury, was on them. Not a single arrow had been fired at him, so astonished had the marksmen been to see a lone figure bearing down on their 30,000 men.

Marcellus crashed through the Romans cutting them away from Spartacus' body. He fought like ten men, wheeling his bucking horse over the corpse of his leader, covering his prostrate body with the blood of Rome.

Nobody else had moved in the gladiators' ranks. They had sat and stood completely dumbfounded by their leader's death. What hope now?

And when half the horde suddenly lost its head in fury and charged the Romans headlong to avenge their leader, half remained, still slow to join, with only Spartacus' ghost for company.

The gladiators' forces were thus cut in two. Those who attacked fought wildly. Roman blood seemed to run as thick as the Tiber.

Crassus, watching on the flank, wondered what, indeed, would have been the outcome of the day's battle had Spartacus lived, had each of his men fought with the wild vigor, the courage of those who attacked.

But of those who still hesitated, some broke and ran for the hills, others put up a bewildered, half-hearted resistance, others again fought as nobly as those who had charged.

But the fight was gone from half the gladiators' army.

At the end of the day, although Roman corpses outnumbered those of their enemy by two to one, Rome was saved, saved with a legion and a half to march triumphantly back.

CHAPTER FIFTEEN

In a mountain clearing in the Appenines, Clodia lay, badly wounded. She was surrounded by a small group of the survivors of the battle.

She had been struck down almost immediately and her horse had bolted. Of those who had fled several had seized her and brought her here to exact full vengeance for their leader's death.

They had soon discovered that she was a woman. Her wound had been staunched and she was stripped to undergo the final indignities.

They kept her for some days, feeding her, submitting her daily to a series of rapes, forcing her with her fading energy to satisfy them.

Then they beat her with whips and the flat of their swords. They turned her over and burned "S" for Spartacus into her buttocks and then into each of her breasts.

Day after day, Clodia lost consciousness, hoping with her last thought that she would not recover. But day after day she came back to lucidity, her body so mutilated and weak that she was beyond the point where pain seemed to matter. Still they found means of torturing her.

They stuck thorns inside her fingernails, inside her toenails. Wild, stinging ants were made to crawl into her vagina until she fainted with horror. They cut out her tongue to stop her feeble screams.

These men became to her like gods. She was completely in their power. If they stopped torturing her for a moment, she felt a great thankfulness for their kindness. When they gave her water or food she worshipped them. When they tortured her again it seemed to her that it was justice and she wished she could die.

Finally, the leader of them pushed her naked body over with his foot one morning.

"It's getting too dangerous for us to stay here," he told her. "Do you hear me?"

His voice seemed to come from a long way off. She nodded feebly.

"So we're going to clear out for a few days," he said. "But we'll be back for you, because there's one thing more to be done."

Clodia heard his words and they meant almost nothing to her. What more was there to be done? She knew she had little time to live.

"If it hadn't been for you, Spartacus would have made us all lords in Rome, by now," the man said savagely. He kicked her and she felt his foot only as a dull, undefined pushing of her flesh.

He scowled down at her for a few seconds. "Well, now you're going to be strung up," he said. "That's what they're doing to those of us they caught—and the dead ones."

Clodia felt no emotion. Her mind was dried up, withered with pain. She was like a dried weed. Nothing could hurt her further.

They strung her up on a tree. They drove stakes through her hands and feet. They left her there alone in the mountains to wait with a great longing for the relief of death.

* * *

Marcus Crassus was annoyed. He and he alone had saved Rome from a terrible fate at the hands of the gladiators. Had it not been for him they would all have been slaughtered. And what had happened?

Pompeius had landed in the south with stacks of booty and slaves. He had cut off part of the gladiator remnants fleeing to the south and was now the hero of Rome—for almost no reason at all it seemed.

With the security of Pompeius' approach, the Senate had disbanded Crassus' army with nothing but public thanks and a medal for him. And he seemed to be back where he'd started.

Money was his only success.

He strolled now through the forum where the crosses were being made. Bands of slaves were making them—huge crosses of cedar wood. Tall and strong to bear the weight of a man.

An overseer walked among the chained slaves cracking his whip. Sometimes the whip cracked in the air, sometimes it lashed across a naked back and a wretch yelped and stumbled before renewing his work with even greater energy.

Slaves making crosses for slaves who had fought against their fate. That was a salutary lesson for them.

This had been Crassus' idea.

On both sides of the Appian Way he would have them placed. They would stretch from the gates of Rome to the far distant south, thousands of them, an interminable reminder. A living, dying and dead monument to Marcus Crassus who had crushed Spartacus and his slave rebellion.

He watched the sweating backs of the slaves toiling. That's where it got them. It would be a long time before there was another such revolt. And they couldn't expect very friendly treatment now, if that was the way they bit the hand that fed them.

"That puts them in their place."

Crassus turned and gave a guilty start. Lucius Crispus stood beside him.

"It's a pity Spartacus isn't still living to be able to see what's become of his scum," Crispus added.

Crassus nodded. He wondered how much Crispus knew about it all.

"He was the first to go," he said.

"Yes. That was a strange thing. Killed by one of his own men, I believe?"

Crassus looked at Crispus thoughtfully.

"Did you see it?" he asked.

"No. Not exactly. It happened so quickly."

"Yes, it was a strange business," Crassus agreed.

"That man Spartacus was a strange one,"

Crispus went on in discreet, confidential tones.

"Oh? I wondered about him." Crassus was interested. He wished he'd met the gladiator. He thought of Clodia, of what she had said of the man. He thought of 10,000 men following an ex-slave to their liberty—and then collapsing because suddenly he was with them no more.

"Oh yes, there was something powerful about him."

This was one of the topics of Rome. A topic about which Crispus was in the proud position to know more than anyone else. After all, Spartacus had been his slave. And now that the man was dead he felt he could speak frankly about him—now that the challenge was gone.

"Other people have told me the same thing," Crassus said.

"Of course he was my chief slave," Crispus said. "I saw more of him than anyone else. I never put up with any cheek from him. But I must confess that I never had him whipped. He was not the sort of man you had whipped."

Crispus paused, wondering if he had made a confession of weakness, if he had said too much. But he could see the interest in Crassus' face.

"They say he was descended from the Thracian princess," he went on. "I must say the man had a certain quality. He took natural command of all the slaves of my household."

"He took natural command of a large portion of the slaves of Italy—much to their present regret," Crassus added.

"Pretty surprising that he lasted so long and did so much damage, eh?" Crispus said.

"Not really," Crassus said. "It was just a question of bad organization against him."

"Maybe, maybe," Crispus admitted. "But he had a power, he had a power."

They stood together in the forum watching the slaves toiling in the sun, the sun glinting off the equestrian statue where Clodia had been strung. Crassus began to feel guilty again. He wondered what had happened to Clodia. She had not been among the dead—a surprising fact. And she had not been among the prisoners.

"How is everything with you?" he asked Crispus suddenly.

"Oh, the divorce you mean?" said Crispus, made frank by the unexpected interest. "Well, as a matter of fact, my wife has disappeared."

"Oh?"

"Yes. She was living in a wing of the house and it was some time before I realized she was gone. I think she must have fled to the north with some of the others who left. I dare say I'll hear from her in due course."

"I see," said Crassus.

"Rather strange, though," Crispus added with a little shake of his head.

There was another silence and then Crispus looked at Crassus nervously. He hesitated and then said suddenly:

"By the way, I'm giving a banquet in a week or so to celebrate the victory. I do hope you'll be able to come."

CHAPTER SIXTEEN

Another morning rose over Rome. It was the same as all the others, except that there was a certain undercurrent of excitement.

The shops were crowded, like the streets,

with crowds of busy people. Wares were spread onto the roads. Barbers were shaving their customers in full view. Hawkers roamed the streets bartering their sulphur matches for anything they could find in exchange.

Sausage, roast fowl and game were displayed piping hot in pans and ovens by owners of cookshops with an eye to business. Money changers clinked their coins on tables in the market, others pounded gold dust.

In the forum a bear-tamer had his great shaggy animal perform tricks for a large, gaping crowd of idlers. Beggars held out their worn hands for alms, invoking the gods and the natural kindness of the passers-by.

Now and again a horseman would clatter up the narrow streets, a group of laughing soldiers would pass, or perhaps a senator in his red sandals and purple-striped toga would stride thoughtfully toward the law courts.

Everywhere was a torrent of people, sometimes flowing into pools, at others narrowing to a back-street trickle. But always unceasing in noise and movement.

The excitement today was at the approach of Pompeius.

Soon the city would be filled with fresh legions, fresh riches, fresh spectacles, led in triumph by the great general.

Late that afternoon, when Pompeius rode at the head of his men up the Appian Way towards Rome, he passed silently through a vast colonnade of crucified men. Six thousand of them, some living, some dead, hanging in anguished macabre welcome.

And when Crispus went through the gates

to join the welcoming crowd, he found a throng at the foot of the cross of the dead Spartacus, the cross nearest to the gates of Rome. He pushed through the crowd, and with a thick feeling of nausea, a mystery was washed away.

As the crowds began to cheer the general's arrival, he found himself gazing at the mutilated, but recognizable body of Clodia, where she had been flung at the foot of Spartacus' cross.

He raised horrified eyes to where the dead man hung.

And it seemed that even in death his power remained.

THE END

Great Erotic Fiction from Carroll & Graf

VICTORIAN CLASSICS (MASS MARKET)
- ❏ Anonymous / AUTOBIOGRAPHY OF A FLEA
  & OTHER TART TALES 5.95
- ❏ Anonymous / THE BEST OF THE EROTIC READER 7.95
- ❏ Anonymous / THE BEST OF THE EROTIC READER II 7.95
- ❏ Anonymous / CARELESS PASSION 6.95
- ❏ Anonymous / CARNAL KNOWLEDGE 7.95
- ❏ Anonymous / THE CUNNING LINGUIST 7.95
- ❏ Anonymous / CONFESSIONS OF AN ENGLISH MAID
  & OTHER DELIGHTS 5.95
- ❏ Anonymous / EROTICON 4.95
- ❏ Anonymous / EROTICON II 4.95
- ❏ Anonymous / EROTICON III 4.50
- ❏ Anonymous / FALLEN WOMAN 4.50
- ❏ Anonymous / INTIMATE MEMOIRS 7.95
- ❏ Anonymous / LAY OF THE LAND 4.50
- ❏ Anonymous / THE LIBERTINES 4.50
- ❏ Anonymous / NOTHING SACRED 4.95
- ❏ Anonymous / THE OYSTER V 4.50
- ❏ Anonymous / OYSTER REDUX 6.95
- ❏ Anonymous / PAGAN DELIGHTS 5.95
- ❏ Anonymous / THE PEARL 6.95
- ❏ Anonymous / PLEASURES AND FOLLIES 3.95
- ❏ Anonymous / PURE NO MORE 6.95
- ❏ Anonymous / ROMANCE OF LUST 7.95
- ❏ Anonymous / SECRETS & SCENTS 6.95
- ❏ Anonymous / SENSUAL SECRETS 4.50
- ❏ Anonymous / SWEET CONFESSIONS 4.50
- ❏ Anonymous / TROPIC OF LUST 4.50
- ❏ Anonymous / VENUS BUTTERFLY 3.95
- ❏ Anonymous / VENUS DELIGHTS 3.95
- ❏ Anonymous / VENUS RISING 7.95

❏ Anonymous / VICTORIAN FANCIES	4.50
❏ Anonymous / WET DREAMS	6.95
❏ Anonymous / YOUTHFUL INDISCRETIONS	4.50
❏ Cleland, John / FANNY HILL	4.95
❏ van Heller, Marcus / SWEET FRICTION	7.95
❏ van Heller, Marcus / UNBOUND	5.95
❏ van Heller, Marcus / VENUS IN LACE	3.95
❏ Villefranche, Anne-Marie / CONFESSIONS D' AMOUR	6.95
❏ Villefranche, Anne-Marie / PASSION D'AMOUR	5.95
❏ Villefranche, Anne-Marie / SCANDALE D'AMOUR	5.95
❏ von Falkensee, Margarete / BLUE ANGEL CONFESSIONS	6.95
❏ "Walter" / MY SECRET LIFE	7.95

Trade Paper

❏ Berliner, Janet (ed.) / DESIRE BURN	9.95
❏ Hurford, Christopher (ed.) / EROTIC VERSE	10.95
❏ Jakubowski, Maxim (ed.) / THE MAMMOTH BOOK OF EROTICA	10.95
❏ Jakubowski, Maxim (ed) / THE MAMMTTH BOOK OF INTERNATIONAL EROTICA	10.95
❏ Lloyd, Joan / BLACK SATIN	8.95
❏ Lloyd, Joan / THE PLEASURES OF JESSICA LYNN	8.95
❏ Lloyd, Joan/ SLOW DANCING	9.95
❏ Scott, G.C. / HIS MISTRESS'S VOICE	9.95
❏ Schimel, Lawrence / THE MAMMOTH BOOK OF GAY EROTICA	10.95

Available from fine bookstores everywhere or use this coupon for ordering.

Carroll & Graf Publishers, Inc., 19 West 21st Street, Suite 601, New York, NY 10010-6805

Please send me the books I have checked above. I am enclosing $ _____ (please add $2.50 per title to cover postage and handling). Send check or money order—no cash or C.O.D.'s please. New York residents please add 8 1/4% sales tax.

Mr. / Mrs. / Ms. _____

Address: _____

City: _____ State / Zip: _____

Please allow four to six weeks for delivery.